Praise for
UPON A MIDNIGHT CLEAR

"Delightful, charming . . ." —*Philadelphia Inquirer*

"Christmas stories from some of the best romance novelists around."

—*The Pilot* (Southern Pines, NC)

"Heartwarming, unforgettable tales from five of today's most talented romance authors."

—*The Literary Times*

"[A] masterly anthology . . . fans of holiday short-story collections will want to read and keep as a treasure to be reread next Christmas."

—Paintedrock.com

"*UPON A MIDNIGHT CLEAR* celebrates this season with the joy of good reading."

—*Romancing the Web*

"Original stories by five bestselling authors . . . which will brighten the holidays and warm the hearts and souls of readers. . . . A great holiday anthology."

—*Abilene Reporter-News* (TX)

"These fictional stories are delightful to read and leave the reader with warm and enduring memories."

—*Pocono Record* (Stroudsburg, PA)

"Heartwarming." —*Chattanooga Free Press* (TN)

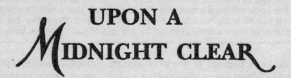

UPON A
MIDNIGHT CLEAR

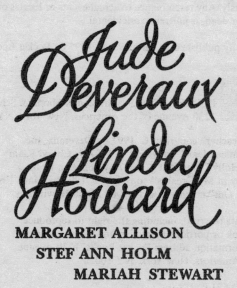

Jude Deveraux

Linda Howard

MARGARET ALLISON
STEF ANN HOLM
MARIAH STEWART

POCKET BOOKS
New York   London   Toronto   Sydney   Tokyo   Singapore

This book consists of works of fiction. Names, characters, places and incidents are products of the authors' imaginations or are used fictitiously. Any resemblance to actual events or locales or persons, living or dead, is entirely coincidental.

Originally published in hardcover in 1997 by Pocket Books

POCKET BOOKS, a division of Simon & Schuster Inc.
1230 Avenue of the Americas, New York, NY 10020

"The Teacher" copyright © 1997 by Deveraux, Inc.
"Christmas Magic" copyright © 1997 by Cheryl Klam
"Jolly Holly" copyright © 1997 by Stef Ann Holm
"If Only in My Dreams" copyright © 1997 by Marti Robb
"White Out" copyright © 1997 by Linda Howington

ISBN: 0-671-01988-0

First Pocket Books paperback printing December 1998

10 9 8 7 6 5 4 3 2 1

POCKET and colophon are registered trademarks of Simon & Schuster Inc.

Cover design by Gina DiMarco
Cover art by Lina Levy

Printed in the U.S.A.

Contents

Contents

UPON A
MIDNIGHT CLEAR

Jude Deveraux

The Teacher

One

Legend, Colorado

"I DON'T SEE WHY—"

"Please don't say it again, Jeremy," his mother said, then had to grab the side of the stagecoach to keep from slamming into the fat, snoring man beside her. Or perhaps *beside* wasn't the correct word. Even before the man had fallen asleep he'd been trying to get even closer to her than the tiny seat forced on them. It didn't help matters that the man kept swearing that she was "the prettiest little thing I ever seen in my whole dad-gummed life," as he put it. When Jeremy had closed his eyes, looking as though he'd fallen asleep, the man had offered Kathryn an extraordinary amount of money to spend just one hour alone with him. "If you know what I mean."

Kathryn certainly did know, and her instinct demanded she tell him she'd rather be boiled in oil than have him touch her, but instead she'd smiled and murmured that she was already "promised."

The man had patted her knee and said he "understood." Maybe he did, but Kathryn didn't have any idea what he meant. Was the American Wild West so without morals that women did spend "just one hour" with a man? As much as she wanted to know, she wasn't about to ask. However, the man's intimate interest in Kathryn de Longe and her son was why they were now speaking in French.

"We could have stayed and fought," Jeremy said, looking up at his mother with eyes much too old for his mere nine years.

Kathryn had no answer for him because over the last weeks she'd exhausted her supply of words. What could she tell him that she hadn't already said? For his entire nine years they had been running. Actually, since Kathryn had had to escape Ireland when she was pregnant, maybe she could say he'd been running since before he was born. But no matter where they went or how well they disguised themselves, the O'Connor money always found them.

Now, Kathryn looked out at the steep mountainside that fell away from the narrow road the stagecoach was trying to climb. This barren, isolated place was their last chance. Their very, very last chance.

Turning, she forced herself to smile at her son. Since he was born she'd tried to protect him. Perhaps she hadn't done a very good job, but she knew she'd done her best. And maybe this time they could settle down. Maybe this time they could stay in one place for longer than three months.

When she'd bought her stage ticket (through a third party so no one would remember a lone woman buying a ticket), she'd asked a man about the isolation of Legend, Colorado, and he'd laughed. "Lady, there are places up in the Rockies that not even God can find. And I figure Legend heads that list." She hadn't smiled as he'd meant her to, but had nodded solemnly. Yes, that sounded like the place she needed.

It hadn't been so easy to persuade Jeremy to the idea of living in an isolated mountain town, as he'd liked Philadelphia very much. He was a quiet child and studious. Like his father's people, Kathryn thought with a melting of her heart. He was very much like his father's uncle with his love of books and music. And he had his father's taste in clothes. And his father's good looks, she thought with a heavy sigh. One look at Jeremy and there was no doubt whose son he was.

"I'm sure there was some other way," Jeremy said for the thousandth time. "We could have—"

"No!" Kathryn said sharply, then wanted to bite her

tongue. Part of her wanted to tell him the truth of how bad the situation was, but another part wanted to protect and shield him.

Sewn inside her corset was a wanted poster bearing excellent likenesses of both her and Jeremy. The poster said that she, Caitlin McGregor, was wanted for thievery and attempted murder, and ten thousand dollars was offered for information leading to her apprehension. It further stated that she was dangerous and should be treated as such.

You'd like that, wouldn't you, O'Connor, she thought to herself. You'd like to see me behind bars. Or better yet, led to the scaffold. You'd probably dance at my hanging.

If she were caught, there would, of course, be no appeal for her. Who would believe her over the money of an O'Connor? Who would step forward and defend her against such a man as he? Especially when he was so very obviously Jeremy's father?

"I'm sure you'll like the place," Kathryn said soothingly to her son. "I hear there's a library and many entertainments are brought from Denver."

"Denver," Jeremy said with a sneer of contempt. "Traveling players? And what do you think they have in the library? Dime novels? Shall I read about Dead Eye Dick?"

"It might do us both a bit of good to get away from the rarified air of Philadelphia for a while. And we might like it here. Stranger things have happened."

Jeremy just snorted and looked out the window at the beautiful, but empty, mountain scenery.

Kathryn wanted to isolate herself in this godforsaken place about as much as her son did. They'd been in Philadelphia nearly three and a half months, and they had begun to make friends. There had even been a man. . . .

But Kathryn wouldn't allow herself to think of that. She knew when she'd run away from Ireland with Sean O'Connor's child in her belly that she'd never be able to have a normal life, a life with a man and a house and maybe other children and—

"Mother!" Jeremy said sharply. "You have that look on your face again."

Kathryn smiled as she reached across the narrow aisle

and took his hand in hers. She knew she'd been wearing what Jeremy called her "dreamy look" when she was far away. She'd told him she was thinking of the sweet greenness of Ireland when she had that look. Better that than to tell him the truth of how she dreamed of a home and husband and safety. No, she couldn't tell Jeremy that, for, knowing him, he'd think she could have those things if it weren't for him and he'd run away. Again.

With a tiny shake of her head, Kathryn leaned back against the seat and looked at her son in awe. He had the refined, aristocratic look of the O'Connors, a look that had taken generations of breeding to achieve. He had long, thin fingers that looked as though they were meant to hold a lace handkerchief. But Kathryn knew the truth. At Jeremy's own insistence, he'd taken boxing lessons (free in exchange for Jeremy's writing letters home for the boxer) and she knew what a punch he could make with those hands.

From the way he was dressed, Jeremy looked as though he'd never seen the outside of a drawing room. No one would guess that they had lived all their lives in tenements where the smell of cabbage always surrounded them. Jeremy had witnessed his first murder when he was one year old, after he'd wandered into a street brawl between two drunken sailors.

It was when he was four that Kathryn finally decided to return him to Sean O'Connor. She was going to take him back to Ireland and allow his father's family to raise him. What did it matter if she were hanged for kidnapping? What did it matter that Sean's family were the coldest, most ruthless people she'd ever met? At least Jeremy would be safe with them in Ireland. And safe was all that mattered to her.

That was the first time Jeremy ran away. Four years old and he ran away from home for three days. Kathryn had been insane with worry, not eating or sleeping for those three days. The police had been no help. What did they care that some slum kid had disappeared? They had leered at Kathryn and offered to give her another child.

After three days Jeremy had sauntered home, clean, well fed, and said that he was not going back to Ireland, that he wanted to live with his mother, and if she tried to send him away, he'd run away again.

That had been five years ago, and since then the two of them had been on the run. But this year Jeremy had been feeling as though he were grown-up and so wanted to stay and fight his father. "He has no claim over me since you never married him," he'd said several times.

Kathryn had tried to explain about money being able to buy anything, but for all the prematurely gained wisdom in his eyes, Jeremy still had a child's belief in justice.

When she'd been offered the job of tutor to a nine-year-old boy in the remote, isolated mountain town of Legend, Colorado, it had seemed like a dream come true. She was to be the teacher of Zachary Jordan, son of Mr. Cole Jordan. And maybe, just maybe, in this remote town, they'd achieve what had become the most beautiful of words to her: *safety*.

"This is it?" Jeremy said with contempt as he stepped down from the stage. *"This* is what we left civilization for?"

"Jeremy, I really don't care for your tone of voice. And I'm sure this is the . . . the . . ."

"Red-light district?" he asked, sidestepping as the stage driver threw their small trunks to the ground.

Kathryn drew in her breath and stared at the awful place around them. There seemed to be nothing but saloons and gambling houses as far as one could see. Noise, dirt, unwashed men, raucously laughing women, great wagons full of rocks, horses and manure, filled the place. There didn't seem to be anything clean or even decent as far as she could see. In front of her was a garish, gaudily painted sign that had a woman's leg wearing a black stocking and a frilly garter. What looked to be a high-heeled bedroom shoe dangled from the toe and the place was called The Lady Slipper. Kathryn didn't have time to look at other signs because she had to step back as a dirty man with graying whiskers made a lunge for her.

"Me first," he said, then when Kathryn sidestepped, he fell into the mud at her feet.

If Kathryn had had so much as two dollars to her name she would have climbed back onto the stagecoach and ridden away, as far from this den of iniquity as possible. Instinctively, she put her arm around Jeremy and drew him closer—as though she could protect him from what she was seeing, hearing, and smelling.

With her arm still around Jeremy, she looked at the stage driver, who was climbing back onto the box.

"Can you take us out of here?" she asked.

"You bet, lady, for fifty bucks each. In cash."

"I don't have—"

He didn't let her finish but just chuckled. "Thought not. Well, there're plenty of ways for a pretty gal like you to earn money in Legend. Giddyup!"

Coughing from the dust of the rapidly departing stage, Kathryn turned back around, the two of them standing alone in the middle of the wide, foul street, three small trunks at their feet. Kathryn didn't have time to think about an alternate plan because a wagon drawn by six horses was coming straight toward them. With one quick gesture she thrust a case at Jeremy, grabbed the other two, and ran for the safety of the boardwalk.

But just as they stepped in front of the saloon, a man came flying through the glass window and hit the board-walk, then rolled into the street, where two men on horses nearly trampled him. Dropping her cases, Kathryn grabbed Jeremy, his back pressed against her front as she tried to pull both of them into the safety between the door and the window. When a shot rang out, she tightened her grip on Jeremy.

Out of the saloon door came a man, his back to her, but she could see the power of his build: shoulders so thick they curved round to his chest, a taut waist with a decorated knife sheath at his side.

"You ever show up in this town again, Bartlett, and you'll answer to me," the big man said to the one in the dirt.

Then, to Kathryn's horror, she saw that the man in the dirt was about to draw a gun, and from the angle of the porch post, she doubted if the man standing in front of her could see him.

"No!" she shouted, and in the next second, with the speed of a striking snake, the man on the porch drew a knife from

8

a concealed pouch down the back of his shirt and threw it. In the next second the man on the ground lay pinned to the dirt, blood pouring from the knife sticking into his shoulder.

Trembling with emotion, Kathryn loosened her grip on Jeremy, and he twisted away from her.

"Don't faint on me now, sweetheart," the man who'd thrown the knife said. He'd turned, and now she looked up into his deep blue eyes. And the feeling that ran through her was nothing that she'd ever experienced before. For a moment, time stood still as her eyes locked with his; it was as though everything else disappeared except this big, handsome blond-haired man.

It seemed natural when his strong arm slipped about her waist and he lifted her off her feet, his one arm holding her as he pressed her body against his, then kissed her.

The only man who'd ever kissed her before was Jeremy's father, and those kisses had been forced upon her. But this man was different, and for the first time in her life, she responded to a man's kiss. Her arms slid about his neck, and she leaned into him as she opened her mouth under his. She could feel her heart pounding and her breasts tingling from the pressure of his hard chest.

The sound of gunfire brought Kathryn to her senses, but when she started to pull away, the man held her firmly so she had to push against his chest to make him release her. All around them was the sound of laughter, unmistakably aimed at the two of them.

Immediately, Kathryn could feel the blood rushing to her face as she glanced up at the man who was staring at her in consternation, as though he were puzzled by something.

Nervously, Kathryn glanced at her son, who was glaring at her—and how could she blame him? She'd just acted—and reacted—completely out of character.

Behind Jeremy was a boy who appeared to be about the same age. They were nearly the same height, but the other boy was large-framed whereas Jeremy was of a wiry build like his father's family. The other boy had sun-streaked blond hair and blue eyes, while Jeremy had dark hair and eyes.

"That your mama?" the boy said into Jeremy's ear, but loud enough that nearly everyone nearby could hear. His implication was unmistakable, that Kathryn was not a woman of high morals.

Jeremy reacted as he had been taught. Pivoting on one foot, he swung around and brought a left uppercut into the boy's chin. And the boy, equally fast and seeming to be equally well trained, hit Jeremy in the eye with a strong right fist.

In the next second, the boys went tumbling into the dirt, while the crowd, already pleased by the show of a brawl, a stabbing, and a passionate kiss, were now further pleased by the sight of two angry boys trying to murder each other.

Kathryn's first reaction was to leap onto the boys and pull them apart, but Jeremy weighed almost as much as she did, and together the boys were considerably larger than she was. Obviously the crowd wasn't going to help, so she looked up at the man she'd kissed. As far as she could tell, he hadn't moved a muscle, but was still standing there staring at her, his big blue eyes wide with an expression she couldn't read.

"Stop them!" she said to him, but he didn't react. "Please stop them," she repeated, then put both her hands on his wide chest.

Immediately, it was as though a current of lightning surged down her arms, and, as though he were a hot griddle, she pulled her hands away.

It seemed that he, too, felt the jolt, because he came out of his trance and turned. For a moment he stood blinking down at the boys as they fought and kicked and held on to one another as they rolled.

Then the man's mind seemed to clear. "What the hell?" he said, then stepped between the boys and pulled them up by the backs of their shirts. When they tried to go for each other with outstretched hands, the man shook the boys as though they were wet puppies.

"Go home," he said to the blond boy, then released him, and when the boy looked as though he might strike Jeremy again, the man gave him a look that made him retreat. In one last act of defiance, the blond boy stopped by a woman wearing an extraordinary dress of shiny red cloth, took a whiskey bottle out of her arms, and downed half its contents in one swig. With a smirk directed at Jeremy, he shoved the bottle back into the woman's hand, then swaggered off as best he could. Which wasn't easy, since he was limping and one side of his face was swelling rapidly.

Kathryn ran to her son, pulling him from the man's grasp, and threw her arms around him, kissing his face copiously while she tried to ascertain where he was hurt. "Oh, darling, did that boy hurt you? I'll get you to a doctor and I promise we'll get out of here as soon as possible. Darling—"

"Mother!" Jeremy said stiffly, very aware of the townspeople watching and laughing at this display of motherly affection. Considering that Jeremy was nearly as tall as his mother, yet she was cooing as though he were three years old, they were quite enjoying the spectacle.

The blond man came up behind Kathryn, and as he put his arm about her waist he said, "Honey, why don't you—"

Maybe it was the proprietary way the tall man slipped his arm around Kathryn's waist, or maybe it was his tone of ownership (the very same tone another man had once used with her), but she turned on him, twisting so his arm no longer touched her. "I don't need you or anyone else to tell me how to raise my son."

"I didn't mean . . . ," the man began, but Kathryn didn't want to hear what he had to say.

"Could someone show me where the doctor is?" she asked.

"Take your pick of saloons, honey," called a man.

With her arm firmly around Jeremy's shoulders, Kathryn led him from the crowd.

"Mother," Jeremy said plaintively, "will you stop fidgeting? I have told you that I am perfectly all right."

Using her best handkerchief, she again wiped at her son's cheek. "You do realize that what I said, I said in the heat of the moment. You and I must remain in this town, at least for a while, at least until I can find a way to earn enough money to . . ." She halted. In the last three hours she had been offered several ways to earn money in this revolting town.

After she had taken Jeremy from the laughing crowd, she had searched in vain for a doctor. It wasn't until she was at the end of the main street, Eureka, that she came to a stone wall patrolled by armed guards. Looking over the wall at what lay on the other side was like standing in hell and looking at heaven. Across the wall seemed to be a pretty little village complete with a library and a church and several houses with white picket fences and flowers growing in front.

"Back on your side, sister!" said a burly man with a rifle, glaring at the two of them.

For a moment, Kathryn's mind was transported back to Ireland and the laws against trespassing on O'Connor land: O'Connor laws, O'Connor punishments.

When Kathryn was speechless and Jeremy could see the blood rising in her neck, he pulled himself up to his full height and announced that they wanted to see Mr. Cole Jordan.

"And what's your business with him?" said a second guard, who had come to see what the problem was.

"My mother is to teach his son," Jeremy said proudly.

At that the two guards looked at each other and started to laugh. "You?" one said.

"Jordan told us you were—" He was laughing too hard to finish the sentence.

"Got any guns on you?"

"I hardly think so!" Kathryn said, at last recovering her powers of speech.

"Think we oughta search her?" the first man said, then the other said, "Not unless you want Jordan cuttin' your throat."

With that pronouncement, the men parted and allowed the two of them to pass, only vaguely pointing the way toward the Jordan house.

Now, she and Jeremy were standing on the porch outside a large, rambling old house, and she was trying to make both of them presentable.

"Yes, I understand that we can't leave now. I'm not a child, you know," Jeremy said.

"You wouldn't have known it this morning. I still can't

believe that you attacked that boy like that. Whatever possessed you?"

"He impugned your honor."

"Really, Jeremy, this is not the seventeenth century, and you do not have to defend my honor."

"I wouldn't have had to if you hadn't . . ." He hesitated as though he still couldn't believe what he'd seen. "If you hadn't kissed that man."

Since Kathryn had no excuse or even an explanation for her behavior, she thought it best to make no comment. "Now please remember your manners. I want both of us to make a good impression on Mr. Jordan." She took his chin in her hand and looked hard into his eyes. "Remember: We *need* this job!"

"Yes, Mother," he said dutifully. "I will do my best, but I hope you give me no further cause to—" The look his mother gave him made him decide not to finish that sentence. One could push Kathryn de Longe only so far, and well he knew her limits.

Raising her hand, Kathryn knocked, and moments later an elderly man ushered her into a nicely furnished parlor where they were told to wait. Minutes later the man returned and asked Kathryn to follow him to Mr. Jordan's office.

Once she was alone outside the room, Kathryn hesitated before knocking as she smoothed her hair and straightened her travel-stained garments. She would have liked to change, but what she had on was the best she had. There had never been money for more than one suit of clothing at a time.

"Come in," said a pleasant-sounding male voice and, smiling, she tucked her little leather portfolio under her arm and opened the door.

"You!" Two voices spoke in unison, both disbelieving. She was staring into the startled blue eyes of the man she'd . . . Well, that she'd kissed just an hour or so ago. So many thoughts went through Kathryn's mind that she couldn't speak. Would he fire her? Would he, as Jeremy said, "impugn her honor"? He *couldn't*, she thought—and prayed. He couldn't take this job away from her. She and

Jeremy *had* to have it. And she *had* to make him understand that she was a respectable woman—all evidence to the contrary.

The man recovered first. "Look, I can't see you now. I have to interview a teacher for Zach, so you're going to have to come back later. Better yet, give me the name of the house you're working and I'll meet you there later. Right now you have to get out of here." While he was making this extraordinary speech he came around the massive desk, grabbed her arm, and started to usher her out a side door in the room.

"Unhand me!" Kathryn said in her sternest schoolteacher voice, but it had no effect on the man, so, with a twist, she freed herself and ran back to the middle of the room. In an instant he was beside her, about to grab her again.

Without thinking what she was doing, she dropped her case, made a leap, and grabbed what looked to be an army sword from where it hung on the wall. "Mr. Jordan, if you touch me again I'll use this on you. I assume you are Cole Jordan, that is."

For a moment Cole stood staring at her in stunned silence, then his handsome face lit up in amusement. Leaning back against the desk, he folded his arms across his broad chest. "Maybe you should remove the scabbard first," he said, eyes twinkling.

"All right," she said with disgust, then with what dignity she could muster, she replaced the sword on the hooks in the wall and picked up her case from where it had fallen to the floor. "So I don't know anything about weapons of any sort, I admit it, but then I'm a teacher not a fighter. Nor am I whatever else you think I am." Turning back, she smiled at him. "I think, Mr. Jordan, that you and I got off on a wrong foot. Perhaps we should start again." With her hand outstretched, she took the few steps toward him.

But Cole did not take her offered hand, and his face went from smiling to a frown. "Where did you hear of this? Who told you I needed a teacher? And who the hell are you?"

"I'm Kathryn de Longe, and *you* hired me."

At that Cole's smile returned. "Oh, I see. So who put you up to this? Henry Brown? Or was it someone else? No, no, don't tell me, it was Lester and that bunch."

"I really have no idea what you're talking about. You put an ad in the Philadelphia paper, and I answered it. After the exchange of two letters, you hired me."

"Sure I did," Cole said with a voice dripping sarcasm, then he straightened and walked back around the desk, opened a drawer, and took out a large leather book—a book filled with bank drafts. "How much do you want?"

"I want what we agreed upon," she said, puzzled. "Mr. Jordan, I really do apologize for this morning, but—"

"You must be one of the players from Denver. Out-of-work actress, are you? Or just a prostitute with ambition?" He said the last with a slow look up and down her form.

Kathryn started to count to ten to control her temper, but instead she opened her case, pulled out papers, and began to put them before him on the desk. "Here are your two letters to me, and here are copies of my letters to you stating my qualifications. Here is the contract you sent me, and I believe that is, yes, I do believe that is your signature just above mine." She could not resist some sarcasm of her own, then, suddenly, doubt filled her mind. *"Is* that your signature? *Did* you write those letters?"

For a moment he looked at her in bewilderment, and she could tell by his expression that he had indeed signed the contracts. But then that knowing little smile of his came back. "How did you get these papers?"

"Through the United States mail service," she said in exasperation. "What *is* the problem? If you'd tell me what is wrong perhaps I could find a solution."

At that he opened a desk drawer and withdrew a piece of folded cardboard and tossed it toward her. "Open it," he said. "Go on. I think you should see it since *you* sent it to me."

Picking up the folder, she opened it to see a photograph of a stern-looking woman in her fifties, steel gray hair pulled back into a tight knot at the base of her neck. She had narrow eyes, a lipless mouth, and from her expression she had never smiled in her life.

"Seen that before?" Cole asked.

"No, should I have seen it?" she asked, putting the folder back onto his desk.

"That, Mrs. de Longe, or whatever your real name is, is you. Or who you wanted me to believe is you."

"I can assure you that I sent you a photograph of myself, not of anyone else, and I also sent you a full list of vital statistics, just as you asked for. I lied to you about nothing, not my age, my looks, or the fact that I am a widow with a nine-year-old son who will be living with me."

"Is this the list you sent?" he asked as he slammed a paper onto the desk.

As soon as Kathryn saw it she knew it wasn't her writing, for the letters were formed with a sharp angularity that her writing did not have. But when she saw her name at the top of the page, she picked it up and looked at it. According to the paper, Kathryn de Longe was fifty-one years old, five foot nine inches tall, and weighed a hundred and eighty-five pounds. She had never been married, had no dependents, and had taught school for nearly thirty years. Kathryn's mouth dropped open when she saw that all the schools "she" had taught at had been correctional institutions, mostly for "incorrigible" boys, but she'd also worked at a place for women who were "criminally insane."

With the paper were two testaments from former employers stating that Miss de Longe could control any boys, no matter how deviant their behavior.

Kathryn put the pages back down on the desk. "I have never worked with deviants or the insane," she said with a slight curl of her lip. "I was under the impression you wanted a *teacher* for your son, not a jailer."

He didn't respond to her barb, but instead picked up one of the pages she had put on his desk. "And is this your true list of qualifications? Miss Satterly's School for Young Ladies and Gentlemen? And what about this?" he said as he began to read. "Miss Kathryn de Longe, aged twenty-six, widowed with a nine-year-old son named Jeremy." He glanced up at her. "Started very young, didn't you? A nine-year-old at twenty-six, that would make you . . . how old when he was born?"

Kathryn didn't answer him, but stood straight, her fists clenched at her sides.

"Seventeen," he said as though he'd struggled for the

answer. "Were you *married* at sixteen? I don't suppose you have your marriage license."

"Destroyed in a fire," she said automatically, glaring at him.

"Just what I would have guessed," he said snidely. "Or lost at sea."

Kathryn moved in a way that she knew would make her corset stays stick into her ribs. She wanted to remind herself of the wanted poster hidden there. Legend was indeed a horrible place, but that was what was so good about it: No one in his right mind would look for her or anyone else here.

"Mr. Jordan," she said, working to control her growing anger at his implications. "I have no idea how you received another woman's photograph and résumé in place of what I sent. All I know is that I have a contract signed by you. The contract guarantees me a job and living accommodation for two years. It further states that if I am not satisfactory, then you will pay me two years' wages in full."

To her consternation, the man threw back his head and laughed. "So that's the game, is it? Really, you have to tell me who set you up with this. Was it Ned or maybe ol' Hog's Breath, as we kids used to call him?"

"I really have no idea what you are talking about. I would like for you to honor your contract: Either give me the job, or pay me so I can leave this town. One or the other would suit me."

At that Cole put his hands on the desk and leaned across it toward her, his face close to hers. "Mrs. de Longe, or whatever your name is, and I seriously doubt the 'Mrs.,' there is no honor in that contract. The way I see it, you aren't the person I hired, so I don't have to give you one red cent."

For a full moment Kathryn's mind went blank. No job, no money. How were she and Jeremy supposed to survive?

"Now, Mrs. Whatever-your-name-is, I would like for you to leave my office and you can tell whoever's paying you that I wasn't as easily duped as you planned. Although I must say I do like the bait they used," he added with a leering look up and down her tightly corseted body.

"Mr. Jordan," she said, and her voice was hardly above a

whisper. "I must have this job. My son and I have invested everything we have in this, and there are . . . other considerations."

"Such as?" he asked, one eyebrow raised.

"I can't say what they are but—"

She broke off because he began moving the papers on his desk and in the process her letters and the contract fell to the floor. Hurriedly, she bent to pick them up, retrieved her leather portfolio, and began to put the papers inside. Her hands were trembling so much she could hardly tie the string.

"Do you need a cook?" she whispered.

"What?" he snapped.

Drawing herself upright, she swallowed something that could only be her pride. She had dealt with enough people in her life to tell by this man's tone as well as his words that he was not, under any circumstances, going to reconsider his stance. Maybe later she could get him to reconsider, but now she didn't so much as have money for a meal.

"Do you need a cook?" she asked louder, then had to stand there and bear the way he looked at her, as though he were trying to figure her out.

After a while a slow smile crept onto his lips, lips that earlier in the day she had enjoyed kissing. "No," he said softly, "I don't need a cook, and I don't need a wife. My son doesn't need a mother, he needs a teacher. And although I do appreciate all the trouble you have gone to to get close to me, I can assure you that the girls in town supply me with all the 'wifely' affection that I can handle." Again he looked her up and down, but this time with lowered eyelids that let her know what was in his mind. "There are other men in town, Miss, ah, Mrs. de Longe. You really don't have to set your cap for the richest man."

Maybe it was the word *richest* that finally broke through to Kathryn, or maybe it was just the whole rotten day in which she had been repeatedly accused of being a prostitute, and had seen her son nearly murdered in the filthy streets while a bunch of dirty ruffians watched. Or maybe it was kissing a man who turned out to be such a pig as this one. Whatever it was, Kathryn's temper broke.

With measured steps, she walked toward the desk, then put her fists on it and leaned toward him. He was sitting, so she was the one looking down at him.

"Let me make myself clear, Mr. Jordan. I have no, let me repeat that, *no* desire to marry you or any other man. I came here because I signed a contract for a job. You hear me? A *job!* And I want nothing else from you. Right now I don't even want that because I have never met a more vain, egomaniacal man than you in my life—and that includes the aristocracy of Ireland. I have no idea how the photographs were exchanged, but I can assure that *I* did not switch them. I represented myself honestly and with integrity, and that is how I expect to be treated in return. Now, I *demand* that you honor your contract with me!" Never in her life had Kathryn demanded anything, except sometimes that Jeremy not do something dangerous, but this man seemed to elicit emotions and responses from her that she'd never felt before.

"Demand, do you?" the man said with a one-sided smile, then slowly he stood up, pulling himself to his full height of well over six feet. "Well, Mrs. de Long, *I* demand that you get out of my house and never step foot into it again. Now which of us is more likely to have our demands obeyed?"

Standing there, Kathryn looked across the desk into eyes that had turned as cold as sapphires, and she knew she had lost. There was nothing she could do or say that was going to make this man give her the job that was hers by right, the job that she and her son so desperately needed.

Trying to retain her pride, she stiffened her back and walked toward the door. If she allowed herself to think for even a second about what this man was condemning her to, she'd collapse.

Once she was outside the odious man's office, she took Jeremy's hand in hers and led him out of the house. Jeremy knew his mother well enough not to ask questions about what had gone on; besides, their voices had been loud enough for him to hear most of it.

Kathryn half pulled him down the dirt road, past the stone wall that separated the two very different parts of town from each other, and into the muddy streets of Legend proper. For all that Jeremy was only nine, he had seen a very ugly side of life, and he knew what jobs were open to women in a place like Legend.

"I can work," he said softly. "I'm strong and I can get a job. There are mines here and I—"

Abruptly, Kathryn halted in the middle of the street and stared at her son. "Going to work in a mine at nine years old?" she said, horror in her voice. "Is that what kind of mother you think I am?" For a moment forgetting his age, she said, "I'll make a living on my back before I—" She broke off as she stared at something above Jeremy's head.

"Mother?" he said, then turned and looked at the sign that was behind him. "Prettiest girls in the West," the sign read. "Highest prices for the best."

"Mother!" Jeremy said in fear, then grabbed her arm when she took a step forward. "I'll work. I'll—"

But Kathryn wasn't paying any attention to him. As though she were in a trance she started walking, half dragging a fearful Jeremy behind her.

"No, no," he began, but stopped when his mother walked past the entrance to the saloon and instead started up the stairs beside the building. For a moment Jeremy stood rooted where he was, then he saw a small sign hanging beside the bottom of the stairs. *I'll sue anybody about anything,* the sign said. *No case too small. I ain't afraid of nobody. John T. Stewart, attorney-at-law.*

"What an extraordinary sentiment," Jeremy said, reading the sign. "Mother, did you—"

But Kathryn was already halfway up the stairs, and Jeremy had to run to catch her. "Mother, whatever are you thinking of doing?"

"I'm going to sue the bastard," Kathryn de Longe said, which made her son stand where he was, his mouth open in disbelief, for he'd never, ever heard his mother use such a word before. She thought *damn* might open the gates of hell.

"Wait for me," Jeremy called and ran to follow his mother into the grimy little office.

Two

"COLE JORDAN?" THE ATTORNEY, JOHN T. STEWART, SAID AS HE pulled on the long point of his drooping mustache. "You want me to sue Cole Jordan?" Turning around in his chair, he glanced over his left shoulder at his plump wife, who was knitting what looked to be a twelve-foot-long scarf. Mr. Stewart seemed to be highly amused by the very prospect of suing such a man—and he didn't seem to have any intention of taking the case.

"Mr. Stewart, your sign says that you are afraid of no one," Kathryn said, her lips tight, and she couldn't resist a bit of sarcasm. "Why didn't you write, 'With the exception of Cole Jordan'?"

She had meant to shame him, but instead, he grinned at her. "I didn't write on there, 'Except for the devil,' either." After a pause, he looked over his shoulder to see if his wife had caught his witticism, and since she was smiling into her wool, she had.

"No sir," Mr. Stewart said, "I'll sue anybody but the devil and Jordan, which in my book is about the same thing. I'll take on murderers and thieves. I'll even take on preachers, but I'll *not* go against the Jordans."

For Kathryn, what she was hearing was too much like what she'd encountered in Ireland over nine years before. No one would stand up to the O'Connors then, and now no one would help her fight the Jordans. "Are you telling me that in a free country like this you'd allow one man to rule you?"

"You can wave all the flags you want, ma'am, but it won't help. The Jordan family owns every inch of this town, and we all do what they say."

"How many of them are there?" Kathryn asked, eyes wide.

21

"A passel, but most of 'em went to Denver years ago. Only Cole stayed behind to run the town."

"This isn't a town, Mr. Stewart, this is a Den of Sin."

"It is nice, ain't it?" Mr. Stewart said, smiling fondly. "This town is a lawyer's dream-come-true. I got so much business, a dozen of me couldn't do all the work. And I can charge whatever I want."

Kathryn would have left as soon as she heard the man's cowardly attitude, but she was hungry and she knew Jeremy was too, and hunger makes a person desperate. Besides, in the last minutes she had been watching Mrs. Stewart. With every word that was exchanged, the woman's head had bent lower over her knitting, and she was now wearing a frown. Her look encouraged Kathryn.

"I have a case that you couldn't lose," Kathryn said. "I have a contract signed by Cole Jordan, and I'm sure someone in town could verify his signature. But then he admits he signed the contract. I'm no longer asking to work for him, but he does owe me money, and I need that money. I traveled a long way on his word, and now he's going back on his word. Doesn't that count for something here in America?"

"Maybe in America it does, but this here is Legend, and the United States government don't own this place, the Jordans do. They—"

"Isn't there someone who isn't afraid of him?" Kathryn asked in exasperation. "I can see by the filth of this town that the decent people here are fighting a losing battle, but surely, someone, somewhere . . ." She was looking at Mrs. Stewart, who still had her head low, her frown deepening. "Maybe someone with children . . . Surely there must be someone besides me who isn't afraid of him. Or maybe there's something he's afraid of," she said as an afterthought.

"Cole's afraid of guns," Mrs. Stewart said, speaking for the first time. "He won't touch a gun ever since he was nine years old. The boy had a dream that his whole family was killed by the people of Legend shooting at some robbers. Of course nothing like that ever happened, but that don't stop Cole. Won't touch a gun."

After that statement the woman looked back down at her

knitting, and Kathryn blinked in confusion. What did that information have to do with Mr. Jordan's refusal to honor a contract?

But Mr. Stewart seemed to think there was some relevance, as he had turned in his chair and was looking at his wife expectantly. "What's your point, sugar muffin?" he asked after several long moments of silence.

"Judge Harry Bascom."

The name meant nothing to Kathryn, but it seemed to mean a lot to John T. Stewart, for he turned as pale as an eggshell. Considering that he had the red face of a budding alcoholic, that was no easy task.

The lawyer turned back to Kathryn. "How much you payin' me?"

"If I gave you a hundred per cent of all I own in the world it would be nothing."

Mr. Stewart looked at Kathryn hard for a moment. "That's good. Beautiful young widow. Hmmm, almost too beautiful. You look like one of Carl's French singers."

At that Kathryn narrowed her eyes at him.

"No offense," he said, then looked back over his shoulder. "Martha, honey, can you do somethin' with her hair? Pull it back a bit and see if you can make her look less . . . well, less appealin'. We don't want people thinkin' she's a floozy."

"You leave it to me, Jake, I can make any woman look unappealing."

"Except for yourself, love bunny," the man said with an adoring look at his wife's bowed head.

Kathryn was embarrassed by the affectionate exchanges between the two of them; she felt as though she'd walked into a honeymoon chamber. She wouldn't have guessed that Mrs. Stewart, her face weathered by many years in the mountains and quite a few pounds overweight, could inspire the name "love bunny."

"Ahem," Kathryn said, clearing her throat and intercepting the looks they were exchanging. "Who is Judge Harry Bascom?"

Reluctantly, Mr. Stewart looked back at Kathryn. "He ain't afraid of even the Jordans."

"Or the devil," Mrs. Stewart said softly, and this witticism sent Mr. Stewart into spasms of laughter.

While Kathryn waited for him to come back to the task at hand, she glanced at Jeremy, who was quietly studying the few law books in a case against one wall. She knew Jeremy well enough to know that he was keenly interested in every word that was being spoken.

"Then you'll take my case?" Kathryn asked when the man had stopped being convulsed with laughter.

"What do you think, Bunches?" Mr. Stewart asked his wife.

Jeremy looked up from a book and mouthed, Bunches of what? to his mother, making her hide a smile behind her hand.

For a moment Mrs. Stewart looked at Kathryn, studying her, and Kathryn could see the intelligence there. No wonder Mr. Stewart asked her opinion.

"I think this woman might do some good for this town. I think it's time that someone fought the Jordans, and I think this woman and you, Jake, are just the ones to do it."

Before Mr. Stewart could say anything, Kathryn spoke up. "I don't want there to be any misunderstanding. I have no intention of helping this town, as you put it. In fact, I have no intention of staying here. I really just want enough money to get out of here so I can go somewhere else. San Francisco maybe." At this she looked at Jeremy, and his slight smile and nod were enough for her. "Yes, just the money and nothing else."

Mr. Stewart looked at his wife at the end of this speech, saw that she was smiling into her knitting, then turned back to Kathryn. "If I can get Judge Harry, I'll be glad to take on your case."

"And how likely is it that you will be able to get this judge?"

At that, Mr. Stewart chuckled. "Three years ago Cole Jordan broke Judge Harry's eldest daughter's heart. He'll come. Don't you worry about that. It's just a matter of when. Now you just tell me where you're stayin' so I can contact you when it's all arranged."

"That is a bit of a problem," Kathryn said, looking down at her hands. "My son and I have no place to stay and no money to rent a room." Her head came up and her mouth tightened in anger. "I thought we were coming here to a job and a place to live. But now we have nothing."

"Oh, that's very good," the man said. "You'll do real well on the stand. Can you make them tears come at will?"

It was on the tip of Kathryn's tongue to tell him that her feelings were genuine and not something she could turn on and off, but Mrs. Stewart spoke.

"You'll have to stay with us," she said, smiling sweetly at both her and Jeremy. "You wouldn't happen to know how to sew, do you, dear?" she asked, thereby establishing that Kathryn was to be a working guest.

"My mother was a cook for a large estate and I learned a bit from her," Kathryn said modestly. "Perhaps I would be allowed to help in the kitchen."

"If you insist," Mrs. Stewart said, smiling as she looked back at her scarf.

"My mother can knit, too," Jeremy said, speaking for the first time.

For a moment Kathryn held her breath. Would Mrs. Stewart be horribly offended by his words?

But Mrs. Stewart looked up, eyes twinkling, and held aloft her long, long scarf. "Then perhaps she might teach me," she said, and all of them laughed together.

Four and a half weeks, Kathryn thought, as she twisted the black cotton gloves on her hands. She and Jeremy had been in this horrible town of Legend for four and a half long, long weeks, and during that time she had learned more than she'd ever wanted to know about Cole Jordan. She'd found out that his family owned all the land, the buildings, the mines, and, some said, he even owned the people.

She'd found out that he was massively wealthy, but he never spent a penny on the town unless he had to. He just lived on his side of the stone wall and pretended that the debauchery on the other side didn't exist.

Except when he came down to visit, that is. Visit the "girls," as they were called. And it seemed that he visited them often. "Twice a day if he ain't too busy," a woman had told her.

The day after she and Jeremy had moved in with the

Stewarts, Kathryn had found herself to be regarded as a heroine, maybe even an avenging angel. "You tell him I wanta buy my place," a man told her, then Kathryn launched into a long explanation about how she had no power to make Cole Jordan do anything.

But no one seemed to hear her, for a few minutes later three women descended on her complaining about their "working" hours. Kathryn knew her face was aubergine purple when she thought about what they worked at, but the women kept on in spite of Kathryn's embarrassment.

By the end of the first week Kathryn began to carry a notepad and pencil with her wherever she went so she could write down the complaints. She had no idea what she was going to do with her list, but it seemed to be the polite thing to do.

By the end of the second week she knew half the people of Legend by name, and the wagon drivers bringing goods up from Denver always saved the best of the produce for her to use in the Stewarts' kitchen. By the third week she was known as the best cook in the country, "maybe even in the whole world" thanks to a fairly continuous round of dinner parties the Stewarts gave.

So now she and Jeremy had been here over a month and she was sitting in a courtroom waiting for the trial to begin. Right after their one and only confrontation, Cole Jordan had left town and had only returned last night, so Kathryn had not seen him during her long stay in Legend.

But now she was sitting at a table on one side of the courtroom, and he was on the other, half hidden behind his three lawyers. This morning the Stewarts had dressed Kathryn all in black, pulling her dark hair back so tightly that her eyes watered, then an old-fashioned black silk poke bonnet had been pushed down onto her head. When Jeremy had seen her, his eyes had widened, and he'd said in a whisper, "You look like a Raphael Madonna." Looking in the mirror, Kathryn agreed that she looked pale and . . . well, untouchable.

"A virgin widow," Mr. Stewart decreed, as he put his arm around his wife's plump shoulders. "I knew you could do it, Honey Lamb," he said to his wife.

"I look ridiculous," Kathryn said, pushing at the high

collar of her heavy black silk dress with the cameo at its neck.

"I think she looks beautiful, Mrs. Lamb," Jeremy said, blinking at his mother. He'd called Mrs. Stewart that behind her back for all the first week, but one night at dinner it had slipped out, and the Stewarts had laughed so hard that he'd called her that ever since. Even Kathryn had slipped twice and called her Mrs. Lamb. It was easy to do since Mrs. Stewart was kind and gentle—and ruled her home and husband with an iron fist.

So now Kathryn was sitting in the courtroom and awaiting the next moments that would decide the course of her life, for Cole Jordan had been called to the stand.

Mr. Stewart had just asked Cole why he hadn't honored his contract and given Widow Kathryn the job she so desperately needed for the support of herself and her dear little son.

"I refused to hire her because she couldn't handle my son," Cole said smoothly, ignoring Stewart's insinuations and smiling at the courtroom with absolute confidence. He even smiled up at Judge Bascom, but Kathryn was relieved to see that the judge did not smile back.

"All of you know my son," Cole continued. "He can run a whorehouse; he can gamble. But look at her. She's never drunk out of anything except porcelain, so what does she know about a boy like mine?"

John Stewart looked puzzled, as though he didn't understand Cole's comment. "But isn't that what a governess is for? To teach things like tea drinkin'? If you wanted someone to teach the boy how to drink out of a beer mug, why bother hirin' someone from Philadelphia? We got beer-drinkers right here in Legend."

At this the courtroom erupted into laughter until Judge Bascom banged his gavel.

"However," Mr. Stewart said loudly, "we concede that your son has the knowledge of a criminal and the manners of a jackass—"

"Just like his pa!" someone in the courtroom yelled, and there was more laughter until the judge shouted at everyone to shut up.

"Now, according to your story, you thought you were hiring an older woman who was experienced in dealing with incorrigibles and the criminally insane. Is that correct?" Mr. Stewart didn't wait for Cole to answer before he continued. "Then am I to believe that you wanted to hire a, shall we say, masculine woman to teach your son to be a gentleman? Can you tell me how that works, Mr. Jordan?"

As far as Kathryn could tell, Cole Jordan was unperturbed by Mr. Stewart's questions. But then she knew how people who owned everything reacted to the law. People like the Jordans made the laws; they didn't obey them.

"I need someone who can control him first before she can teach him anything," Cole said smoothly.

"Mr. Jordan," John Stewart said, "tell me, how tall are you? Over six feet?"

"An inch or two," Cole said modestly.

"I see," Mr. Stewart said, walking away from where Cole was seated, all six feet two of him sprawled out, lounging in the chair as though he hadn't a care in the world. "Six feet two and a couple of hundred pounds, right?"

Cole gave a one-sided smile. "Better ask some of the ladies. They might know something about the size of me."

His meaning was unmistakable, and the courtroom filled with feminine laughter. Cole looked up at Kathryn. She thought maybe he expected her to smile at him, but the look she gave him would have turned him to stone if he'd had a heart. He winked at her, then looked back at Mr. Stewart.

"Mr. Jordan, what I'd like to know is, if you can't control that hellion of a son of yours, how do you expect any *woman* to?"

There was more laughter from the court, but the judge just waited for it to subside as he leaned across his desk and looked expectantly at Cole. "You wanta answer that question, boy?" the judge said, and Kathryn was pleased to hear the hostility in his voice. She had been told in full the story of how Cole had "jilted" Judge Bascom's eldest daughter. But, to be fair, from what Kathryn had heard, most of the pursuit had been on the daughter's side, and the complaint had been that she had not been able to snare Cole Jordan into being the husband she wanted so much.

"The point of this whole thing is," Cole said evenly, "I don't think she was going to try to control him or even to teach him." He leaned a bit forward as though confiding a secret. "I think her concerns were with the father, not the son."

"Oh?" Mr. Stewart said in a stage whisper. "What makes you say such a thing?"

Slowly, as though he had all the time in the world, Cole withdrew a newspaper clipping from a Pennsylvania paper from his shirt pocket and handed it to Mr. Stewart, who took a few moments to read it.

"I see," Mr. Stewart said after a while, then held the article up toward the courtroom. "I'd like to tell the court that this here article states that Cole Jordan of Legend, Colorado, is rollin' in dough and ain't bad to look at either." When the laughter had stopped, he turned back to Cole. "Do I have that right?"

"You do," Cole said stiffly.

"So let me guess at your reasonin'," Mr. Stewart said. "You think this woman saw this article in the Philadelphia newspaper, then did everything she could to win a teaching contract from you? And she did this all for the sole purpose of tryin' to marry you?"

"In a word, yes."

With a look at Judge Bascom, Mr. Stewart said, "You seem to think a *lot* of women want to marry you, don't you, Mr. Stewart?"

The judge didn't bother trying to make the courtroom stop laughing at that because from the way the sentence was stated, it made his daughter seem to be one of many whom Cole Jordan had thought wanted him.

It was Mr. Stewart's booming voice that made the laughter stop. "Tell me, Mr. Jordan, how did she know what you wanted? Let me remind you of the advertisement you put in the Philadelphia paper sayin' you needed a governess. It said that you needed a mature, responsible woman. Is that correct?"

Cole gave a curt nod of assent.

"Mrs. de Longe is old enough to have a nine-year-old son and responsible enough to take care of him, so I believe she answers your request. So how did she know to send a photo of a much older woman? For all Mrs. de Longe knew, you were lookin' for a young woman." He looked at the courtroom. "For all she knew, you were a lonely cowboy lookin' for a wife."

"That's what every woman thinks a man wants, isn't it?" Cole said, but Kathryn could see by his face that he didn't get the laugh he'd expected. By now the courtroom was sitting on the edges of their seats and waiting to see where John Stewart was leading.

"Could you please tell the court what happened to make you believe Mrs. de Longe was after somethin' other than a teachin' job?"

Cole gave a one-sided grin and seemed to relax in his chair. "The first time I saw her, she threw herself into my arms. And kissed me!" He smiled at the courtroom. "Later she pretended she hadn't known who I was, that it was merely a chance meeting, but what's the likelihood of such a coincidence? No, I think she planned it all from the beginning. She may have the face of an angel, but she has the heart of a scheming, conniving little—"

Judge Bascom interrupted. "Mr. Jordan, please refrain from your comments. It is the court's job to decide what lies inside Mrs. de Longe's heart. However, I think it is safe to say that we can all agree with you that she has the face of an angel."

At that there were whoops of agreement from the men in the room.

"And that's the problem," one of Cole's attorneys yelled, coming out of his seat. "This woman is too much temptation for any man. How would it be for a man to be lusting after his son's teacher? It is our belief that the woman planned all of this with matrimony in mind. Cole Jordan is an eligible bachelor and she is a widow—if she was ever married, that is. She answered the advertisement, lied about her age, even sent a bogus photograph. Not that our client isn't flattered by this elaborate hoax in an attempt to win his very rich hand, but he's just not ready for the old ball and chain yet. He—"

"I do *not* want to marry him!" Kathryn shouted, coming

out of her seat. "I sent a photo of myself and no one else. I did *not*—"

"Are you trying to make us believe—" Cole's lawyer began, but the hoots of the audience and the banging of the judge's gavel made him stop.

When the noise began to subside, Mr. Stewart's voice rose as he made an elaborate show of helping Kathryn to sit back down. "I think I can clear up this matter, Your Honor, if you'd just let me call my next witness."

"Do it!" the judge said, letting everyone see that he was glad to get Cole off the stand.

"I call Zachary Jordan," he said, and immediately a hush fell over the courtroom.

In the turmoil of the last weeks Kathryn had forgotten all about the boy she was to have taken charge of, but today's testimony had made her curious. Twisting about in her seat, she first saw Jeremy, sitting just behind her. When his face began to turn an unbecoming color of purple, she knew that what was coming wasn't going to be pleasant.

Swaggering in an exaggerated imitation of his father, the boy who had fought with Jeremy on that first day moved to the front of the courtroom and took the witness seat.

Kathryn grabbed Mr. Stewart's coat sleeve. "I just want the money due me," she said in a ragged whisper. "I don't want to try to teach that . . . that violent child. He and Jeremy would kill each other."

"Leave it to me," Mr. Stewart said confidently, then turned to the smirking young man slouching in the chair.

"You wanta tell everyone what you did," Mr. Stewart said, then waved his hand at the boy.

"I switched the letters," the boy said proudly. "Pa wanted to hire some old crow, so when I saw this lady's picture, I just switched 'em. Pete the forger helped me a bit with the letters, but I done a real good job, don't you think?"

When the laughter from the court had stopped, Mr. Stewart walked over to the boy. "You tampered with the United States mail?"

"Yes, sir, I did," the boy said proudly, looking about the courtroom as though he expected to be congratulated.

"I'm going to tan you," Cole said to his son, but loud

31

enough for half the courtroom to hear him. "When I get you home—"

The judge brought down his gavel. "You can carry out your domestic quarrels at home, Jordan. This is a court of law. But it seems you were wrong and this young lady was telling the truth all along. And it seems that you need somebody to keep constant watch over that brat of yours. I hereby decree that you give her the job you promised her."

"No!!" came the combined shouts of Kathryn, Mr. Stewart, Jeremy, and Cole.

"Your Honor," Mr. Stewart said quickly. "My client just wants the money so she can leave Legend forever. She's suffered horrible distress while she's been here and she needs to—"

"Bull!" the judge bellowed. "She's become the town celebrity. Walks around with a notebook taking down orders of what people want her to get from Cole Jordan. If you ask me, the two of them deserve each other. Of course, if your client can't handle this young scalawag, then that would invalidate the contract. Does she want to back out?"

"No, Your Honor," Mr. Stewart said. "But she don't wanta stay either."

"Then she shouldn't have come here in the first place." He banged his gavel. "That's it. She stays and teaches or she drops the whole thing. Those are the choices. Which is it gonna be?"

Mr. Stewart looked at Kathryn with apology on his face.

"I have to take the job," she whispered.

Mr. Stewart looked back at the judge. "He pays court costs?"

"He pays for everything," the judge said with just the tiniest bit of a smile.

"Then we take the job on one condition. Mrs. de Longe wants the biggest padlock this town has for her bedroom door."

As the courtroom was laughing, Mr. Stewart turned back to Kathryn. "Real sorry about the verdict. There ain't nobody can teach that brat of Jordan's. He's got bars on the kid's bedroom window, but he still escapes."

"And drinks whiskey," Kathryn said as she blinked up at

Mr. Stewart, still unable to comprehend the verdict. "I have to *live* with the two of them?"

"Looks like that's what the judge said," Mr. Stewart said as he shoved papers back into a leather case. Kathryn was going to say more, but by then people were shoving each other to be able to congratulate both of them. To the town's mind, Kathryn had won a case against the Jordans, something no one believed would happen.

"Now you be sure and tell him what I told you," a beefy woman pumping Kathryn's hand was saying. Her breath smelled like old sheets.

"And you help me buy my own store. A man oughta own his own place," a man said as he thumped Kathryn on the back. "You tell Jordan that—"

But Kathryn wasn't hearing anymore as she looked across the people to see Cole Jordan standing and glaring at her. His look said she may have won the battle but the war was yet to come.

"Come on, Zach," she heard him say as he cupped his hand at the back of his son's head. As they turned away, the boy winked at Kathryn.

"Oh lord," she whispered to herself. "What in the world have I got myself into?"

Three

KATHRYN STRAIGHTENED HER SHOULDERS AND TRIED TO PUT some steel into her spine as she raised her hand to knock on the door of Cole Jordan's office. It had been a mere two hours since the verdict had been given, and only minutes ago, Mr. Stewart had dropped her and Jeremy off in front of the Jordan house. Now Jeremy was sitting in the hallway, their small trunks on the floor at his feet, and it was Kathryn's job to find out what Mr. Jordan had planned for them.

"Courage," she said aloud to herself, then knocked on the door. The gruffness of the "Come in" almost made her turn and run, but she took a breath and opened the door.

He was sitting behind his big desk, his head down. "Mr. Jordan," she began, but he interrupted her.

"So you won, did you?" he said, leaning back in his chair and scowling.

"I want you to know that what I did was out of necessity. I would never have resorted to a court of law if I hadn't been in desperate need."

"Desperate need," he said. "Ah yes, I know that feeling." Looking like some great prowling beast, with his brows drawn into a scowl, Cole rose and came around the desk to glare down at Kathryn.

With stiff arms and her hands made into fists, she stood her ground. She was not going to let him see how much she regretted everything that had happened.

"Mrs. de Longe, let me tell you about 'desperate need.' I own this town, and that means that everyone and everything in it is my responsibility. On top of that responsibility, I have the sole care of a hellion of a son. His mother, may she rest in peace, dumped him on my doorstep the night before she ran off with a circus performer."

At that Kathryn raised her eyebrows. A circus performer?

He was advancing on her, but Kathryn refused to retreat. "I need someone who can handle that boy. You don't know what he is like."

"I can see what you have allowed him to become," she said with more courage than she felt.

"Oh?" Cole said, one eyebrow raised. "Should I have kept him tied to me as you have that son of yours? Pardon me, Mrs. de Longe, but I do *not* want my son raised to be the puny, frightened little creature that your son is. I want my son to grow to be a *man.*"

Kathryn could take anything anyone gave to her, but she couldn't take what he was saying about Jeremy. "How dare you?" she said, moving toward him and standing on tiptoe so she was closer to his level. "My son is more of a man than that ill-mannered, selfish creature *you* have raised. *My* son isn't halfway to being hanged for the criminal he is."

"Criminal?" Cole said, his face furious as he was nearly nose to nose with her.

Then suddenly, he seemed to change. As he stepped away, there was a smile on his face, a wicked little smile. "Yes, Mrs. de Longe, Zachary is on his way to becoming a criminal, which is why I needed someone who could handle him. You . . ." He looked her up and down with contempt. "You can only handle boys who say, Yes ma'am and No ma'am, and know which fork to use."

"I can handle anyone," she said under her breath, still seething at his remarks about Jeremy. "I can teach your son and discipline your son and—" She broke off because he was laughing at her, as though what she'd said was extremely amusing—and ridiculous.

"You?" he said, laughing. "I have a dog that outweighs you, and a prison warden couldn't handle that son of mine."

Truthfully, Kathryn agreed with him, but she couldn't back down now. "I can and I will control your—" She broke off as he picked up a check from off his desk and handed it to her. "What is this?"

"It's a bank draft for two years' salary. When I'm wrong I admit it. It was my son who was the liar, not you. I pay my debts, so there's the money I promised you in the contract."

Kathryn stood there looking at the check in her hand. It was what she wanted, what she'd gone to court to get. So why wasn't she halfway out the door by now? She looked up at him. "Who will you get to teach your son? Will you hire that woman who has worked with the criminally insane?"

"Yes," he said simply.

"Then I don't want this," she said as she put the check back onto his desk. "Your son needs a teacher, and I have been hired to be that teacher, as well as being ordered to by the court."

"That's very noble of you," Cole said. "But also very stupid. My son is not for the likes of someone like you."

"And what am I, Mr. Jordan? Since you seem to know a great deal about me, I'd like to know what it is you do know about me. Other than that you think I'm trying to trap you into marriage, that is."

At that, the corner of Cole's mouth quirked into a bit of a smile. "You're a lady," he said as he sat on the desk, his long legs stretching into the room. "And since you're in this hellhole of a town, my guess is that you're running from something or someone. People in Legend often come here to hide from something. You say you're a widow, but *lady* widows usually have rich relatives to take care of them. So where are your rich relatives?"

It was Kathryn's turn to smile. "You are not a good judge of character, Mr. Jordan. I am not a 'lady,' as you call it. My mother was a cook for a large estate, and my father worked in the stables until he died when I was five. When the daughter of the house proved too stupid to educate, it was decided that perhaps if she had a companion she might better learn, so I was schooled with her. But even though I was educated in the main house, I was never, ever treated as anything except the cook's daughter. As for Jeremy's father, that is none of your business. Now, would it be possible that someone could show me where my son and I are to stay?"

"Stay?" Cole asked. "You can't stay here. And you can't possibly take on Zachary. He—"

"Double my salary says that I can and will get that young man under control, and I'll do it within a week. As long as you give me a free hand, that is."

Cole opened his mouth to speak but closed it, then he smiled in a knowing way. "You're on. One week. Double your salary." Putting out his hand, he shook hers, and the look in his eye said that this was one bet he was sure he was going to win.

For a moment Kathryn felt exhilarated that she had won, but at the same time she felt terror running through her as she remembered the way young Zachary had pulled a whiskey bottle from the arms of a woman and downed half of it. "W . . . where do we stay?" she asked, taking her hand from his because he had not released it. Instead, he was standing there staring at her in a way that was making Kathryn feel decidedly uncomfortable.

"Anywhere," he said, then turned his back on her as he looked at some papers on his desk. "Take whatever rooms you want. The house is mostly empty."

"All right," she said softly, then started for the door.

"Mrs. de Longe?"

She paused with her hand on the door.

"I'll be away in Denver for the next week. I usually take my son with me, but since you seem convinced that you can handle him, I'll leave him in your care."

"Yes, certainly," she said with as much courage as she could summon. How in the world was she going to control that horrid boy for a whole week? Should she ask where the whips and chains were stored?

"If you should change your mind after the first day or so, I'll leave this draft here. You can cash it at the Legend bank, and you and your son may leave at any time."

"And who will look after your son?"

"He seems to be rather good at taking care of himself," Cole said. "I've never found that he needs anyone."

"Like you, Mr. Jordan?" she said. "Perhaps he is merely echoing your sentiments, that you believe you need no one else on earth."

Turning, Cole gave her that little smirk again. "I see. Now let me guess, Mrs. de Longe. You think *you* are just the person I need."

Kathryn gave him a very sweet smile. "Mr. Jordan, I hope your horse steps into a hole and you fall and break your neck. Good day, sir." As she firmly shut the door behind him, she heard his laughter.

"Mother, you have gone mad," Jeremy said when he heard what she had done. "You should have taken the money and we could have left this horrible place. Zachary *is* incorrigible. And the father is as bad. I've heard that—"

"Jeremy, you are not to repeat what you've heard about either of them. Zachary Jordan has no mother, so we must be forgiving and—"

"I have no *father,"* Jeremy said and there was the unmistakable tone of jealousy in his voice. "But that fact has yet to excuse me from any misbehavior."

"Jeremy, my darling, you have been blessed with a mother who is sane and sensible and loves you very much. That poor child has had no one except a man who lives under the illusion that every woman on earth is dying to spend her life with him. He is vain and arrogant, not to mention ignorant of the simplest courtesies and—" She broke off because Jeremy was staring at her oddly.

"Come on," she said, picking up one of the cases at his feet. "Let's see if we can find someone to tell us where *his* rooms are, so we can live as far from him as possible."

Jeremy grabbed the other bags and started to follow his mother up the stairs. "And a room that we can put a padlock on."

"I think that was just Mr. Stewart's little joke," Kathryn said as she paused on the landing, looking at the two hallways in front of her, one branching right, the other left. With her free hand she ran it along the surface of a table, then frowned as her hand came away dirty.

"I don't think it was a bad idea," Jeremy said as he followed his mother down the right corridor, his shoulders pulling under the weight of the bags. "Really, Mother, a padlock could be quite an asset."

Kathryn was opening doors, looking inside the rooms, then clucking in disgust. It was obvious that the house had once been beautiful, but now neglect had been allowed to make the rooms almost uninhabitable. Dirt and dust were everywhere. In one bedroom there was a mouse nest in the feather pillow on the bed. One bedroom's window had blown open, and it looked as though it had stayed open for days, because the floor and the surrounding furniture were damaged severely.

When Kathryn opened the door at the end of the corridor, she said, "Ah," in such a way that Jeremy came to peer over her shoulder. He could see that this was obviously *his* bedroom, as Jeremy thought of the man who had made his mother so unhappy. There were clothes and dirty boots slung everywhere. A pile of socks that looked as though they hadn't been washed in years were heaped by the door.

With thumb and one finger extended, Kathryn picked up a sock and held it aloft. The toe was worn through. "Disgusting," she said, dropped the awful object, then shut the door. "Come, Jeremy, we will move into the opposite end of the house."

"Where does the other one sleep?" Jeremy said under his breath as he followed his mother's swift footsteps.

Kathryn didn't say anything, but she silently thought that poor Zachary could probably sleep in town in one of those . . . those houses, for all his father knew.

"Mother, you must rest. And you must admit defeat."

Kathryn ran the back of her hand over her sweaty brow, pushing the fallen hair out of her eyes, and looked up at her son. She was on her hands and knees scouring the kitchen floor, which she was sure hadn't been washed in the last ten years or so. "Darling, if I had ever admitted defeat I would have been hanged for kidnapping long ago and you would be living a life of leisure with your father."

At that Jeremy smiled and sat down at the big pine kitchen table that now gleamed from his mother's efforts. "You could always help me, you know."

Jeremy picked up an apple from the bowl on the table and bit into it. "I am an O'Connor, you know. Blood of kings, that sort of thing."

Kathryn threw her dirty rag, and it would have hit him smack in the face if he hadn't caught it midair then dropped it disdainfully on the floor. She got off her knees and lowered herself onto a chair near her son. "Jeremy, darling, what in the world am I going to do? Mr. Jordan will return in a day or two, and I haven't made any progress at all."

For a moment she closed her eyes and thought back over the last several days, and involuntarily, she gave a bit of a shudder. Zachary Jordan was afraid of no one and nothing. There was nothing she could threaten him with that made any difference to him. She couldn't intimidate him with, "I'm going to tell your father," because he knew very well that his father wanted her to fail—if for no other reason than to be able to say, I told you so.

She had talked to Zachary twice to try to persuade him of the value of an education. Like his father, he had just laughed at her, then turned away and left the house.

She had tried to make a home for him. Well, truthfully, maybe she had tried to make the Jordan house into a home for her and Jeremy, but Zachary lived there too. It seemed that Cole Jordan only had male employees, and cleanliness was not something they considered important. Neither was good food. They fried everything in lard, poured it onto platters, then put them into the middle of the table.

For her and Jeremy's own health, she had started cooking for the two of them and young Zachary, who, she quickly discovered, had an appetite that matched the size of him. And of course Kathryn couldn't cook in a kitchen as filthy as that one had been, so she'd cleaned it. Then she'd cleaned two bedrooms for herself and Jeremy, and since their rooms turned out to be next to Zachary's, she cleaned his too, even sending the sheets out to the Legend laundry.

"There is nothing I can do to force him to study."

"Too bad you can't starve him," Jeremy said as he bit into his apple. "The boy eats as much as the town blacksmith, who, from what I hear, might be his father as well as any other man. And he certainly likes those shirts you had ironed."

Days ago Kathryn had stopped correcting Jeremy's unpleasant comments about Zachary because she'd found out that his jealousy was stronger than her attempts to inhibit him. No, she wasn't worried about Jeremy; her concern was Zachary. How did she get him to agree to be her pupil? She had figured out that that's what it would take with Zachary because he was too willful to be forced to do anything he didn't want to do.

"You can see that he looks just like Cole Jordan," Kathryn said, her chin resting on her hands and thinking about what Jeremy had just said. She might not have been able to get Zachary to open a book, but she had made inroads into other parts of his life. Who would have thought that such a grubby little boy would actually be a hedonist?

Over the last few days Kathryn had seen the pleasure he had taken in putting on freshly washed and ironed shirts. She'd seen him flick a speck of dust off his newly polished boots. Maybe she couldn't get him to want to learn geography, but she'd had no trouble getting him to bathe.

And Jeremy was right about the food. The first night when she and Jeremy had sat down to a dinner of roast chicken and tiny vegetable tarts, Zachary had scoffed and ridiculed the meal even as he was filling his plate. That night

Kathryn had been past exhaustion and she had snapped at him, "Either you mind your manners and act like a gentleman or you eat in the bunkhouse with the men." After that Zachary had quietly sat down across from Jeremy and had watched everything Jeremy had done and imitated it perfectly.

At least I taught him something, Kathryn thought. Then, suddenly, her head came up and she stared, wide-eyed, at her son. "What did you say?"

"That the town blacksmith could have been his father. I was told that his mother——"

"Jeremy, you must stop listening to gossip. No, what did you say before that? Something about food."

"Oh. I said it was too bad you couldn't starve him into submission."

"Yes," Kathryn said as she stood. "That's it. Jeremy, I want you to go into the bunkhouse and get the dirtiest sheets you can find."

"The men don't have sheets, just blankets."

"Then get the dirtiest blankets you can find. And I want you to have the men use Zachary's clothes to wipe down their sweaty horses this evening."

Jeremy stopped chewing his apple as he looked up at his mother in disbelief. It was one thing for him to think up hideous things to do to Zachary, but his mother was a firm believer in returning good for evil.

"And I want you to get Manuel back in here. I want him to cook dinner tonight."

"Mother! You can't mean——"

"Go! Do it! Now!"

Jeremy dropped his apple and began running.

As Zachary Jordan rode home that night he was smiling in anticipation of the hot dinner waiting for him and the smell of lemon oil that now filled the house. Every time he'd entered the house in the last week he congratulated himself on his cleverness. It was due to him that Mrs. Kathryn de Longe was now living with them. If it had been left up to his father, they'd now both be imprisoned by that bull of a woman his father had wanted to hire.

But Zachary had foiled him. With a little help from his

friends in Legend, Zachary had been able to hire the sweetest woman he had ever met. And in the last week he had lived in heaven. He would have died before he admitted it to anyone or let the men see how he actually felt, but he loved the cleanliness of the house. He liked being able to put on a clean shirt every day.

And he loved the food the woman cooked. Instead of two-pound beef steaks that took a Bowie knife to cut, he now ate beef cooked in wine, chicken wrapped in herbs, trout smothered in slivered almonds. She served salads and cooked vegetables with delicious sauces ladled over them. There were desserts that made him nearly weep when he put them into his mouth.

And all he had to do to get this wonderful food and service was to sit at the same table with that little prig, Jeremy, and mirror everything he did. Which, of course, hadn't been difficult. What great intelligence did it take to pick up one fork instead of another?

He did feel a tiny bit bad about his refusal to comply with Mrs. de Longe's other request, that he spend his days with his nose in a book, but how could he give up life for something like that? How could he stay away from mountain streams of water so clear you could see fifty feet down? How could he forgo hearing the eagles' songs or sitting around a campfire and listening to old Golden Hawk's stories of the old days? Was he supposed to give up shooting lessons from the 'Frisco Kid? Maybe he was old now, but he could still shoot and still spin a yarn about gunfighters and what it had been like long ago. And then there were what he considered his duties in Legend. The ladies told him what their problems were and he told his father and, most of the time, his father fixed what was wrong. His father had banned more than one bad-tempered cowboy from town because he was mistreating the ladies.

Smiling, Zachary remembered the day he had first seen Mrs. de Longe. A lot of the men of Legend thought Mrs. de Longe was one of the ladies, but Zachary knew she wasn't. She was beautiful, true, but there was an air of quality about her. The ladies were fool's gold, but Mrs. de Longe was like twenty-four-carat gold. The real thing. He'd known that when he saw her photograph, and he'd been even more sure of it when he'd seen her in person.

On that first day, as he'd stood on the sidelines and seen the way she had held on to her son, a wave of jealousy so strong had overtaken Zachary that he could hardly bear it. All his life he'd heard too many rotten stories about his own mother. She had been one of Legend's ladies, but she had also been ambitious and had set her cap to become Mrs. Cole Jordan. After Zachary had been born, he knew his father had refused to marry her, so she'd dumped her baby on the doorstep and run off. She hadn't been back or even enquired about the son she'd left—or probably sold—since.

Zachary could still remember how he'd felt that day, seeing a boy his own age with a mother like that. All he could think to do was make that perfectly clean boy feel as bad as he did, so he'd acted as though he thought Mrs. de Longe was one of Legend's ladies. How good it had felt to fight with the boy, even if he was a much better opponent than Zachary would ever have thought! Later, he couldn't refrain from taking a bottle from a lady and drinking half of it down. He knew the city boy wouldn't know that the ladies filled their bottles with cold tea.

So now, returning to the house, Zachary was smiling in memory and anticipation. What delicious thing had Mrs. de Longe cooked for him tonight?

But when Zachary reached the house, he found the front door to his own house locked. Since when was there need to lock the Jordan house, he thought. His father had armed guards patrolling the Jordan Line, and who would dare attack their house anyway? He pounded on the door, but no one came to answer it. In the end he had to climb up the porch post, walk across the porch roof, then climb across two windowsills before he reached his own bedroom window.

As soon as he slid the window open, he smelled the room. And as soon as he did, he knew exactly what Mrs. Kathryn de Longe was up to. And, immediately, he admitted defeat. If he was going to have to pay for clean clothes and good food with multiplication tables, then so be it. And if that prig Jeremy could do them, then he could too. Besides, some of the things she'd been telling Zachary about foreign countries sounded a bit interesting. He could do without spelling, but maybe he'd conquer that too.

Zachary walked through his dirty room, grabbed a pillow from a settee in the hall, and went to sleep outside Mrs. de Longe's door. That should get her, he thought as he settled down to sleep, for Mrs. Kate, as everyone had come to call her, had the softest heart he'd ever seen. Except when it came to his father, he reminded himself. When it came to the elder Jordan, she didn't give an inch.

You're slippin', Pa, he thought as he drifted into sleep. You need to do some work, like maybe *you* should start sleepin' outside her door for a few nights. Then you'll get all she has to give.

Four

"MOTHER," JEREMY SAID FOR THE FOURTH TIME. "I DON'T think you're listening to either of us."

"My dad's choppin' wood," Zachary said without looking up. "Got his shirt off."

Kathryn certainly did hear that remark, and she moved away from the window swiftly, because she had indeed been watching Cole Jordan with his shirt off. "Yes, Zachary," she said as efficiently as she could manage, "could you show me on the map where Borneo is?"

"Sure thing, Mrs. Kate," he said with a cocky grin. "But maybe we oughta work on biology today."

One look from Kathryn made him close his mouth and go to the map pinned to the far wall. And for the rest of the day Kathryn made herself stay away from the window. But it was later when Zachary spilled a bottle of ink that she knew she'd have to leave the room they were using for their classes.

"I'll go, Mother," Jeremy said when he saw the look of

dread on her face. Most of the school supplies were kept in Cole's office.

"No," she said, "finish your lessons. I'll be back in a few minutes." She knew that if she sent either one of the boys, Cole would show him something that was infinitely more interesting than geography, such as roping or branding or how to throw a knife accurately. The schoolroom was the only place that Cole respected as off-limits to him. That and Kathryn's bedroom, she thought as she walked down the stairs.

Straightening her shoulders, smoothing her dress, Kathryn made her way toward Cole's office. In the few weeks that she had been in the house, it was amazing how successful she had been in avoiding him. For the most part she tried to act as though he didn't exist. She and the boys ate at different times than he did, or at the very least at one end of the table while he sat at the other. And Kathryn scrupulously avoided wandering about the house when she knew Cole was home.

But who did she think she was kidding? Certainly not Zachary, who seemed to be nine going on fifty. The "child" seemed to know everything that was going on in her mind, for Kathryn secretly watched Cole as though he were the most fascinating person on earth.

For one thing, he didn't seem to be who she originally thought he was. He was an excellent father—to both of the boys. He never included his own son in something that he didn't ask Jeremy to join. And he was wonderfully fair. If Zachary was better on a horse than Jeremy, Cole would ask Jeremy to recite the multiplication tables. If Jeremy began to think he was smarter than Zachary, Cole would ask his son to tell them how to mine silver, including all the technical aspects of it.

Yes, Kathryn thought, Cole was an excellent father. And he was true to his word that he hadn't so much as tried to touch her since she had been in the house. Truthfully, their relationship was one of great formality. For all that they addressed polite words to one another, they could have been living in different cities. But then Kathryn went out of her way to be where Cole Jordan was not.

Now, after giving a soft knock to make sure he wasn't

inside, she put her hand on the doorknob to his office and took a deep breath. Then she reminded herself that this was ridiculous. Mr. Jordan meant nothing to her. This was a job and nothing more.

But then she remembered the day he had joined her and the boys on a nature walk when they'd been trying to identify trees by their leaves. Out of nowhere Cole had appeared and surprised them all with an extensive knowledge of plants.

"I only know what's good to eat," he'd said when Jeremy had asked him where he'd learned so much. "Not that Manuel ever uses any of these plants, but when I was nine I became interested in herbs, and my mother helped me learn what was what. And, too, there was Wendell."

At that Zachary had let out a whoop of delight so, grinning, Cole stretched out on the ground, his long legs almost touching Kathryn's skirt, and had told what Zachary called a "Wendell story"—his favorite. And Kathryn had to admit that the story—untrue, of course—was indeed entertaining. It seemed that Cole had been telling his son about this extraordinary woman who wore black leather clothing, ever since Zachary was left with him by his mother.

By the end of the story, Kathryn found herself as eager as the boys, only barely able to keep from asking questions about where this woman came from, what had happened to her, and were the outrageous stories of the future she told true.

But Cole had ruined the moment by leering at Kathryn as though to let her know he knew she was intrigued by him. So Kathryn had closed the picnic basket just as he was slipping his hand inside.

Cole had drawn back with an expletive, then sucked at his fingertips, which she had caught with the lid. "What is wrong with you?" he muttered, then looked at her with anger in his eyes. "Don't you ever forgive a man?"

"There is nothing whatever wrong with me," Kathryn said firmly. "And I do forgive people, but not when they put me through the humiliation that you did," she said, referring to the trial. With her back rigid and her resolve strengthened, she had led the boys back to the house.

So now she was going into his private domain in order to

get a bottle of ink, which she was sure he kept there just so she'd have to come after it. There was no answer to her knock, and since she knew he was still outside, she went into the room. The first thing she saw was that a wall safe was open and scattered on the cabinet below were a stack of papers. Rushing toward the safe, with thoughts of robbery in her head, she saw that there were stacks of what appeared to be hundred-dollar bills inside the safe. So there was no robbery, she thought, relieved, just someone's carelessness at leaving a safe open.

With a few stern thoughts about the irresponsibility of some people, she began to put the papers away, but then one of them caught her eye. It was a bank statement for an account in Denver, opened in the name of a man in Legend who had begged Kathryn to get Cole to allow him to buy his store.

With interest, Kathryn began to go through more of the papers. There was a book that showed that Cole was paying for a retirement home in Denver, and the names of the tenants were things like Diamond Sue and Tricky Jane. There were huge bills for the repair of the houses of Legend.

"Seen all you want?"

Kathryn nearly jumped out of her skin when she heard Cole's voice, then spun on her heel to see him sitting in a chair in the far corner of the room, at least half a dozen ledgers on his lap.

"I . . . I came for a bottle of ink," she said, and even to herself she sounded as though she had something to hide.

"I rarely keep ink in the safe," he said, one eyebrow raised.

"I didn't mean to pry," she said as she put the papers she held back onto the cabinet below the safe. She knew she should leave now. She should forget the ink and leave, but instead she looked at him. "What are all these documents? Why don't you sell Legend to the inhabitants? Why do you have to be such a, a . . ."

"Despot?"

He was laughing at her, but she didn't care; she wasn't going to back down. When he took a while to answer, she knew he was trying to decide whether or not to trust her.

"I'm sure you won't believe me, but I'm doing this town a

favor." Standing, he walked across the room to reach above her head and put the ledgers back into the safe. "The mines are playing out. Colorado is no longer in a silver boom, and most of the towns that were near here when I was a kid are now ghost towns. And the people who put their money into them have lost everything."

As he turned his back on her and walked to his desk, she tried to put together what he had just told her, and when she did understand, she gave a little laugh. "Am I to believe that you are retaining sole ownership of this town out of some altruistic motive? When the mines do give out, every person in this town can walk away without losing a penny because you've allowed no one to buy any property? Is that what I'm to believe?"

When Cole looked at her his eyes were cold. "It doesn't matter to me what you believe. But what I have just told you is the truth."

"And I guess there is nothing in this for you," she said, one corner of her mouth tilted up in a smile of disbelief. "You don't get riches beyond belief? You don't get power to control a town full of people? To make their decisions for them? To—"

"Power?" he half shouted at her. "You think that running a place like Legend is *power?* Have you actually *looked* at this place? There are more whorehouses than there are businesses."

"But that's because you won't allow decent people into this place. You encourage only the lowest people to come here."

He advanced on her. "That's exactly right, and have you ever stopped to ask *why* I encourage such decadence as this?"

Kathryn was backing toward the door, and he was moving closer to her, leaning over her.

"Have you ever asked yourself why my own family moved to Denver, yet I stay here *alone?* I'll tell you why, Mrs. High and Mighty de Longe. It's because there is no future for this town. My father wanted to close the place down; he said it made him ill."

"Then why not bring in some decent people? Why not allow—"

Her back was against the door, and he was so close to her now that she could see the tiny flecks of black that were in his blue eyes. And she could feel his breath on her skin.

Abruptly, he turned away and walked to the center of the room, then stood there looking down at his desk. Kathryn knew this was her opportunity to escape, but instead she took a breath and said, "Why?"

He didn't answer for a while, and when he did his voice was soft and low. "My family has made a lot of money from this town, enough to keep us for generations if we have any sense. A few years back when my father found out the mines wouldn't last much longer, he could have sold every inch of land to anyone who wanted it, then left here forever."

"But he didn't," Kathryn said. "No, *you* didn't. You stayed behind to run the town."

He turned back to her. "Yes, I stayed behind. I had Zachary so I wasn't totally alone, and my grandmother had long ago fenced off this part of town so we could have some semblance of life that didn't involve liquor and bets being wagered." He gave her a little half smile. "But I haven't done so well with my son. He's grown up knowing more about a roulette table than about . . ."

"The Bible?" Kathryn supplied.

"Exactly," Cole answered, then gave her a genuine smile.

Kathryn moved away from the door and went to the safe, where she picked up a handful of papers. "So what are these?"

"Just a bit of management," he said, taking the papers from her, as though he were embarrassed at her seeing his good deeds. When he'd put the papers away and closed the safe, he walked away from her, and his gesture was a dismissal, but Kathryn didn't move.

"Why have you done this?" she asked. "I can understand why you didn't sell the land, but the rest of this is not something I can comprehend. The people of Legend are adults; you are not their father or their guardian. You don't have a right to decide their futures for them."

"A right?" he asked, turning back to her, his face angry. "I have an obligation to them. I have—" Halting, he put his hand over his face. "That's right, Mrs. de Longe. I have no

49

right. I am rich, therefore I am bad. Isn't that what you believe? Isn't that what everyone believes? Now, would you please leave so I can get back to my work of duping poor innocent people out of their hard-earned money?"

When Kathryn just stood there without moving, he barked, "Go!" and she had to work to keep herself from running away as though she were a schoolgirl. Calmly, she opened the door and left the office.

It was after that encounter that she began to ask Zachary questions about his father's business. At first the boy was very secretive, until Kathryn told him what she already knew.

"He told you the mines are playin' out?" Zachary said in disbelief. "He told you that? Don't nobody know that."

"No one knows of that," she corrected him automatically, then waved her hand before Zachary started one of his "That's what I said" routines that could go on for half an hour. "Why has he stayed here?" she asked.

"A dream," Zachary said as he bit into a piece of apple pie, then grinned at the look Kathryn gave him. "All right, I'll tell you, but it don't make no sense to me."

Kathryn had to bite her tongue to keep from correcting his grammar, and the imp knew it. Finally, Zachary told her that when his father was nine years old he'd had a dream that changed his life. In the dream his whole family had been shot by the people of Legend, and as a result all the townspeople were sent away and died terrible deaths.

"And because of this dream he now takes care of the inhabitants of this town?"

"Don't make no sense to me, either, but that's the way he is. He won't carry no gun, and he makes sure that when this town goes under, nobody is hurt but him. He's put money into banks in Denver for the people who have been here the longest."

"And knowing that the mines are going to give out, he doesn't encourage family people to come here. They'd lose their homes in a few years," Kathryn said thoughtfully.

"That's right. My grandpa wants Pa to stop tryin' to be a hero and move to Denver with the rest of the family, but Pa says he owes something to these people and he has to keep them from cursing the Jordan name for all eternity. That seems to be part of the dream too. Oh, and that woman Wendell told him some things too. I think she's a distant cousin to my pa."

It was later, as Kathryn felt her resolve melting toward Cole Jordan, that she renewed her distance toward him. Hadn't he made it abundantly clear that he wanted no woman who was interested in him in a matrimonial way? And as for Kathryn, she knew where such closeness could lead. Jeremy was evidence of that.

Five

"DAMN HER!" COLE MUTTERED AS HE PULLED THE BARBED WIRE even tighter.

"Hey!" Joe yelled. "You almost caught my hand in that." He started to say more, but then a bolt of lightning flashed nearby, the horses let out screams of fear and tried to get away, then Cole yelled something that Joe was sure he didn't want to hear. All in all, Joe decided it was better to keep his mouth shut, which was what all the men who worked or lived in Legend had decided of late.

Ever since Mrs. Kate had come to live in the Jordan house, Cole's temper had been like that of a wildcat caught in a trap. Couldn't nobody talk to him or even look at him for fear of having his head bit off.

The only way the people of Legend could stand Cole's temper was because they knew what was going on, since everybody who worked near the Jordan house made sure they told everything they saw. And they saw plenty!

Mrs. Kate had indeed tamed that brat Zachary. Everyone was amazed at what she had been able to do with him. Who would have thought that the boy was smart? Clever, yes, but not book-learnin' smart. But he was.

After Mrs. Kate showed that hellion Zachary that if he

was going to eat anything besides Manuel's swill, he had to apply himself to the books just as her perfect, prissy son did, Zachary settled down to become a real scholar. Of course it greatly helped matters that one day the two boys went behind the barn and young Jeremy knocked the stuffing out of Zachary. Everyone on the place had gone running to watch that fight. Everybody except Mrs. Kate, that is. Of course she must have known that it was going on, what with all the hollerin' and swearin' that she was sure to have heard in the house, but maybe she decided not to try to stop what was bound to happen.

Manuel said that when the boys came to breakfast she didn't say a word about their bloody faces and bruised, sore bodies. In fact, she made them both sit on hard benches without a break for three hours. And when both boys were nearly falling asleep from fatigue, she said their problem was that they needed some exercise, so she took them outside and made them run halfway up a mountain then back down. By the nightfall both boys were united by a common enemy: Mrs. Kate.

So now, three months later, the boys, if not exactly friends, certainly were together a great deal, both of them challenging each other to be the best at whatever they tried.

No, the problem was not the boys. The problem was Cole. For all that weeks had gone by, Mrs. Kate had not relented in her complete and absolute disregard for Cole Jordan. Manuel reported that for all the notice that Mrs. Kate took of Cole, he might as well not exist.

At dinner she and the boys sat at one end of the table and ate what she cooked, while Cole sat at the other end and ate the greasiest mess Manuel could manage to come up with. And considering Manuel's expertise in that area, Joe hated to think what that was like.

With Zachary's help, Mrs. Kate had hired a couple of women who had retired from "other" work in Legend to do the cleaning, washing, and ironing. Except they didn't clean or iron or wash for Cole. His room was left a pigsty and she left the care of his clothes to Manuel, who made sure they stayed dirty and rumpled.

The result of all this was that Cole Jordan's temper was

enough to send bears running for cover. Half the hands had quit and moved to Texas. "Or hell," they'd said. "Hell couldn't be worse than this place."

Now, when the sky opened up and cold rain poured down on them, Cole didn't seem to notice, so Joe kept on holding the fence posts for him while he strung the wire. But when the sleet started and icy pellets hit the two of them, Joe didn't bother to tell Cole he was going back to the bunkhouse. After all, it was already ten o'clock at night, they were working by moonlight (which wasn't there anymore), and they'd both been up since four A.M. And if that weren't enough, it was Christmas Eve.

After another half hour, Joe just turned away, got on his frightened horse, and started riding away. Even over the storm he could hear Cole behind him shouting that he was fired and that a man couldn't find anybody today who knew how to work.

"Damn them all to hell," Cole muttered under his breath as he pulled on the wire again, but it slipped from his gloved hand and landed . . . He had no idea where the wire went, and it was much too dark to see. Reluctantly, he stuck the hook in his back pocket and mounted his horse. When the animal was skittish, Cole pulled back on the reins until it knew who was master.

The sleet was so bad that it took nearly an hour to find his way back to the house, and when he rode into the barn he was shivering. Shaking one of the men awake, he told him to rub his horse down, then Cole staggered to the house.

As always, the back door was bolted closed, and the sight of the Christmas wreath on the door just angered him more. "Damn her!" he yelled just as thunder cracked and drowned his words. Her and her obsession with locking him out of his own house! In one of her rare moments of addressing actual words to him, she'd handed him a key and said that he could use it. But now his hands were too cold to find a key in his pants pocket.

After fumbling for a few moments he said, "Oh, the hell with it," then raised his foot and kicked the door in. "Fat lot of good a lock does," he muttered, then stumbled toward the big cast-iron stove along the far wall. But of course the stove was cold; the coals had been banked for the night. With hands that were like pieces of wood, he tried to pick up the iron lifting handle and insert it into the plate so he could throw some kindling on the coals and get a fire going. But his hands weren't responsive, and he dropped the plate so it went clattering onto the stone floor. The crash of the iron plate knocked about half a dozen homemade Christmas decorations down with it.

"Take another step and I'll shoot you," came a woman's voice from the shadow of the doorway.

"Go ahead," Cole growled. "Might as well kill me since you're trying to starve me anyway."

"Oh, it's you," Kathryn said flatly. "I thought you were—"

"I was who?" he said angrily as she lit a lantern and golden light flooded the room. But she didn't waste any time looking at him; her interest was in the door. "Look what you've done! You've broken it. Now the lock won't work." Bending, she picked up the wreath that had fallen when the door crashed back.

"Lock?" He half yelled at her. "Can you tell me why the hell you need a lock when there are armed guards around the place night and day? And where the hell did you get a gun?"

After Kathryn put the wreath on the end of the table, she pushed the shattered door closed against the wind, then braced it shut with a kitchen chair. "I don't have a gun. It was a bluff." When she had the door relatively well shut, she turned toward him. "Well then, good night," she said stiffly and started toward the doorway.

But when she glanced at him, she paused, her eyes widening as she stared at him. He was thoroughly wet, and ice had formed on some of his clothing and in his hair. He was holding his gloved hands close to his chest, as though they were lifeless things somehow attached to the end of his arms. With a glance at the pot handle and the stove lid on the floor, it didn't take much to figure out what he had been trying to do.

With a grimace, she said, "If you get sick and die, I'll be out of a job so I guess I'll have to help you."

If Cole hadn't been so cold he would have laughed. As it was all he could do was curl one corner of his mouth up in amusement. "That would be very sensible of you," he said, then stepped away from the stove as she quickly moved to stand in front of it and build up the fire.

Standing to one side, he stood there looking at her for a few moments. Her thick dark hair was in one fat braid down her back; she was wearing an old robe that looked as though it had been made from a blanket, and the front was gaping open so he could see the front buttons on his flannel nightgown. Cole was sure he'd never seen a more beautiful or desirable woman in his life.

But then he'd felt that from the first moment he'd seen her. When he'd turned that first day and seen the woman who had called out and warned him that Bartlett was about to shoot him, Cole had been shocked at the beauty of her. No, not just her beauty. There were lots of pretty girls in Legend. But what Cole saw in her eyes that day was the kindness of her, the sweetness—and the strength. At that moment if someone had told him that he'd die if he kissed her, he still would have done it.

"Are you just going to stand there?" she snapped.

But all Cole did was stand there and stare at her. For these last weeks he had been able to stay angry enough to keep away from her. And he'd used trips to Denver and working from early to late to keep himself out of the house. Anything to keep from seeing the coldness in her eyes. He couldn't bear seeing that day after day.

And he couldn't bear to hear the laughter of her and the two boys as they decorated the house for Christmas, a Christmas that didn't seem to include him.

"Sit down," she said, then half shoved him into a chair and began to pry the gloves off his frozen hands. "If one of the boys stayed out until he was this cold I'd turn him over my knee," she said, sounding like the teacher she was.

"Feel free to do the same to me," he said softly to the top of her head as she bent over his hands.

"Stop it!" she said, looking into his eyes, which were almost level with hers. "And if you make any attempts at . . . at . . ."

55

"At what?" he asked softly.

Kathryn tossed his cold gloves on top of the wood box, then moved away from him. "Seduction, that's what."

As the kitchen began to fill with warmth, feeling was returning to Cole's body. "Seduction?! How can you accuse me of such a thing? You've lived with me—*lived* with me!— for weeks, and I've never so much as touched you. I've seen you bent over your desk and reaching for apples and asleep in your bed, and I've never so much as laid a finger on you. So how can you accuse me of trying to seduce you?"

In spite of herself, Kathryn had to turn away so he wouldn't see her smile. Cole Jordan was a difficult man to hate. Just seeing the way he loved his son was enough to melt a woman's heart. And then there was what he was doing, anonymously, for the people of Legend. How many men paid for retired "ladies of the evening" to be taken care of?

Kathryn didn't bother to answer Cole as she raked the coals then added kindling and began to build up the fire in the stove. Turning toward the pantry, she said, "I'll see what Manuel has left for you to eat."

But before she could take a step the door blew open, and she ran for it, but Cole beat her to it. Leaning over her, he shoved the door closed, then told her to pull the loose board off the kindling box and to fetch hammer and nails. Kathryn scurried to obey him, then held the board up as he nailed it in place across the door.

When he'd finished she turned to walk away, but her body was pinned between the door and him, and it didn't look as though he was about to move.

"What is it you want?" he asked softly.

Kathryn tried to look around him, but that was nearly impossible considering how big he was. "Please let me by," she said, trying to still the trembling in her voice.

"No, you can't go. Not until you talk to me. Not until you tell me why you've turned against me."

That made her look up at him! "Turned against you? You tried to deny me a job that was rightfully mine. You called me a liar and worse in front of the whole town. You humiliated me in front of . . ."

She broke off because he was wrapping her braid around one hand, while his other hand trailed down her shoulder.

"Why is it that even though you have a child I get the feeling that you know nothing about men?"

"I know everything about men," she said, trying to tighten her lips into a line. "I know that they are liars and cannot be trusted, that they take everything from a woman and leave her nothing. I know they . . . they . . ." His hands were on her neck now, and she turned her head away. "Please don't do that," she whispered. "Please."

Abruptly, he dropped his hands, but he didn't step away from her. "You're free," he said. "Free to go wherever you want."

Kathryn started to step away, but then she turned and looked up at his face. The room was dark except for the soft glow from the lantern; she could feel the heat rising from the stove. And the Christmas decorations she and the boys had hung about the room gave it a festive, happy look. Outside a bolt of lightning flashed, making her jump, and when she did, she came in contact with Cole's big body, his clothing still wet and cold, but she could feel the heat from his body as though he were a raging fire.

Her mistake was in looking up at his face as another flash of lightning illuminated it, and all she could think of was that first day and his lips on hers. Without conscious thought, Kathryn's arms went around his neck, and she kissed him with all the pent-up desire that had built in her over the weeks. No, the desire that had built up over years was in her lips.

For a second, Cole pulled back from her, then looked at her in puzzlement because she kissed like a child, with her lips tightly closed. With great pleasure he showed her how to open her mouth under his, and when the tip of his tongue touched hers, she seemed to melt into his arms.

"Kathryn," he whispered as he buried his face in her neck. "I have dreamed of you every night and every day. I've thought of nothing else except you since that first day. I can't fight you anymore. We must—"

With a great push, she got away from him. "No," she said, moving away, her breast heaving. "Don't say any more. You mustn't say any more. There cannot be anything between us."

Cole was smiling at her and slowly moving closer. "I know that there have been some unusual things between us, and maybe I shouldn't have thought you were trying to trick me into hiring you, but I really did think you'd tried to play me for a fool. And can you blame me for being angry? There I'd found who I thought was the one woman for me, only to find out that she was a conniving little actress, so I—"

"Don't come any closer," Kathryn said under her breath.

"Sweetheart, I plan to get a lot closer than this," he said as he reached out for her, then only smiled when she moved to the other side of the kitchen. "Look, honey, I'll court you if that's what you want. I'll buy you flowers and candy and—"

"No!" Kathryn said fiercely. "You can't. We can't. You don't know—" Suddenly her head felt as though it were going to explode. In Philadelphia she had dreamed of falling in love with a man and having a complete family, but now she knew what it felt like to love a man, for only love could make her feel this awful. And with the knowledge of love, she knew something else: She knew that she could not endanger Cole and Zachary. She and Jeremy were already in danger, and it must not extend further.

"What in the world makes you think I'd ever be interested in a cowboy like you?" she said, with a toss of her head that she hoped looked convincing. "Look at yourself. You smell like horses, and I doubt if you've ever read a book in your life and—"

She didn't say any more as Cole pulled her into his arms and kissed her until she could hardly breathe. When he moved his mouth away, she was limp in his arms, her eyes closed.

"I don't know why I ever thought you could have been a good actress," he said softly as he began to kiss her neck. When she didn't respond, Cole swept her up into his arms and carried her up the stairs to his room, where he gently laid her on his bed.

"But I . . . We . . ."

"Shhh," he said, kissing her as he quickly stripped off his

cold, wet clothes, then climbed into bed beside her. When a flash of lightning illuminated the room and he saw Kathryn's expression as she saw his nude body, he smiled. "You'd think you'd never seen a naked man before."

"I haven't," she said without thinking, as he started unbuttoning her dress and kissing the skin that was exposed, inch by slow inch.

He chuckled at her words. "And was Jeremy's father some phantom lover, a man you never saw?" he asked as his hands moved over her breasts.

Kathryn didn't answer, but closed her eyes as she felt the new sensations of this man's touch.

Then abruptly, Cole stopped touching her and leaned over her, staring down into her eyes. "How did you get pregnant with Jeremy?" he asked forcefully.

Turning her head away, Kathryn wouldn't look at him, then she drew her dress together and started to get off the bed, but Cole stopped her.

"The bastard," he said under his breath, and those words told that he knew how Kathryn had been made pregnant. After a moment, Cole slowly began to kiss her neck again. But when she didn't respond, he took her face in his hands and looked at her. "You may not think so, but I'm an honorable man. I keep my word. Kathryn," he said with his eyes piercing into hers, "I love you. I think I fell in love with you that first day when you saved my life. I knew I had never kissed anyone who made me feel as you did, and that's why, later, when I thought you were just one of the girls from town, I was in a rage."

He was caressing her cheek and neck, and Kathryn's eyes closed. "Later," he said, soft and low, "I decided that I didn't want to be in love. I didn't want this feeling of rage one minute and . . . and . . ."

"Blithering idiocy the next?" she asked.

"Exactly," he said, smiling.

All the while he was talking to her, he was touching her, his hands gentle and tender, moving along her waist, along the edges of her breasts.

Then suddenly, he rolled away, to the far side of the bed so he seemed to be miles from her. "I can't do this," he said as he put his hands behind his head and stared at the ceiling. "I thought you were a widow or at least that you were familiar with a man. But you're almost a virgin."

For the last hour or so she had been swept off her feet and unable to think. Yesterday she had told herself that she despised him. When they passed in the hall, she had looked past him. So how had they come to be in his bed together, he naked with only a sheet covering him? How had she come to have her dress unfastened so that her breasts above her corset were exposed? But most importantly, what had happened to make him move away?

She rolled toward him, pressing her body against his, then put her hand on his bare chest. She'd never touched a man's bare body before. When O'Connor had done to her . . . what he had done, he had not bothered to remove his clothing.

"I can't very well be a virgin if I've given birth to a child, can I?" she said as she planted a kiss on his shoulder.

Cole didn't move. "But still, you're not experienced in these matters, so we'd better wait. Until after the wedding, that is."

Kathryn paused in kissing his arm, but only for a moment. Right now she didn't seem able to remember anything about safety. How could she and Jeremy not be safe if they were protected by a man like Cole Jordan? And a wedding might be very nice.

She ran her hand across his wide chest, then, daringly, she moved it downward, below the sheet that was draped over him. "What do a few days matter?" she said as she moved upward and began to kiss the soft place just below his ear. It was when she felt his pulse that she knew he was lying. He was as excited as a man could be, and one glance downward confirmed that knowledge. Maybe she wasn't a good actor, but he obviously was.

"You're right," she said as she moved away from him. "We should wait. We should get to know each other. We hated each other yesterday, and today we love each other. Who's to say that we won't hate again tomorrow? And if we've done this, we won't be able to go back. Yes, indeed, we should wait."

But as Kathryn rolled to the edge of the bed, Cole caught her arm.

"You put one foot on that floor and you're dead," he said in the voice of a man who was serious. Very serious.

With a giggle, Kathryn turned back to him, and the next moment he was on top of her, and her clothes came off in one fluid motion. "You are never, never going to get away from me again, Mrs. Kathryn Jordan," he said as his lips descended on hers. "Never."

"I don't think I want to," she whispered, but didn't say any more because he began to make love to her, and she didn't think after that.

In the morning, when Cole awoke with a smile on his lips, Kathryn was not in the bed beside him. Thinking she'd gone for necessary purposes, he put his hands behind his head and looked at the ceiling. So many years ago, when he was just a boy, that woman he'd seen only once, a beautiful woman with black hair to her waist, had told him to marry someone who could cook. And that was what he was going to do.

But in the next instant his happiness was shattered by the door bursting open, and a wild-eyed Zachary was there. "They're gone," he said.

For a moment Cole couldn't comprehend what his son was saying. "Who's gone? More hands? I'll hire—"

"No! Mrs. Kate and Jeremy are gone!"

In a flash Cole was out of the bed and pulling on his trousers, and moments later he was running down the hall toward Kathryn's bedroom. Her bed had not been slept in but Jeremy's had. Turning, Cole looked at his son and the boy handed him a note that Zachary had obviously already opened and read.

Dearest Cole, he read. *There are things in my life that I can tell no one. I cannot expose you to what Jeremy and I must face every day of our lives. Forgive me, but I love you and Zachary too much to put your lives at risk. Good-bye, my loves.*

Cole looked at his son. "Get my horse ready. She can't have gone far."

"You'll bring her back?" Zachary said, and for the first time that Cole could remember, the boy looked as young as he actually was.

"While there is breath in me I will look for her," Cole said, then grabbed his son in a quick, fierce hug as he was running for the door.

But in the hall, he paused, for there on the floor was a piece of paper. Before Cole picked it up he sensed that it was important, and his intuition told him that Jeremy had secretly left the paper behind.

Bending, Cole picked it up, and what he saw made his breath catch in his throat. It was a wanted poster with a drawing of Kathryn and a younger Jeremy. The poster said Caitlin McGregor was wanted for thievery and attempted murder, with ten thousand dollars being offered for information leading to her apprehension.

When Cole read that the woman was known to be dangerous and should be treated as such, he crumbled the paper in his hand.

But not before his son had seen it. As Cole looked up, he saw the Christmas tree in the living room, gaily wrapped gifts under the tree. The idea of putting up a tree was something that Kathryn had brought with her from England and Cole had surreptitiously watched as the three of them had decorated it.

Now, the tree and the gifts were a reminder that he had a son and he owed something to him. Cole looked into Zachary's eyes. "Today is Christmas," was all he could manage to say, but his son understood that his father was torn between duty and action.

"Won't be much of a Christmas without that sissy boy to show off to," Zachary said, and Cole could see that the boy was hovering between tears and abject terror. "And won't be no real dinner if Manuel has to cook it." The tears were winning.

Zachary's head came up. "She didn't kill anybody, did she? They ain't gonna hang her, are they?"

"Not while I have breath in me," Cole said, then bent and hugged his son fiercely. "How about we hold off on Christmas until we can share it with them?"

Immediately, Zachary's head came up as he pulled away

from his father. "Maybe if you bring them back it will help make up for the low-life snakey way you've treated her since she's been here."

Cole opened his mouth to chastise his son, but closed it again. "Let's hope so. Don't cause any trouble while I'm gone," he said, then ran out the door.

Six

IT TOOK COLE AND SEVEN DETECTIVES SIX MONTHS TO FIND Kathryn and Jeremy. And by the time he did find her, he knew more about her life than he did about his own. It was amazing how many Irish people who were in the United States now had once worked for the O'Connors. And each person was willing to tell all that he knew—or thought he knew.

Cole found Jeremy first, and immediately, his stomach lurched, for the boy, already too thin, had lost weight. And the usually fastidious child was dirty, his clothes nearly worn through. The worst was that in his eyes was a look of hopelessness.

When Jeremy looked up from his shoeshine kit and saw Cole, he didn't say a word, but walked away from his rich customer and stared up at Cole, his eyes filled with questions. Cole opened his arms, and Jeremy fell into them, his body shaking from emotion. When Cole lifted the boy and carried him to the waiting carriage as though he were a baby, Jeremy didn't protest, but put his head against Cole's strong shoulder and buried his face, as though he no longer wanted to see what was around him.

Cole had rented a two-bedroom suite in San Francisco's finest hotel, so he took Jeremy there and ordered half the menu brought upstairs. As Jeremy sat at the table and ate as though he were starving, which he was, Cole said, "Where is she?"

"She won't want to see you," Jeremy said, mouth full, his

usually impeccable table manners forgotten. "She says you'll be killed if you take on my father."

Cole didn't allow the boy to see his wince at the thought of someone else being Jeremy's father. Instead, Cole stood by the door and looked at Jeremy.

The boy got the message, for a moment later he gave Cole the name and address of a soup kitchen. "She waits in line there for free soup. Wait!" he called when Cole bolted out of the room. "She's—" Breaking off, Jeremy looked down at his plate, his face red.

"I'll take her whatever she is," Cole said, not bothering to wait to hear if Jeremy had any more to say.

When Cole at last made his way through the back streets of San Francisco to the soup kitchen and scanned the long line of people, at first he didn't recognize Kathryn, for she was heavy with child. His child, he thought, as several emotions went through him at once. First there was anger that she'd not told him, then there was more anger because she had taken something away that belonged to him. But then Kathryn turned and saw him, and when he looked into her eyes he didn't seem to remember what he had ever been angry about.

For a moment all he could do was stand there, on the other side of the street from her, and grin. But when he saw her put her hand to her forehead and start to faint, he ran in front of carriages, freight wagons, and over pedestrians as he made his way to her.

He caught her before she hit the ground, swept her into his arms, then carried her to the carriage.

"I can't stay here," Kathryn was saying as Cole put more shampoo on her filthy hair. "And you have no right to do this. *We* have no right. We shouldn't—"

She broke off because Cole had dunked her head under water in the bathtub. Kathryn came up sputtering.

"If you're about to tell me that we're not married, and I have no right to strip your clothes off and bathe you, I think that belly of yours is evidence that I have every right."

"It's not your child," she said, chin up as he used a rough cloth to scrub her back. "I have been to bed with so many men that— Ow! That hurts."

"Oh?" he said. "Maybe if you stopped lying and—"

"What makes you think I'm lying? I had to support my son and myself so what better way than prostitution? Jeremy and I—"

He was now using the cloth to soap her face so she couldn't finish the sentence. "First of all," he said, "you would die before you sold your body."

"But I—"

"Second of all, you're so beautiful that if you went into prostitution, you wouldn't be in the starved condition you're in now."

"Oh?" Kathryn said, looking up at him. She should, of course, be too embarrassed to speak, since she was in a bathtub naked and he was washing her as though she were a child. But somehow being with Cole seemed almost natural.

"You have to listen to me," she said with urgency. "There are things going on that you don't know about. I am a hunted woman. There is a reward for me. I—"

"You ready to get out?" he asked, holding out a thick Turkish towel.

Kathryn grimaced. She had to get through to him, had to make him understand how dangerous being around her was. "Turn your head."

"Not on your life," he said without a smile, then when she didn't move, he said, "You can stay in there all night if you want, but when you do come out I'm going to be here holding the towel for you."

"You're a very stubborn man," she said, then, with her eyes on his, she stepped from the tub into the waiting towel.

"I'm trying to match you," he said as he wrapped the towel around her and began to dry her. Then he carried her into the bedroom and set her on the edge of the bed while he picked up a hairbrush from the dresser. "And just where do you think you're going?" he said when she started to rise.

"I'm just going to check on Jeremy one more time," she said.

"Jeremy is fine. He's young. He'll recover. At least he'll recover if all this ends. Sit!" he ordered when Kathryn remained standing.

When she didn't move, Cole climbed onto the bed, spread his long legs across the bed, then motioned for her to sit between them so he could comb the tangles from her hair. She opened her mouth to say that it wasn't decent for them to be in this position, but his look made her close her mouth and give herself over to the deliciousness of having his big hands on her hair.

When he'd finished, he pulled her back against him, tightening his arms about her protectively. For the first time in six months she was warm and clean and fed. But it was too much for her as she leaned her head back, and she began to softly cry.

"I want to hear all of it," Cole urged, his lips on her ear. "Every word. From the time you were born."

Kathryn started to protest, but instead she began to tell him the story of her life. She repeated how she had been the daughter of the cook of a large estate in Ireland, nothing more than the child of a servant. But the daughter of the house had, according to her tutor, the intelligence of a parsnip, so Kathryn was taken from the kitchen to study with the daughter in the hopes that the young mistress would learn by osmosis.

It didn't happen. Over the years the tutor gave up, let the girl ride her horses all day, and instead taught Kathryn everything he knew.

The problem came when the daughter's older brother, the young man who was to inherit the estate, the tall, handsome Sean O'Connor, returned from school.

"I was quite mad about him," Kathryn said, ignoring the way Cole's arms tightened about her. "He was beautiful and elegant and his words were nothing but honey." She smiled. "I would have given in to him if it hadn't been for my mother, who said all the O'Connors were sweetness on the outside and treachery within. And besides, she made sure that Sean and I were never alone."

"But you were," Cole said softly.

"Oh, yes," Kathryn said with anger. "He got me alone all right, but not until after he'd gone to a great deal of trouble. Do you know what he did to me?" She didn't wait for an answer. "He put on a pretend marriage, is what. He got one of his friends from Oxford to dress as a priest, and he put on a marriage. Just like one would put on a play."

"What made you think it was a false marriage?"

"I was young, but I wasn't stupid. Or maybe I was, I don't know. After the . . . the ceremony, Sean took us all to a pub. He was already drunk, so I don't know what he wanted with more whiskey, but then I have never understood drink. There was a barmaid there, and she said, 'If that one's a priest, I'm a nun.' Then she asked me if my mother knew that I was out with these men. Suddenly everything became clear to me."

"And you ran away," Cole said as he pulled her closer.

"Yes, I ran. But I didn't get very far. I was halfway back to the cottage where my mother lived when Sean caught up with me."

When she said no more, Cole urged her to continue. "Then what happened?"

He could feel her body tense into a knot. "It was dark and Sean was drunk. He said that after all the trouble he'd gone to, I owed him. He said he'd never worked so hard to get a woman, and he was going to have me—whether I wanted him or not."

For several minutes Cole rubbed her shoulders until he could feel the tension beginning to leave her body. "I went to London," she said softly. "I got a job as a cook's assistant, but I was fired five months later because it was evident that I was going to have Jeremy."

Kathryn took a deep breath. "I stowed away on a ship bound for America, and since then . . ."

"Ssssh," Cole said. "Be still. It's over now."

"But it's not!" she said fiercely, twisting about to look at him. "Can't you see that it will never be over as long as I'm alive? Sean knows about his son. He wants him, and he'll do anything to get him back."

Putting her head in her hands, Kathryn began to cry. "I can't give Jeremy up. And he won't allow me to send him back."

"Jeremy's father can't do anything to harm you because he's dead," Cole said above her sobs, and it took Kathryn a moment before she heard him.

"What?"

"Sean O'Connor died of a fall from a horse years ago. He was drunk, he took a fence, and he didn't make it. Died instantly."

A thousand questions tumbled through Kathryn's head. "But if he's dead, how can he be chasing us? Why would anyone else want us?"

"Jeremy is his son," Cole said softly, then waited for her to understand.

"His bastard, you mean," she said bitterly.

Cole smiled at her. "Tell me, was the barmaid who told you O'Connor's friend wasn't a priest, was she pretty?"

"Yes, very, but what . . . Oh, I see. You think she and Sean were lovers?"

"What do you think? Was O'Connor the type to have a mistress in the local tavern?"

"Sean O'Connor went to bed with any woman anywhere," Kathryn said bitterly. "He was rich and gorgeous, and he had a way about him that was as charming as the devil." Her eyes began to fade to dreamy. "All he had to do was talk to a woman in that low voice of his and a girl would—"

She broke off because Cole kissed her, kissed her hard and thoroughly, and when he pulled away, she was limp in his arms.

"Did he kiss you like that?" Cole asked angrily.

Kathryn's first thought was to tease him, but she saw the hurt in his eyes. She had yet to comprehend what he must have done to be able to rescue her. She had never thought to see him again. Yet she couldn't continue to see him because there was danger and—

"If Sean is dead, then who put those posters out saying I was wanted?" she asked, eyes wide.

Cole was watching her closely, and he was relieved to see that she was not grieving over hearing that her son's father was dead. "Why did you marry him?"

"I didn't love him, if that's what you mean," she said with a grimace.

"But, according to you, he was the most handsome man on earth. Even the angels must have praised him."

Kathryn smiled at his jealousy. "Yes, he was beautiful to look at, but the truth is he was as stupid as his sister. If it didn't have four legs he didn't understand it. I doubt if the man could read a nursery rhyme."

"Yet you married him."

"It was either that or have my mother discharged. Besides, I told you, the marriage was fake."

"The marriage was real," Cole said softly. "Whoever told you the priest wasn't real was lying."

"But it wasn't real! I accused Sean of faking everything, and he admitted it."

"Maybe he didn't like being called a liar. We men tend to be like that," he said, smiling, and she smiled back, thinking of the lawsuit she'd brought against him.

Suddenly, Kathryn sat up straight. "But if the marriage was valid, then Jeremy is—"

"Exactly," Cole said. "Jeremy is the rightful owner of the O'Connor estates."

For a few moments Kathryn sat there blinking at him, then she leaned back into his arms. "It was Sean's aunt, wasn't it? I never met a more spiteful woman than she. She was older than Sean's father, her brother, and she told anyone who would listen that, had she been a man, she would have been the owner of the estates." Kathryn gave a little one-sided smile. "Of course there were those who said that the woman *was* a man, certainly more of a man than Sean's father ever was."

"So what are you going to do now?" Cole asked.

"I . . . I don't know. How does one go about claiming an estate for one's son?"

"Maybe I could help," Cole said softly.

Kathryn's mind whirled with too many thoughts. If she and Jeremy went back to Ireland to live, she'd never see Cole again. But how could she give up such a future for her son?

To her disbelief Cole began to laugh as he snuggled her close to him, nuzzling her neck.

"Could you tell me what it is about me that you find so amusing?" she said stiffly.

"I can read your mind, that's what," he said. "And I am glad to see that I'm included in your dilemma."

"If you can see my problem, then why are you laughing?"

"Kathryn, my love, I'm going to take care of you."

"I can take care of myself!" she said angrily, trying to twist away from him, but he held her fast.

"Yes, I can see that you can take care of yourself. You,

Jeremy, and now my son are starving. You also have, or had, actually, lawmen and bounty hunters chasing you."

"What do you mean, had?"

"I got rid of them. I got a judge to sign papers clearing your name."

"And how did you do that?" she asked with tight lips. "Pay them?"

"No, I hauled half a dozen witnesses before him and they told him the truth. The judge knew jealousy and revenge when he heard it."

"But the posters—"

"Gone. I got rid of them. Oh, there may be a few about here and there, but for the most part they've been destroyed. Now, are you going to listen to what I have planned for your future?"

Kathryn started to say that her future was her own to plan, but she was too tired to fight any longer. The last six months had been too horrible for her to survive. A pregnant woman with no husband is not employable.

"We will be married," Cole said, then paused to see if she was going to protest. When she said nothing, he continued.

"Then we're going back to Legend and celebrate Christmas."

"Christmas?" she said. "In the middle of the summer?"

"Zachary and I decided to wait until we could share it with you and Jeremy, so the tree and the gifts and all the decorations are just as you left them."

"Oh my," Kathryn said. "By now that tree is—"

"The size of a redwood," Cole said in disgust. "Remember that you wouldn't let anyone chop it down. Instead you had the men dig it up and put it in a pot, and now the thing seems to like living indoors. Zach's last letter said that they'd had to stick the top of the tree out the window or it would have gone through the roof. And half of those little bells you and the boys put on it have grown into the wood. When we get it planted again, it's going to be one funny-looking tree."

Kathryn couldn't help laughing.

Snuggling her closer to him, Cole continued. "I've had a long talk with my grandmother Ruth, and she's going to move back to Legend for the next few years and start closing the place down."

"How can you close a town down?"

"Better to do that than to have it die overnight when the mines give out. She's going to find places for the residents to live."

"But—"

"Why is she doing that?" Cole asked. "My grandmother is very strange about the town of Legend."

"As you are."

"Yes, I guess I am. I've always felt that I owed it something. My grandmother feels the same way, so she's going to take over my job. There isn't much left to do before the silver is gone, but she'll see to it."

"And what are you going to do?" Kathryn asked hesitantly.

"Zachary and I are going to Ireland to live with you and Jeremy, of course," he said as though there were no other choice. "The boy has to learn how to run an estate properly, and I don't think that aunt of his is going to teach him. Besides, with her turn of mind I'd be afraid the cinch on Jeremy's horse would be cut and his neck would be broken."

At that, Kathryn's hands clenched on his. "Then I can't—"

"Yes, you can," Cole said, cutting her off as he turned her in his arms and lifted her chin up so he could look into her eyes. "You and I together can do anything," he said softly, his lips against hers. "Let me take care of you, Kathryn. Please. Let me take care of you and Jeremy, and in return you can take care of us. Zachary and I need you. We need you desperately. Will you let us take care of you and protect you?" He smiled against her lips. "And this child. Will you let me take care of him?"

"Her," Kathryn said, smiling in return. "I think she's a her."

"Whatever," Cole said, as he kissed her, and after that he didn't ask any more questions. Sometime during the night he thought he heard Kathryn say, "Yes," but he wasn't sure.

When the dawn made the sky pink, he pulled her into his arms, both of them sated with lovemaking, happy to be together again, and Cole smiled just before he fell asleep. Ireland, he thought. What was it like? But, truthfully, it didn't really matter because he and Kathryn and the children would make a home wherever they were.

"I love you," he whispered into her hair. "And from now on you'll be safe."

He wasn't sure, but he thought he heard Kathryn murmur sleepily, then he heard no more as he fell asleep with his arms about her.

JUDE DEVERAUX is the author of twenty-two *New York Times* bestsellers, including *An Angel for Emily, Legend, The Heiress, Remembrance, Sweet Liar, A Knight in Shining Armor,* and *The Duchess.* She began writing in 1976, and to date there are more than thirty million copies of her books in print. Ms. Deveraux lives in a 300-year-old house in England, and is currently at work on her next novel.

Margaret Allison

Christmas Magic

For my parents . . . Merry Christmas.

One

KIM LEANED BACK IN HER CHAIR AND STUDIED THE ABSTRACT OIL painting in front of her. Strong bold red lines accented a deep green background. She picked up her paintbrush and hesitated. She tilted her head, as though trying to get a different perspective. She had been working on this painting for months, but she just couldn't finish it. The painting needed something. Unfortunately, she was having trouble determining what it was lacking.

Frustrated, she set her brush back down and glanced out the window. The house she rented was small and old, but the location had made her fall in love with it immediately. It was perched on a small grassy hill overlooking a large stretch of beach in Hudson, Florida. She walked over to the window and opened it, allowing a warm breeze to flow through the room. It was November twenty-seventh, the day before Thanksgiving, but the temperature gave no indication that winter was right around the corner.

"Deck the halls with balls of holly, fa la la, la la . . ." Barbara, Kim's friend, burst through the door singing her own rendition of a Christmas carol.

"Hey!" Kim yelled out.

Barbara set down her bag of groceries. "What's the matter? Do you have a headache?"

"No. I just don't feel like hearing Christmas carols. I'd

77

like to get through Thanksgiving first. And besides. It's *boughs,* not *balls.*"

"Balls, boughs, big dif. You get the gist. And Thanksgiving is tomorrow. As everyone knows, Thanksgiving is the official beginning of the Christmas season." She looked at Kim accusingly as she put her hands on her hips. "Are you always such a scrooge?"

"Most of the time," Kim admitted. Christmas was one of those holidays that reminded her of everything she didn't have. "What did you bring?" Kim asked, motioning toward the bag.

"Stuff for tomorrow."

Barbara and Kim had volunteered to make Thanksgiving dinner for several of their friends who had decided to forgo having turkey with their families. "But I've already got everything," Kim said.

"Nope. Not hors d'oeuvres."

"Hors d'oeuvres?"

"Yeah. I went all out. I was missing my family so I needed some comfort food." Barbara began pulling the groceries out of the bag. "Cheez Doodles. Chips. Dip. Salsa. Bugles . . . God, I *love* Bugles. Assorted nuts. Cheez Whiz for inside the celery sticks, which I . . . forgot. Oh, shoot," she said, slapping her forehead.

Kim looked at the snacks in front of her and smiled as she shook her head. "Don't worry," she joked. "We'll just dip the Bugles in the Cheez Whiz."

Barbara's eyes opened wide and she nodded. "Excellent idea!" She opened the refrigerator, admiring the feast Kim had already purchased. "Everything looks beautiful. Cranberry salad. A giant turkey. And this?" she said, opening up a casserole dish and peering inside.

"Green bean casserole."

"God! You're so organized," she said, slamming the refrigerator door. She opened up the bag of Bugles and tramped toward Kim's painting. "I like it," she said, nodding as she popped a Bugle into her mouth. "It's very Christmassy."

"Christmassy?" Kim asked, walking over beside her as she opened up the jar of Cheez Whiz. She took a Bugle from Barbara and dipped it inside. "How do you figure?"

"Green and red. Looks kind of like a big, weird wreath," Barbara said, following Kim's lead and dipping the Bugle in the Cheez Whiz. "Don't you think?"

Kim tilted her head and looked at it again. "I don't know. Right now it doesn't look like much of anything to me." She shrugged. "I'm sorry. I woke up in a lousy mood. I think it's the holiday." She nodded toward the jar of Cheez Whiz. "We better put that stuff away. It's addictive."

"No!" Barbara said adamantly. "This is all part of the holidays. You start eating, and you don't stop until January. It's an eatathon. Anything and everything you can stuff in your mouth."

"I think I'll pass," Kim said. "But you go right ahead. I'll leave this out for you."

"So why are you so crabby? Getting nervous about your show?" Barbara asked, referring to the second major show of Kim's career. Her first show had been six months earlier at a local gallery in town. A buyer from a prestigious Miami gallery had seen her work there and had offered Kim a showing at his gallery, one frequented by wealthy clients. It was an important break for Kim. Her career had demanded long hours and hard work, with little financial reward.

"No. I don't think so. I mean I'm nervous, but I don't think that has much to do with my mood."

"Are you missing Ed?" Ed was Kim's most recent boyfriend, a fellow artist who had recently decided to move to L.A. and become an actor.

"Ed? No." Kim had been relieved when Ed had decided to move. It was an easy, almost painless way to end a relationship that had been going nowhere fast. "I'd have to be a masochist to miss him. I mean, I guess I miss having a date every now and then, but I don't miss always paying for his dinner, watching him flirt with other women in front of me, and being told I could benefit from hiring a personal trainer—as he's squeezing my rear end. . . ."

"Yeah, right! As if he was Mister Stud-ly!"

"Exactly," Kim said, shoving another Bugle into her mouth. The mere thought of a hard-core workout was enough to make her stomach rumble.

"Anyway, you're a toothpick. He's crazy!" Barbara said enthusiastically.

Kim shrugged. "According to him, my body is not *toned.*"

"I should be so unlucky," Barbara said wistfully, staring at her pretty and thin friend as she ate a spoonful of Cheez Whiz. "You know what you need?"

"To lay off the Cheez Whiz?"

Barbara stuck the spoon back inside the glass jar and said, "You need to relax a little. Get out there and date, instead of always working."

"I'm busy. And I'm happy with my life. My time is important to me—and I'm not going to waste it dating just to . . . date."

"Mr. Right could be out there waiting for you, and you'd never know it. You'll never meet him holed up in here all day and night."

"I'll never meet Mr. Right because he doesn't exist."

"Tell me what you're looking for. Maybe I can fix you up with someone."

"No thanks."

"C'mon. What kind of guy are you looking for?"

"Someone who puts family above . . . well, his career."

"Better look for a guy over sixty-five. If you want to come before his career, stick with retirees."

Kim laughed as she took a hair band out of her pocket and skillfully pulled her long brown hair back in a ponytail. "Whatever happened to old-fashioned romance?"

"Old-fashioned? Forget sixty-five, maybe you better try a guy over seventy."

"You know what I mean. The "Hey, it's cold out here, let me give you my coat" type of love. The kind of guy that brings flowers. . . ."

"I've got just the guy. My grandpa—Grandpa Willie. You'll love him. Want to see a picture?"

"Does he have gorgeous eyes, nice hair . . . ," Kim replied, playing along.

"I think he has a nice hair. How many do you want?"

Kim smiled at her friend. "Grandpa Willie, huh?"

Barbara nodded. "He *is* cute." She laughed. "Let's say you can choose three things about your Mr. Right. What are they?"

"Things?"

"Characteristics. Qualities."

"The coat thing, that's a definite."

"Okay, we've got the guy giving you his coat . . . very chivalrous," Barbara said, drawing a number one in the air.

"And the flowers."

"Okay, we've got a guy giving away his coat and bringing flowers," she said, drawing a big number two in the air. "One more."

"And he must like my rear end."

"Just your rear end?" Barbara asked. "Why not go for the whole package? Don't you want a guy that thinks you're perfect? This *is* Mr. Right, after all."

"Exactly," Kim said good-naturedly, pretending to slam her fist down as she played along with her friend. "He must like my whole package!"

"Excellent!" Barbara said, laughing and clapping her hands together. "He must think you're perfect."

As their laughter died down, Kim shook her head. "Listen to me. Rambling on about my dream man. Good thing you're not taking me seriously."

Barbara nodded knowingly. "So that's why you're so cranky. Depressed about your love life."

Kim shrugged. "Usually I don't mind being single," she said, "but the holidays can be tough when you're alone. I always get this kind of vague, uncomfortable feeling that I'm missing something." She sighed. "I don't know. It's like New Year's Eve. I'm always convinced everyone is having a really good time except me."

Barbara's lips curled up into a dreamy smile. "I had a great time last New Year's. I was dating Frank, remember? I had been dating him for . . . well, we'd been on five dates, and he hadn't even tried to kiss me. He waited until the clock struck midnight on New Year's Eve. It was so romantic," she said dreamily. She shook her head as her mood suddenly changed for the worse. "Of course, I had to go and dump him for Rick." Then she added quickly, "The doctor," as if to distinguish him from any other Rick she might have dated. Barbara had dated Rick for about five months. When he left town for a new residency program, their relationship had ended.

"Don't feel bad about Rick," Kim said. "I know you were

impressed by the whole doctor thing, but believe me, being the wife of a doctor stinks. They work all the time. You'd never see him."

Barbara shrugged. "I can think of worse things."

"They're a strange breed. Especially . . . what was Rick . . . a surgeon or something?"

"A thoracic surgeon," Barbara said. "Just like your dad."

Kim's father was the chief of thoracic surgery at St. Mary's Hospital in Ann Arbor, Michigan—at least, that was his job fifteen years ago, when Kim had last spoken with him.

Kim rolled her eyes. "Take it from me, you made the right decision," Kim said, "dropping him."

"I didn't drop him, he dropped me."

"He did you a favor. My mother was one of the loneliest people I knew. She gave up everything for my dad, and he never even noticed." Kim hesitated as she remembered her mother. She had died last year and Kim missed her terribly. She remembered the anguish her mother had suffered, loving a man whose obsession with his career rendered him incapable of returning her feelings. "My dad's patients and his career always came first—before my mother, before me. If you had kids, you'd have to raise them yourself. He'd be on call all the time, and when he wasn't . . ."

"He'd be with me in our eight-bedroom house on the water. . . ."

"He'd be trying to arrange a way to sneak out with one of the nurses he had his eye on."

"Oh! That snake!" she said, smiling as she raised her fist up in the air. "I'll throw the book at him. I'll take him for every cent he has." She smiled. "That's a pleasant thought. Do I get to keep the house?"

"If you're looking to live in a huge house on the water, can I give you a suggestion?"

"Marry a dentist?"

"No, something even more novel. How about getting that law degree you keep talking about?"

"So I can defend myself in my divorce settlement with my doctor? Excellent idea," Barbara joked. "Think of all the money I'll save." Barbara's smile faded and she hesitated.

Kim rarely spoke of her past, and Barbara thought she might try to take advantage of the direction the conversation had taken. "Kim," she said finally. "What happened between you and your father? What made you stop speaking with each other? Did you have a fight?"

Kim shook her head. "Nothing so dramatic. After the divorce, when my mother and I moved to Florida, he just seemed to lose interest in me. He sent child support payments, but never included a note. He never even called."

"Did you call him?"

Kim nodded. "Quite a few times. But he wasn't home and I never called him at work. I wrote him every now and then, but as I got older, I stopped trying."

"Aren't you tempted to call him now?"

Kim smiled sadly as she shook her head. "I don't know what good would come of it. I'd probably just end up opening old wounds."

Barbara could tell by her expression that her friend was beginning to get upset. She decided to change the subject. She pulled a container of salsa out of the refrigerator and opened it up. "Maybe we should move on to a happier subject . . . like New Year's Eve. I can't remember what you did last year," she said, swirling a Bugle in the salsa and offering it to Kim.

"Hmm," Kim said, thinking as she shook her head, declining the unusual snack. "I'm not so sure it's a happier subject. At least, not the New Year's Eves I usually have. Last year I went on a blind date with that nutcracker guy. The one that kept cracking those nuts in his teeth. Remember? He kept telling me that wasn't the only way he could crack a nut."

"Oh yeah," Barbara said.

"Actually it was one of my better New Year's. In terms of entertainment value."

"You deserve a really great man to show you how to enjoy the holidays."

Kim laughed. "I have a man. Grandpa Willie."

"You just need to meet a good guy," Barbara continued. "Christmas can be so romantic. The soft holiday music, the sparkling gold lights . . ."

Kim rolled her eyes and nodded toward the salsa. "I thought you said it was an eatathon. Doesn't sound too romantic to me."

Barbara shook her head, as if giving up. "You're hopeless. Go ahead and be a scrooge. I, however, happen to love the holidays."

"A lot of people do," Kim said, feeling a little guilty about not sharing Barbara's enthusiasm. "My mother always said that Christmas was a wondrous, magical time."

Barbara laughed. "Magical, huh?"

"That's what she said. Every Christmas she'd tell me to think about what I wanted most and make a wish. She promised it would come true."

"And did it?"

Kim shook her head. "I never took her seriously. I don't believe in magic, especially at Christmas. Christmas is . . . well, it's just like any other time of year. Only people are more irritable."

"I think your mother was right," Barbara said enthusiastically. "Like last year, I stayed here, remember? The whole time I kept thinking about how much I wished I was with my family. And this year, my whole family is meeting back in Maine. My sister is flying in from L.A., my brother from Baltimore . . . what else but magic could get us all together? And what else but magic could keep us all from killing each other?"

Kim glanced away. Barbara was lucky. She had a brother and a sister, parents that loved her and each other. Kim could understand Barbara's looking forward to Christmas—she would, too, in her place.

"Hey, I have an idea," Barbara said excitedly. "Why don't you make a wish? If it comes true, then you'll know your mother was right; if it doesn't, well . . ." She stopped speaking.

Kim was shaking her head.

"C'mon, Kim," Barbara said. "Humor me. You've got one wish. What's it going to be? Are you going to sell all your paintings next month?"

Kim knew what she would wish for. And it had nothing to do with her career. She wanted what Barbara had: a family.

Barbara paused, noticing the wave of sadness that had

crossed Kim's face. "What's the matter? Thinking about your wish?"

Kim forced herself to laugh. "Yes. I wish for a better date on New Year's."

"That's it?"

"Uh-huh," Kim said, turning away so that Barbara couldn't read her expression.

But she didn't turn quickly enough. One look at Kim's face told Barbara what Kim had wished. "Maybe you should break down and call him," Barbara said quietly.

"What? Who? Ed?"

"No. Your dad. Every now and then you get like this, and I know it's because you miss him."

"I don't miss him," Kim lied. "How can you miss someone you don't even know?"

Barbara sighed. "I don't blame you for being upset. You're a good person, Kim. You deserve better."

Kim opened the refrigerator, absentmindedly shoving the Cheez Doodles inside.

"The man's been a jerk from the get go," Barbara continued. "I mean, cutting off all communication just because you moved with your mother. . . ."

"He did send me money. . . ."

"He can afford the money," Barbara said. "But no letters? No phone calls?" Barbara shook her head, disgusted.

"Okay, Barbara. Thanks. Next subject."

Barbara shrugged. She knew better than to push her luck. Kim had always been a very private person, and Barbara knew she had to respect that. "What time is everybody coming tomorrow?"

"Chris and Lisa are coming at three. Kate will be here at four. I told them that if it's a nice day, they should come early and bring their suits."

"Thanksgiving on the beach," Barbara said wistfully. "I mean, I miss my family, but I love the idea of a swim before turkey."

The phone began to ring, and Barbara snatched it up. "Hello? Sure. Just a minute." She held the phone out toward Kim. "It's for you. A man," she said devilishly, raising her eyebrows.

Kim frowned as she accepted the phone. "Hello?"

"Is this Kim Risson?" a deep, unfamiliar voice inquired stiffly.

Kim glanced up at Barbara. Probably a sales call. "This is Kim," she admitted.

"I'm Dr. Steve Harkavey. Your father's doctor." He hesitated. "His cardiologist."

Kim slowly sat down in a chair. "Yes," she said, stunned.

"Your father . . . had a heart attack last night. He's in the intensive care unit here at St. Mary's."

Kim was silent.

"The good news is that as head of the Thoracic Unit, he's getting the absolute best treatment possible. We've got a top-notch team working on him, but . . . ah, it looks like we're going to have to replace his mitral valve and do some bypass surgery. We're waiting for him to stabilize."

She paused, feeling everything and nothing at all. "Did he ask for me?" she managed.

"He hasn't been able to talk. Fortunately, I found your phone number in his address book."

My father has my phone number? "How serious is this?"

"Well, that depends on the damage to his heart. As you know, this isn't his first heart attack."

No, she thought. She did not know that. She knew nothing about the man this doctor was talking about.

She heard the doctor ask, "Are you planning on coming out here?"

Kim was silent.

"Kim," the doctor repeated. "We may need you to make some decisions."

Decisions. "Of course," she said automatically. "I . . . ah, I'll be there as soon as I can."

She put the phone back on the receiver.

"What's the matter?" Barbara asked, alarmed by the look on Kim's face.

Kim glanced up at her friend. "My father. He's had a heart attack. I guess they need to do surgery."

"How weird," Barbara said, her eyes opening wide. "It's like karma or something. You just make your wish, and then you get a call. . . ." She hesitated as she saw Kim pick up the phone book. "What are you doing?"

"Calling the airlines. I'm going to try and fly there this afternoon."

"What?! This afternoon? The day before Thanksgiving? It's the busiest travel day of the year! It'll be a nightmare."

Kim scanned the airline numbers.

"Did he ask for you?"

Kim began to dial a number, not answering.

Barbara crossed her arms in front of her. "How do you even know he wants you there?"

Kim glanced at her. "You're the big believer in magic, or wishes, or whatever you call it. And now you're telling me not to go?"

Barbara shook her head. "I'm not telling you not to go. I just want you to be . . . careful. I know you. I know how much you want to have him back in your life. I just . . . well, what if he wakes up and doesn't want you there? For all you know he could even have other kids, another family, by now. Just think about this, Kim. Think about what you're doing. And why."

"I don't know what his personal situation is. All I know is that the doctor called *me* and said I needed to make some decisions. So I'll stay and make decisions until he's either well enough to make decisions for himself or somebody else shows up to make them for him. And if he has other kids, great. A perfect opportunity to meet my new family." She glanced into the kitchen. "The turkey is ready to be put in the oven. Can you handle it without me?"

"Of course." Barbara hesitated. "What about your show?"

Kim glanced toward her painting, concerned. "Hopefully I won't have to stay in Michigan all that long."

Barbara shook her head. It was obvious she was not going to be able to talk her friend out of this. And she wasn't sure she should, anyway. "You're a good daughter, Kim." She shrugged her shoulders. "I just hope Santa's watching. It might make up for some of the naughty things you've done this past year."

Two

THE AIRPORT WAS EVEN WORSE THAN KIM HAD EXPECTED—
which was saying quite a bit. And, unfortunately for Kim,
she had been unable to get a direct flight—or even a
semidirect flight. On the busiest travel day of the year, the
best the airline could do was to fly Kim from Miami to
Chicago. In Chicago she had to transfer planes and jump on
a flight to Pittsburgh. In Pittsburgh, she was wait-listed on a
flight to Detroit. It was an extremely circuitous route, but
considering the circumstances, Kim didn't have much of a
choice.

And now, as she waited in a terminal in the Pittsburgh
airport, she could feel her patience begin to wear thin. She
kept an eye on the two gate attendants, flashing them a look
that alternated between pissed off and sugary sweet, as
though she had not yet decided which tactic would work
best. She had missed the previous flight and this was her last
chance. The next flight wouldn't be leaving until tomorrow
morning. She checked her watch. Boarding would start at
any moment, which meant in a few seconds she would know
whether she would arrive in Detroit this evening or tomorrow.

She glanced around her. Everyone seemed to be scurrying
as fast as possible. Haggard-looking parents held on to tired
and cranky children as they rushed to make their flights. As
she scanned the crowd her eyes focused on a tall, handsome
man moving in her direction. Although he was definitely
not her type, he was striking nonetheless. She had always
thought of herself as a good judge of people, and she judged
him to be a California beach bum. He certainly looked like
it. He was all muscles, with lean, handsome features that
were framed by tousled, wavy brown hair. He had a deep
tan and at least a two-day beard growth. He was wearing a

88

bright tropical shirt, jeans, and sneakers and carrying a large red backpack over his shoulders. Kim knew the type. The, "Hey ladies, look at me" type. Handsome and aware of it. His only concern was the height of the waves.

She watched as he walked up to the gate and began to speak to the attendant. He pulled out a ticket and showed it to her. It was obvious that he was not confirming his seat, but was asking her a question about the flight.

The other gate attendant began to board the flight. Concerned, Kim grabbed her luggage and began to move forward, just as the man pulled out his wallet and flashed the gate attendant what appeared to be ID. Kim stepped up to the ticket counter and interrupted. "Excuse me," she said, sensing disaster. "Can you tell me when you'll announce the names of the wait-listed passengers that can board?"

The attendant didn't even look up from her computer screen. "I'm sorry, ma'am. There's only room for one wait-listed passenger. And that would be this gentleman right here."

"What?! But I was here first," Kim said, trying desperately to remain calm. "He just got here!"

"Look," the man said quietly to Kim. "I can explain."

"This is not fair," Kim said, tears welling in her eyes. "I've been waiting here for two hours, and you're letting some guy just bump me right off?"

"I'm sorry, ma'am," the attendant said insincerely. "It's not up to me. He was priority-ranked."

"Please. Just let me explain . . . ," the man began.

"Priority-ranked?" Kim said incredibly. "What kind of a system is this?"

"I'm sorry, ma'am," she repeated simply as she handed the man his boarding pass. "It's out of my hands. I'll be happy to book you on a flight leaving first thing in the morning."

"Please," the man said calmly to Kim. "I can explain . . . ," he began.

"You don't understand!" Kim interrupted, as the tears began to flow. "My father is very sick. He's in the hospital . . . intensive care. Tomorrow morning may be too late."

The gate attendant rolled her eyes as though she had

heard it all before. Sick aunt, sick grandpa, sick dog, sick dad. It made no difference to her. It was the busiest travel day of the year, and Kim wasn't getting on that flight.

Kim glanced back at the man with the seat assignment. She may have lost the gate attendant's sympathy, but it looked as if she still had the man's attention. "We're very close, my father and I," she explained, lowering her voice but keeping the intensity. "He's on his deathbed. If something happens to him before I get there, I don't know if I could live with myself." Hmm. Well at least part of it was true. The part about him being her father.

The final boarding call was made, and the man glanced down at his ticket.

"Please," Kim said. "He could die before I get there." Okay, now she *was* really upset.

The man glanced toward the boarding gate. He looked at Kim as if evaluating her for truthfulness. He sighed. "Here," he said, handing her his ticket. "Go ahead."

Kim glanced down at the boarding pass. It was issued to an A. Hoffman. She smiled at him appreciatively. "Thank you, Mr. Hoffman. Thank you so much."

"Good luck," he said matter-of-factly.

Kim held her Styrofoam cup of thick black coffee in her hands as she glanced around the critical care waiting room. It was quite a bit more comfortable than the emergency waiting room, with clusters of well-worn, plump beige couches and chairs, and a small kitchen area.

At ten o'clock in the evening, the waiting room was practically deserted. In fact, only one family remained in the room with her, anxiously awaiting news of their loved one. The parents sat on the couch, holding hands as they stared blankly at a large TV screen. Two girls, sisters, Kim guessed, sat on the floor beneath their parents, working on a jigsaw puzzle that they had spilled out onto the coffee table.

Kim glanced up at the TV. The sound was turned down so low she couldn't even hear it, but the images were familiar enough that she didn't need any sound. In an advertisement for a local car dealership, a man whom she presumed to be the owner of the dealership was dressed up like Santa, pointing his finger and chatting at the camera. She had no doubt he was promising great prices this holiday season.

"Excuse me, Kim?"

A man with silvery white hair and a long doctor's coat stood in front of her. Kim jumped up, almost spilling her coffee.

"I spoke to you on the phone. I'm Dr. Harkavey, your father's cardiologist."

"Hi," Kim said, not certain which questions to ask first.

"I've met you before, when you were about this big," he said, raising his hand to his waist. "You probably don't remember."

Kim squinted as though trying to recall.

"Why don't you set that down," he said, motioning toward her coffee. "Let's take a walk."

Still silent, Kim set her coffee down on the counter. She glanced over at the family, who were staring at her sympathetically. She flashed them a brave smile before following the doctor out into the hall.

"What's going on?" she said. "They wouldn't let me see him."

"I know. I'm sorry about that. They're just trying to be extra careful. You're father's an important man around here." Kim knew that. She also guessed that her father was an unpopular man around there. He had never been an easy man to please, at home or at the office.

"But why can't I go in?"

"They're worried about infection. His system is very weak right now. But I think it'll be all right if you want to see him for a moment. We won't stay very long."

"But is he . . . will he be all right?"

"Well," he said carefully. "We were lucky. He was here when he had his heart attack so he was able to get medical attention immediately, which probably saved his life. However, he's got a serious problem with his mitral valve, as well as several of the arteries that lead to the heart. But we've assigned one of the top thoracic surgeons in the country to your father. As soon as your dad is stable, we're going to go ahead and operate . . . replace the mitral valve and unclog the arteries. Assuming," he said, pushing open a set of swinging doors as he checked his watch, "the surgeon has arrived by then."

They stopped at the nurse's station at the end of the corridor. "This is Kim Risson, Dr. Risson's daughter," Dr. Harkavey said to the nurse behind the desk. "I'm going to take her in for a few minutes." The nurse nodded as she flashed Kim a sympathetic glance. "Here, Kim," he said, handing her a mask. "Why don't you put this on."

Kim slipped the mask over her face.

"I have to warn you, your father won't be conscious. He's heavily sedated, and he's intubated as well," he said, leading Kim down the chilly, antiseptic white hall. He stopped at a door at the end of the hall and pushed it open.

Kim hesitated in the doorway. She felt an eerie sense of numbness overtake her as she slowly stepped inside the room, her eyes focusing on the form in the bed. This couldn't be her father. The man under the covers looked much smaller than her dad. Much older.

She stepped closer. There were tubes everywhere, coming out of her father's nose, his mouth, and his arm. This was not the strong, handsome, intimidating man she remembered. This man looked frail and weak. Helpless.

Kim was seized with a sudden, intense sense of impending loss. Until now, everything had seemed so surreal, almost as if she were having some sort of vivid dream. But now, for the first time in fifteen years, she was standing in front of her father, the man she had for so long held responsible for much of her pain and suffering. And surprisingly enough, she no longer felt any anger toward him. All she felt was love. Regardless of how he felt about her, he was her father, her only family, and she needed him to get well. "Dad," she said quietly. "Dad, it's me. It's Kim. You're going to be okay." Her father lay still. Kim doubted that he had even heard her. She glanced back at Dr. Harkavey, and he nodded encouragement.

"Dad, I'm going to stay here with you. We're going to get through this. You're going to get better. Okay?" She picked up his lifeless hand and gave it a gentle squeeze.

She felt a touch on her arm. Dr. Harkavey gently steered

her out into the hall, shutting the door behind them. "I know it means a lot to him to have you here, Kim."

Kim pulled off her mask. The top of it was wet.

"Here," Dr. Harkavey said, handing her a tissue.

Kim touched her fingers to her cheek. No wonder the mask was wet. She was crying.

"Can I get you a glass of water? Some coffee?" Dr. Harkavey asked.

Kim shook her head. What a nice man he was. With a decent beard he could even pose as Santa.

Like a kindly grandfather, Dr. Harkavey took her arm and steered her back toward the waiting room. "If you like, I'll ask the surgeon to stop by when he arrives. He can answer any questions you have about the procedure."

"Yes," she said, nodding, as they paused outside the waiting room door. "Thank you. When is he going to get here?"

He glanced at his watch. "When he called he was in Toledo, and that was about two hours ago." Which would mean he should arrive at any minute. "He would've been here sooner," he continued, "but he was vacationing in the Caribbean this morning. He interrupted his vacation to come back here and take care of your father. Apparently he had some trouble with his flights. I haven't talked to him, but somebody said he got bumped from one of his connections, so he had to rent a car to get back here."

For some strange reason Kim had a sudden sense of dread. Just tired, she told herself. Tired and stressed. "Where did he have to drive from?"

"Pittsburgh or something."

"What's his name?" Kim asked hoarsely.

"Hoffman. Dr. Anthony Hoffman."

Three

KIM SAT STILL ON THE COUCH, HER BACK STIFF, HER FOREHEAD
creased with worry. The TV was off and the only light, a
floor lamp beside the couch, cast an eerie glow about the
room. It was almost eleven o'clock, and she had not yet
seen Dr. Anthony Hoffman. She stood up and walked over
to the glass windows that separated the waiting room from
the hall, anxiously awaiting his arrival. She gently rested
her fingertips on the pane of glass as she leaned forward,
stretching her neck to look down the hall. *Please,* she
thought, praying for the arrival of the doctor. *Please hurry.*

She walked back to the couch and forced herself to sit
back down. She stared at the half-finished puzzle in front
of her. She could understand why they kept a hearty supply
of jigsaw puzzles in this room. They were just about the
only thing you could do when your entire body was
consumed with a mind-numbing pain.

"Kim?"

Kim glanced up. Dr. Harkavey stood in the doorway.
Beside him stood the same man she had met earlier that
day. The only difference was that he had traded in his jeans
and luau shirt for hospital-issue blue scrubs. It looked like
he hadn't even had time to go home to shave.

"This is Dr. Hoffman. He's in charge of your father's
heart surgery."

Kim nodded, waiting for him to say, *Hey! You're the girl
who gave me that sorry song and dance and swiped my
ticket.*

"Hi, Kim," he said instead, shaking her hand. "I'm Tony
Hoffman. I thought you might have some questions."

Tony, she thought, focusing on how he had introduced
himself. She preferred calling her doctors "doctor." But
still, she was appreciative that he had not mentioned their

94

earlier meeting. At least, he hadn't mentioned it yet. "Thank you . . . thank you for interrupting your vacation. . . ."

"Of course," he said, letting her off the hook. Both he and Dr. Harkavey looked at her, as if waiting for her questions. "Um," she said. Her mind was a blank. "How long do you think the operation will be?"

"About seven hours. We have to take the heart out, stop it, and fix the problems and put it back."

"You have to stop the heart?" Kim said, looking worriedly at Dr. Harkavey.

He nodded. "The blood will be pumped mechanically." Tony smiled at her encouragingly before checking his watch. After a brief, empty pause, he said, "If you don't have any more questions, I should get going."

Kim nodded, still finding it difficult to believe that this was the same man she had met in the airport. He may be one of the best heart surgeons in the country, but he certainly didn't look the part.

"Your father's going to be just fine," Tony said, as if sensing that she needed to be reassured.

She felt as though she couldn't breathe. She must have looked ill, because Tony said, "There are rooms here if you'd like to lie down."

She shook her head. "I'll wait here."

"All right," Tony said, with a quick nod of his head. "I'll come back and see you when we're finished."

After he had left the room Kim glanced up at Dr. Harkavey. "He's not quite what I expected," she admitted.

He smiled as he said, "He's a little unconventional, but he's one of the best in the country, if not *the* best."

Kim nodded. She must not have looked convinced because he then added, "I promise you."

Kim paced the floors, checking her watch every five minutes. She made several quick trips to the coffee machine, although she didn't need any help staying awake. Every time anyone walked past the waiting room, she jumped, certain that it was someone with news for her. Bad news.

She forced herself to focus on the jigsaw puzzles. At four-thirty in the morning she was on her fifth cup when she heard someone say her name. She looked up. Dr. Hoffman stood in the doorway. Fearful of what he might say, Kim felt her body go rigid. He stepped inside the room and sat down next to her. "Everything went well," he said. "Your father did just fine."

Kim breathed a sigh of relief as the tears began to flow. "Thank you."

"He's resting now. I think you'll be able to see him tomorrow morning, if you like."

Kim nodded, delicately wiping her face with her forefinger. "I was so worried," she said. "When I found out that I was the reason you weren't here on time . . ."

"It didn't make any difference," he said quietly. "Don't torture yourself. You were right. You should have been here with him. There was nothing I could do until he stabilized, and he didn't stabilize until after you arrived. I think you were responsible. Your being here gave him the strength he needed."

Kim's tears slowed. "Really? He wasn't even awake when I saw him."

He nodded. "He may not have been awake, but I'm sure he sensed your presence. So it was perfect timing. Because by the time I arrived we were ready to begin surgery." He smiled again. It was a nice smile. A reassuring smile.

"Well, in any case, I'm sorry."

"You shouldn't be." He smiled at her. Kim stared into his hazy green eyes. One could forget one's troubles staring into eyes like that. "Why don't I show you where the rooms for families of critical care patients are," he continued. "They're in a building next to the hospital. You can get some sleep."

She shook her head. "No," she said adamantly. "I want to stay here."

He nodded. "That's fine, too." He smiled reassuringly. "I'm sure I'll see you tomorrow."

What a thoughtful man, Kim thought silently, as she watched him walk out of the waiting room. He seemed to honestly care, not only about her father but about her comfort as well.

Kim drifted toward the couch and prepared to settle in for the night. She glanced around the empty room and recalled her first meeting with her father's surgeon. She appreciated his not mentioning her "little outburst" at the airport in front of Dr. Harkavey. Instead, he had been sweet and kind, reassuring her that she shouldn't feel guilty for her actions—despite the inconvenience she had caused.

Kim smiled as she remembered what she had said to Barbara about surgeons only hours earlier. And now it appeared, sitting alone in a waiting room miles away from her life in Florida, doctors were her only friends. Maybe . . . just maybe, she had been wrong about the type of men and women who went into this intense, high-pressure career. Perhaps they weren't all like her father.

At the thought of her father, Kim lay down on the couch, brushing away a tear as hours of delayed fatigue washed over her. She pulled her sweater around her shoulders, using it as a blanket. Within moments she was asleep.

Tony took a sip of black coffee as he waited for the elevator. He glanced over at the clock on the wall. Five-thirty. It was already morning.

It was hard to believe that twenty-four hours ago he was asleep with his window open in the balmy Bahamas. It had been his first vacation in years. And it had lasted exactly two days.

It had been difficult for Tony to go on vacation in the first place, mainly because he knew he would be traveling alone. He was not dating anyone whom he cared enough about to share his valuable vacation days. In fact, he had recently resigned himself to the solitary life of a confirmed bachelor, a life filled with first dates and casual relationships. He had not yet met any woman who had captured his heart, and he had promised himself that he would not settle for anything less. He had learned his lesson in his last painful breakup, with the woman he had been involved with for six years. They had both sensed that they were not right for each other from the beginning of the relationship, yet that had not made the demise of their relationship any less painful.

He squinted his eyes as though trying to squeeze out the fatigue. He had to exorcise the Bahamas from his mind. He had been given one of the most important cases of his career. He couldn't afford to be tired. He had his boss and his nemesis under his care: Dr. Harold Risson.

The elevator arrived and the doors opened. Tony stepped inside and pressed the button for the third floor. The critical care ward.

He had worked for and with Harold Risson for almost five years. Their relationship had been strained from the start. He had little in common with the rigid, conservative chief of the department. But their differences had little to do with style or social opinions. Risson seemed to possess a hearty and intense dislike for Tony. Rumor had it that when Risson retired, Tony was in line for Risson's job. Risson seemed to take these rumors to heart, making it clear that he had no intention of retiring anytime soon. In reality, Tony was not "after" Risson's job. He had made a point to stay out of office politics, and had even made it clear to the head administrator that he would never accept the position unless Risson himself nominated him for it. But that simple act hadn't eased the tension between them. In fact, just last month Risson had attempted to transfer Tony to a smaller, less prestigious hospital. Risson had long complained that Tony lacked discipline, but others, including the head of the hospital, disagreed. Fortunately for Tony, not everyone was as conservative as Harold Risson.

Of course, Tony thought, he had to give Risson credit. He had been a trailblazer in his day. A gifted and talented surgeon, he had been one of the first doctors in the state to do transplants. But Risson was from the old school, where doctors were next to God in terms of power. They received their MD, learned their craft, developed their specialty, and that was that. Tony was from the new school of doctors, the ones who viewed medicine as part of a growing field that included holistic and natural approaches to healing. Tony liked to think of medicine as an art, a field that was constantly changing, a field in which he needed to try new techniques just to stay on top. In a field with little room for rebels, Tony pushed the conservative thinking to the limit.

He stepped off the elevator and began walking toward the critical care unit. As he approached the waiting room, his thoughts drifted back to Kim. Who would've thought that the woman who had talked him out of his plane ticket was Risson's daughter? *It figures. She's probably every bit as tough as her father.* He chuckled as he remembered the expression on her face when she demanded he give up his seat on the plane. Like father like daughter.

In fact, he had not even been aware that Risson had a daughter—and the news had surprised him. He had never heard Risson, or anyone, for that matter, mention Risson's family. But then again, Risson never socialized with anyone in the hospital. Tony doubted if Risson socialized much with anyone. He was always working. Always at the hospital. Tony had assumed that the reason why Risson would never step down as chief of the department was because he had no life to retire to. Risson was known as a lonely, unhappy man. In fact, if Tony hadn't seen it with his own eyes, he would've bet money that Risson didn't even have a heart.

Still, he thought, remembering the concern he had seen on Kim's face, his daughter seemed to love him.

Tony stopped at the window and peered inside the waiting room. Kim was by herself, sleeping curled up on a couch, using her small sweater as a blanket. The light was still on beside her.

Tony paused for a moment. She was a beautiful woman, with strong yet delicate features. He shook his head. He felt sorry for her. This was a hell of a way to spend a holiday. Alone in the critical care ward, waiting to see if her father would live or die.

He stepped away and walked briskly into an empty hospital room. He snagged an extra blanket and headed back toward the waiting room. Careful not to wake her, he slipped inside the room and laid the blanket on top of her. Turning off the light, he bid her a silent good-night.

Four

KIM SPENT THE MAJORITY OF THANKSGIVING DAY IN THE critical care waiting room. She was allowed to spend exactly ten minutes every hour by her father's side. By five o'clock that evening, she was ready to fall over. Her father had been in a drug-induced slumber all day and had not even known she was there. As she made her way back to the critical care ward, she waved hello to the nurses, who smiled at her and nodded. She didn't need to check in anymore. She had done this drill ten times so far that day, and everyone who worked there knew who she was and where she was heading.

She walked into her father's dimly lit room. She could see her father lying in bed, his eyes closed. She sat down next to him and took his hand. She could never remember holding her father's hand when she was growing up, and under normal circumstances, she never would have dreamed of such a gesture. But every hour on the hour it was just about the only way she could communicate with him. It was a simple yet universally understood sign of affection.

She looked down at his thin, white hand. "I'm here, Dad." She was beginning to worry that he would never wake up. She glanced up at the heart monitor, watching the regular, steady graphs duplicate across the screen. "Oh, Dad," she said with a sigh. "You've got to get better. I'm sorry we haven't spoken in such a long time. I'm . . . well, I'm sorry for a lot of things." Kim stopped. She could have sworn she felt something. A slight tightening of his hand, as though he was attempting to communicate. She looked up at him. His eyes were open.

"Dad?" she whispered. She knew he couldn't answer her with the breathing tube down his throat. Again she felt the weak squeeze. He attempted a smile, but the simple act appeared to exhaust him and he shut his eyes again.

"How's he doing?" a nurse asked, popping her head in.

"He's awake," Kim said excitedly.

"Dr. Risson?" the nurse said loudly, leaning over him. She picked up his wrist and took his pulse. "He seems to be coming out of it. That's good. Dr. Hoffman will be pleased."

Kim smiled. She felt a sense of accomplishment and relief. Her father was not only waking up, he was happy that she was here. She could feel it. The nurse motioned toward the clock. Kim nodded as she stood. Her ten minutes were up.

As she left the room, she practically bumped into Dr. Hoffman. "Hi, Kim," he said, flashing her his shy smile. "How's the patient?"

She practically beamed at him. "He was awake."

He nodded. "Good," he said. "C'mon back in. I'm just going to look him over."

He walked past Kim, close enough so that she could detect the faint smell of aftershave. Kim stepped back into the room and watched as he picked up her father's chart and flipped through it. "Good," he repeated matter-of-factly. He put down the chart, took out a small pocket light, and opened her father's eyes, flashing the light in his pupils.

Tony slipped the light back into his white jacket and nodded for her to follow him. As soon as they were out of the room, he said, "Your father's doing well, but he probably won't regain full consciousness until tomorrow. Dr. Harkavey's got him scheduled to have his breathing tubes removed first thing, so he'll be able to speak." He walked with her out of the critical care ward and stopped at the elevator. "If I were you, I'd go home and get some sleep. He'll be all right," he said, pushing the elevator button.

She frowned. Home. That might be a problem. She had no idea where her father lived, or if he'd even be comfortable with her staying in his house.

"Is something the matter?" Tony asked.

"I . . . um, I can't remember where he lives."

Tony looked at her curiously. "I'm afraid I can't help you. I've never been there myself."

"I . . . ah, I haven't spoken with my father in quite a while," Kim stammered. "What I said at the airport, about our being so close . . . it wasn't exactly true."

"It's okay," he said, nodding understandingly. He paused, thinking. "There're some decent hotels around here. Of course, the closest ones are pretty expensive."

Kim hesitated. Her airline ticket had cost her almost all the money she had in her savings. Maybe she should just stay at her father's house. As long as . . . well, as long as there wasn't anyone else already living there. "Is he . . . uh, my father . . . Is he married or anything? I mean, I haven't seen anyone around here, but I wasn't sure. . . ."

"No. Your father's definitely not married. And as far as I know, he's not dating anyone. At least, no one I've heard of. And I make it a point to stay on top of hospital gossip," he joked.

The elevator arrived and the doors opened, but Tony ignored it. "C'mon," he said, nodding toward the waiting room. "Why don't you grab your stuff and we'll go find a computer."

He followed her into the waiting room and picked up her suitcase.

"You don't have to . . . ," she began, uncomfortable that he was carrying her luggage.

"I've got it," he said, motioning for her to follow him. He led her out of the waiting room and made a left. "This way," he said, heading toward the nursing station. "Hey, Melva," he said, smiling at the pretty brunette nurse who was sitting behind the desk. "Look up Dr. Risson's address for me, will you?"

She walked to the computer and leaned over, typing in some information. "222 Sycamore Street."

Kim exhaled. Easy. "That's where we used to live. I guess he never moved." She looked at Tony and smiled. "Is there a place where I can rent a car around here?"

He shook his head. "They won't be open today. If I were you, I'd just drive your father's car."

"I don't have keys."

"Hey, Melva," he said, calling the nurse back. "Where are Dr. Risson's valuables? His keys and stuff. Do you guys have them? If so, cough 'em up."

She raised an eyebrow. "Why?" she asked suspiciously.

"Because I want to go to his house tonight and rob him. I figure it's a good time since he'll be busy for a while."

Melva shook her head as she put a small plastic basket in front of him that held a wallet and a set of keys. "If anyone's head rolls because of this, it better be yours."

"I'm taking full responsibility. By the way," he said, fishing out the keys. "Have you met his daughter?"

She nodded, making it clear by her cold, stony stare that it made little difference that it was his daughter who was taking the belongings. She was still holding Tony responsible.

Kim smiled politely. She had seen the nurse quite a few times, but she had never introduced herself.

"Nice to meet you," Melva said curtly.

"Thank you for doing this," Kim said appreciatively.

"Yes, thank you, Melva," Tony said, pushing the little plastic basket back toward her. Melva raised an eyebrow as if she definitely did not approve.

"Do you know which car is his?" he asked, focusing his attention back on Kim,

Kim looked at him blankly.

"C'mon," he said, nodding toward the elevator. "I'll show you. You can't miss it." He led her to the elevator and caught it just as the doors were closing. They stepped inside and he pressed the button for the lobby.

Her eyes wandered toward his ring finger. No band. When she glanced back up at him, he was looking at her with a little smile that let her know he was fully aware of what she had been trying to determine. Embarrassed, Kim glanced away and busied herself by focusing on a piece of lint on her pants.

"You must be exhausted," he said quietly.

She nodded as she picked lint off her sweater. "It's been a rough few days."

"I bet." He paused. "Do you mind if I ask you a personal question?"

She nodded. "Go ahead."

"Do you have anyone that could help you with this?"

"What do you mean?"

"I mean family."

She shook her head. "My mother is dead. And I'm an only child. So," she said, tilting her head to one side and shrugging, "I'm afraid I'm my father's only family."

He gave her a small, admiring smile. "He's lucky to have a daughter like you."

She blushed. "He's lucky to have a doctor like you." She inwardly winced. What was she doing—flirting?

"I don't know that he'd agree."

Kim glanced at him, confused. "What do you mean?"

Tony hesitated. "Your father and I have had our issues."

"He can be difficult," she said diplomatically.

Tony smiled appreciatively. Risson's daughter was very different from her father. Despite her obvious personal strength, there was a softness in her demeanor that Tony found enticing. "He's a damn good surgeon, though," Tony said. "One of the best. He's the reason why I came here. I wanted to study under him."

"Oh," she said, trying to hide her disappointment. "You aspire to be like him?"

He laughed. "You don't sound as though you think that's a worthy goal," he said as the elevator doors opened.

"No, of course not," Kim said vaguely and followed him toward the front door.

He stopped suddenly and looked at her. "Where's your coat?"

"I stuck a windbreaker in my suitcase. I don't really have a winter coat," she said.

"No coat?" he said incredulously. "Where are you from?"

"Florida."

"Wait here," he said, setting her suitcase down. He took off running down the hall.

"I don't need one," Kim called out, but he didn't bother to stop. He returned a few minutes later carrying a warm-looking down jacket. "Take this," he said, holding it out to her.

"What's this?" she asked, looking at it.

"Boy, you *do* live in Florida," he said, laughing. "This is called a winter coat," he said, holding it open for her.

Kim paused and smiled at him. "I know what it is. Who does it belong to?"

"Me."

"I can't take your coat," she said, putting up her hands in

protest. "It's very sweet of you to offer, but if I take your coat, what will you wear?"

"I'll be fine. I've got a ton of sweaters in my locker, and I've got plenty of coats at home."

Just then a man walked into the hospital and a blast of cold air shot down the hall. It was enough to make Kim reconsider.

"Take it," Tony said, handing her the coat.

"Are you sure?" Kim asked, impressed by his generous and chivalrous offer.

"Absolutely," he responded, helping her put it on.

Despite the chilly air circulating in the hall, Kim felt a warm, cozy feeling melt through her as he slipped the jacket onto her arms.

"Thanks," she said, feeling awkward and embarrassed, although she wasn't sure why. "Thanks very much."

"You're welcome very much," Tony said as he finished helping her on with the coat. He nodded toward the door. "Shall we?"

Kim stepped outside and experienced the same sense of frozen lethargy she always felt in cold, miserable weather. "It's freezing," she said.

"It's not freezing. It's just a little brisk."

"It's freezing," Kim repeated matter-of-factly, hurrying to catch up with him.

She followed him to a large, blue Cadillac. "This is your father's car," he said, his arms crossed in front of him to keep himself warm.

Kim glanced at the car with disbelief. It looked like the same car she remembered her father driving. Perhaps it *was* the same car. After all, they long ago stopped making cars as big as this.

"I hope you have gas money, because this car probably goes through a tank in about five minutes," Tony said.

Kim stepped forward with the key. She felt uncomfortable, as if she were breaking into a stranger's car.

Tony opened the driver's door for her. "I think the button for the trunk is . . ."

"Right here," Kim said, popping open the glove box and unlocking the trunk.

Tony smiled as he walked around to the back and set her suitcase inside the ample trunk.

He walked around to the front just as Kim was using the windshield wipers to scrape off the light dusting of snow that had fallen. "Are you going to be all right?" he asked, leaning over the top of the door. "You remember how to get home?"

"Like it was yesterday. That's the problem."

He nodded as though he understood, though what she had said really didn't make any sense, even to her. He stood up straight.

"Thank you," she said. "For the coat, for everything."

"No problem," he said, still leaning over the door. His teeth were chattering and his lower lip was turning a shade of blue.

"You better get inside," she said. "Before you freeze."

He shook his head. "Nah," he said, looking up at the sky. "I like the cold. I'd stay out here all day . . . and night, if I could." He smiled at her as he stood back from the door. "Have a good Thanksgiving evening."

Thanksgiving. She had forgotten about that. "Same to you," she said as he shut the door. She smiled and waved good-bye as she fired up the Caddy.

Kim drove through the deserted, eerily familiar roads. She felt funny driving her father's car. Especially this car. This car made her feel tiny, which was not a simple feat. At five feet nine inches, she didn't often feel small. But in her father's Cadillac, she had to lean forward to be able to see out the window.

This was not the first time she had been behind the wheel of this car. She had driven it once before, when she was fourteen years old. She had been angry that her father had not allowed her to go on a date with a boy three years her senior, so she had retaliated by getting up in the middle of the night and driving her father's pride and joy, his brand-new big blue Cadillac, around the block. That was it. She had simply driven it around the block and parked it back in the driveway and he had never found out. It hadn't been much of a retaliation, but the truth of the matter was, her father scared the hell out of her, especially then. Not because he had a temper, but because he didn't have one. He was always so controlled. So cold. Even when he was angry.

Kim glanced at the mileage. The car incident was almost seventeen years ago, and her father had only 70,000 miles on the odometer. It was obvious he only used the car to drive to and from work.

Kim turned onto Sycamore Street, and her breath quickened. She stopped in front of her father's house—the same house she had grown up in. She looked at the willow tree in the front yard, the same tree she had fallen out of, breaking her leg. Feeling as though she had stepped back in time, Kim nestled her nose in Tony's jacket, his deep musky scent bringing her back to the present day. She loved the fact that he had given her his jacket. It had been a gallant, sweet act on his part, and she respected that. *Whatever happened to the "Hey, it's cold out here, let me give you my coat" type of guy . . . ?*

Obviously he was alive and well and living in Michigan; she'd be sure to tell Barbara when they spoke that evening. She smiled as she straightened in her seat. Of course, the whole coat incident really didn't count, because she wasn't dating this man—he was simply being nice. But she was grateful, not only for the warmth the jacket provided but for the sweet reminder of her present-day life. She was not a child returning to an unhappy home, but an adult, returning to her father's house not because she had nowhere else to go, but because she had chosen to return.

Kim grabbed her suitcase out of the trunk and walked down the front walkway to the door. The back door seemed too personal a way to enter this house. It was for family. And she was a guest. Not even an official guest. A visitor.

She opened the door and walked in, shutting the door behind her. The house smelled like she remembered it, a mixture of Pledge and fresh laundry. She took it as a sign that her father had kept the same housekeeper all these years.

She glanced inside the large living room off to her right. The same rust brown shag carpeting covered the floor. A familiar white, furry rug was still lying in front of the fireplace. The walls were paneled with the same heavy oak paneling. Even the furniture was as she remembered it. Kim stepped inside the room and stopped. The portrait of their family still hung over the fireplace, as though she, her mother, and father were still the occupants of this big, old lonely house.

Kim had a sick feeling in her stomach. This was weird. Very weird. Apparently her father had suffered a little bit more than she had suspected. Why else had he never changed the decor?

Kim couldn't bear to look at anything more. She walked up the stairs and made her way to her old bedroom. As she suspected, it was neat and clean, but appeared to be exactly as she'd left it. Exhausted, she slipped into her old twin bed and closed her eyes.

Kim reached the parking lot at five minutes after seven. The heat in the Cadillac was blasting as high as it could go. So hard, in fact, that her hair was blowing back. "Ahhhh," she sighed out loud, as she adjusted the vents so they were aimed at her toes. *They just don't make cars like this anymore.* She could understand why her father had wanted to hang on to it.

Kim had woken up bright and early, and even a little cheerful, although she wasn't sure why. She suspected it was because of the house. She was encouraged by the fact that her father hadn't changed anything. Perhaps he had left everything the way it was because he missed them. For whatever reason, it had certainly been helpful this morning. Kim had rummaged through the front closet and had found one of her mother's old winter coats with a pair of brown leather gloves still tucked into the pocket. Kim glanced down at the slightly moth-eaten blue wool. She wasn't going to win any fashion awards, but at least it was warm. And the best part was that it had been her mother's.

As she pulled into the hospital parking lot, she checked her watch. She had made it there in under five minutes. She glanced at the parking lot instructions. Visitor parking to the right. Maternity parking to the left. Patient parking to the left. Physicians parking . . . right in front. Kim hesitated as she glanced at the special parking sticker posted in her father's front window. Maybe she should park in the physicians parking. After all, who knew what time she would be leaving? Did she really want to stroll through a dark parking lot in the cold of the night?

Cold was the key word.

She drove slowly toward the front, making a wide turn into a parking spot. As she stepped out of the car, she realized that she had inadvertently taken up two spots. She got back inside, fired up the engine, and slowly backed out and pulled back in again, this time pulling in closer to the car to her right. Perfect, she thought, stopping the car and turning off the engine. She glanced to her right. She was definitely close to the car next to her. Very close. But what could she do? If she parked any farther away, when someone pulled in on the other side, they'd be so close to her she wouldn't be able to get back into her car. She stepped out of her car and walked over to check the distance between her car and the one on the right. Just fine, she thought. As long as the driver was slim. Make that very slim.

She was distracted by a thundering roar and glanced back. A man in a motorcycle pulled into the open spot behind her. He pulled off his helmet. It was none other than Dr. Anthony Hoffman. Tony to her.

He made a point of staring at the *Physicians Only* parking sign. Then he looked at her and winked.

Kim could feel herself blush. Busted.

"Good morning," he said, hopping off his motorcycle.

Kim nodded. Her eyes scanned his outfit as he walked toward her. Black motorcycle jacket and jeans. His wavy brown hair fell over one eye.

"Isn't it a little chilly to be riding a motorcycle?" Kim asked incredibly.

He shook his head. "It's nice outside."

"Speaking of which," she said, reaching back into the car and pulling out his jacket, "thank you very much. I really appreciated it."

"Are you sure you don't need it? You can hang on to it if you want. . . ."

"No, I'm fine," Kim insisted, handing it back to him. She nodded toward her coat. "I found an old coat of my mother's."

"Oh," he said, nodding in approval. "That's nice. And it's in style, too."

"Yeah, well, there's no accounting for taste, I guess," Kim said with a smile, and they began walking toward the hospital.

After a pause, Tony said, "I was thinking about you last night. How did everything go? Did you find your way to your dad's house?"

"Yes, thanks. I found my way and got inside without any trouble. It was all a little weird, but I survived. I feel much better today."

"Well, good," he said, opening up the hospital door for her. As she stepped inside, their eyes locked for a split second before Kim glanced away.

"I'm sure I'll see you upstairs," he said casually as he turned down a long, narrow hallway.

Kim paused for a moment, glancing after him. She realized that she was warm. She pulled off her glove and held a hand to her cheek. Either she was getting a fever, or she was still blushing. She thought back to his grin, which she had decided was definitely one of the sexiest she'd seen. She had a feeling she knew why she was warm.

Watch yourself, she commanded. He may be nice, but she had little desire to end up in a cold, unhappy marriage with a man who worked night and day. And at this point, she wasn't much interested in a casual fling. At least not with Tony. It was too complicated with his working with her father. She had best focus on the matter at hand. She picked up her pace as she headed toward the elevator.

"Dad? Dad, it's me. Kim." Kim paused as she waited for a reaction. She glanced at the clock on the wall. It was almost noon. Time for her to leave. She patted his hand. "I slept at the house last night. I hope you don't mind." She left out the part about driving his car. If he was awake, that might be enough to send him back into cardiac arrest.

His eyes fluttered and he opened them. "Kim?" he said in a voice that was barely audible.

"Hi, Dad," Kim said, her eyes welling with tears.

Her father squeezed her hand. "Thank you . . . for coming."

Kim nodded. She couldn't think of anything else to say.

"My throat . . . ," he began. "So dry."

"Want some ice?" Kim asked, anxious for something to do. Her father gave her a slight nod.

She stepped back out into the hall and hurried to the nurses' station. Melva was sitting behind the desk. "Ice!" Kim said, in a low, anxious whisper. "My father wants some ice."

"He's awake?" Melva asked, exchanging a glance with the nurse next to her.

Kim nodded. "He's awake and he wants some ice," she repeated, as though his very life depended on it.

Melva shot Kim a glance that said, "Calm down" as she filled a Styrofoam cup with some chipped ice and began to walk quickly back toward Kim's father's room. She pushed open the door. "Good morning, Dr. Risson. Here's your ice."

He nodded. He tried to sit up but was too weak. Melva skillfully grabbed his arm and helped move him up on the bed as Kim stood helplessly off to the side. Like a feeble old man, her father accepted the ice from Melva and attempted to suck on the chips.

Melva began to take his blood pressure. "You have a lovely daughter, Dr. Risson," she said. "She's been here with you every day."

Kim's father gave Kim an appreciative smile. "Yes," he said simply. Melva finished taking his blood pressure, marked it down on his chart, and walked out of the room, leaving father and daughter alone once more.

"Kim," he said, staring at her with tears in his eyes. "So much time . . ." His voice trailed off. He smiled at her weakly. "You've grown up."

Kim nodded. "Yes."

"How did you find out about me . . . my heart attack?"

"Dr. Harkavey called. He got my number out of your address book."

Harold nodded. "And you came," he said weakly, as though he didn't quite believe it.

Kim nodded. She paused, biting her lower lip. "Of course. You're my . . . my dad."

He smiled. "I'm happy you . . . thank you for coming,"

he stammered, putting the cup of ice back down on his bedside table. He closed his eyes briefly from exhaustion and pain. He gingerly slid back down on his pillows.

"How long . . . ," he said, his voice heavy with sleep. "How long can you stay?"

She didn't hesitate. "As long as you need me."

He opened his eyes once more and again attempted to smile. "Thank you, Kim."

After her father had fallen back asleep, Kim wandered back toward the waiting room. She stepped inside and hesitated. She had begun to hate this room. She felt so sorry for the people who had come and gone since she had arrived. Some left crying, others left hopeful, but all left exhausted. She glanced out the window and saw Tony step out of the elevators. She immediately walked into the hall, happy to see a familiar face.

"Dr. Hoffman," she called out.

He stopped and turned around. "Kim," he said, his face brightening as he walked toward her.

"My dad's doing much better," she said.

"That's what Dr. Harkavey said. I was just speaking with him. He said your father was already quizzing him about his medications. A positive sign."

Kim grinned.

Tony caught himself staring into Kim's tired, big brown eyes. He felt sorry for her. She looked like she was in dire need of a break from all the stress. "Look," he said, hesitating. "I could really use a cup of coffee. Would you care to join me?"

Kim nodded, anxious to avoid the waiting room. "That sounds good," she said, happy for the distraction.

Kim and Tony took the elevator to the main floor. As Tony led her through the cafeteria, she said, "Thanks again for last night. Helping me get my dad's address and everything."

"Sure," he said as he poured them both a cup of coffee.

"I've got this," Kim announced, nodding toward her purse as she picked up her Styrofoam cup and headed for the cashier.

"That's all right," he said.

"No. I insist," she said adamantly. She didn't want it to

appear even slightly romantic. He was not buying her coffee, nor did she even want the issue to arise.

"Well, thanks. I owe you one." He followed Kim to an empty table near the window and sat down across from her. "So," he said.

"So," she repeated. "You probably think that it's kind of weird that I didn't even know where my dad was living."

He shook his head. "Not really. Family relationships can be complicated."

Kim nodded. "Yeah, well. That certainly describes our relationship. Complicated." Kim looked into his deep green eyes. They radiated a gentleness, a sensitivity, that encouraged her to confide in him. "My mother died last year," she continued, "but my parents had been divorced for quite a while. It was, as they say, acrimonious. My mother moved to Florida. With me. My father never quite got over it." As she remembered the decor of her father's home, she added quietly, "Apparently."

"Sounds like you've had a tough year."

She nodded. "Not to mention, JFK Jr. got married."

"My condolences," he said, smiling. "So I take it you're not married."

She shook her head. "No." Before she could stop herself she asked, "And you?"

He shook his head. "No."

After an awkward pause, he said, "So—you and your dad—how long has it been since you've seen each other?"

"I don't know," she said, thinking. "I guess . . . geez. It must be almost fifteen years."

He raised his eyebrows. "Wow. What happened?"

"Nothing really *happened*. There wasn't any fight. He just . . ." she said struggling, searching for the right words to describe the demise of their relationship. "He was very angry at my mother for leaving him. And he wanted me to stay here with him. But . . ." She shrugged again. "My mother and I were very close. Unfortunately, I think my father viewed my decision to stay with my mother as some sort of betrayal. It was difficult staying in touch with him after that. You know," she added quickly, "the distance and everything. I guess it was bound to happen."

Tony nodded sympathetically, although he didn't really

understand. He came from a close-knit family, and he couldn't imagine his parents cutting off contact with him, regardless of what he had done or where he lived.

She seemed to read the expression in his eyes. She sighed. "Who am I kidding? You know my dad. I'm sure you think he's a pain in the neck, don't you?"

He almost spit his coffee out. "I . . . ah, I don't know your father very well," he said, avoiding her eyes.

She smiled as though she had caught him in a white lie. "Like I said last night, he can be difficult. My mother loved him, but even she couldn't take it anymore. She had given him so much of her life, and although she had me, and a lovely home, she said that she couldn't deal with the loneliness anymore."

"Did she work?"

"She did when my parents first met. She was climbing the corporate ladder at an insurance agency, and she loved her job. She put my father through medical school. When he graduated, he decided that she should stay home, and my mother, not being as liberated as . . . well, for instance, as I am . . . agreed. In any case, after my parents' divorce, she got a job as an executive assistant, but I think she always wondered what her life would have been like if she had continued working after she married." She paused. "What do you think? Do you want your wife to work?"

He laughed. "Not having a wife, I think the question is moot."

She shrugged. "I would have to work. I love my job. It's part of who I am. So I know right off the bat that I'm going to need a husband who can help me raise the children and be an integral part of my life."

"Sounds like you've got it all figured out."

She laughed. "Not really. I just know that I don't want to make the same mistake my mom made when she chose my dad. His main priority has always been his job."

"He is a brilliant surgeon," Tony said.

"Yes," Kim agreed almost sadly.

"I first heard about him when I was in college. I knew I wanted to be a doctor, and my parents got me a subscription to the *Journal of American Medicine*. I remember reading an article written by your father about a sick little girl who was in need of a transplant. The child had no insurance so your father offered his services for free and convinced the hospital to donate their care. Unfortunately, the transplant failed and the girl died. Your father took it very hard because he had formed an attachment to this child. To make matters worse, the parents turned around and sued him and the hospital for malpractice."

Kim sat back in her chair. Her father had tried to save a poor child? It certainly didn't seem to fit with the mental picture she carried of him. "When was this?" she asked.

Tony squinted his eyes, thinking. "I was a senior, so . . . 1982."

The year she and her mother had left. Kim didn't speak. She thought back, remembering that year. She had had little idea of the professional chaos her father had been dealing with.

"Kim?" Tony asked, leaning forward. "Are you okay?"

"Yes, sorry," Kim said, forcing herself to focus back on Tony. "I just . . . I'm surprised," she stammered. "I didn't know about that." She thought back to the child her father had tried to save. "Why did the parents sue?" Kim asked. "Without a transplant the child would've died, right?"

Tony nodded. "Yes. But people are so upset when someone they love dies that they don't always think rationally. They were angry that their little girl was taken away, and they blamed the doctor. Unfortunately, it's not that unusual." He sipped his coffee. "Your father has taken some risks, operating on people that other doctors refuse to touch—simply because they feel the patient's chance of survival is not all that good. Your dad believes that every patient deserves a chance. If he succeeds, he's lauded as a hero. But if he fails—and occasionally we all do, not necessarily because of an error but because the patient simply wasn't strong enough—the doctor is often viewed as the villain. We're used to it. But in that particular case involving the little girl, there was a lot of publicity—negative publicity. If your dad had been anyone else, he probably would have been fired. But he was . . . and is, one of the best surgeons in the country. The hospital couldn't afford to lose him."

Kim had always thought of patients as the enemies. They took her father away from her. But now she was realizing how immature and selfish she had been. She had never given the patients names or faces, nor had she imagined them as husbands, wives, sons, and daughters whose only chance at life might be held in the hands of their doctor—her father. She felt as though she should say something, in some way atone for some of her immature thoughts, but the best she could do was to say, "I guess you guys have a pretty stressful job."

Tony nodded. "It can be."

"I mean, in most jobs when something goes wrong, or when you make a mistake you can say, 'Well, at least it's not life or death.' I guess you can't really say that, can you?"

He laughed. "Not really." He paused, looking at her. "What kind of work do you do?"

"Me? I'm an artist."

"Really," he said, leaning forward slightly as if fascinated by her response. "What kind of an artist?"

"A painter. An oil painter. Basically abstract, although I do some portraits."

"Are you commissioned to do them?"

"Some of them. And some I just paint and hope that I'll sell them. As a matter of fact, I've got a show coming up in a couple of weeks at an art gallery in Miami."

"Congratulations." He nodded, impressed. "So you must be good," he said.

"Well, I support myself, but not in style. I just stopped waitressing a couple of years ago."

"I like to think I appreciate art. A beautiful painting always seems to remind me that there's more to this life than work—and I definitely need to be reminded of that sometimes."

"So you're a collector?"

"I wouldn't go that far. I just know what I like. I can't tell if a painting's any good or not."

"If you like it then the artist succeeded."

He nodded. "Are you working on anything right now?"

"Actually, I brought a piece with me. I've been having trouble finishing it. And a bunch of supplies. I always have to have my supplies with me."

"I'd love to see your work sometime."

Kim nodded, feeling a slight blush creep over her face. "Sure," she said as casually as she could.

"Hi, Tony." A bubbly blonde in blue scrubs appeared at the table. An attractive tall brunette, also in scrubs, stood beside her. "We waited for you last night. How come you never showed?" the brunette asked.

"I had to work," Tony said, shrugging his shoulders.

"You missed a lot of fun, Teddy," the blonde said, winking at Tony as she called him by what was obviously a nickname. "Well, we've got to run. We're due in surgery in two minutes. Call me later?"

Kim felt a pang of jealousy tug at her heart. She forced herself to sip her coffee, avoiding Tony's eyes.

"Those two are doctors here," Tony said self-consciously. "More surgeons."

"I should have known by the way they were rushing out of here," she said calmly. "Is Teddy your nickname?"

"No," he said. "She calls me that. She thinks it's funny."

Kim put down her coffee. You have nothing to feel jealous about, she reassured herself. You have no claim on this man. He's simply your father's doctor. "She's cute," she said, nodding toward the blonde. "Do all your girlfriends give you nicknames?"

He shook his head. "Whoa. She's not my girlfriend. We're just friends."

"Oh?" Kim said hopefully.

Tony just smiled. He was intrigued by the woman sitting across from him. From the first night he had seen her he had been aware of the intense personal strength that seemed to radiate from within her. He knew that it couldn't have been easy to come back to Michigan to help care for a father whom she hadn't spoken with in years. Yet the minute her father had needed her she had flown to his side, not sure of where she would stay or if she would even succeed in arriving in Michigan before he died.

Kim raised her hand as she sneezed.

"God bless you," he said.

"Excuse me," she said, blinking her eyes. "Allergies."

"It's this hospital air. You should get outside. Get some fresh air. You've been spending all your time in that stuffy waiting room."

"I don't know. I just can't get used to this weather. I'll freeze to death in about a minute."

"Only if you stand still. You have to keep active to stay warm." He paused. "Hey, I have an idea," he said, leaning back slightly as he stared into Kim's eyes. "I like to skate . . . it's my exercise. I do it whenever I have a chance. Why don't you come with me tomorrow?"

"Ice skate?" she asked incredibly.

He nodded.

She emitted a small laugh as she shook her head. "No," she said. "No thanks."

"Are you sure? I leave from the hospital, and I'm only gone for about an hour or so. Then I come right back."

Kim hesitated. "I haven't skated in years."

"C'mon, it's like riding a bike."

"I don't have ice skates."

"You can rent them."

She shrugged. He seemed to have an answer for everything. "All right." It might be worth a few frozen toes just to see him twirl around. "Thanks."

"Okay," he said, standing. "I'll meet you in the lobby at three."

"See you then," Kim said, holding back a smile.

At nine o'clock Kim left the hospital and walked back out to her father's car. Tony's motorcycle was gone, and a red Mercedes was parked in its place. Kim held her breath as she scooted through the tight space left between the two cars.

She turned on the radio, and classical music flooded the car as she drove the short ride home. When she arrived back at her father's house, she walked in the front door and flicked on the light. She had so many memories of this house, many of them pleasant. Her parents had rarely fought, and although she was aware of her mother's deep unhappiness with her father, Kim had had a happy childhood. There was summer camp, and birthday parties, ice-skating, skiing, and tennis. Unfortunately, her father had been so busy with work that she had few memories of him.

Kim put her purse down and walked into the kitchen.

The same heavy dark oak cabinets. The same fake brick vinyl floor. She opened up the refrigerator, looking for a bottle of wine. Nothing. Her father obviously still did not drink.

She shook her head. Her poor father—didn't drink, exercised regularly, ate healthy foods, and he's in the hospital with a heart condition.

She wondered if he had even known that he was critically ill before his most recent attack. She guessed not. Her father would have ignored the signs that he was once again having heart troubles, just as he ignored everything else that did not fit into his tightly structured world.

She poured herself a glass of water, made a mental note to pick up a bottle of wine tomorrow, and wandered toward her father's office, otherwise known as the den.

She flicked on the light and peeked inside. Her father's heavy mahogany desk sat in the corner. Kim noticed some pictures on top and walked over. She picked them up and turned them around. They were pictures of her, taken the summer before she left.

Kim set the pictures back down on his desk and sighed. If he had loved her, why hadn't he bothered to try to maintain a relationship with her? How could he cut her off, disown her as he had? Maybe not disown her totally, she reminded herself, remembering the child support payments that her mother had received regularly. But certainly he had cut off contact with her. She had written him letters that he had never bothered responding to.

Kim sat behind his desk and opened up the top drawer. Paper clips, pens, everything neatly arranged. Everything in its place.

She pulled open the large drawer to the right. Two pictures that she had painted with watercolors in grade school were neatly placed at the top of the drawer. Kim smiled as she picked them up. One was a picture of the sun and the earth, the other a picture of what she knew was supposed to be a little girl standing next to her father. *To Daddy, Happy father's day,* was written in neat cursive handwriting on the bottom. She set the pictures down and glanced back inside the drawer. She saw a group of letters neatly rubber-banded together. She knew they were hers immediately. It looked as though her father had saved every single letter she had ever sent him. She picked up the bundle and took the rubber band off. Taking the top letter out of its envelope, she saw that it was dated Christmas of 1982. She scanned through the letter, which was basically filled with details of her plans for Christmas. It was boring, really, just details of where she and her friends had shopped and what the weather was like. What was extraordinary about the letter was where the blue ink had run. The letter had tear marks on it, as though her father had cried when reading it.

Kim quickly folded the letter up and put it back on top of the bundle. Slipping the rubber band back on top, she put the bundle back in the drawer. After she replaced the pictures she had drawn, she picked up her water and turned off the light.

Back in her room, Kim tried to busy herself with unpacking but was unable to stop thinking about her father. She needed to understand the feelings that were flooding through her. The guilt, the anger, the confusion. If her father had loved her, why hadn't he made more of an effort to stay in touch with her?

Kim took out her portable easel and the painting she had been trying to finish.

She needed to express her feelings the only way she knew how. The same way she had when she was six years old. She wanted to paint a picture for her dad.

Five

KIM WAITED INSIDE THE LOBBY. SHE TRIED TO APPEAR AS CASUAL as she could, even though her heart was racing. Why was she so nervous? It's not as if this was . . . a date or something. It was merely a chance to get out of the hospital and do something different.

The elevator doors opened, and Tony walked out with his skates swung over his shoulders. He was wearing jeans and big heavy construction boots. He had his hands tucked into his Patagonia jacket. "Hi, Kim," he said with a smile.

"Hi . . . Dr. Hoffman," she replied.

Tony grinned at her. "C'mon," he said, nodding toward the exit. As soon as they stepped outside, he said, "Can you call me Tony now? I mean, we're not in the hospital anymore."

"I don't know," she said with a laugh. "I can try."

"Are you bundled up warm?" he asked.

"Warm enough."

"Good," he said. "Because I had to bring the motorcycle today."

His motorcycle? It couldn't be any warmer than thirty degrees. "Don't you have a car?" she asked suspiciously.

"I have a car, but it's got a hundred and fifty thousand miles on it, so it's continually in the shop. I need to go pick it up, but I haven't had a chance to get over there. Up until recently, though, it's been a great car. I can't quite bring myself to trade it in. Anyway," he said, nodding to the left, "my bike is right over there."

"We can take my car. Or rather, my dad's car," Kim offered hopefully.

"I like the fresh air. Do you mind? The park isn't far. It's right up the street."

"No," she said, resigned to making the best of the situation. "It's fine."

He stopped at his motorcycle and slipped his skates into one of the containers he had fastened on the back. He handed her a helmet. "You keep an extra one?" she asked. Smooth operator.

He shrugged. "Sometimes." He slid onto the bike and motioned for her to get on behind him.

She winced as she pushed up her coat, straddling her legs over the banana-shaped seat, and sat up against him. This was *way* too intimate. What was she doing with this doctor without a cause? She looked for a place to hold on and, not finding any, folded her hands neatly in her lap. "So what kind of car do you have," she yelled. "A Jeep?"

"No."

"Saab?"

"No."

"Volvo?"

He lifted off his helmet and twisted around. "Wrong again. This is Detroit, remember? I drive a Ford. A Taurus."

She looked at him as though she didn't quite believe him. He didn't look like the kind of guy who would drive a Ford Taurus. Too practical. She thought at the very least he'd be in a Jeep.

She must have looked confused because he bit back a smile and said, "Have you ever ridden on one of these before?"

She shook her head.

He laughed. "Well, you better hold on. I don't want to have you fall off. I'd have a hard time explaining it to your father." She uncomfortably placed her hands on either side of his waist. He revved up the engine, and they were off.

Kim tightened her legs around the side of the motorcycle and leaned forward. The cold, damp air sprayed in her face as she turned back toward the hospital. She wondered what her father would think of Tony taking his daughter for a spin on his bike. She had a sneaky suspicion he wouldn't approve. Still, he must like Tony. Of all the doctors he could have chosen for his team, he had picked Tony.

Tony pulled the bike into the park and drove down to a pond that had frozen over. "C'mon," he said, pulling off his helmet and nodding toward a large wooden building. "That's the lodge. They rent skates in there."

Kim followed Tony inside. Before she could stop him, he had rented her a pair of skates.

"You didn't have to do that," she said.

"Do what?" he asked.

"Rent me skates."

"Why? Did you plan on wearing those?" he said, pointing toward her cute little suede flats. She had lived in the south so long, she had found herself without boots or anything even close to resembling snow shoes. "You'd probably get the same effect."

"True," Kim said good-naturedly. "Well, thanks, Dr. Hoffman," she added somewhat awkwardly.

"Tony," he corrected her patiently, sitting down on the bench. "Please call me Tony. That's my name. I don't call you Artist Kim. Besides, it makes me feel old."

"Hmm. Old. I'm sure that's a word that's not usually used to describe you," Kim teased.

"Oh? And why not?" Tony asked hesitantly, not certain he was going to like her answer.

"Well, you certainly try your best to act young."

"Oh, really?" he said, looking at her playfully. "That wasn't meant to be a compliment by any chance, was it?"

"Well, you know what I mean. Motorcycle. Leather jacket. You just have an aura about you. You probably date college girls."

"I have a college girl aura?" He laughed. "The last time I dated a college girl was when I was in college." He looked at her and shook his head. "You think you've got me figured out, don't you?" he said as he stood up and skated onto the ice.

He turned around to face her and started skating backward.

Kim stood up to follow him, but hesitated, still at the edge of the pond. It had been a long time since she had been in a pair of skates—and she couldn't say she felt like a natural. "I wouldn't say I've got you figured out . . . but I think I understand you. Your type."

"My *type!*" he said incredulously, skating forward to help her onto the ice.

"You know . . . you're a doctor, so you feel like the creative side of you is being . . . well, denied. So you adapt this bad boy persona—i.e., motorcycle and leather jacket. Single guy—never been married . . . it's your way of letting people know that you're really a creative, multitalented individual."

"Is that so?" he asked, amused. "I'll have to remember that the next time I'm with a woman. I'll let her know that I can't possibly marry her, because, well, my bad boy image would go down the tubes."

"That's right," she said.

"Would you like some assistance onto the ice?" he asked, his eyes twinkling mischievously. She smiled, looking into his eyes as she accepted his outstretched hand.

"So what else do you think you know about me?" he said, resting one arm around her waist as he pulled her in close so that they were skating side by side.

She paused, thinking. "You're up on hip music," she said. "You're definitely a Democrat. You typically date about three women at the same time. You're spontaneous and . . . a little wild."

"Wrong, right, wrong, right, not really sure. What's wild?"

She smiled. "Trust me, you're wild," she said, breaking away. She skated toward the edge of the pond, her confidence increasing with her speed.

"Oh yeah?" he teased, following her. "You were wrong about the three women. I'll have you know I date no less than four women at a time," he joked. "And they're quadruplets to boot."

Kim laughed as she skated around the rink, her arms outstretched. Tony followed her, and soon they were doing turns around the ice, showing off their limited skills and laughing like schoolchildren. After a while, Kim got a little cocky, and when she completed her spin, she finished it off with a clumsy half-jump.

He clapped his hands in approval. "Excellent!"

Kim pretended to bow. "Now you," she said, moving out of the way.

He skated away. She watched him pick up speed, and then, in an exceptionally graceful move, he jumped up and spun around, landing on one foot.

She clapped her hands, which turned out to be a mistake. She fell down, her rear end hitting the ice with a loud *thump*.

Tony was by her side in a flash, helping her up. He began to brush the snow off her rear end. Embarrassed, she said, "I'm fine. Really." She pushed him away and proceeded to fall right back onto her rear.

This time, embarrassment gave way to laughter. Kim sat on the ice and threw her head back as she howled with laughter. Smiling himself, Tony helped her up. He stood in front of her, gently holding on to her arms.

"How do you do that?" she asked. "That spinning around thing?"

"Practice. You could do it, too."

"I don't think so," she said, laughing. "It would take a miracle."

She suddenly realized that he wasn't letting go. Nor did she want him to. She glanced up at him.

Both of them stopped smiling as they stared at each other, aware of the electricity between them. "Now it's my turn," Tony said softly, still staring into her eyes.

"For what?" she asked, swallowing.

"Let's see . . . ," he said, thinking. "I'd say you're the opposite of what one would imagine an artist to be. You prefer classical music to, as you called it, 'hip' music, you're a Republican, you're compulsive to the point of driving your friends crazy, and you have trouble dating more than one person at the same time."

"Right, wrong, right, right," she said.

"So we're more alike than you thought. Because I, too, like classical music. And I also don't like to date more than one person at a time."

"And are you dating anyone right now?" she heard herself ask.

He shook his head. Kim glanced away, mortified that she had been so forward. And so obvious. She noticed that he hadn't bothered to ask her that question. He may not be dating anyone, but he still wasn't interested in her. He was just being nice. And she had misinterpreted it.

She heard a quiet beeping noise. Tony pulled out a small black beeper and looked at it.

Turning it off, he stuck the beeper back into his belt. "That's the hospital," he said, all trace of humor gone from his face. "We should get back."

Kim stayed with her father until he went to sleep. Before she left she tucked the blankets in around him. He had seemed quite a bit improved from the day before, but he was still groggy and tired.

As she walked down the hall she continued to think about her father. He had asked her several questions about her life, like if she was married, if she had kids. He asked her about her career and seemed happy that she was doing well.

Despite good intentions from both of them, they were

still a bit awkward and unsure about each other. So much time had passed since they had last spoken that Kim wondered if they would ever be able to completely heal the broken bond between them.

Leaving thoughts of her father and the hospital behind her, Kim stepped out into the parking lot and saw that white, powdery snow had coated the streets and the cars. It had been so long since she had seen snow that she had forgotten how beautiful it could be. Zipping up her coat as she made her way toward her car, she stopped and glanced around the snow-covered lot. As she rounded the corner of the hospital she saw Tony standing beside his motorcycle, shaking his head.

"Tony?" she called out as she walked over to him.

"Hey, Kim," he greeted her. "Don't say it."

"Say what?"

"What you're thinking. 'This guy should know better than to drive a motorcycle in December.' "

"Okay," she agreed, trying to keep the laughter out of her voice. "Can I ask you if you want a ride somewhere?"

He nodded. "If you give me a ride, then you can say it." She smiled as she led him back toward her car.

"Whoa," he said, sliding inside. "Now this is a car."

"Same car he drove when I was in high school."

"Does it bring back memories of driver's ed.?"

"Almost." She turned the key in the ignition, causing the engine to spin to life. "Where do you live?" she asked, backing the car out of the space.

"Not very far from here. Off of State Circle. On Michigan Avenue."

"Apartment?" she asked, effortlessly steering the car through what must have been at least eight inches of powdery snow.

"Is that where you'd think I'd live?"

"Well," she said, smiling, "I would've said yes, but I can tell from the way you asked that you live in a house. Don't you?"

"Very perceptive, Holmes."

"Thank you, Dr. Watson . . . or Hoffman, as the case may be."

He smiled at her. A friendly smile, she decided. But not

an "interested" smile. She made a left-hand turn onto Michigan Avenue.

"It's this house up here on the right," he said pointing to a two-story colonial. Nice, but not ostentatious. It was a family house, not the type of house she expected him to have. She thought he'd have something a little flashier, showier.

"It's nice," she said simply.

"It's a little big for me right now. I haven't done much with it since I bought it."

She pulled up in front of his house and stopped. Before he could open the door she blurted out, "About earlier. I'm sorry if I seemed a little . . . forward."

He put his hand on the door handle and hesitated. "What? I was just about to apologize to you."

"For what?" she asked, surprised.

"Well, I . . . I damned near kissed you on the ice."

"You did?" she asked hopefully.

"I, well, do you . . ." He hesitated for a split second. "Would you like to come in for a cup of coffee or tea? Actually, I could use your opinion on something. A couple of holiday decorations I bought for the yard."

Kim checked her watch, playing it cool.

"And I'd also like you to meet Geena."

"Geena?"

"My dog."

Kim nodded. Of course. His dog. "Um, sure," she said, turning off the car. As soon as she stepped outside she realized that she was going to have to walk through quite a bit of unshoveled snow. Her little flats—or what was left of them—would be finished off. Oh, well, she thought. All for a good cause.

Kim followed Tony to the house, trying to step into the imprints of his shoes. When he opened the door a golden retriever stood in front of them, wagging her tail in greeting.

"Hey, sweetie," Tony said, bending down to greet his pet. "This is Kim."

Kim leaned over and patted the dog. "She's adorable."

"Thank you," Tony said, glancing at Kim's feet. "Your shoes are soaked," he said.

"It's no problem," she said, stomping her feet on the welcome mat.

"Give them to me," he said, adding, "I'll put them in the furnace room to dry."

She slipped off her shoes.

"And your socks," he said.

"My socks?"

He nodded.

She slipped off her socks and handed them to him, trying to ignore the chipped red nail polish on her toes.

He headed toward the furnace room with Geena following behind. As Kim listened to Tony gabbing amiably to Geena, she wandered into the room across from her and turned on the light. The large room was empty with the exception of a black leather couch placed in front of the fireplace.

"Like what I've done with it?" he said from behind her. She turned around. He was holding a pair of thick wool socks.

"Impressive."

"Here are some socks for you to wear while your shoes dry."

"Thank you." She took the socks and smiled. "Where's Geena?"

"She's outside. She seems a little tired. I pay the kids in the neighborhood to come over and play with her during the day. She tells me it's been a rough one. I think they wore her out."

Kim smiled. "So what did you want my opinion on?"

"These," he said, heading toward the room across from them. He turned on the light. The dining room was empty with the exception of an inexpensive-looking giant plastic Santa and snowman. Instead of appearing cheery, the Santa had an eerie, almost jack-o-lantern grin. And the snowman's eyes were painted so haphazardly, they appeared crossed.

All in all, they were two of the ugliest, not to mention scariest, Christmas decorations Kim had ever seen. She glanced at Tony. So much for his art appreciation.

Tony was looking at her intently, waiting for her opinion.

"Nice," she said, trying to sound sincere as she bent over to slip on the socks.

"Do you think they look good together? Or should I put one in the front and one in the back?"

God forbid they be together. One was bad enough. "Ah, one in the front, one in the back."

"Done!" he said just as the teakettle whistled. She finished pulling on her socks and followed him into the kitchen.

"What kind of tea do you like?"

"Um . . . ," she said, staring at the wallpaper. She guessed that it had been installed by the previous owners. It was bright yellow with clusters of fruit all over.

"I've got Cinnamon Apple . . . and Cinnamon Apple. I also have some beer if you're interested."

"Cinnamon Apple sounds great."

She glanced at him as he pulled the tea bags out.

He handed her a cup of tea and then opened the back door, letting Geena back in. Geena walked into the room, gave them both a sniff, and then went to her bed and lay down. "What did I tell you," he said. "She's bushed. C'mon," he said, nodding for Kim to follow him. "Let's go back to the other room. I'll start a fire."

A fire? A fire was almost synonymous with romance. "I really can't stay that long," she said as she followed him back into the living room.

"It'll take a minute. If you're going to be indoors in the winter, you should have a fire."

She sat down on the couch and watched as he crumpled up some newspapers. "How long have you lived here?" she asked, looking around at the empty walls.

"I don't know. Five years or so."

"And you don't have any furniture?"

He nodded behind him. "I have a couch. Doesn't that qualify?"

"You know what they say about guys that don't have furniture," she said, sitting on the couch.

"I have a feeling I'm going to find out."

"No couch, no commitment."

"I have a couch," he repeated, lighting the fire.

"Well, you get the drift. Men who can't commit to furniture are certainly not going to be able to commit to a relationship."

He stood up and tilted his head, looking at her curiously. "I've got to admit I've never heard that before."

She shrugged her shoulders as she daintily sipped her tea.

"Just for your information," he said, leaning on the fireplace mantle, "the reason why I don't have furniture is because I *was* committed. And when we broke up, she got the furniture."

"Oh?" she asked as innocently as she could. "Ex-wife?"

He shook his head as he sat back down next to her. "No. Serious girlfriend. We dated for five years, lived together for one. When we split up, she got the furniture, and I got Geena. Which is exactly what I wanted."

"Oh," she said again, staring into the fire.

"Well?" he said, leaning over to look her in the eyes.

"What?"

He flashed her a sly grin. "You're going to let it drop? You're not going to ask me why it didn't work out?"

"Okay, doctor," she said amicably. "Why didn't it work out?"

He shrugged. "I really don't know," he said thinking. "It was just one of those things. We never fought, we just . . . drifted apart. Actually, there was never that . . . spark, you know what I mean? I guess I always knew that we would never marry. And so did she."

She nodded.

"In retrospect, I think we were both too much alike. There wasn't enough . . . balance."

"Was she in medicine?"

He nodded. "A surgeon. And, just FYI, she was a couple of years older than me." He took a sip of his tea. "So much for your theory of my dating younger women. Although," he said, hesitating, "I have to admit I've been out with a few younger women since my breakup with Robin."

"Playing the field?"

"Not really. I just . . . well, my time is pretty valuable to me. I don't have much of it. And I've decided not to keep seeing a woman when I know we're not right for each other. I learned that lesson."

Kim nodded. She understood. After all, she felt the same way—which unfortunately, meant that she usually ended up spending the holidays by herself—or worse, sitting across from a blind date.

"What about you?" he asked. "Any marriages in your past? Close calls?"

She shook her head and furrowed her brow, thinking. "I was serious with someone earlier this year, but it didn't work out."

"Too bad."

She shook her head. "Well, not really serious. I guess I should qualify by saying serious for me, which is probably casual for you . . . am I making sense?"

"How many dates?"

"Dates? I don't know. A lot."

"Let me ask you this: Did he ask you out for Saturday night or was it just assumed you were doing something?"

"Assumed."

"Sounds pretty serious."

Kim laughed.

At just that moment, Geena walked into the room and let out a deep bark, causing them both to jump. Tony laughed and shook his head. "Sometimes she just does that. For no reason."

Kim smiled at him.

"What do you think of dogs?" he asked.

"Do you mean, do I like them? Or what does it mean when a guy has a dog?"

"Both."

"Yes, I like them and yes, it's a very good sign. About commitment," she added quickly. "Helps to make up for the lack of furniture."

Tony nodded and grinned. He shook his head as if in admiration. "You know, I'm getting the impression that you have a wild, stubborn streak yourself."

Kim laughed. "I think you're right—on one account, at least. But I'm definitely not wild. I'm the type of girl who goes to bed at nine o'clock."

"Nine o'clock sharp?"

"Every night. And you?"

"I burn the midnight oil."

"See? Wild man."

"Yeah. I'm usually out escorting college girls around town or doing transplants," he joked. "I alternate nights." He paused, looking at her as if he was deciding on something. "You know, Kim," he said, raising an eyebrow. "I really didn't ask you in to get your opinion on those plastic . . . things," he said, nodding toward the dining room where the snowman and Santa were stored. "They're a joke present for one of the administrators at the hospital."

Kim started to smile.

"But I'll have you know, I was impressed by how . . . delicate you were about your disapproval."

"So," she said carefully. "Why *did* you ask me in?"

He glanced back at the fire. "I guess I just want to get to know you better. Most of the people . . . or rather women . . . that I meet are somehow connected to the hospital. It's not often I get to spend time with an artist."

She nodded. "So you like my profession."

He shook his head. "I like you," he said softly. He sighed. "I just . . . well, it's a little awkward. The fact that you're Harold Risson's daughter."

"I'm of age," she volunteered. "Barely, of course."

"I know, but it could still be awkward."

She shrugged. "As you're aware, he and I have had our differences." She hesitated as she put down her teacup. "I've been making up my own mind for years."

Tony turned toward her and brushed a strand of hair away from her eyes. "There's that wild streak again."

She felt a tingling down her spine. He had a gaze that made her want to melt into his leather bachelor-pad sofa. Suddenly, Tony leaned forward and kissed her. Kim kissed him back, welcoming his tongue as it slid inside her mouth. But when he gently began to push her back on the couch, she broke away.

"What is it?" he asked quietly.

"I . . . I'm not sure I'm ready for this . . . for us," she stammered. "Not that we're an *us*, or anything," she added quickly. She didn't want him to think that she was assuming they were about to begin a relationship. For all she knew, he was interested in a one-night stand. "It's just that I've got a lot on my plate right now . . . with my dad and everything.

I'm not going to be in town that long, and I'm not looking for a fling. I just . . ."

He put his index finger to her lips. "It's all right," he whispered, pulling her in to him. "You should know that if I was looking for a fling, I wouldn't choose Harold Risson's daughter." *That's right,* he realized. He wouldn't. So what was he doing here with her if he wasn't looking for just a casual friendship? Perhaps, just perhaps, it was because he knew that Kim Risson was special.

Tony smiled sweetly and slowly pulled away from her. "I know you've been through a lot recently. We'll take it as slow as you want. There's no rush."

Except for the fact that she planned on heading back to Florida as soon as her father left the hospital. Their time was limited, and they both knew it. Tony kissed her forehead as he wrapped his arms around her. "I just like being with you." He leaned over and looked into her eyes. "Hey," he whispered in her ear. "Why do you look so sad?"

She sighed. "I don't know. The holidays always get me down, and with all that's happened in the past few weeks . . ."

"This Christmas will be better," he said, hugging her close. "I just have a feeling."

Kim was practically humming as she walked down the hospital corridor. She felt like a teenager in love. She glanced at the Christmas tree some of the hospital staff were decorating in the waiting room. Maybe her mother had been right. Maybe this was a magical season.

It had certainly been a magical night. She and Tony had talked for hours before finally drifting off to sleep in each other's arms. She had woken at four, found her shoes and socks, given Geena a pat good-bye, and slipped out without waking Tony.

After knocking on her father's door, she quietly walked into his room. He was sitting in bed and smiled when he saw her. "Kim," he said.

"Hi, Dad." She went over and gave him a quick kiss on the cheek. "You seem like you're feeling better."

He nodded. "They're moving me out of critical care today."

"That's wonderful," Kim said.

He smiled. "Kim," he began. "I've been thinking. I . . . well, I feel like I've been given another chance. Another chance to make things right again."

Kim nodded.

"I'm sorry for never writing you back. Those letters that you sent me . . . they meant a lot to me," he said, struggling with every word. "I just couldn't bring myself to write back to you. If I did, our separation would become real. Instead, I made myself believe that it was just like when you wrote me from camp. That I'd see you again before I even got a chance to write you . . ."

"Oh, Dad," Kim said sadly, keeping an eye on the EKG machine. The last thing she wanted was to upset him. "We both made mistakes. I never really understood before what stress you were under . . . all the pressures from your job. I know it wasn't easy for you. I just . . . well, I was a child. All I knew was that my father wasn't around. I didn't—I couldn't understand why. But I do now," she said, thinking about the little girl who had died. The little girl he had tried to save.

"I want you to know . . . I'm sorry that I wasn't there for you. But I never stopped caring about you."

She nodded, touched by the sincerity in his eyes. She blinked back tears as she said, "I know that, Dad."

He nodded, blinking back tears himself. "I was sorry to hear about your mother."

Kim nodded.

"I loved her. I know she didn't think so, but I did. I just . . . I had a hard time showing it."

Kim glanced at the floor. She wasn't ready to discuss her mother with him.

"When you and your mother left, a part of me died. I . . . I couldn't deal with it . . ." He looked at her and wiped away a tear.

She smiled weakly and gave his hand a squeeze.

Harold swallowed. As if embarrassed by his display of emotion, he shook his head slightly as he glanced at the clock. Suddenly he barked out, "Oh, for Pete's sake."

"What?" Kim asked, taken aback.

"Oh, Tony Hoffman was supposed to come here this morning at eight," he said, as if disgusted.

Kim checked the clock. It was already eight-thirty. Kim felt slightly guilty, realizing that there had not been an alarm clock in the living room. She wondered if he was still asleep on the couch.

"There's no excuse for this behavior. As usual, he's testing me. He's trying to annoy me."

"Calm down, Dad," she said, disturbed by his vehement reaction. "I'm sure he's not trying to annoy you. He just saved your life. Why would he want to upset you?"

"It's a power play. These young, cocky surgeons are all alike. Tony is a decent surgeon, but he knows it. He's a wild card, and that's going to cost him some advancements around here." Her father glanced at her. "Have you met him yet?"

She nodded. "Ah, yes," she said quickly. She had done more than just meet him, but for some reason, she didn't feel like this was an appropriate time to discuss her budding romance.

Tony knocked on the door and peeked his head in. "Good morning, Harold," he said. "Kim," he said quickly.

"Doctor," Kim said, acknowledging him as she avoided his eyes. Talk about timing.

"You were supposed to be here a half an hour ago," her father said sternly.

"I'm sorry," Tony said, picking up her father's chart and looking at it. "I . . . well, I was delayed."

"I bet," her father said, irritated.

Kim stood up. "I . . . um, I'm going to go get some coffee. Dad, do you want something?"

Her question seemed to soften him. He smiled at her warmly. "No thanks, dear."

She nodded. "I'll be in the cafeteria," she said, glancing at Tony as she headed for the door.

Kim was on her way out of the cafeteria when she saw Tony. He was scanning the room and smiled when he finally saw her. "Ms. Risson," he said, hurrying to catch up with her. "Why didn't you wake me up when you left?" he whispered in her ear as he walked alongside her.

"Because you were sleeping," she said casually. "Besides, I didn't know you had an early morning appointment with my father."

"That's all right," he joked. "When I explained that I was late because you forgot to wake me, your father understood completely."

Kim looked at him, alarmed. "What?"

He smiled as he discreetly took her arm. "I had a feeling you didn't tell your father who you were with last night."

"The subject didn't come up."

"Hmm," he said, steering her into a deserted storage room. "Come here for a minute," he said, pulling her inside. He shut the door behind them and kissed her passionately.

She pulled back to say, "I feel like a schoolgirl necking in the boys' john."

"Oh, really," he said, nuzzling her ear. "Is that something you did often, you wild girl, you?"

"Not really. Never, actually. But I always thought it was a great idea."

He pulled down the collar on her sweater and began to leave a trail of soft, butterfly kisses on her neck. "Will I see you tonight?" he whispered in between kisses.

She stretched out her neck as she closed her eyes. "A second date? I'm flattered you're willing to invest the time in me," she teased him.

"How about dinner?" he asked softly, brushing his lips up her neck toward her ear.

"Maybe," she murmured.

He delicately ran his tongue around the inside of her earlobe.

She swallowed. It was becoming increasingly difficult to concentrate.

"Maybe I'll pick you up at seven-thirty?" he breathed into her ear.

"Do you know where my father lives?"

He pulled back and smiled at her, cupping her face in his hands as he brushed her lips with his fingers. "I'll find you. Don't worry." He gave her a hug good-bye, just as his beeper went off. "I'll see you at seven," he said, holding her hand tightly before they parted in the hallway.

Kim glanced at her watch. It was almost eight o'clock. Tony had called earlier to let her know that he was delayed, but she was starving.

Get used to it, she told herself. If she was embarking on a relationship with a heart surgeon of Tony's stature, she'd have to get used to eating meals by herself.

She walked into the kitchen and opened the cupboards. Her eyes lit up as she spotted the jar of Ragú. She hoped Tony liked Italian.

Kim hesitated as she remembered all the meals she and her mother had eaten by themselves, in that very kitchen. She knew that her mother had not lived the life she had intended. Her mother had come from a large, warm, loving family, where everyone had sat down to dinner together. She had never adjusted to having a husband who left early in the morning and did not return until late at night.

Kim poured the Ragú into a pan. She reminded herself that she was not her mother, nor was she in the same situation. She was not marrying Tony—she was simply enjoying his company. He was a fun, talented man, and doctor or not, she liked him. End of subject.

She busied herself with dinner, and by the time the doorbell rang, dinner was ready and a fire was blazing in the fireplace.

Kim opened the door, anxious to see Tony.

He stood on the porch, his fit athletic form outlined in the moonlight. He was wearing a turtleneck, jeans, and an L. L. Bean jacket and was holding a bouquet of flowers in front of him.

"Hi," he said, leaning down to kiss her. "These are for you," he added and handed her the flowers.

"Thank you," Kim said, admiring the bouquet. First his coat, then the flowers. She'd better watch out for this one.

She glanced up at him. Her enthusiasm faded as she looked into his eyes. His beautiful eyes were a bloodshot red, and deep, dark circles were etched beneath. He looked as if he was ready to fall over from exhaustion.

"Sorry I'm late," he said.

"What's the matter?" she asked, ushering him inside.

"Bad day," he said.

"How bad?" she asked, taking his coat.

"I was on my way out the door when one of my patients simply stopped breathing."

"Is the patient okay?"

He nodded. "Now he is. But it was touch and go for a while. The guy is young, too. Only forty—with a wife and a baby." He sighed. "It just tears you apart."

Kim nodded in sympathy as she thought of the pain the family must have experienced. She turned her attention back toward Tony, trying to comprehend the terrible duress of his day. In the dim light of the hall he looked older than his years, weighted down by the heavy burden of sadness and responsibility. She wondered how many times her father had come home suffering from the same burden.

Standing in the hall of her parents' home, holding Tony's coat in one hand, the flowers in the other, Kim couldn't help but compare herself to the ghosts that had stood in this very hall twenty years before.

Tony glanced at Kim and flashed her a tired half smile. "I'm sorry. I'll snap out of it. I know I have to work on leaving it all at the office, but it's difficult. I haven't developed that tough outer shell that, according to your father, is a necessity in this business. He feels that if a physician becomes too personally involved with his patients, it not only affects his professionalism, but can lead to early burnout as well."

"But I thought you said that he did get involved . . . with the little girl that needed a transplant. . . ."

Tony nodded. "He did. I guess even the masters have their weak moments." He shrugged and ran his fingers through his hair. "In any case . . ." he said, then hesitated as though he was seeing her for the first time. "You look beautiful." He wrapped his arms around her waist, pulled her to him, and kissed her. "Mmm," he whispered, smiling. "I feel better already." Still holding her close, he paused, looking into the living room.

Kim almost laughed at the expression on Tony's face as

he caught a glimpse of the decor. "Kind of makes you want to head out to a disco, doesn't it?" Kim asked.

He glanced around at the heavy wood paneling and the rust brown shag carpeting. "Now that you mention it."

"My father hasn't changed anything since my mother and I left," she said, breaking away from Tony's embrace. She carefully set the flowers on the entrance table before hanging his coat in the closet.

"What's that," he asked, pointing to the thick wool rug in front of the fireplace.

"The rug?"

"It's a rug? I thought it was some kind of animal," he joked.

"My high school boyfriends used to call it the make-out rug."

"Were they speaking from experience or are these the same guys you were meeting in the bathroom?" Tony eyes seemed to brighten as he watched the corners of Kim's lip turn up in a smile.

"These would be the bathroom guys," she said.

He grinned as he turned back toward the portrait over the mantle. "Is that you?"

Kim shut the closet door and picked up the bouquet. "Me when I was five. And my mother and father."

Tony stepped down into the living room and walked in front of the portrait for a better look. "Your mother was beautiful."

"Yes. Yes, she was."

"And look at you," he said, admiring the portrait. "You've always been beautiful, haven't you?"

Kim rolled her eyes. "Thanks."

"You are, you know."

For some reason, Kim always responded to flattery as though she was still an adolescent. And this time was no different. "Are you hungry?" she asked, changing the subject.

"Is that dinner I smell?" he responded, surprised and pleased.

Kim nodded. "Since you were running late, I thought we'd just eat here. I hope you don't mind."

"Mind? I love it! So you can cook, too," he said teasingly.

"As a matter of fact," she replied, "we're having my specialty," she said, heading to the kitchen to find a vase for her flowers.

After they had eaten and put the dishes in the dishwasher, Kim gave Tony a tour of the downstairs.

"You have a pool back there?"

Kim nodded. "My father does. Yes."

"You should take the cover off. It would make a great rink."

"Oh, sure," she said and laughed, certain that he was joking. "Right."

"No, I'm serious."

"I'll mention it to my dad. I'm sure he'll get right on it. I can just envision him doing a few pirouettes in the middle there."

Tony laughed. "Your father needs to start exercising. He's thin, but he's in terrible condition."

"So tell him."

"Harkavey's already told him," he said. "Your father can be very stubborn—a trait he's passed on to someone else I know." He smiled. Holding on to his glass of wine, he stepped into the den and pointed to a canvas that sat on the easel. "Is that yours?"

She nodded.

"Can I take a look?"

"Sure," she said. "It's almost finished." She turned on the light and nodded toward the painting. "It's a Christmas present. For my father."

He moved closer to the painting, visibly affected by the stunning impact of colors and shapes. A rich deep purple now twisted around the strong red lines. Clouds of a light, ethereal yellow lifted out of the dark green background. "It's wonderful."

Kim glanced at him, trying to determine the truthfulness of his reaction. He seemed to be sincere. "I was having a lot of trouble with this. When I decided to paint it for my father, it all came together."

"How so?"

"Purple represents my father. It's a strong, stubborn

color, a lot like him. The red is a signal of love, the yellow . . . hope."

"And the green?"

"A good background color." She smiled. "I hope he likes it."

Tony nodded as he swirled his glass of wine. "You know, Kim," he said, hesitating. "I spoke with Harkavey today, and your father should be getting out of the hospital in a couple of weeks. I was just wondering . . . do you think you'll be staying in Ann Arbor when he gets out?"

She shook her head as she glanced back at the painting. "I don't know. I wasn't planning on it. But it depends on how my father is doing."

He took a step toward her and set down his glass. "Your father is going to be just fine. I was still hoping that you might stay, though," he said.

She sighed as she brought the conversation back to her father. "How do you know for certain he'll be fine? How does anyone know?"

"Trust me," he said quietly, tracing the outline of her lips with his index finger.

She smiled as his lips drifted toward hers. "Sounds like you've said that before."

He took her hand and led her back into the living room. He sat down on the couch facing the fire and pulled her on top of him, so that she was straddling his lap. "I know you think you know all about me, but you may not be as perceptive as you think you are."

"I find that hard to believe," she said, her eyes twinkling playfully.

He took her in his arms and kissed her so deeply she heard herself sigh with desire. "If you just give me a chance," he whispered while she attempted to catch her breath, "you might find out that we're more suited for each other than you think."

"I should tell you now that doctors aren't my type," she said, as his lips wandered to her neck.

"Even ones that can fix broken hearts?" he asked, his hand slipping inside her shirt. His fingers swept over her chest, lightly massaging the area over her heart.

"Even ones that talk like they write for Hallmark," she murmured, closing her eyes as he skillfully unsnapped her bra.

"Then it's very kind of you to let me stay here and nibble on you," he said, his hand grazing her bare breast.

"I'm like that," she said, as his fingers found her nipple, tugging on it gently. "Very kind." She hugged him tightly, feeling the warmth of his body meld with hers. She slid her hands under his shirt and ran them up his muscled back.

Tony gently lifted her chin, forcing her to look at him. "You're shaking," he said quietly. "Are you frightened—or cold?"

"I'm a . . . a little of both," she admitted.

He smiled a kind, sweet smile. "Don't worry. There's nothing to be frightened of," he said, brushing her hair back away from her face. "I really care about you—I mean that."

Kim closed her eyes as she ran her hand up his toned arm, holding it against her. She kissed his hand. "I care about you, too. I just—I didn't plan on this."

He lifted her hair and began kissing her softly on the back of her neck. "Being here with you . . . I can forget about everything else. It's just you and me. That's all that seems important."

All her fears melted away as a slow burning desire began to creep over her. It was enough to make her stop behaving like a frightened little girl.

Kim pulled away from his arms and stood up, so that she was facing him with her back to the fire. He leaned up on one arm, watching her, curiously awaiting her next move. She slid out of her pants and shirt, standing in front of him wearing only her unsnapped bra and panties. She saw him inhale slightly with excitement as his eyes held her, encouraging her to continue. "I don't want to get cold," she said, teasing him.

"I promise that you'll never have to worry about that when I'm around," he said, enjoying the intimate banter.

Kim smiled slightly as she pulled off her bra, leaving on only her silky white panties.

Tony's eyes drifted over the curves of her pale form, drinking in each detail. "What kind of spell have you cast on me?" he murmured. He slid down onto the floor, kneeling in front of Kim as he pulled her to him, running his tongue lightly over her firm stomach.

"Tony," Kim teased as she glanced down at him, running her fingers through his thick, curly hair, "I'm curious. What's involved in this broken heart treatment of yours?"

He lay down on the soft white rug and pulled her on top of him. "I've already done the most difficult part."

"Oh?" she said curiously.

"I gave you my heart," he explained softly as he took her index finger and traced it around the right side of his chest. "But now, I have a very special recovery in mind for you."

"And what might that be?" Kim teased softly, enjoying the effect she was having on him.

Still holding on to her index finger, he brought it to his lips and kissed it gently. "It's very important that you close your eyes, relax . . . and let me love you," he said, his voice growing heavy with desire.

He gently pulled her down in front of him, so that her back was facing the fire. Shifting his weight so that he could lean on one arm, he stared intently into her eyes. He lifted her chin with his finger so that she was looking at him, and then he used that same finger to draw an imaginary line down her body, starting with her shoulder and ending with her little toe. "You are perfect," he said, as his finger drifted back up her body, lightly brushing the tip of her nipple.

Kim smiled. "That's three," she said out loud. First the coat, then the flowers, and finally the sweet comment about her body.

"What?"

Kim leaned over and slid her hands around the inside of his jeans. "I think I'm ready for my treatment."

He grinned as he pulled her beside him. It was an offer he had no intention of refusing.

"I've decided to stay through the holidays," Kim announced.

Her father smiled. "But," he said, becoming concerned, "what about your show?"

"I called the gallery owner this morning. I explained what

was going on, and he said he didn't think it was necessary for me to be there. He said it might even add to my allure if I wasn't there—make me seem more mysterious."

"Mysterious?"

She shrugged. "I don't know. I wasn't quite sure what he meant either. But I didn't want to push it. I was just happy I didn't have to go back."

He nodded, his face solemn.

Kim said, "I thought you'd be happy."

He took her hand. "I am. I just don't want you to harm your career because of your concern over me. I'll be just fine."

She glanced away. "Don't you want me to stay?"

"Of course," he said quietly, giving her a weak smile. "It'll be the first Christmas I've celebrated in quite a while."

Kim had often wondered what her father had done on the holidays. She just assumed he had spent them with friends. Or a new family. But from the lack of visitors in his hospital room, she was beginning to realize that had not been the case. "What do you usually do?"

He shrugged his shoulders. "Work."

"Well, this year will be different. I'm going to get a tree later on today. This Christmas you're going to have a traditional Christmas dinner."

He nodded as a wave of sadness crossed his face.

"What's wrong?" she asked.

"I just . . . I've missed so much. I . . . I just . . . well, I'm glad that you're here," he said, repeating her something he had told her many times already. "I've always tried to keep tabs on you, even when we weren't speaking. Many times I picked up the phone . . . but I just couldn't bring myself to dial the number." He shook his head. "I've been a lousy father. Stubborn pride."

Kim shrugged. "Fortunately for both of us, we still have the future to look forward to."

"Yes," he agreed. "And Christmas."

"How about this one?"

Kim shook her head. Tony was standing beside a tree that had to be at least fifteen feet tall.

"Too small," she said, laughing. She pointed to a tree that

was tucked away in the corner. "That's the one. That's the one I like," she said excitedly.

Tony nodded as he headed over to it. He took out his wallet and paid the vendor. "All right, m'lady, it's yours."

Tony grabbed the tree and hiked it over his shoulder.

Back at the house, he helped her set the tree in the stand. Only after they had wrapped several strings of tiny gold lights around the thick green branches did Tony's beeper sound. He pulled the beeper off his belt and looked at the number. "My service," he said, automatically recognizing the number. He kissed Kim on the lips. "I have a sneaky suspicion I'm going to have to go to the hospital for a while."

She nodded. "The phone is in the kitchen."

She understood. Even before he volunteered to help her pick out the tree he had warned her he was on call.

A few minutes later, Tony reappeared behind her. "Unfortunately, I have to go back in," he said as he wrapped his arms around her, pulling her in close to him. "I can't remember when I've had a better afternoon."

"Will you stop by later?" she asked.

He kissed her forehead before he spoke. "I thought you'd never ask."

"In case I fall asleep," she said, handing him her key. "Let yourself in."

When Kim opened her eyes the house was completely dark with the exception of the lights on the Christmas tree. Bing Crosby's "White Christmas" played softly on the stereo. She glanced over at the fire, which had died down except for a few embers that were still smoldering.

She smiled to herself, recalling her day. After Tony left, she had rummaged through the basement and found the old box of Christmas ornaments that she and her mother had always used to decorate the tree. In a box beside the decorations were the old Christmas albums her parents had collected through the years. Kim had spent the rest of the afternoon and evening on a date with Christmas past, listening to Christmas carols as she unwrapped the old, familiar ornaments and hung them on the tree.

She heard the lock turn and smiled to herself.

Tony crept into the room and knelt down beside the couch where Kim lay curled up.

"Hi," he whispered, putting his hand to her cheek.

"Hi," she answered.

"I thought you'd be asleep by now."

"What time is it?" she asked, yawning as she pushed herself up.

"Close to eleven."

"Did you see my dad?"

"I checked in on him right before I left. He was sleeping and doing just fine."

"Thank you," she said.

He sat up on the couch next to her, picked up her hand, and kissed it. "The tree looks beautiful," he said, wrapping his arm around her.

"Thanks. Do you want something to drink?"

He shook his head. "I didn't want to leave you today," he said quietly, caressing her fingers. "I've had a hard time thinking about anyone—or anything else."

She inhaled slightly as he began to lightly kiss each fingertip. "As a matter of fact," he said, his eyes settling on hers, "I've had a hard time thinking of anything else since I met you."

She leaned forward and kissed him. She slid her fingers inside his shirt as she drew him toward her. "I'm sure you say that to all the girls."

He shook his head. "Never," he said seriously. "I don't play games. I don't have time for them." He kissed her forehead and ran his lips down the side of her face, breathing in the faint, clean smell of her perfume. "I've known what I wanted for a long time. Until recently, I was beginning to give up hope that my wish would ever come true."

"What exactly did you wish for?" Kim asked as innocently as she could manage.

He held her hand to his lips and kissed it. "A woman . . . ," he said, thinking. "A woman that I, . . . well, could never forget."

"And what happened recently?" Kim teased as she leaned back on the couch.

His eyes locked with hers as he slowly began to unbutton her blouse. He whispered, "I met you."

Six

HAROLD RISSON SAT UP IN BED AND IMPATIENTLY HIT THE buzzer for the nurse. He had always been self-sufficient, and he found himself resenting the fact that he was dependent upon others for so many things. Swinging his legs over the side of the bed, he grabbed his robe and wrapped it around his slender frame. Cautiously he stood up and made his way to the door, slightly embarrassed that his staff would see him walking around clad only in a bathrobe and slippers.

The whole experience of being a patient in the same unit that he presided over had been a humbling one. But still, he did not feel sorry for himself. Instead, he felt gratified that his illness had allowed him to be with his daughter once more. Her being there had helped heal his heart more than any of the many medications he was forced to take each day.

Harold shuffled awkwardly into the hall and looked both ways for a nurse. The hall was practically empty. He made his way toward the pantry, determined to get his own water.

Outside the doorway he stopped. There were people inside the pantry. People saying his name.

". . . Risson. Imagine my surprise. Who would've even thought he had a heart!" There was the sound of a woman's laughter.

"Well, you've heard the news, I'm sure," a man's voice piped in. "Guess who Hoffman's latest conquest is? Kim Risson."

"No way!"

"I saw her riding on his motorcycle the other day. And this morning I drove by Risson's house on my way to work . . . Hoffman's car was parked outside."

Harold stood still for a moment, not quite believing what he had heard. Surely they were mistaken.

147

"Can you imagine? Risson would have another heart attack if he found out his daughter was dating the same guy he'd been trying to fire."

"What does Risson call him again?"

"An immature kid masquerading as a doctor."

There was laughter, then a man's voice again. "I wish they'd just fire Risson. I'd rather work for Hoffman any day."

"Hoffman?" the woman asked. "You think he'll succeed Risson?"

"I think he wants to." The man laughed. "Whether he will or not is another story."

Harold Risson turned away from the pantry and slowly made his way back to his room. Kim and Tony? He refused to believe it. Surely his daughter had more common sense than to be taken in by a man like Tony Hoffman.

He had made it back to the doorway to his room when he heard the woman from the pantry call his name.

Harold stopped, his hand on the doorknob.

"Dr. Risson?" the woman repeated as she ran up to him. She was a pretty nurse in her fifties. Harold had seen her many times before. Never would he have imagined himself as the object of her gossip. "What are you doing?" she asked. "You shouldn't be up walking around."

He touched his throat. "I need a glass of water. Please."

Kim drove the Cadillac into the parking lot, pulling in in front of a large, unruly-looking snowbank. She jumped out of the car and smiled. The sun was shining, the sky was blue, and two large fresh green wreaths had been placed outside the hospital doors in honor of the approaching holiday.

Kim had to admit she was enjoying this Christmas season. She was with her family—her dad. And of course, there was Tony.

When she had opened her eyes and seen Tony lying there beside her, his arms still wrapped around her, she had been filled with a warm, calm sense of intimacy. She didn't want the morning to end.

In fact, when Tony left, she had found herself unable to think of anything else. So she had done the only thing she could think of. She had started work on his Christmas present. She had had little trouble deciding what to give him. She would paint him a picture.

Kim stepped inside the hospital, glancing around for Tony, even though she knew that he was in surgery. She took the elevator to her father's floor, clutching the fresh-baked bagels she had brought for him. She knocked on his door and stepped inside. Her father was sitting straight up in bed. When she entered the room, he raised an accusatory eyebrow.

"Hi, Dad," she said, giving him a kiss on the forehead. "How are you feeling this morning?"

"Sit down, Kim," he said sternly. "I want to talk to you."

She put the bagels on his tray. She may not have had any contact with her father in fifteen years, but she still recognized that tone of voice. Not to mention the old hairy eyebrow. "What's the matter?" she asked.

"Why don't you tell me what's going on around here?"

"What?" she asked, confused.

He sighed. "Look. I know that you have not been here all that long, and . . . well, sometimes it's difficult to ascertain a person's truthful intentions when inundated with—"

"Dad," Kim interrupted him. "Cut to the chase. What's wrong?"

"Tony . . . Hoffman," he added quickly.

Kim hesitated. "You've heard that Tony and I are friends."

"Friends?"

Kim nodded as she smiled slightly. She was glad that her father knew. "I like him. He's very sweet . . . and interesting. . . ."

"Oh, for Pete's sake, Kim," her father said angrily. "You don't know him. Tony Hoffman has been a troublemaker around here since he began his internship."

"I don't know about that. But I do know that he's a good surgeon. He did *your* surgery," she said defensively.

"Any decent doctor could've done it." He shook his head. "Look," he said, softening his tone. "Tony Hoffman dates a lot of women around here. He's immature and . . . well, I don't want to see you get hurt."

"I know he seems a little wild," she said. "I thought so too. But he's really not . . ."

"Listen to yourself!" He shook his head. "I don't like my daughter falling into the same traps that I've seen so many other women fall into."

"I don't know what you're talking about," Kim said stiffly. "We're friends."

"I know about motorcycle rides and cars parked outside each other's homes . . ."

"Dad . . ."

"He's using you, Kim. He thinks if he's got you on his side, I'll name him division chief. . . ."

"Oh, for God's sake, Dad. He's not using me."

"I'm not blaming you, Kim. I just don't want you dating him. . . ."

"Blaming me? For what? For living my life?" she said incredulously. "You seem to be forgetting that I'm not a little girl anymore. If you wanted to be a parent, you should've been one," she said angrily, her eyes filling with tears. "But it's too late now. Your little girl has grown up—*without* you. And I'm more than capable of making my own decisions." She shook her head as she stood to leave.

"Kim," her father began.

"It's too late, Dad," she said, wiping away a tear. "I'm an adult. And I have been for a long time. You missed your chance to be a parent."

The phone rang several times at the house during the day, but Kim ignored it. She didn't care who it was, she didn't feel like talking to anyone. Her argument with her father had upset her so much she hadn't been able to eat anything all day. Her first thought had been to hop back on a plane and leave him there, to run away from the whole mess. She was embarrassed and angry. Her father had treated her like a child who had gone astray, a child that needed strict parental guidance to get back on track.

She thought back to his accusations about Tony. Perhaps she had been too harsh with her father. She really didn't think Tony was using her, but on the other hand, she hadn't known Tony all that long. She pushed aside the momentary feeling of doubt as she reminded herself to trust her feelings.

If Tony was not the person he appeared to be, then she intended to find out for herself.

Besides, the issue was not whether Tony was right for her. She wasn't sure about that herself. The issue was whether her father had any right to "forbid" her to see anyone.

She sighed as a pang of guilt stabbed at her conscience. She was acting like an indignant, self-righteous child. Her father was ill—and not only that, he was in a time warp. She was sure that part of him believed that she was still a little girl. He was trying to protect her in the same way he had protected her from dating a boy three years her senior. She should be happy that he was finally demonstrating paternal feelings. Expressing his dismay must have been a big step for him. At least he was communicating—even if he was telling her something that she didn't want to hear.

Since his surgery, he seemed to be trying hard to change . . . perhaps he just needed time. In the meantime, they both needed to realize that it was not going to be easy becoming a part of each other's lives once more. And she hadn't made it any easier by getting involved with the surgeon who had saved his life.

But what her father didn't realize was how being with Tony had helped her to understand him better. Until she became involved with Tony, she had had little idea of the stress her father had suffered. Tony had helped her to see her father not as a cold, distant, hard man, but as a man who was coping with a traumatic and difficult job as best he could.

The phone began to ring again. Kim knew it wasn't Tony; he was in surgery until later that night. She assumed it was her father calling to apologize. And she had now cooled off enough to accept.

But it was not her father on the phone. Nor was it Tony. It was Dr. Harkavey.

And he was calling to tell her that her father had suffered another heart attack.

Kim sat in the critical care waiting room. It was almost ten o'clock, and she hadn't had anything to eat or drink since Dr. Harkavey had called. All she could think about was that her father might die. And that it would somehow be her fault. Why had she upset him by getting involved with one of his peers? She had sacrificed the only family she had left for a relationship that would probably turn out to be no more than a . . . fling.

"Kim."

She looked up. Tony sat down beside her, putting his arm around her. "I just heard."

She nodded.

"Sometimes this happens. I've spoken with Dr. Hark-avey, and your father's already stabilizing. It was a very mild attack. He's responding very well to the medication. He'll be okay."

"Tony," Kim said calmly. "We need to talk."

Tony stiffened slightly. "Sounds serious."

"I've enjoyed spending time with you, I really have. And I appreciate everything you've done for my father. . . ."

"What are you saying?" Tony asked quietly, the surprise evident in his bloodshot eyes.

Kim took a deep breath and then said, "I think we should redirect our relationship. You know. Just be friends."

Tony just looked at her as the impact of her words settled. "What?"

"Look," she said reasonably. "I came back here to be with my father. I just . . ." She paused, her willpower suddenly crumbling. She blinked back the tears as she said, "Please try to understand."

"What's the matter, Kim? Is this because of how your father feels about me? Are you worried that he won't approve?"

"It's true that I don't want to upset him, but I'm not doing this because of him." She paused, as she quickly attempted to gather the thoughts that were darting around her mind. "My whole career . . . my *life* is in Florida. This is an important time for me. I'm just making a name for myself there. . . ."

"You can make one here."

She shook her head. "No," she said, stubbornly. "I can't leave now."

"I'll wait. I'll wait as long as necessary. . . ."

"I can't be with you, Tony. I'm sorry. I just . . . I know what your career demands. I know what my mom went through with my dad. She wanted more . . . and because of that, neither she nor my father was happy."

"What are you talking about? I have a busy, demanding job, that's true. But so do you . . . ," he said, frustrated.

Kim shook her head. "I know how difficult it is to love a man who's obsessed with his work. I don't blame you . . . I think you're a wonderful doctor. I just . . . that's not what I want for my life. I want someone who's there for me when I need him, someone who can be there for my children."

"You have children?" he asked, trying to throw in a little humor.

She didn't smile.

"I'm not your father, Kim," he said as the smile faded from his mouth. "I don't live just for my career. I want a family, too . . . I want a wife to share life with. . . ."

"Look at you, Tony," she said sadly. "You live in a house with no furniture. It doesn't bother you because you're never there. Why? Because you're always at work."

"I see," he said quietly. He shook his head. "I thought . . . after last night . . . I . . ." He paused searching for the right words as his eyes locked with hers. "I thought I had found the person I wanted to share my life with. Was I wrong?"

Kim glanced away.

"Kim, don't do this just because you're frightened. We can slow things down . . . take time to get to know each other," he said quietly, putting his hand on top of hers.

"Last night was a mistake," she said. "We're opposites, Tony. We had a good time, but it's not going to go any further than that."

Tony slowly withdrew his hand. "I know that you're going through a tough time right now . . . ," he began.

"I'm sorry," she said definitively. "My mind is made up."

Tony looked into her eyes. It was obvious that there was no reasoning with her. At least not tonight.

He stood up. "All right, Kim. I . . . well . . ." He shrugged. "You know where to reach me if you change your mind," he said, still shell-shocked by the sudden turn of events.

She glanced away, not bothering to answer.

* * *

Her father opened his bloodshot eyes. "Kim?" he murmured.

"Hi, Dad," Kim said, smiling.

"I'm sorry . . . so sorry . . ."

She squeezed his hand. "I am, too. It was silly."

"I thought . . . I thought you were going to go back to Florida." His voice was thick and slow, but Kim could still detect the fear in his words.

"No, Dad. No. I was just angry. I'm sorry. I'm going to stay here and help you. We're going to spend Christmas together. Just you and me."

"Tony . . . ," he began weakly.

She raised her hand as if to brush away his comment. "It's over. It was never any big deal, anyway. My focus is getting you well enough to come home for Christmas."

Her father closed his eyes as a mixture of sadness and guilt washed over him. His daughter had been kind enough to rush to his side when he needed her, and he had repaid that kindness by criticizing her choice in men as though she were a mere child. When he awakened after his surgery and saw her by his side, he had promised himself that he would try to make up for years of bad parenting. He would attempt to be the father he knew she always wished she had. Instead he had disappointed her—once again. "I'm sorry for what I said about Tony. I wasn't being fair," he mumbled weakly.

"Dad," she said patiently. "It's over. Tony wasn't right for me. It didn't have anything to do with you."

He looked at her, not believing her words.

"Really," she said, although she wasn't convinced herself. "I need someone who's more settled. More . . . well, someone who doesn't work as much. Anyway," she said, smiling at him. "I don't want to discuss it anymore. I just want you to get better, so that we can go home. In time for Christmas."

"I want you to be happy, Kim," her father said.

She smiled. "I know you do, Dad."

He nodded, watching her.

"By the way," she said. "I was thinking about taking the pool cover off, turning it into an ice rink."

Her father nodded. "Does this mean that you're thinking about staying?"

"Yes. For a while. Maybe even . . . well, permanently. I mean, you're going to need some help, and I want to spend some time with you."

His eyes welled with tears. "So what do you want for Christmas this year, Kim?"

"I'd like to have my father home."

A voice from behind her said, "I think we can arrange that."

Kim turned to see Tony standing in the doorway. He gave her a weak smile as he focused his attention on Harold. "Good morning, Harold. How are you feeling today?"

"Better," Harold managed, looking at his daughter. She had turned a shade of pink and was glancing around uncomfortably for her purse.

"Kim, I'm glad you're here," Tony said. "Harold, I know you don't want to hear it, but you're going to need some assistance for a while after you return home. Just for a month or so. Maybe a nursing assistant. Someone to help you grocery shop, cook dinner . . ."

"That won't be necessary," Kim said quickly.

Tony shrugged. "Maybe not necessary, but it would be helpful. He's going to have to take it easy for a while. . . ."

"I understand. But a nurse won't be necessary," Kim said, speaking to Tony across her father's bed. "I'm staying."

Tony was silent for a split second. "For how long?" he asked. It was clear to everyone in the room that he was not asking for professional reasons.

Kim met his eyes directly. She was not staying because she had changed her mind about dating him, she was staying because she was trying to rebuild her relationship with her father. "I don't know. Maybe permanently." She shot her father a quick smile as she grabbed her purse. "I'll see you later, Dad."

As Kim walked out of the room, Tony looked down at the chart, though he was too upset to focus. He had received Kim's message—loud and clear.

Harold stared at Tony, aware of the pain the young man was suffering. "You care about her, don't you?" he asked quietly.

Tony shrugged as his eyes focused on his patient. "Yes.

Yes, I care about her. Very much." He sighed. "Anyway," he said, forcing himself to concentrate on the matter at hand, "I'm glad to see that you're stabilized."

"It helps to have Kim here," Harold said, watching Tony carefully.

Tony smiled sadly. "Yes, I'm sure it does."

Harold paused, pushing himself up slightly. "I hear you've been running the department in my absence."

Tony shifted his feet uncomfortably as he glanced toward the door. "Yes, well, not officially. Just filling in for you until you get back."

"I've been hearing good things about you," Harold said.

Tony glanced at him, surprised. "Well, that's nice to know."

Harold nodded, signaling to Tony that he was dismissed. "Keep up the good work," he said.

Tony just looked at him. It sounded like Harold Risson was giving him his blessing. But his blessing for what? "Thank you," Tony said quietly. He hung the chart back up on the wall and left the room, shutting the door behind him.

Harold Risson closed his eyes. But he wasn't ready to go to sleep. He needed time to think. He wanted his daughter to be happy, and it was obvious to him that she cared about Tony. He needed to arrange for them to meet outside of the hospital . . . but how could he do that?

He smiled as he began to formulate a plan.

A few minutes later, he heard the door creak and opened his eyes to see Kim enter the room.

"Kim," he said tiredly. "How do you feel about representing me at the hospital Christmas party this Saturday night?"

"Hey, doc! Where do you want this?"

Tony walked to the front door. On the stoop, two men were holding an overstuffed armchair. "Next to the other one," he said, glancing into the living room.

"One more thing and you're not going to be able to move in here," the delivery man said.

Tony nodded. The room was totally furnished, couch, chairs, end tables, lamps. His entire house, in fact, was now completely furnished.

"What's going on?" the delivery man asked, looking at Tony. "You sure bought a lot of stuff. You getting married or something?"

Tony shook his head. "No. Not that fortunate, I'm afraid."

"Fortunate," the guy said, chuckling. "Take my word for it. You're fortunate right now. Big house, nice dog. No wife. Very fortunate."

Tony smiled as he shook his head. He didn't feel fortunate. All he could think about recently was Kim. And what might have been.

In fact, he had been struck with the sudden urge to decorate when all of his other advances toward Kim had been rejected. Since the night of their breakup, she had been pleasant and polite, but unwavering in her decision for them to stay "just friends." He had been surprised by his unwillingness to accept the end of the relationship. He knew why. For the first time in his life—he was in love.

Kim stood next to Jason Neerbore, a radiologist who was even less exciting than his name suggested. He was talking to her about the difference between Bach and Mozart, a difference that in most situations she would have been happy to discuss. But right now, she was distracted. She had received a call from the gallery owner this morning, informing her that her show had been a success. They had sold almost all of the work she had presented and had received commissions for several more paintings. But tonight, on what should have been a night for celebration, all she could think about was Tony, and whether or not she would see him.

Still nodding at Jason's monologue, she shifted her position. She had inadvertently bought a pair of nylons that were a size too small, and she could feel the crotch drop a little each time she moved.

She felt a hand on her arm. It was Jason. "My partner just arrived," he said. "I'd like to introduce you to him. He did his residency in Florida."

"Oh, great," Kim murmured, trying to sound enthusiastic. "But I have to go to the ladies' room. I'll be just a minute."

"Okay," he said, sliding his glasses up his nose. "I'll be right here."

"Got it," Kim said. She made her way into the ladies' room and yanked up her nylons, causing the small run at the top to rip down the side. She shook her head as she turned before the mirror, trying to ascertain how noticeable it was. Considering they were off-black, and her dress was a snug, velvet green mini, it was just about as noticeable as it could get.

Kim hesitated before pulling them off. She threw them in the trash and slipped her black high-heeled shoes back on her bare feet. She turned away from the mirror, not happy with the reflection. She probably should have bought a dress that was a little more conservative, but she had postponed shopping for it until just that afternoon, a time crunch that inspired impulse buys. She made a mental note to hold in her stomach as she left the ladies' room.

As she walked by the bar, she was too busy holding her breath to notice anyone. "Kim," a voice called out. A voice so familiar it made her jump.

She turned around and found herself staring right up into Tony's deep green eyes. He looked handsome in his suit and tie, a change from his usual wardrobe of hospital scrubs or faded jeans. She exhaled quickly, allowing herself to breathe. "Hi, Tony," she said as casually as she could manage.

"I'm surprised to see you here," he said, not bothering to hide his excitement.

"Yes, well," she said, shrugging, trying to play it cool, "my dad asked me to come."

He tilted his head slightly forward as though he was tempted to kiss her. He suddenly paused and straightened, as he said, "I'm glad I ran into you. Your show . . . it was last night, wasn't it? How did it go?"

Kim smiled, impressed that he remembered. "It went very well. Thanks for . . . remembering."

He smiled at her, his eyes wandering toward the swell of her breasts above the tight green material. His eyes drifted down toward the rest of her body and then back up slowly, as if he wanted her to realize that he was appreciating every delicate curve. "How could I forget?" he asked, his eyes meeting hers.

"Kim! There you are," Jason said, loosely grabbing her arm. "Don't try and steal her away from me," he joked to Tony.

"Steal her away?" Tony asked, glancing at Kim. Was she here with him?

"Tony!" a woman said, practically pouncing on top of him. "Or should I say, Dr. Hoffman. Ah, hell, we're not at the hospital!" She laughed.

Kim gave her a quick once-over. She was a petite, gorgeous blonde for whom Kim felt an immediate, almost inherent dislike. Kim had a feeling that her dislike had something to do with the way the woman looked in her tight, little black dress. Or maybe it was the way she casually looped her hand around Tony's arm.

"Let's dance," the woman said. "You promised."

Kim glanced at Jason uncomfortably, trying to ignore the jealousy that was yanking at her heart.

"Jenny," Tony said, talking to the woman on his arm even though his eyes hadn't left Kim. "Do you know Jason Neerbore?"

The woman nodded. It was obvious she had already had more than a few drinks. "I think so. . . ."

"And this," Tony said, "is Kim Risson. Dr. Risson's daughter."

"Nice to meet you," she said, giving Tony a sloppy tug on his arm. "Come on, Tony."

Tony forced himself to break away from Kim and Jason. "Have fun," he said, accepting Jenny's hand as she pulled him onto the dance floor.

Jason smiled as he watched Tony and Jenny weave their way through the couples entwined together in front of the band. "That Tony. He's always got some beautiful girl on his arm. He's too much, isn't he?"

Kim stepped out of her car and adjusted her sunglasses. It wasn't as though she needed them to protect her eyes against the sun. In fact, even though it was nine o'clock in the morning, the day was dreary and overcast, making it look as though the sun had not yet appeared. But she was suffering from a lack of sleep, and her tired eyes were sensitive to the slightest glare. She wouldn't have minded if she was suffering from a good cause. But her bloodshot eyes were not a result of a good time; they were a result of a restless night spent thinking about Tony. After Jenny had pulled him onto the dance floor, Kim had lost track of him temporarily. Unfortunately, when she saw him again, he was following Jenny out the door.

Kim had left the party shortly after, tormented by emotions she did not want to admit.

Kim glanced to her right as a bright red car pulled in alongside her. Her heart stopped beating when she saw that inside the bright red car were none other than Tony and Jenny. Together.

"Hi, Kim," Tony said, swinging open his door.

"Hello," Kim replied, giving him a curt nod. She suppressed an instinct to run away and instead stood still, politely waiting for them to join her.

"Jenny," he said, standing up. "You remember Kim Risson?"

Jenny hesitated as she slammed her door.

"From last night," Tony said.

She laughed. "I don't remember much about last night." She glanced at her watch. "Oh boy, I've got to hustle. I'm late. All because of you," she said, nudging Tony with her elbow.

Kim swallowed as she picked up her pace. So much for Tony changing his ways.

Tony scurried to keep up with Kim. "Jenny works with the thoracic team."

"How nice," Kim said, giving him a look that she hoped would stop him in his tracks. It didn't.

"Transplant coordinator," he said, as if Kim cared. She didn't. The only thing she cared about was never seeing him again.

Jenny made a sharp right turn as soon as she headed into the hospital. "Bye, guys. Tony, I'll see you tonight around six," she said, taking off her coat as she ran toward Administration. Kim and Tony were left alone. Kim continued walking, hurrying toward the elevator.

"Jenny is . . ."

"I don't really care about Ginny. . . ."

"Jenny," Tony corrected her.

"Whatever her name is," she interrupted, pressing the elevator button.

"She's a transplant coordinator. She lives—" he began.

"Look," she interrupted him, impatiently hitting the elevator button again. "You don't have to explain anything. It's none of my business who you spend your time with."

The elevator doors opened and an elderly woman stepped out. "Good morning, Dr. Hoffman," she said, breaking into a smile. "I'm glad I ran into you. I have a question about my husband . . ."

Kim used the distraction to escape inside the elevator. The doors snapped shut before Tony could join her.

"What's the matter," her father asked. "Didn't you enjoy yourself last night?"

Kim forced a smile. "It was all right."

"That bad, huh?"

Kim smiled. "The shrimp was good."

"Did you, ah . . . run into Tony there?"

Kim nodded. "Yes," she said. "He was there."

"Did you talk to him?" he asked hopefully.

She paused, looking at him suspiciously. "Dad . . . what are you up to?"

"Nothing."

"Look, Tony is not my type. I'm not sure what my type is, but he's not it. End of subject. Besides," she said, looking at him suspiciously, "I thought you didn't like him."

"I never said that. I just . . . well, I had made some assumptions about him. But I've decided that if you want to marry him—"

"Marry him?" Kim interrupted loudly. "Where the heck did you get that idea?"

He shrugged. "It seemed obvious that you cared about him. . . ."

"Whoa," she said, raising her hands. "Look, Dad, he's a nice guy and all, but we . . . well, we're not right for each other. If I married Tony—which, by the way, is ludicrous even to mention," she rambled on, "considering we only went out a couple of times—but, if I did, which I won't, my whole life would revolve around his schedule. I have a career, a career that means everything to me."

Her father wrinkled his brow, confused. "You're an artist," he stated. "You can't marry a doctor? How come?"

"It's not just the doctor thing. It's the marriage part. I mean, I spend all my time working, unencumbered with thoughts like: What time is he coming home? Do I have to fix dinner? Do I have to pick up dry cleaning? Do I have to . . . take a shower?" She sighed, as if exhausted by the very thought.

"Your career is everything to you, huh?" he said, thinking. "Sounds like you're more like me than you care to admit."

Kim paused, thinking about what her father had said. For so long he had represented everything she resented. Was she so busy resenting the choices he had made that she hadn't noticed herself doing the same thing?

"You're a beautiful, warm girl," her father said paternally. "And you're not married. You've never even come close. How come?"

She shrugged. "I haven't met anyone interesting. I work by myself all day, and at night I'm too tired to go out."

"I don't know Tony very well, but he certainly seems interesting to me . . . and I know a lot of women at this hospital would agree."

"Then they should marry him."

"He doesn't want them. He wants you."

Kim shook her head. "You're wrong."

Her father watched her carefully. The pain was evident in her eyes. She cared about Tony, and regardless of what she said, her eyes could not deny the intensity of her feelings. "Are you afraid that Tony will treat you like I treated your mother?"

"What?" she asked, surprised.

"Tony isn't like me. He's a different man . . . from a different generation—"

"Dad," she interrupted.

He raised his hand, silencing her. "Your mother and I had our issues. They were ours, and our alone. My job didn't drive a wedge between us, Kim. I did. It wouldn't have mattered what kind of job I had."

"What are you trying to say?"

He paused. "I don't think Tony should pay for my mistake."

"What is this? I thought you didn't like him!"

He shook his head. "I like him. I just don't like what he represents."

"Which is?"

"Change. I think there are some people around here that would like to see Tony replace me as head of thoracic surgery."

Kim shifted her eyes downward.

He continued, "I'm beginning to think that might not be a bad idea. You see, I'm not afraid of change anymore—or the future. In fact, I look forward to it. I have a chance to change, a chance to correct some mistakes I've made."

Kim smiled sadly. "I look forward to the future, too.

Her father hesitated. "Where's my wallet?"

Kim wrinkled her forehead, confused. "Your wallet?"

He nodded.

She pulled open a drawer next to his bed and pulled out the worn, brown leather case. "Right here."

"Look inside the top fold there. Behind the credit cards."

She opened the fold and glanced at a worn piece of paper, neatly folded up. What's this?" she asked.

He nodded. "Read it."

She unfolded the note. In large, light script was written:

Dear Daddy,
Because I haf skwandired my alowance, I am giving
you Max for Christmas. Plese take care of him.
Love, Kimberly Risson

When she was finished reading the note, she looked up at her father, surprised that he was sentimental enough to have kept this letter in his wallet for all these years.

"You were six years old when you wrote that. You probably don't remember, but I was always telling you . . ."

"Not to squander my allowance."

He smiled.

"Who's Max?"

"Max was a stuffed duck that you took with you everywhere. It was a total, unselfish gift of love."

"And you've kept this note in your wallet . . . ?"

"Ever since."

Kim smiled. Her father was certainly full of surprises. Surprises that she was more than happy to discover.

"I learned a lot from that gift . . . and I've learned a lot from you. I hope this Christmas I can give you something that will mean as much to you."

"You already have," Kim said.

Harold just smiled. He knew what his daughter really wanted, and he had every intention of getting it for her.

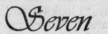

Seven

"WELCOME HOME, DAD," KIM SAID, AS SHE PULLED INTO THE driveway. It was the evening of December twenty-third, and as Tony had promised, her father was coming home. Tiny white lights glimmered from the branches of the trees.

"Who helped you put the outdoor lights up?"

"No one. I did it myself."

"You climbed up on a ladder?"

"Yes," Kim said. "Wait until you see the back. I've strung lights all around the ice rink."

"How do you like that," her father said, smiling proudly.

Kim stopped the car and hurried around, helping her father inside the house.

"A Christmas tree," her father said happily, glancing inside the living room. "I don't think there's been a tree in this house since . . . well, since you were here last."

Harold sat down on the couch as Kim turned on the tree lights. He smiled. "Beautiful."

"Do you want dinner, Dad?"

He shook his head. "Actually, I'm feeling a little tired.

And I want to be well rested for tomorrow." He pushed himself up and Kim hurried to assist him. "That's okay, Kim," he said. As he stepped into the hall he glanced in the den, his eye catching sight of her easel. "What's that?"

"Oh," Kim said. "I've been working in your den. I hope you don't mind."

"Of course not," he said, stepping inside and turning on the light. "What are you painting?"

"Well, actually, it's your Christmas present."

He smiled. "Can I see it?"

"You don't want to wait until Christmas?"

He shook his head. "I've never seen your work before."

She led him around the easel. He nodded his head slowly, a proud smile creeping up his lips. "It's beautiful. Absolutely beautiful."

"You really like it?" she asked, analyzing his expression. She had feared he might not like it; after all, not everyone enjoyed abstract art.

"I love it," he said with uncharacteristic enthusiasm.

He touched the stiff canvas of the painting, and it fell forward slightly, revealing another finished painting underneath. "What's this?"

"Oh, just something that I did for fun."

Her father gently held his painting as he looked at the canvas behind it. In a magnificent, almost blinding display of colors, little lines shot out from a large red heart.

"I like this. It looks like fireworks."

Kim laughed uncomfortably. "I started painting that one for Tony. It was going to be his Christmas present. I don't know why, but I finished it anyway." She shrugged. "I guess I thought it might help to exorcise him from my system."

"And did it?" he asked, looking at her intently.

She smiled sadly as she stepped away. "Come on, Dad," she said. "I'll help you upstairs."

"Can I get you anything, Dad? Are you comfortable?"

Kim's father looked at her as he flashed her a kind smile. Since he had arrived home the day before, Kim had been scurrying around the house, making him breakfast and lunch, making sure his pillows were fluffed and his ice cubes solid. As much as he loved her, he didn't like having her fuss over him so. "I'm fine," he said. "Look, you don't have to stick around here with me all day. Go on out . . . get some fresh air. It'll be good for you." He paused. "Do your own thing, isn't that what they say?"

"Maybe twenty years ago," Kim said with a laugh.

"Well, go. I don't want you sitting at home all day, taking care of me."

"Well," she said, thinking. "I was going to run to the grocery store . . . "

"Then go."

Kim checked her watch. It was four o'clock. "Maybe I'll just run to the corner store . . ."

"Go," her father said. "And enjoy yourself."

"I'll do my best," Kim promised. Although she could think of more enjoyable things than running to the grocery store on Christmas Eve. Her instincts told her it was going to be packed. Still, she was making a traditional Christmas dinner tomorrow night, and she had realized a few minutes before that she had forgotten cranberry sauce.

"I'll be back in a flash," Kim said, grabbing her coat.

"Take your time," her father commanded.

"Aye, aye," Kim said, saluting him as she stepped outside.

Her father just laughed.

Kim walked down the crowded aisle, two bags of fresh cranberries stuffed under her arm. She let out a silent moan when she saw the long line wrapped around the single open register. She was standing at the end of the line, shifting her weight back and forth impatiently, when she saw someone she recognized. Someone she was not anxious to see. It was Jenny, the same woman who had been with Tony the morning after the hospital Christmas party. She had a cart full of groceries and a baby strapped into the child seat.

As Jenny pushed her cart behind Kim, Kim grabbed a trashy magazine and pretended to immerse herself in an article.

After a few minutes Jenny said politely, "Excuse me. You're Dr. Risson's daughter, aren't you?"

Kim glanced up at her. "Oh, hi," she said, pretending that she had just this moment noticed her. "Yes. I'm Kim. And you're . . ." She paused, as if searching for her name.

"Jenny. Jenny Treeby. And this is Kirby. My son."

"Your son?" Kim inquired. He didn't look to be more than a year old.

Jenny nodded.

So she was a single mother. Kim gave her credit. She knew that couldn't be easy. "He's adorable," Kim said politely.

"Thank you. So, do you live around here?" Jenny inquired, making friendly chitchat as the line moved slowly forward.

"My dad does. I live in Florida, but I'm staying with him until he gets back on his feet. Although I'm considering moving here myself," Kim replied.

"Oh, there are a lot of nice neighborhoods around here. I live on Michigan Avenue. Off of State Circle."

Tony's neighborhood, Kim thought. How convenient for them both.

Jenny continued, "When my husband and I bought our house—"

Kim tilted her head. Husband? "You're married?" she interrupted.

Jenny nodded. "Yes."

"But . . . I thought, I thought you and Tony were . . ." Her voice drifted off.

Jenny just looked at her blankly.

"Seeing each other," Kim continued weakly.

"Tony Hoffman?" Jenny asked, repeating his name slowly. "You thought . . . ?" The woman squinted as though the idea had never occurred to her. She burst into laughter so loud that her child started to cry. "Oh my God, no. Although I guess I could see how you would think that. We come to the party together. We leave together. We show up for work the next morning."

Feeling like an idiot, Kim flashed her a half smile.

Jenny shook her head as she popped a pacifier into her son's mouth. "Tony lives next door to us. He and my husband are best friends. My husband didn't want to go to the party, and Tony's car was in the shop, so I took him. And I drove him to work the next day, too. But he just bought a new car, thank God. He's been going a little crazy lately, buying everything in sight."

"What do you mean?" Kim said, handing her cranberries to the cashier.

"He completely furnished his house. In about one hour. Can you imagine? What inspired him, I'll never know."

Kim paid for her cranberries. "It's been great talking to you, Jenny," she said, grabbing her brown bag. "Have a merry Christmas."

"Sure thing," Jenny called out. "Same to you."

"What's the matter," Kim's father asked, leaning forward slightly. "You've been distracted all evening."

"I know," Kim apologized. "I'm sorry. I just . . . well, have something on my mind."

"Something or someone?"

Kim smiled sadly. "Am I that obvious?"

"Want to talk about it?"

"Oh, it's nothing. I'm just . . . I don't know. Mad at myself."

"What? Why?"

"Just because I'm pigheaded. Opinionated. Stubborn . . ." She hesitated. "Feel free to argue with me," she joked.

"Pigheaded, opinionated, stubborn. Sounds like you're talking about me."

She laughed. "I guess we grow up to be our parents. That's what they say."

The smile drifted from his face. He thought for a moment. "What if your parent changes?"

She smiled. "I don't know. I'm pretty set in my ways. I think it's too late."

"If there's one thing I've learned over the past month, it is that it's never too late."

Kim nodded. "Speaking of which," she said, changing the subject as she glanced at her watch. It was eleven-thirty, a little late to be eating dinner. "Are you sure you want to wait until midnight to eat?"

Her father nodded enthusiastically. "Absolutely. And to exchange gifts . . ."

"Dad," Kim said. "I've already told you, I got what I wanted . . ."

He smiled at her. "I haven't seen you use that new ice rink yet."

"Maybe tomorrow," Kim said.

"How about right now? I can watch from the window," he said standing up and turning on the outside light.

Kim looked at him curiously. "Right now?"

"Why not? It is Christmas, after all."

Kim nodded. If she bundled up, she might be able to withstand the cold. After all, if she *was* going to move here, she'd better get used to it. "All right," she said, going off in search of her new skates.

Harold stood at the window, watching Kim wander onto the ice. She waved back at him as she skated cautiously toward the middle of the rink. He smiled proudly and watched her skate around the perimeter. He would have liked to stay there and watch her until she came back inside, but unfortunately he couldn't. He had some work to do. And he didn't have much time.

Tony used the windshield wipers to brush away the snow that had started falling a few minutes earlier. Christmas carols played on the radio as he pulled up in front of the Risson house. He was a bit curious as to why Risson had insisted he come out to his house as soon as he was finished at the hospital. After all, if Risson was having problems, he should have contacted Harkavey. He was his cardiologist, not Tony.

Tony parked the car and walked up the walk. The house was dark with the exception of the lights from the Christmas tree. Tony shook his head. Maybe Risson had wanted to speak with him and had waited until Kim had gone to bed before summoning him over.

Tony walked up to the door and hesitated. There was an envelope taped to the door with his name on it. He pulled it off and opened it.

Dear Tony,

I'm afraid I've brought you out here under false pretenses. The pain I'm suffering right now is not from any mistake you have made . . . it is due to a serious error of my own. I've made many such errors in my life; however, the most recent was when I seriously misjudged you and your caring for my daughter.

I ask you both to forgive a silly, selfish old man. I not only approve of you for my daughter, I have spoken with the chairman of the hospital and have nominated you for my replacement as Chief of the Thoracic Unit when I retire next month.

Congratulations and Merry Christmas,

Harold

P.S. Be patient with Kim. Just remember—she loves you.

Kim was getting into it. Too bad I don't have any music, she thought, picking up her speed as she stretched out her arms. She twisted, intending to spin herself around. Instead, she lost her balance and fell flat on her rear. She started laughing as she slid backward on the ice. As she drifted to a stop she looked toward the window, taking a mock bow toward her father. But it was not her father that she saw. It was Tony, standing at the edge of the rink, watching her.

Kim sat on the ice, not even feeling the cold wetness as it seeped through her jeans. "Tony?" she asked softly, brushing a snowflake off her eyelash.

He smiled at her as he stepped onto the ice. He stopped in front of her and extended his hand in an offer to help her up.

She slowly accepted his hand and he lifted her to her feet. Still holding on to her, he showed her the note.

Kim read it slowly, her brown eyes filling with tears. She looked at Tony and smiled.

Tony was the first to speak. "Kim, I . . . well, I'm sorry if . . ."

"You have nothing to apologize for. I do. I'm sorry. I was worried about repeating the mistakes of the past, and in doing so, I almost made the most terrible mistake of my life."

He traced his finger underneath her eye, wiping away a tear. "You changed your mind about us? Were you visited by the ghost of Christmas past?"

She smiled and nodded. "As well as the ghost of Christmas present and future. I saw what my life would be like without you."

"And what were you doing . . . without me?"

"I was sad and lonely. I had been offered something more priceless than money or fame, and I was too frightened to accept it."

He hugged her close. "I love you, Kim. I can understand why you were concerned about me . . . or rather, about us . . . but I think as long as we make a conscious effort to balance love and work, we'll be okay. Even your dad could see that. Speaking of which . . ." he said, nodding toward the house. "I don't know how you did it, but you've even changed him. His letter . . . well, it's a miracle."

Kim grinned with happiness as she grabbed him, pulling him in closer. "It's no miracle," she said. "It's magic. Christmas magic."

And then, just as the distant church bells began to chime midnight, he kissed her.

MARGARET ALLISON, a graduate of the University of Michigan, is a former advertising and marketing executive and has also worked as a model and as an actress. Margaret currently lives in Maryland with her husband and is working on her next novel for Pocket Books.

Stef Ann Holm

Jolly Holly

For my father and mother,
Frank and Gloria Wysocki,
who've always believed

One

1900, Limonero, California

JOHN WOLCOTT LOUNGED IN THE DOORWAY OF THE CALIFORNIA Republic Saloon with a cold beer in his hand. Sticky black petroleum gummed the bottom of his boots and the denim of his Levi's. A cotton shirt with the armholes frayed stuck to his sweaty back. Caught by wind, the light hem at his lean hips rippled.

Gazing at Main Street, he watched the goings-on. The temperature on the wall thermometer behind him registered near one hundred. It sure as hell didn't feel like Christmas was just over a week off.

With the beer bottle poised at his mouth, John's attention landed on a woman walking down Sespe Avenue. She'd come from the tall stands of dried-up mustard and wild grass, and carried a bucket in each hand. With every step, water sloshed over the rims, spattering the thirsty earth and spotting her sage green skirt. To keep the scalding sun from beating on her face, she'd tied the ribbons of a straw hat beneath her chin; the crown was adorned with a clump of matilija poppies.

Crazy Isabel Burche.

He knew who she was, but he'd never talked with her. She was as nutty as a walnut orchard. She'd actually forked over twenty-five bucks for the five acres of land she lived on—which wasn't worth a plug nickel to anyone who had a lick

177

of common sense—to grow lemon trees. The parcel boasted more rocks than a river bed, making it useful only for grazing, if that. And Isabel didn't have a horse or a cow.

Taking a sip of beer, he watched as she turned onto a barely visible lane. She momentarily disappeared from his view. Then that hat stuck out from the wavy sea of field as she gained higher ground and headed toward the broken-down cabin that had been abandoned back in ninety-one. Isabel had surrounded the decrepit place with a variety of plants she'd dug up from the hills. Damned if the poppies hadn't taken root and grown taller than the sagging veranda porch; dusky greenery waited for early summer to bloom.

He could see her set the buckets down, wipe the sweat from her brow with a back-swipe of her wrist, then proceed to water two lemon trees. It was a hell of a thing. Because as soon as she finished—one bucketful for each tree, she retraced her steps to Sespe Avenue once more. Since she had six trees, she did this a dozen or more times a day. Her land had no tap access to the town pipeline, so she had to bring water in from Santa Paula Creek. The hike was a mile each way.

John drank his beer as she faded from his line of vision. Isabel Burche had been in Limonero nearly a year. She'd held and left more jobs than him—which in itself was no small feat.

For a day, she'd taken up residence at the Blossom as one of the girls. He'd been over in Ventura at the time, but Newt Slocum said she'd been a real merry bit in bed. The following morning, she'd strode out the doors without a backward glance and had gotten work at the mill stitching flour sacks.

From there, she'd packed lemons, then clerked for the mercantile, served as a waitress at the Calco Oil Café, and a score of other things he'd lost track of—not that he was keeping track of Isabel. In a town this size, a man noticed a person's business just by turning around.

A gust of hot air breathed beneath the saloon's awning, sending a multitude of green paper flyers across the boardwalk. They tumbled and somersaulted down the street, seemingly coming from nowhere. Bending down, John snagged one as it stuck to his tacky boot heel. He didn't take the time to read it just yet.

As he stepped away from the railing, a clattering noise struck overhead on the awning, then came a *ping* as something rolled down the roof. A tiny white ball ricocheted off the hitching post and sailed straight for him. The damn thing belted him on the shoulder, then dribbled to his feet. He stared at it.

Perfect Flight golf ball.

Looking up and down the street and seeing no one searching out a ball, John shrugged and left it there. Shank shot. Some idiot.

His thirst sated from the beer, he went back into the Republic to order a tequila. The cash from today's pay burned a hole in his wallet, and he doubted he'd have a cent left over by tomorrow.

Never having the patience to settle into one trade and stick with it until the effort paid off, John Wolcott lived each moment as it came. Part-time oil driller; part-time dowser; part-time big talker; part-time drunk. Put them all together and one could say he was a professional good-for-nothing.

John liked to think of himself as holding out for the right opportunity to come along.

Isabel Burche sat on her porch in a rocker made from peeled willow boughs. A fiery sunset bathed the undulating grasses before her in deep brass and copper shadows. The Santa Ana winds still blew, but not with as much force as they had earlier. She'd opened the windows in the cabin, hoping a distant ocean breeze would be able to wend its way to the valley, but the small interior remained uncomfortable.

Her muscles ached, and her palms hadn't toughened enough to form calluses. Blisters made the skin tender and painful. Even though she wore gloves to carry the buckets, the wire handles were merciless; the constant care her plants and the lemon trees required in this heat was wearing her down.

But she wouldn't give up. Those trees represented the first

real hope she had of making her own way. She'd never solely relied on herself. At twenty-eight, the time had come for her to be self-sufficient.

Once her trees began bearing enough fruit to turn a profit, she intended on using the harvest as the foundation for her business. The lemon sauce and syrup she made could be sold. With as slow as the lemons were growing, so far all she'd canned was a case. There was a market for such a thing. In the last six months, she'd had Duster ask the roughnecks if any of them would be interested in buying sweets. Every one of the oil drillers said they most surely would.

Now all she needed was for the lemons to multiply and ripen faster.

Broad shoulders filling a tattered shirt with the sleeves torn out came into her view through snippets of the wind-blown field. When the wild mustard parted on a gust, she could see the entire figure for a moment.

Tall and built as strong as the rig he worked on, John Wolcott strode up Sespe in the twilight. Obscured by the deep cut of dark shadow in her porch, Isabel could freely stare at him.

He's early, she thought. He never left the Republic until after ten o'clock—if at all. There were times when she took her first morning walk to get water, and she'd catch him stumbling out of the saloon with a liquor bottle in his hand. On hot evenings when sleeping in the stifling house was unbearable she'd stay outside waiting for exhaustion to overcome her and she couldn't keep her eyes open any longer. She'd sometimes doze in her rocker, then awaken with a jolt to a drunken voice as John sang in Spanish to a midnight moon. He was as crazy as a loco coyote.

Isabel's eyes narrowed, following him through the opening of her lane. He was too handsome for his own good. She'd never seen him up close, but a woman didn't have to. Just by the manner in which he walked, held his head, and wore his masculinity so effortlessly, she knew he would be trouble.

In the waning light, she saw a slip of green in John's hand. The slow chirp of crickets and the Santa Anas whispering through her poppies disguised the crinkle of papers as they suddenly tumbled and careened into the yard. Sheets fluttered up the porch steps with the breeze. One landed smack in her lap.

Isabel lifted the flyer and tried to make out what it said. It was too dark. So she rose from the rocker and went inside to turn up the lamp. Kerosene hissed and gave off a soft orb of light by which she read the green paper.

JOLLY HOLLY CONTEST

Will award the person who collects and delivers the most holly berries for stringing on a Christmas tree to be erected in the yard at Ninth and Mill Street this Friday. Deadline is December 24, 1900, at the stroke of midnight. The prize will be unlike anything you've ever known. Riches beyond your wildest dreams. The key to eternal happiness. Prosper in a way you never thought possible. You will be forever grateful. 'Tis the season for the holiday spirit so join in and reap the rewards.

—Bellamy Nicklaus

Isabel didn't know any Bellamy Nicklaus. And the last time she was by the house on Ninth and Mill—which was just yesterday, it had been vacant and in horrible neglect. This could be a prank.

While mulling over the possibilities, a dull rattle sounded in the pipe to her pot-bellied stove. *Squirrels*. She absently tapped the black cylinder with a spoon. The noise stopped. But then oddly, the grated door drifted open and a sooty white ball rolled to her feet. She dismissed it as a child's errant toy. The plum-sized ball must have gotten wedged in the flue. It was amazing that she hadn't filled the house with smoke when her stove was lit.

Isabel turned her thoughts back to the contest . . . she could really use the winnings. How much money was the prize? The paper didn't say. Even if it was minimal, she could afford small improvements. A well on the place was financially out of her reach right now. She'd sunk most of her savings into the land and repairs on the old cabin—

which still wasn't completed, but more livable than it had been. The money could tide her over so she didn't have to get another job. She'd had just about every position in Limonero. There weren't many options left open to her.

With a tired hand, she smoothed her brow and straightened her shoulders to relieve the ache. She gazed at the flyer once more. John Wolcott had one of these. Maybe everybody in town did.

Deadline—December twenty-fourth at midnight.

She had eight days.

Thoughts about going to bed vanished. The image of holly bushes loaded with big scarlet berries pulled at her. She knew just the spot. Down by the first barranca across from Santa Paula Creek where willow patches grew.

Going quickly to the kitchen counter, she snatched her gardening basket; it was an old lunch hamper, but sound and sturdy with a lid. The inside could hold a lot of berries.

Isabel was going to win that contest.

Calco Oil had started a spur out to Dutch Flat No. 3, but abandoned it when the well went dry after six months.

With a slice of moon beaming light down, John followed the length of iron railroad track. He'd slung his pillow slip over his shoulder and walked with hands shoved deep into his pockets. The wind flared up every now and then, but without any kind of cool bite.

He would rather have been drinking tequila, but the contest's lure had been too much for him to forget about. His third drink had come before he'd finally read the paper. *Riches beyond your wildest dreams. The key to eternal happiness. Prosper in a way you never thought possible.* No wonder the Republic had been deserted.

This was just the kind of opportunity he'd been looking for—easy money, a way to cash in at the bank and sit back and spend it. He could win this contest. It wasn't hard to find berries. He knew where a cache of them grew: in various spots around the valley; some in the foothills; more patches over the ridge toward the beach. He would pick the bushes clean. Then after he got his reward, he'd draw up to the bar in the Republic, drink a beer, and ponder what to do with all that cash.

John wasn't opposed to hard work. He'd done it most of his life, first on his father's dirt farm in Texarkana, then across the western countryside. He never put down roots. No place interested him enough. But he liked California's climate. Every chance he got, he rode to the ocean to watch the sunset fall in a sizzling ball over the waves. Limonero he could call home.

That money could buy lumber, a band wheel, manila rope, a boiler, and a twelve horsepower engine. Building his own derrick and drilling for his own oil instead of sweating for Calco—now that would be something.

John let the idea gel as he walked across Santa Paula Creek.

As he wove up the path and stared hard for signs of holly bushes, a beacon of light flashed across his face for an instant. He froze. Whoever had shot him with the reflecting lamp hadn't realized he was there or they would have kept the beam on him. The person was moving. He could see the sway of the lamp's bright shaft as the sound of footsteps rose upward toward the slope.

John fell in behind the moving light, eyes widening as he recognized who held the handle.

Isabel.

Being in a state of semi-drunkeness, his attempt to quiet his footsteps didn't succeed. Isabel turned sharply, the lantern in her hand swaying outward with her movement. The brilliant white flame blinded him, and he swore beneath his breath. She lowered the beam. The manzanita-bordered path on which they stood was bathed in enough light for them to view one another.

They stared for a long moment.

He noticed she held a hamper and wore an apron but no hat. Her black hair had been plaited in a thick braid that rested against the pale curve of her neck and fell across her breast like a caress. He couldn't decipher the color of her eyes. But her face was prettier than he would have thought for a crazy woman, its shape a perfect oval, her lips with a kissable bow. The arch in her brows lifted in a way he thought sensual.

She spoke first, eyeing his pillowcase. "What are you doing here?"

"Same thing as you, I expect," he drawled, a leftover remnant of his native Texas slipping into his words.

"Well, do what you're going to do over there." She pointed beyond him. "I've already got a stake on this spot."

"Says who?"

"Says me. I'm ahead of you."

Waving the lantern between them, she showed him their positions—which was like writing up a thimble shot on a bar tab: There was no reason to. She didn't own the ground. He could go wherever he damn well pleased.

"Just by one step," he said, then cut the space with a long stride. "Now we're even. What are you going to do about it?"

Her frown made her lips go pouty. He lowered his eyes and stared. She had a tempting mouth. They stood close enough that he could feel the slow fire from the lamp heating his thigh. At least he figured it was the kerosene flame. He'd never burned up over a woman before.

She breathed lightly between parted lips. "I'm going to ignore you."

Lost in the fullness of her mouth, he'd forgotten what he'd asked her and was slow to figure out what she meant. Her words hit him when she walked away and took the light with her. Like an idiot, he stood in the darkness.

A breeze knocked the pillowcase off his shoulder. He still didn't move. Then he muttered an oath, bent to pick up his sack and followed her.

Isabel could hear him coming closer. She did her best not to let him know she knew he was there. But it was very difficult. His presence took up the night and filled it with a commanding air of virility.

He was taller than she'd thought. He stood a full head higher than her. She hadn't been prepared for the tingling in the pit of her stomach when she'd looked into his face. The reaction disturbed her. Handsome didn't begin to describe his features. Even in the muted light, she could see the power in his face—the square jaw that had thrust forward, straight forehead, and mouth firm and sensual.

Her husband had been a good-looking man. They'd been married less than a year when he disappeared one day. He hadn't snuck off. In fact, he'd been seen in a variety of places before he'd gone to San Diego. She gave him two years to come back. He didn't, so she filed for divorce on the grounds of abandonment. It was a hard cross to bear, and now she was wary of men.

She didn't hate them. But after her disastrous experience with marriage, she was cautious and protected her heart. She'd never be hurt in such a manner again.

From the corner of her eyes, she could see John climbing the embankment to the bushes. He appeared granitelike, unyielding. The set of his shoulders told her he didn't like being told what do to. Still—she'd been here first.

The lower hillside and opposite bank of the Santa Paula had been thick with people going after the berries, but she'd gone farther up to the willows because she knew more berries grew there. Obviously John knew it, too.

Isabel raised her light and shone it on the glossy shrubbery. The California holly had leathery leaves with bristle-pointed teeth. She'd brought her gloves with her so she wouldn't get pricked. She'd also packed a canteen of water, a biscuit and jam, and hard lemon candy to keep her throat from parching.

Lowering the lamp, she did her best to forget that John was thrashing around in the bushes. She chose the left side of the patch while he chose the right.

She had a crisp view of her work area, while her competitor foraged in near dark. Unbidden, a smile snagged the corner of Isabel's mouth. She tried to bite it back, but couldn't. His arrogance over deeming the ground fair game nettled her, and she liked having pulled a small something over on him: intelligence.

He was a nitwit for not bringing light and food. He must not have expected to be out here long. She, on the other hand, was equipped to stay up the entire night.

Isabel went to work, keeping her mind occupied by thoughts of the prize and what she would do with the money. Later on, she made a check of the time on the watch pinned to her bodice. She noted the three o'clock hour and forced herself to endure. There were a lot more berries to collect.

Her back ached from bending over. Her knees felt

bruised, even though she'd thought to bring a small braided rug on which to kneel.

As the night wore on, she and John sidled closer and closer toward the center. Not a word passed between them. Fine with her.

He swore a lot, and yanked the berries off rather than plucking. She bet he squashed quite a few.

Seeing her creep up to his position, John gave her what appeared to be a scowl. It was hard to tell. She was tempted to beam the light on him to check for certain and call him out on his audacity. Then he did something that caused her to gasp.

He jolted sideways toward the bush she was going to pick from and blocked it from her with his well-muscled legs.

Staking his claim, he announced, "This one's on my side."

Isabel set her hamper down. "There are no sides."

"There are now."

She folded her arms beneath her breasts. Making an ownership argument out of a public berry bush was beneath her, so she merely bent, opened her rug, and sat down. She took out the biscuit thick with jam and drank some water.

She did gain a small amount of satisfaction while watching John sweat and wipe his forehead, then lick his lips as if he were dying of thirst. Once, he eyed her canteen, and she took a long, exaggerated drink. Then she brushed the crumbs from her lap and rose.

"I know who you are." John's resonant voice broke through the night.

Her skepticism couldn't be contained. "Do you?"

"Isabel Burche."

Packing away her things, she returned, "Well I know who you are, too."

"Is that a fact?"

"John Wolcott."

He lifted his pillowcase. "Now that we've got each other's names out of the way, that's all we have to know about one another. That—and the fact that I'm going to win this contest."

"I agree about the name part. But it'll be me who wins."

"Don't think so."

"Why's that?"

"Because now I'm ahead of *you*." On that, he headed down the hillside with an easygoing stride, that pillowcase of his all knobby and filled to plumpness with berries.

Isabel fell in behind him and kept her distance. She hoped he'd trip—the arrogance of the man.

Shining her light on the ground as she walked, Isabel minded her steps. At first, she couldn't be sure, but then, not only one but three . . . then four . . . a half dozen, then one-two-five-ten . . . sixteen! Berries! Bright red berries! The rolling fruits were littering the dirt trail!

She paused and shone the light ahead of her to John Wolcott's back. With each step, the pillow slip bounced against his right shoulder. And with each bounce, a sprinkle of berries fell through a hole on the bottom of his sack.

Isabel wanted to laugh. She quickly crouched down, scooped up the berries, and dumped them into her hamper. She scrambled a few feet ahead and did the same thing, cringing when the wicker hinge on her basket creaked.

Working with nimble fingers, she alternated her gaze between the strewn berries and John's retreating silhouette. Surely he'd feel his sack growing as flat as a pancake. She quickly stood, stepping on a twig and crunching it beneath her heel. The corner of her hamper crashed into a manzanita bush, making an awful rustling sound. Before she could rush ahead and collect the next batch of strays, John looked over his shoulder to glare at her.

She acted fast and knocked the light off the evidence-bearing trail. Aiming the beam on him, she saw a wide arc of berries fly out of his pillowcase as he swung around.

"What in the hell are you doing?" He brought a hand up to keep the bright light out of his eyes.

"Nothing," she said flatly.

"You're walking funny. I can hear it."

"I'm walking the way I always walk. You wouldn't know because you don't know me. . . . How I walk, that is."

"Get that damn light out of my face. You're blinding me."

Isabel shot the reflecting lamp's bright shaft toward the hillside, purposefully avoiding the path.

"No wonder you're walking funny, you can't see where

you're going." He took a step toward her. Her eyes widened. She couldn't let him come back up the trail. He might find the berries. She ran down to meet him and nearly crashed into his chest. She would have if he hadn't grabbed her wrist—the very hand that held the lantern. The beam swayed back and forth over the sage and mustard weed.

Isabel stared into his shadowed face, glad she couldn't see his expression clearly. Her heartbeat tripped against her ribs. She felt utterly foolish. Under any other circumstances, she wouldn't have thrown herself at him.

John's fingers were warm and strong around her. She hoped he couldn't detect the erratic thrum of her pulse. His voice went through her with a husky grate. "What's the matter with you?"

She couldn't tell him. She needed a diversion. Turning her head toward the hillside, she exclaimed, "Oh—look! There's a rabbit."

"So what?"

Slowly she faced him once more. "I thought you might want to shoot it."

He released her, suspicion in his tone. "I'm not wearing a gun. Besides, why would I want to shoot a rabbit?"

"For your dinner."

"I eat dinner at the café."

"Oh . . ."

"I always knew you were . . ." The thought trailed off.

Isabel frowned. *He always knew she was . . . what?* He couldn't possibly know a thing about her.

"Stay the hell away from me," he barked, then swung around once more.

With his motion, Isabel was peppered with berries. They hit her bodice, shoulder, and one on her cheek. He disappeared, and she had a good mind to holler out good riddance. But she kept quiet. She had one up on him.

As soon as she felt it safe to move, she foraged the hillside for the berries that had scattered; then she resumed her clean sweep of the path.

All the way down the hill, Isabel picked up John's fallen berries and claimed them for her own. Yes, there was a great deal to say about being the wiser sex.

Women kept their pillowcases mended.

Two

"POUR ME A TEQUILA, SAUL." JOHN PROPPED HIS ELBOWS ON the Republic's bar and turned to acknowledge Duster Hobson, the only other patron in the saloon. The old-timer sat in one of the chairs at a table, too bowlegged to keep his foot on the brass rail. "Hey, Duster. Haven't seen you in a while."

"Went over to Ojai to visit with my sister." His chin glistened with snow white stubble, his hair the exact same color. A weathered hand lifted a beer bottle to his mouth.

John turned, his eyes following the drink as Saul put the shot glass in front of him. Sliding the coin beneath his fingertip, John paid the barkeep. Except Saul didn't remove his grasp from around the crystal rim. "Money's no good today. Twenty-five berries for the liquor."

"What was that?"

Saul motioned to the sign hanging above the cash register.

> *On account of the Jolly Holly Contest, the*
> *California Republic Saloon ain't taking money for*
> *the next seven days. All drinks are to be paid for with*
> *berries, at a predetermined price set by the barkeep.*
> *Yours truly, Saul*

John leveled his gaze back on Saul, who shrugged. "I've got a bar to run. I can't go out and scour the countryside for berries. I want to win as much as the next guy. This is how I'm going to do it. Some men just won't give up their liquor and they'll pay top berry to get a shot."

Irritability churned inside John. "Well, this is a hell of a way to run a bar." The drink sat not but three inches from him. He could smell the liquor. He could almost taste it.

189

John could let days pass without a drink. He wasn't dependent. Only today he didn't want to go without the fire burning sweetly across his tongue. Right now, he wanted that tequila. "Saul, I've got some berries at home. Float me for an hour and I'll bring them by."

Saul's hand didn't flinch. "Sorry, John. No berry credit."

The glass began to slide back, away from John's reach. He swore up a storm inside his head. He yanked his hat off, creased the crown, then smashed it back on. Thumping his boot off the rail, he turned around.

Duster's face lit up as he enjoyed his cold one. John scrutinized the bottle.

"Duster, can you loan me twenty-five berries?"

Setting the beer down, Duster leaned back in his chair. "I'm a man of few needs. Never carry extra money or berries on me. Goes against the simplicity of my nature."

"Well dammit all."

John strode through the saloon, shoved at the batwing doors, and slumped a shoulder against the boardwalk post.

The irony of it was—*he had cash!* The morning after a payday he was almost always flat busted. But since he'd left the Republic early last night, he'd left with money in his pocket.

And he had berries, too. What was left of the big cleanup he made.

John shot Isabel Burche's rundown cabin a frown.

Crazy Isabel had stolen the berries he'd picked. John figured that out when he got back into town early that morning, dropped his pillowcase on the bed, and stepped on a few berries at his feet. The sack had a hole in the bottom. Not so big he lost everything he'd gathered—but a good part of it. All that fumbling behind him had been Isabel picking up what had dropped.

Then when she'd slammed into him . . . for a moment he'd thought she might be a tad attracted to him and flaunting it. Not that he wanted to attract a walnut.

John's eyes hardened as he remembered her words. Rabbit his butt.

Damn . . . but he had to give her credit for ingenuity.

Rubbing his jaw and the bristly growth of day-old beard at his chin, John pondered his next move.

He'd slept half the morning away, right into the afternoon. He missed going out to Ferndale No. 8 and working on the rig. But he wasn't worried Calco would give him the boot. John knew so much about drilling, he had a job whenever he wanted one. He could man every hand position: tool pusher, floor, lead tong, chain, and derrick.

Seeing as he had the berries at his place—a small bungalow off Grove—he could walk home, get them, and sit in the Republic for a while and think up a plan for going after more berries.

He spied Isabel leaving her house, a hamper hooked in the crook of her arm. She had a sneaky air about her as she walked swiftly out of town on the main road, then veered off on Junipero Avenue—a long and dusty country lane that led up to Chumash Mountain. And Chumash Mountain, on the eastern side, was chock-full of holly bushes.

John pushed away from the awning post and made a run for the livery, striding over the golf ball rolling down the powdery street.

Isabel stopped her climb to take a drink of lemonade and dab her forehead with a handkerchief. She'd almost made it to the little bluff on Chumash Mountain. Gazing at the valley below her, she saw most of Limonero's rooftops and a few of the streets—and the Sun-Blessed Growers Association's endless lemon tree groves.

She had a job there once that lasted nearly four months. She'd been let go for excessive peel polishing before packing. But the lemons had looked so much better with the pretty yellow sheen to them.

As she proceeded, Isabel kept a close watch for contest competitors. She'd encountered parties of berry pickers on the town side of Junipero Avenue. This area of the mountainside was remote so she felt fairly confident she wouldn't be discovered. A person would have to walk over three hours to reach it or ride on horseback.

Isabel didn't have a horse.

A corner of shale jutted from the mountain, and just around its bend: holly bushes. Ignoring the perspiration gathered on her upper lip, Isabel continued. At the turning point, she stopped in her tracks. There on the bluff, sitting on his duff, lazed John Wolcott.

He had the audacity to wave at her.

Trudging forward, Isabel drew up to him and cast John in her body shade. If she allowed herself a small consolation, his face appeared sun-browned to crispness beneath the brim of his hat; his wide hands sported numerous fresh scratches from holly leaf spines. His legs were casually spread, and the boulder he sat on also had a pair of saddlebags as large as the long defunct Pony Express's mail pouches. One had its flap open, exposing the hoard of berries inside.

"You've been busy, I see," she managed in a tone tight with agitation. *How had he known about Chumash Mountain?*

He injected his reply with accusation. "I had to make up for all the berries that fell out of my sack and *somehow* got *lost.*"

Isabel feigned an air of innocence. "How did you get up here ahead of me? I saw you at the Republic three hours ago."

The lopsided grin he gave her would have been bone-melting if it had come from anyone but him. "I have a horse. He's tethered up there." He tilted his head toward his left.

"I didn't think you owned anything."

His mouth fell in a grim line. "What the hell's that supposed to mean?"

Scanning the bushes to see if he'd left her any berries, Isabel vaguely commented, "You aren't ambitious. You spend more time in that bar than any other place." Her eyes landed back on him. "And you dress like a tramp."

John gave himself a cursory inspection.

He wore denim pants so thin in the knees the indigo had faded to pale blue. His shirt had been rolled up at the sleeves, the thread for the hem missing.

"I like comfort."

"You like liquor and loafing," she muttered beneath her breath, the breeze snatching her words.

"What was that?"

"I'm not going to stand here loafing."

Isabel went past him and inspected the bushes. Very few berries were left. Either others had been here earlier, or John had shucked them naked. Since she'd come all this way, she began to pick what little there was.

Every once in a while, she checked to see if John still reclined on the boulder. He did. And she felt he dissected her every move. It was unsettling. Why didn't he just leave?

When she'd finished, she quenched her thirst with a long drink of lemonade. As she lowered the canteen, she noted John's gaze lowering as well. It was affixed to the canteen.

She walked toward him. "Did you forget to bring provisions again?"

"I left in a hurry."

Inhaling and straightening the kink from her spine, she bit her lower lip in contemplation. Then she slowly extended her arm. "Here."

"Obliged."

John took the canteen and drank. When he lifted his chin, she noticed for the first time that his eyes were gray-blue, like campfire smoke in twilight. Eyelashes the same tawny brown as his hair framed his eyes.

Just as she was admiring his handsome face and admonishing herself for doing so, his mouth soured. "What is this?" He grimaced so visibly, she grew offended.

"Lemonade."

"I was expecting water." He handed the canteen back.

"Next time, don't expect anything."

He rose to his feet, towering over her with his inordinate height. He looked down into her face, and she was helpless to turn away. There was something about him that just naturally pulled her toward him, an invisible magnetism that exuded more masculinity than a traveling rodeo's paste-up poster. "I apologize, Miss Isabel."

She hadn't expected that from him. To her dismay, the heat of a blush stole onto her cheeks. Anxious to escape from his arresting presence, she snatched her hamper and began walking down the hill but dreaded every step of the walk in this unrelenting heat.

She'd barely gotten past the bend when the methodic clop

of hooves sounded behind her. John and his horse fell in sync with her steps.

"Damn hot afternoon," he commented, pushing his hat back with his thumb. "One wouldn't think Christmas was coming."

Isabel held her tongue and kept on walking.

"Saw a lot of folks in town with baskets and the like going after the berries."

She kept silent.

"They're wasting their time. I'm going to win."

Minding her footing, her eyes remained on the trail.

"Probably buy me a plot of land and drill for oil. Calco isn't the only outfit in town who can get rich off petroleum."

The horse nickered.

"You aim to walk all the way back or are you going to let me give you a ride?"

"I didn't know you were offering."

"I was hoping you'd take the hint when I was talking."

"I didn't know talking meant offering."

"It does." He steered around a manzanita, then back next to her once more. "So are you?"

Isabel thought of the time it would take her to return to her cabin—precious too much of it. The sun would be going down in another two hours. If she got home ahead of it, she could water her trees. However much she didn't want to be beholden to John, she had to think of her future business.

Slowing to a stop, she nodded.

John reined the horse to a halt, then held out his palm. Grasping it, she gave a slight hop as he propelled her upward in front of him into the saddle. She landed with a small cry as he tucked her in tight, both her legs dangling off to one side.

His thighs were hard as steel against her bottom. She clutched her basket to her breasts as an unconscious defense against the tension winding through her. As much as she wanted to deny it, he was all man.

As he nudged the horse forward, she tensed with the swaying jolt and would have grabbed the horn had she a free hand. Instead, John's arm came around her midriff to steady her. The mere touch of his hand sent warm shivers through her.

They rode the way back without speaking, Isabel sitting rigid and making her joints ache. Once they came to her porch, she slipped out of the saddle so fast he didn't have the chance to give her aid.

"Well . . . thanks," she said climbing her rickety steps to put as much distance in between them as she could. She still clutched her wicker hamper as if it were a shield against him.

"I'll say it was my pleasure and that I hope our paths never cross again."

Isabel lowered her chin so her hat brim could keep the sun from her eyes. "I hope likewise."

Then he turned around and loped down her lane, kicking up clouds of dust.

Only after he disappeared, did she lower the basket to the porch and let her muscles go slack. Needing something to take the dryness out of her throat, she unscrewed the cap to the canteen and drank. Once her mouth touched the opening, she remembered John Wolcott's lips had been on it.

Bringing the canteen in front of her to look at, she thought about wiping off the rim. Rather than do that, she slowly brought it back to her lips, closed her eyes, and drank . . . swearing she could taste his mouth. . . .

All the while she ignored the heat that coiled in her stomach.

John had thought to get one up on Isabel by beating her to the top of Chumash Mountain, but now he wasn't so sure he'd outfoxed her. She'd turned the tables on him with that heavy-lashed gaze of hers that could make a man forget he'd ever looked at another woman.

Her eyes were the shade of coastal lupines . . . a blue yet violet. He'd never seen such an eye color in a person. Each time she gazed in his direction he felt as if he ought to give up liquor, buy a new set of clothes, and swear undying love for her.

Now if that wasn't stupid.

She'd worked at the Blossom, of all places—the town whorehouse. Newt had had a good ol' time with her. Unbidden, the image of Newt and Isabel in a room up at the

Blossom came to him. The picture put a twist in his belly and made his teeth ache where he clenched them. John wondered how many times Newt had kissed her full mouth . . . how many times he'd . . .

John made himself shrug out of the thought. He had more important matters on his mind, namely winning the Jolly Holly contest.

The day had dawned sunny and bright. Not a single breeze. Air hung low in the sky, warming the rocks and trails through the valley. John sat astride his horse wearing a shirt with the sleeves cut short, a bandanna around his forehead—his beat-up Stetson over that, and a pair of worse-for-wear cotton duck pants.

He was headed for Oak Grove Gulch, an out-of-the-way place known only to those who'd come across it by accident—which was damn few, as the grassy ravine was off the beaten path by many miles. The ride was a good half day, but worth the effort. The hills were covered with holly bushes.

Steering clear of an outcropping of boulders that had slid down the mountain, John reined in and then gave his horse some spur. Just over the other side of this ridge and he would be there.

A whorl of dust caught his eye. From the west, a horse and rider approached at what seemed a fair gait. Slowing, John squinted against the sun; then he swore up a blue streak when he made out who it was bearing down on him.

He damned his luck—or lack of it, and rested his forearms on the pommel of his saddle. There was no sense in proceeding. They were both going in the same direction.

Dust clouds swept over the ridge as Isabel slowed her horse. John gave the animal a cursory inspection, then swallowed a laugh as he stared at the rider.

Isabel wore a split skirt and boots, and a blouse that defined her every curve. If he hadn't been gaping at the slow rise and fall of her breasts, he would have seen the fire in her eyes before her words ignited him.

"*You!* You're following me."

He took offense and leaned toward his left the better to view her, to see the blush of pink across her cheeks and the column of her throat. "You've got that turned around. You're following me."

"I don't think so. How come you keep ending up in the same place I'm at?"

"How come you keep ending up in the same place *I'm* at?" he shot back.

Isabel sat straighter, glaring ahead at the terrain—the same terrain they seemed destined both to cover. Now why in the hell was that? There had to be a reason. The only person who knew this country like the back of his hand was . . .

John faced her. "You know Duster Hobson?"

Quizzically, her eyes widened. "You know Duster Hobson?"

"I just asked that. And I'm still waiting for your answer."

"I know him. He was at the Blossom when I was . . ." The sentence trailed off.

John grew unexplainably angry. Had she acquainted herself with Duster as well as Newt?

"Why do you want to know?" she questioned.

"When Duster's not at the Blossom, he's at the Republic." Were his words as peppered as he thought, or had he imagined jealousy oozed from his tone?

"Well, now that we got that straight—what does knowing Duster have to do with us both being here?"

"I think you know the answer to that."

"Do I?"

"Duster talks a lot."

"Yes, he does. About the landscape."

"Got that right. He used to hold up stages in these parts."

"He did?"

"Hell yes. Why do you think he knows the landscape?"

"I assumed he knew it because he used to drill for oil . . . and came up dry all the time. That's why they call him Duster."

"That reputation came a long time after he gave up his illegal ways."

"Why . . . I never would have figured Duster for an outlaw. He's just too sweet."

John grew annoyed by the way she stuck up for the old

man. "Well, some people can lead a surprising life. And Duster's one of them. He goes on and on about this rock cut and that creek—"

"—this ridge and that ravine . . ."

"Where white alder grows and where purple sage is thickest."

Isabel nodded. "And where black sage is compact or junipers are the tallest." She gave an audible sigh. "Rigby Glen."

He knew the spot—the next logical place to search for hollies if a man . . . or a woman . . . had been listening to Duster go on. After that—John threw up his hands in resignation. "Foster's Hideout."

"And the day after . . . ?" Isabel baited him, but he remained quiet.

Then after a long pause, they both said: "Moontide Ridge."

"Well, damn," John muttered.

"Damn," Isabel seconded, surprising him. "No wonder we keep stepping over each other. We both think like Duster."

Isabel plucked her gloves off, wet the kerchief at her neck with water from a canteen, and wiped the damp cloth over her cheeks, nose, and mouth. He watched in fascination. Then he fixed his stare on her horse weighted down with ungainly panniers—a much safer target for his preoccupation.

"That's the sorriest horse I've ever seen."

The liver-spotted nag with a swayback deeper than a gully, and knock-kneed to boot, looked ready to keel over.

"It's a rental," Isabel replied.

"It's a standing corpse."

"Well, she was free for the day." Her lips pursed. "Or almost free."

"How many berries did she cost you?" John had seen the livery tacking up a big sign out front saying deals would now be made berries on the barrel or no deal at all.

Isabel's face lit up, as if she felt real proud of herself. He liked the spirit and merriment in her eyes; they made her look lively. "She didn't cost me any berries. Just a case of my lemon syrup. I wanted a pretty piebald mare, but the livery said she was two hundred and forty-eight berries for a day's use. Highway robbery."

"Yep, it was highway robbery to give you this one."

"Well, I didn't have to give up a single berry for her, so she's good enough for me."

He wondered about her lemon syrup, but not enough to ask her about it right now. The problem at hand took precedence.

"Seems we're bound to keep tripping over one another."

"Seems like it."

The reins in his fingers tugged as his horse shook his head. John looked down, thought a minute, then looked up into Isabel's expectant face. Even though his plan made sense, his words surprised him. "We could work together."

Wariness crept into her features. "How so?"

"Collect the berries together, then split the prize money down the middle. Fifty-fifty."

She pondered this with a gnawing of her lush lower lip, then a gaze at the sky where a condor soared overhead. After a moment, she stared at him. "How do we know this Bellamy Nicklaus is for real? Has anybody seen him?"

"Somebody's had to. Lights go on and off in that house at night. That I've seen for myself."

"Well, what if this contest is a hoax?"

"Can't be a hoax. I've heard it said Nicklaus is the main man for Calco Oil."

"I heard he owns the Pacific Coastal Railroad."

"Whatever the case, he took that rundown house on Ninth and turned it into a show palace overnight. That takes money and power. He's some big man from someplace, and for reasons I'm not going to question, he's willing to part with a bundle of his cash." John adjusted his hat against the afternoon glare. "You may think a lot of lowdown things about me, but I've never battled a woman. The best thing would be for us to pair up."

"As much as I hate to admit it . . . you may be right." She tucked a wisp of hair behind her ear, then slapped the dust off her gloves against her thigh. "But there's a problem with your plan."

199

"Which is?"

"We don't trust each other." She laid the gloves next to the fork of her saddle. "Where do we keep the berries?"

John mulled this over. She had a point. They didn't trust each other. She'd no sooner have him hold the berries than he would her. So where to put them as they built up their store?

The idea of hiding them out in the countryside didn't thrill him. Animals might come across the cache and have a real feast. The possibility of discovery was even stronger out in the open without being guarded—not to mention that berries shouldn't be in the heat. A dark cool place was best—like beneath the floorboards of his bungalow . . . or the inside of a cabin—where they would be behind a locked door.

It was a choice between the two. But before he made up his mind, he had to know if she was playing with a full deck.

"Why are you growing trees in dirt that's no more than rocks? And with no water on your property?" He refrained from adding: Only a crazy person would do such a thing.

She bristled, her posture going erect. "My trees aren't planted in rocks. I cleared every last one from that bed. And I'll get a well just as soon as I can afford to have one dug—which will be when I get the contest money. I know there's water. Then I'll have a lot of lemons and I'm going to sell lemon syrup."

He gave her a sidelong stare, thinking over her explanation. She seemed to know what she was doing and her efforts weren't misguided. He liked lemon syrup on his pancakes. Knowing what she was up to greatly relieved him and gave him the reassurance he needed for what he had to say next.

Amid the buzz of grasshoppers, John asked, "What's your word worth to you?"

Isabel's violet eyes unflinchingly measured him. "Everything. My word is everything."

John eased back in the saddle. "Then we'll keep them at your place if you give me your word you won't take off with them."

"I give you my word."

"So, then, are you in?"

Slowly she replied, "I'm in."

"Partners," he said.

"Partners," she agreed, extending her hand.

John took the offering and they sealed the deal with a handshake.

Three

ISABEL DRIFTED AWAKE TO THE CHITTER OF FINCHES AND A WARM shaft of sunshine that spilled across her bed. Snug and drowsy, she didn't feel like getting up. Eyes still closed, she relived the dream that clung to the edges of her sleepy mind.

John Wolcott had been kissing her.

And she'd been kissing him back.

Rolling from her side, Isabel put her arm over her forehead. Dreams of such a passionate nature hadn't snuck up on her in longer than she could remember—and never as vivid a one as she'd had about John's mouth covering hers. It was as if he'd actually been kissing her. Her lips tingled even now.

With a lift of her hand, she ran her fingertips over the seam of her mouth. A kiss as tender and light as the breeze . . . that's how it had started. Then it turned to an intensity that sent spirals of ecstacy through her.

Reckless abandon, that's what it had been.

How could she? Even in a dream?

He was a good-for-nothing, a serenader to full moons— not the kind of man she wanted.

Isabel became aware of a tinny sound that didn't belong outside her window. Her heartbeat faltered. Sitting up and flipping her braid behind her, she grabbed the tiny derringer she kept in a bedside drawer. The gun wasn't very powerful, but it was enough to persuade any intruder to think twice about trespassing or harming her.

Not bothering to slip into her wrapper, she crept onto the porch and walked to the side of the house, pistol raised. She paused when she saw John.

He was watering the last lemon tree with her metal bucket. All the other trees had sloppy wet pools at the bases of their trunks. He must have been at this for hours. Why hadn't she heard him before?

Her mind had been too occupied with thoughts of kissing him . . . that's why.

Lifting his head, John spied her. The sides of his mouth curved down. "I didn't think you'd stoop this low."

Nonplused, she murmured, "What . . .?"

"Shoot me and take the berries for your own."

"I'd never do that." Indignation laced her reply. Isabel gazed at the gun, then at John. She lowered the pistol to her side. "I heard a noise. I didn't know it was you out here."

"Somebody had to get these trees watered if we're going to get an early start over to Rigby Glen. Half the damn morning's been wasted."

Embarrassment clutched Isabel. She normally did rise early. It still was early, by the looks of the sun. Usually she'd have been up by this hour and already had half her trees watered. That John had gone out of his way to help her . . . it just . . . well, the gesture flustered her. She didn't know what to make of him.

She caught him eyeing her nightgown with a smoldering stare. To be precise, he was eyeing the thin muslin covering her legs as the rays of sunlight poured through it left the fabric as transparent as white poppy petals.

"I'll get ready," she said and turned toward the house, unable to rid herself of the longing that gnawed inside her. With a single gaze, John made her feel like she ought to be in his arms.

Inside the cabin, Isabel collected herself and rushed to dress and pack a meal for the day. A couple hours later, they sat beneath a pungent eucalyptus eating the tortillas with brown sugar, powered cocoa, and cinnamon rolled into tubes that she'd made, and handfuls of dried apricots.

They'd gathered a good share of berries, having dodged a group to the south by riding west several miles, then doubling back in the higher country and heading for the glen undetected.

John had surprised her with that piebald mare she'd wanted—saddled and waiting in the yard next to his mount. When she asked him how he'd managed to get the horse when he'd given her all the berries, he wouldn't tell her. For a few flickering seconds, she wondered if he'd held out on her . . . if he'd kept some berries for his own vices.

She knew that nearly all the businesses in town were now taking only berries as payment. And she knew that John liked his liquor. . . . But she didn't press him for an answer. She had to trust him. They were partners now.

"Goin' to be a cooker today," John mentioned as he brought his leg up and rested his forearm on his knee.

His accent made her ask, "Where are you originally from?"

He turned toward her. They shared the small blanket she'd brought, John leaning his back against the eucalyptus trunk. "Texarkana, Texas."

"You sound like you're from Texas."

"Do I? I didn't think my drawl was that noticeable."

She shook her head while smiling softly.

"Where're you from?"

"Los Angeles," she replied.

Isabel faced forward and looked at the expanse of wide open country growing wild with lilac, spicebush, and California juniper. It was hard to believe that she'd actually lived in the city, been confined by brick buildings, the first motor cars, and street noises so loud she'd grown used to them.

"You lived alone?"

"No. With my sister and her husband."

She thought about the two years prior to her arrival in Limonero.

She'd been living in a tiny apartment with Kate and Andrew while working as a maid at the Hotel Ramona. As much as she loved her sister, Isabel found the close quarters disquieting, especially when tensions rose between the couple.

Having gone through a bad marriage herself, Isabel

hadn't wanted to add to Kate and Andrew's troubles by being in the way. So she'd packed her belongings, wished her sister well, and left on the first northbound train with the promise that she'd write. She did stay in touch, and was glad to hear the couple was working out their differences.

"Do you have family back in Texas?" she asked, folding her napkin and John's and putting them back in her picnic hamper.

"Nope. My dad and his new wife live in Mexico. My mother's dead. I've got a brother—Tom, who lives in Montana. I haven't seen him in ages." His expression grew distant, as if talking about his brother wasn't something he was used to. "You see your sister much?"

"No."

"Sometimes families just drift apart, I expect."

Quietly, she nodded.

They shared something, and it somewhat unsettled Isabel. Both of them had family; both of them were on their own. Both of them seemed to be . . . loners. She didn't like the word. She hated even using it on herself. But it was the truth. She didn't get close to people. The only person she could call a friend was Duster, and even so, she didn't see him as often as she used to. Except for that night in the Blossom, she hadn't sat with him for a long spell and had a conversation.

"You sure have had a slew of jobs since coming to town," John commented, pulling Isabel from her thoughts.

The dry inflection in his tone put a pebble in her shoe. It sounded as if he wondered what was wrong with her that she couldn't hold the same position for more than a few months.

"Yes, I have." She stared at him, daring him to make a smart remark.

He held his hands up in mock surrender. "Don't bite my head off. I was just making an observation. Hell, the same could be said about me."

"You're right. It sure could."

She'd seen him working at the feed and seed, the livery, repairing the engines Calco used on the rigs, and warming the bench in front of the Republic while eating peanuts and drinking beer. The latter was his favorite occupation.

Since he'd admitted to employment shortcomings, she was willing to let the subject go—until he added, "But at least I've worn my clothes in my jobs."

Pinning him with a glare, she choked, "What did you just say?"

"Think you heard me, Isabel." With that, he went to his feet. She shot up next to him.

"You have no call to be saying such a thing to me."

"Wasn't me who worked at the Blossom." His eyes locked with hers. If she could have calmed her jagged pulse for a moment and looked at him rationally, she would have seen the jealousy in his gaze. "And we know what kind of place that is."

"I suspect all of Limonero knows exactly what kind of place the Blossom is. And don't you try and tell me you've never been there. Jacaranda told me all about you."

John adjusted his Stetson—that habit of his; there was never anything wrong with the angle. He just rearranged the brim when he got mad and always set the crown exactly the way it had been before he messed with it. "She did? What in the deuce did she have to say?"

Isabel wasn't about to tell him that Jacaranda said *she* should have been paying *him* instead of the other way around. Jacaranda had claimed John was the best—

"Somebody's coming," John hissed between his teeth.

Snapping her chin up, Isabel searched the dull horizon. A dust cloud rose in a thin plume: one rider.

"Get on your horse."

Isabel protested. "But we haven't picked all the berries. Why let somebody else have the rest?"

He brought his face close to hers, his nose and forehead inches from her own. The smoldering fire of his blue eyes grounded her to the spot. She could smell the sweetness of cinnamon and cocoa on his breath. "It's not the berries on the bushes I'm worried about. It's the ones we already picked. Some people would do anything to win this contest, even if it means thievery at gunpoint. I don't know about you, but I don't feel like getting killed today."

* * *

They loaded the horses with their gear, and rather than ride out, John told Isabel to take the reins and follow his lead. Where they'd stopped for breakfast had been flanked by an outcropping of sandstone directly behind them. He knew of a narrow canyon inside that had been carved out by water some hundreds of years ago. The stream that meandered through it now was low, but crystal clear. He had a good mind to go swimming as soon as whoever the rider was had either passed this way and left, or got his fill of berries.

Guiding his horse around the twists and turns of the soft rock incline, John reached the top and tied off the reins, motioning Isabel to do likewise. Once their animals were secured, he crouched low and went to the ground. Crawling up to the edge of the cliff, he peered down at the scene below just as Isabel scooted next to him.

The flashy gray roan tipped him off as to who the rider was reining in and dismounting.

"It's Newt," John stated dully.

"Who?"

He flashed her a sideways stare. "Guess you didn't go by names."

Nudging toward him, she said, "I don't like what you're hinting at."

"I'm not hinting at anything." John kept his gaze fixed on Newt, who was in a hurry to pluck berries and throw them in a burlap sack. "Newt told me all about it."

"All about what?"

"You and him at the Blossom."

"There wasn't anything between me and him at the Blossom."

"Not what he told me."

The censure in her voice had slapped him as sure as if she'd used her hand. "Well there wasn't and he's a damn liar!" With that, she cuffed him for real and they both went sliding backward down the ledge.

He put a hand over her mouth to muffle her scream and she latched on to him with both hands on his shoulders. John lost his hat, swore, and yelled at Isabel to shut up. She kept on with her cries. He cupped his fingers tighter over her mouth; she bit him. He swore once more.

Looking about for a strong foothold to stop their decsent,

he wedged his boot into a flannel bush. They came to a sliding halt. Pebbles showered their heads and dust clogged the air.

John didn't remove his hand from her mouth and arm, fearful he'd reach for her throat if he did. She'd come after him as if she was some kind of crazy woman. To think, he'd watered her stupid lemon trees to help her out.

Hell, he'd thought she was sound—her reasoning about the lemon syrup and all. But he guessed he was wrong. She was still nutty and her hull had just cracked.

Violet eyes glowered at him; dusty lashes blinked in rapid succession. She was spitting mad. He couldn't release her yet.

"Now listen." He brought his nose smack up to hers. "If I let you go, you'd better not be screaming because these canyons carry noise—if Newt didn't hear us already. I've known him for a while, but I can't vouch for a man's character when money's at stake. No telling what he might do if he finds us up here. He travels with a Colt, and I don't want to be on the barrel end of it."

John gripped her arm tighter. "I'm going to take my hand off your mouth. If you open your lips to do more than whisper, you're going to be sorry."

Slowly, he pulled his hand away.

Isabel's nostrils flared. In a low voice, she ground out, "I was never one of the girls in the true sense."

Her words sluiced over him like warm rain after a drought, bringing solace and . . . relief. Why, he didn't want to confront. It shouldn't have mattered to him.

With brows furrowed, she asked, "What's this Newt look like?"

"Lanky. Sandy hair. Small gap between his front teeth. Chews tobacco."

To his surprise, she laughed. She rolled onto her back and softly laughed.

He kept his hand on her arm, only now he stretched across her waist . . . just below the swells of her breasts.

"Oh, him. I know who he is."

That niggling feeling rose in John again, green and ugly. She knew who Newt was.

207

She quieted her laughter and turned to him. "I locked Newt in the closet."

"What for?"

The mirth in her eyes faded. "Because I couldn't go through with it, that's why. I thought I could."

John eased onto his side, but kept his arm draped over Isabel. She made no move to fling him off her. "Why'd you go there in the first place?"

"I was down on my luck and the Blossom seemed a sure way to improve it. All I was thinking about was the money." Her lashes swept down. "And that I wasn't giving anything up, so I had nothing to lose."

The implication came across clear. She wasn't a virgin.

"I wasn't cut out to be a floozie. I had to wear this scrap of silk Fern told me to put on. The skirt was lemon yellow and the bodice had white lace all over the top and straps—like blossoms. And it had lemon-scented sachets sewn into the hem. . . ."

John listened, but didn't really hear her. He was picturing Isabel in a yellow dress and smelling like lemon blossoms. Maybe with her inky black hair all curled and piled high on her head. If he'd been in the Blossom that night, he would have paid Fern whatever she wanted for a chance to be with Isabel. . . .

". . . Fern gave all the girls names the night I started. Said it was a costume party in honor of my . . . well—" A blush brought a stain of color to her cheeks. "My first time. She called me Miss Lemon Blossom. It was downright humiliating."

Watching her lips as she spoke, John grew mesmerized.

"I had to sit in the parlor and socialize. Then that friend of yours—Newt—he and Fern started talking, and the next thing I'm being told to go up to my room and he's following. Once inside, he starts getting all hands with me right away. I told him I kept a pretty wrapper in the closet and asked him to get it for me. Once he was in the door's opening, I shoved him inside and locked him in the closet."

In spite of the serious set of Isabel's brow, John couldn't help smiling. Newt must have blown a gasket.

"I can't imagine why he'd go around telling people that he

and I were . . . well, you know. That no-good bluffer. I ought to shoot him with my derringer."

"What did you expect him to say? Can't have a man go upstairs with a wh—" He cleared his throat. "A floozie, and then tell the local bartender he got locked in a closet. Wounds a man's pride. He had to say you were a real mer—" John cut his words short.

Isabel looked into his face. "I suppose he said a lot of indecent things about me."

John lied, "Not much," then slowly added, "No more than the deputy and foreman from Sun-Blessed."

Fire lit her eyes to amethysts. "They couldn't have boasted about getting any different treatment than Newt did. I handcuffed the deputy to the bed and left the foreman on the balcony. I let them all go after their hour was up."

Shrugging, she went on, "I thought they'd want their money back, but when Fern didn't stir up a fuss . . . I assumed they were too embarrassed to ask for a refund."

Her line of rationalization sounded convincing—*convincing* from a woman's point of view. But from a man's, that was another story. A man would never let on he'd been gypped out of his frolicking by a woman smarter than him. And John had to admit, Isabel was a smart woman.

"Then Duster came in," she said, brushing the talc off her white blouse now soiled with reddish dirt. "He didn't want a thing from me other than conversation. We stayed in the kitchen the rest of the night and drank coffee until sunup. After Fern closed the doors, I told her I quit and I walked out." Musing replaced the soft curve on her mouth. "It was the first time I wasn't fired from a job. No, wait . . . I take that back. I quit the Ramona Hotel. I guess it was the first time I wasn't fired from a job in Limonero."

She stated the fact without any grudge in her tone. Compassion overcame John's usual live-and-let-live manner. He wanted to console her.

John reached out and tucked a strand of hair behind her ear. The gesture felt natural, and he marveled in the glossy softness of the wisp. When she didn't swat at his hand, he let the sense of pleasure he'd been holding at bay work through him.

For a wavering few heartbeats, they shared an intense

physical interest in the other. They were focused only on each other's face, and John wanted to bring his mouth over hers but didn't want to move and lose the moment.

Then Isabel half-smiled and sat up. "I don't know why I told you all this."

As if a hot Santa Ana wind had come down on him, John's thoughts of kissing Isabel Burche evaporated. He pushed himself to sitting, knocking the twigs and sand from his pants legs.

John couldn't rid the tightness in his voice when he said, "I expect you'd have told somebody sometime."

"But I told you."

"Yep."

She heaved a great sigh. "I never have enough to do what I want. I thought working at the Blossom could give it to me."

"Money, you mean."

"Yes . . . money."

"I never have any extra either."

"That's why we *have* to win this contest."

For a haphazard couple of seconds, John had allowed himself to think Isabel was glad they were partners. But he wasn't so sure. Hell, she would probably have been better off if they weren't—because his mind wasn't clear at the moment. He was thinking of her more as a desirable woman and less of a fifty-fifty partner.

"Well, we aren't going to win it sitting on our duffs."

John got to his feet and held a hand down for Isabel. She grasped it, and he berated himself for reveling in her touch. Gruffly, he knocked the stems of flannel bush from her shoulder and hair, forcing himself not to feel.

"Best we make sure Newt's gone. Then we'll ride up farther and finish out the day."

She nodded.

A little later, they were on their horses. She rode in front of him. John got to watch the gentle motion of Isabel's shoulders; see the way the sun shone on her black braid; appreciate the outline of her backside in the split skirt she wore.

The view was worth all the stalls he'd be mucking out for the next couple of months in order to work off the loan of her piebald mare.

Four

JOHN BELLIED UP TO THE POLISHED BAR AT THE CALIFORNIA Republic Saloon and spilled twenty-five berries on the counter.

"Pour me a tequila, Saul."

As Saul went for the liquor, John avoided his reflection in the back bar's long mirror. It wasn't as if he couldn't face himself. He had every right to these berries. He'd gone on a late-night scout and had only picked the twenty-five needed for a midnight drink. He shouldn't be feeling guilty. There was no reason to share with Isabel. He'd thrown in everything else he picked. His intentions were still on the up and up.

But for right now, he needed the tequila to smooth over his rocky emotions.

He'd never been so . . . heroic . . . around a woman—first, getting her a horse by promising to shovel its apples, then making a half-dozen trips for water at dawn when he could have been catching a few extra winks in bed.

What had gotten into him?

No liquor is what. His brain had dried up. As soon as he had a drink, he'd be back to his old self. John licked his lips in anticipation.

Saul turned around, set the drink down, and slid it toward John.

"You can take your hands off the glass, Saul," John said confidently. "It's all there. Twenty-five berries. Count 'em if you don't trust me."

The barkeep's fingers remained on the shot glass's circumference. "I trust you, John. But tequila's gone up to fifty berries. Berry inflation."

John's spirits plummeted. "What was that?"

Motioning to the sign, Saul read, "All drinks are to be

paid for with berries, at a *predetermined* price set by the barkeep."

"Well, hell!" John erupted, removing his hat and then smashing it back on. "Pour me a damn beer then."

With quiet emphasis, Saul explained, "Beer's thirty berries."

"But I only have twenty-five berries!" Taking off his Stetson once more, he was vaguely aware of creasing the crown and resettling the brim over his forehead again. "Pour me a damn half a beer!"

"Sorry, John. No discounts."

Muttering a string of oaths, John stood.

Newt Slocum had the misfortune of entering the Republic with a grin on his mug. "Hey, John. Haven't seen you around."

Without a word, John coiled his arm back and hit Newt square on the jaw with a punch that sent him reeling backward into a limp heap. "That's for lying about Isabel."

Then John stormed out of the saloon and left thoughts of Newt behind.

Somebody was out to get him. He didn't know exactly who, but somewhere, somebody, was thinking this was a hell of a funny one to pull over on John Wolcott—shut off the tap to his liquor by decreasing the value of berries.

He shoved the swinging doors and stood on the darkened boardwalk. A thin moon spilled down on Main Street. In its pale milky cast, a golf ball flew past like a shooting star, diving into the horse trough in front of John. The force of its impact splashed him with murky water.

John took a sharp look to the right where the ball had come from.

Nothing stirred. He couldn't see anybody.

To the night shadows, he shouted, "I've got news for you, whoever you are! I'm not laughing!"

The speculative buzz in the growing crowd escalated the closer the hour got to noon. Isabel had heard Bellamy Nicklaus would be stepping onto his porch to announce the arrival of his Christmas tree—the very one the berries were going to decorate. Supposedly a big Douglas fir had been cut near Santa Barbara and was being shipped down on the Pacific Coastal Railroad.

Gazing at the freshly painted house with its old gold half-timbered gables, Indian red trim, straw body color, and medium brownstone roof, Isabel couldn't believe it was the same decrepit place it had been less than a week ago.

Box elder that had been overgrown and gangly was neatly clipped. Monkey flowers thick with sticky foliage and trumpet-shaped flowers in a colorful profusion bookended the house's sides leading to the front path. How had Bellamy managed to do so much overnight? It was as if he were . . . magic.

Through the gathering, a gray felt Stetson stood out above the rest catching Isabel's attention. John. Although a short distance separated them, she could see he hadn't slept well. His long hair had been combed behind his ears and he hadn't shaved. Their eyes briefly held, then she looked away, feeling inexplicably self-conscious. Yesterday, she'd known he'd wanted to kiss her. But she'd pretended not to notice, too afraid to let herself melt beneath his sensual gaze. Doing so would be easy. Effortless. But she'd have to live with the repercussions.

A hush fell over the group as soon as the *pop-pop* and *ca-pow* of a rarely-ever-seen-in-Limonero motor car sounded, putting in from Main Street. Isabel hadn't even heard the noon train's whistle announcing its arrival. And here came a dusty black Olds with a festive wreath mounted on the center headlamp.

Sticking up at least ten feet from the tonneau poked the tallest Christmas tree Isabel had ever seen, a fir with dense and fluffy foliage. The bluish-green needles spread all around the branches.

"Olds Motor Vehicle Company—Curved Dash model," the man next to Isabel said.

The fellow beside him added, "Nicklaus must have a bankroll. Only twelve of these have been made so far."

"You don't say."

"Four-point-five horsepower with a single cylinder engine of ninety-five-point-five cubic inches mounted horizontally under the seat."

"Bet it can really open up on the road with all that power."

"Yep. One of these beauties goes for six hundred and fifty simoleons."

In the driver's seat and commandeering the automobile sat an extremely tall and broad-shouldered man in a white touring duster. He was burly enough to be a prizefighter. The chap next to him was just as husky.

Everyone cleared an opening for the Olds to pull up at the house's picket gate. The two men hopped down and swaggered toward the front door. Isabel stood on tiptoe so she wouldn't miss anything.

"What do you make of all this?" John's deep voice tickled the shell of her ear, bringing a cascade of shivers out on her arms.

Turning her head toward him, she said, "I don't know what to make of it. I've never seen anything like this. Have you?"

"Reminds me of a Jig Top tent menagerie I went to with my brother. A lot of strange exhibitions."

"The front door's opening!" somebody shouted.

Isabel craned her neck to watch the door swing inward and a portly man fill its opening. A scotch plaid cap covered the snow white hair on his head. His bushy brows, full mustache, and long beard were the same aged hue. His plump cheeks had a ruddiness to them.

He wore argyle knickers and ribbed socks that sagged in spite of the elastic button-clasp garters holding them up to his pudgy knees. On his feet—felt house slippers. He smoked a pipe and dangled a metal, canelike stick in his hand.

My . . . but this Bellamy Nicklaus was an eccentric-looking man.

"Well, hell," John muttered at her side. "He's the guy who's been slicing chip shots at me."

"What?"

John didn't get the opportunity to answer. Bellamy began talking.

"Glad to see you folks came out to watch the arrival of my tree," he said with a chuckle. Then, to the gargantuan men, he announced, as the corners of his eyes creased with glee, "You've done a fine job, Yule and Tide. This one's even better than last year's when we were on Pago Pago. Sure do miss those prickly fruits—what were they?"

"Pineapples," Yule replied.

"*Ja,* pineapples," Tide seconded.

To the crowd, Bellamy enthusiastically smiled. "I hope you've all been busy gathering berries." He stared directly at John and Isabel. Mostly Isabel.

The bottom dropped from her stomach, as if she'd been on a swing and had gone too high, then plummeted backward. Nordic blue eyes reached inside her and touched her heart. She couldn't explain it. But immediately she felt a kindred spirit, a fondness . . . and even the overwhelming desire to tell him everything about herself.

But the way Bellamy looked at her, he already knew every detail of her life: that she had never really favored the pink hair ribbons she'd gotten for Christmas when she was seven—she'd wanted cardinal-colored ones like Kate; and that she'd fibbed to her mother about losing one of the bisque china dogs from her pug-dog family . . . when she'd really broken the puppy and hadn't wanted to get into trouble for taking the set outside when she'd been told not to; or the time she'd "borrowed"—but she'd given it back!—Mabel Ellen Littlefield's dolly with long curly real hair and moving glass eyes because the one she'd gotten Christmas morning had been muslin with yarn hair and button eyes.

A wave of guilt knocked at Isabel. Suddenly, she felt as if she needed to say she was sorry . . . to Bellamy Nicklaus.

Then Bellamy's gaze turned on John and she felt him tense. The two stared eye-to-eye a long moment, then John swore beneath his breath. He shifted his weight onto the other foot . . . stuck a hand in his pocket . . . removed the hand . . . took off his hat and fiddled with the crown, then fit it back on his head.

Bellamy returned his attention to the audience. "We're going to put up the tree today, and Mother has some trimmings she'll be using for decorations to spruce it up. All that will be left to hang on Christmas Eve will be the berry strings."

A surge of nods and smiles swam through the crowd.

"The lucky winner of the contest will be chosen that night. Mother has a keen head for numbers and can count them up quickly."

Again, Bellamy's eyes briefly met Isabel's and she didn't think it was an accident. It was as if he was sending her a message . . . a private one. He said he didn't need her to apologize. . . . He understood.

Yule and Tide took up shovels and began digging in the middle of the yard. Behind them were buckets of sand that would be used to fill in the hole and keep the tree from toppling.

As they worked, they spoke a foreign language that Bellamy chattered just as fluently. Then they came for the tree and hoisted it into their arms. It would have taken at least a half-dozen normal-sized men to lift it, but the two managed fine on their own.

Once the tree was secure, Bellamy clapped. This in turn, excited all the others in attendance to do so, too.

Isabel did.

John didn't. His glare lay hard on Bellamy.

"What's the matter with you?" she asked in a whisper.

Through a frown, he grated, "I don't like this guy."

"Why not? He seems so kindly."

"Kindly my butt. This is a circus. All we need is the fat lady."

At that moment, an ample-waisted woman with ash gray hair wearing spectacles and an apron over her dress appeared behind Bellamy. "Papa, are you ready for the trimmings?"

John raised his hands in resignation. "There you go. This is a farce. It's a damn joke."

He began to walk away, and as much as Isabel wanted to stay, she felt she should go after John.

Pushing her way through the crowd, she caught up with him as he stalked down the middle of Main Street.

"Forget it, Isabel. The jig's up. Bellamy's a crackpot. With a mashy club."

"With a what?"

"Mashy golf club. I've played the game before. This guy's brain is just as mashy as that club he's holding. The old bird has been duffing balls at me."

Isabel had to walk fast to keep up with John. "Him? Really . . . I don't think he'd hit you on purpose. He looks so . . . harmless."

"Harmless as a busted pump rod."

"But what if he really does have money he's giving away?" she reasoned. "We can't risk somebody else getting it."

He stopped and faced her. "Isabel. There is no money. The guy's flat busted after the renovations he made on that house. This Jolly Holly contest is a fake."

She understood why John was skeptical. Deep down she had her doubts as well. But there was something about Bellamy's eyes: the crinkling blue with lines in the corners; the warm depths; the merry cheeks; the way his tummy sort of shook when he laughed.

"You have to want him to be real," she said with firm conviction. "Bellamy Nicklaus's contest is all we have."

John pointed his forefinger toward the direction of the house on Ninth and Mill. "That guy reminds me of somebody."

"Me, too," she conceded. "But I can't put my finger on it."

"Yeah . . . like somebody I knew when I was a kid or something."

"Right . . ."

Rubbing the stubble at his jaw, he pondered aloud, "A lot of land swindlers in Texas when I was growing up. Could be he's one of them and this is his new scam. Holly berry contests."

"I doubt that. I grew up in Los Angeles, and I'm sure I know him. I think my mother and father showed me his picture . . . but I can't remember why."

"Too bad Limonero doesn't have a telephone. You could call them and ask them who this Bellamy is."

Unexpected tears filled her eyes. "My dad died some ten years ago. And my mother's been with him for three."

John let out his breath and laid a comforting hand on Isabel's shoulder. "Isabel . . . I'm sorry."

"You didn't know." She blinked her eyes, thinking her mother hadn't lived to see her become divorced. The shock of such a thing would have wounded her—even though Isabel had been deserted by her husband. Her mother had old values and old ideals. To her, marriage was forever no matter what.

Isabel was no longer a romantic woman. But that didn't mean she'd given up on love. She was hopeful that maybe one day she'd meet somebody . . . and he'd be everything her husband hadn't been.

Giving her shoulder a gentle squeeze, John lowered his arm. "Okay. We'll keep collecting the berries."

Gratitude made her smile bright.

John added, "But if Bellamy doesn't put up, I'm having the sheriff lock him behind bars."

"He'll make good on his word. I know it."

"All right. Pack for overnight. We're leaving for Foster's Hideout just as soon as we water those lemon trees of yours."

The hair on the back of John's neck still prickled as they rode through the narrow canyon. Bellamy Nicklaus had gotten to him, had unraveled him right out of his skin and muscles . . . had stared at him down to his bones.

John knew him.

And Bellamy had sorely disappointed him in the past.

But what exactly that past was . . . John couldn't be sure. It was too vague. Too cloudy. But he kept seeing a scene play out in his head.

He'd been about five or six. It was Christmas morning. His dad hadn't come home the night before, and he must have promised his mother because she'd kept a vigil at the window. That's where he and Tom had found her when they'd come down to see what was under the tree.

Nothing.

His mother had tried to make up for it by baking them special gingerbread cookies for breakfast. Then his father had finally come through the door and his parents had argued a long while; afterward, Dad had stormed outside and gone into the barn.

It was then John stopped believing that penny whistles and wind-up dancing bears and pull toys came from some magical being. They were from his dad. And his dad had drunk their gift money at the Lucky Spot bar. From then on, John had known Christmas was for dreamers.

As he nudged his horse onward, John reflected on the years after that winter day. He'd changed. Rather than being an optimist like his brother, he'd turned into a bitter young man. From then on, he knew he could never count on anyone but himself. Discovering he had a talent for a divining rod, John would make a little money from time to time.

Mostly he worked the fields with his father, giving his elder no more than a few words when necessary. He hated having the plow strapped on him, so much that one day he'd said he'd had enough and had never gotten behind one again.

He'd left Texarkana and made his own way, doing just enough to stay afloat. Enjoying a game of cards. A glass of liquor. The soft and willing flesh of a woman.

A disturbing musing filled John's head. How did he get to be so much like his father? Why couldn't he be more like his younger brother, Tom?

Tom, who was ambitious enough to open his own sporting goods store. Tom, who saved enough earnings for it to amount to something. Tom . . . to whom John owed a pocketful of money. Every time John asked his brother for a loan, Tom complied. When would he wise up and realize John would never pay him back?

John lived day to day. It had been the smell of flowing oil that had attracted him to Limonero. But what did he have to show for years of working for Calco? Not a damn thing.

When Bellamy had looked at him, a single word had played over and over in John's head, knotting him up with apprehension:

Change. Change. Change.

What did Nicklaus want him to do? Change his ways? How could he? It had taken him thirty-four years to get this way. He didn't know any other existence but the one that had him living by the seat of his pants.

Change. Change. Change.

The branches of valley oaks stretched overhead, framing Isabel as she rode through them. They traversed oil country—all of it owned by Calco. The vast spread of shale glistening with a rainbow of petroleum and water oozing from the slopes made John think. If he could just get enough money together and buy a piece of land . . . he could drill for himself . . . be rich . . . have something to offer a woman.

A woman like Isabel.

Where that thought came from John didn't want to go. He didn't even know her very well—other than to know she worked hard, was trustworthy, and was more pleasant to look at than the sunset over Ventura beach. And that was saying a lot, because he surely enjoyed that hour when the sun slipped into the ocean.

"How much farther?" Isabel called over her shoulder.

"Not that much. Across the creek and over that ridge." He pointed and her gaze followed his hand.

Along the hillside stretched an endless length of pipeline. Calco's. They'd finished it some five years back and saved a bundle on transporting fees through the railroad. The oil flowed from the fields all the way to the pier in Santa Barbara, making for one hell of an enterprise.

The distant gallop of horses caught John's ear in the windless canyon. The cliffs and large grove of oaks muffled sound, so the horses had to be well inside the canyon's mouth for John to hear them. They were close. Too close. He didn't want anyone giving them a run for the berries, so he trotted up to Isabel.

"We're crossing here." He steered his horse down the incline, Isabel falling in behind.

As he cantered toward the water, he flushed a flock of buzzards looking for a little wind to ride up over the ridge. But nothing moved down here except dust and heat. Not even the gunmetal layer of clouds that hung low in the sky could give any respite from the simmering air. Rain would be a salvation. And while he thought it, several fat drops hit him on the face and arms. John didn't want to be near the creek when the downpour hit. Flash floods could strike swiftly.

He urged his horse fast up the incline, making sure Isabel could keep up. He didn't see the riders behind them, but a swirl of dirt rose from an area in the canyon about a mile back. Whoever else was on the berry chase wasn't that far away.

Isabel caught up to him and they rode side-by-side in the peppering rain. "Do you think we're being followed?"

"Not followed. It's just that there aren't any bushes left around Limonero that have berries. People have to spread out. And after that speech Bellamy gave, I reckon the frenzy is only going to get worse."

Although he hadn't heard all of what Bellamy had to say, whatever it was had put the angst of a stirred beehive into town. When he and Isabel rode out the main street, shop windows had been painted with signs offering a penny for every berry brought into the store. The mercantile had upped their payment to two cents for every berry. And the Republic had done one even better—three cents.

While exiting Limonero, voices had been raised with excitement. Some said Bellamy was giving away five hundred dollars in gold. Others claimed it was one thousand in cash. Another assured the prize was the key to Bellamy's house. As the speculation increased, so did the fervor.

That was why John had buckled on a gun belt with a loaded Remington in the holster. He wasn't about to get shot over berries. Nor was he about to let anything happen to Isabel.

The need to protect her welled inside him and he rather liked the feeling. It made him think he had a worthwhile purpose, something important and more of a cause than sitting in the Republic drinking beer.

After a few miles, the climb grew steep and the oaks gave way to evergreens. A meadow loomed ahead, and with the rain coming down as hard as it was, John decided to make camp here on the sleek grass.

He reined in and dismounted. Keeping hold of his leathers, he dipped under his horse's neck and went to help Isabel. She was light in his arms as she sprung to the ground. He would have lingered a moment if it hadn't been for the need to put up the tent.

"Hobble the horses," he directed, his gaze on the rain-drops clinging to her full mouth.

She set out to do so.

John began cutting poles for the tent and worked fast to stake it down. When he was finished, both he and Isabel were soaked through.

Sitting beneath the canvas and listening to the pulse of rain, John tucked a striped Mexican blanket around Isabel's shoulders.

"Cold?" he asked.

"No. The rain's warm."

Her hair had come loose from its twist. She lifted the length from beneath the blanket and the glossy black hair fell in a wet river down her back. He wished he had a brush on him . . . he would have liked to run it through her hair to get the tangles out.

She gazed through the part in the tent flaps, sitting Indian style and with a pensive set to her profile.

With a leisurely sweep of his eyes, John admired the beautiful view. Then he asked something he'd never asked a woman before—because he'd never cared . . . until now. "What are you thinking, Isabel?"

A soft smile overtook her mouth. "I was thinking about how I got here."

He grew puzzled a moment, then realized she meant the grander picture. Not here on the meadow . . . but here as in her life.

"Why's that?"

"Well . . ." She licked her lips, and as she blinked, dewy sweet rain fringed her lashes. "I'd planned to be a modern woman. A teacher, to be exact." She gave him a quick glance to look for his reaction.

He had none that was ill-willed. He thought being a teacher was an admirable thing. But he just couldn't imagine Isabel hiding her womanly figure in a shapeless crow-black dress and with a severe bun in her hair for the rest of her youthful years. "And once I was a teacher," she continued, "I was going to save all my money and every summer I'd travel and go on a grand tour of Europe. While in Rome, I'd sit in the piazza and write poetry. Then I'd pen a novel while staying in an English cottage." Her expression fell somber; the luster left her eyes. "And I'd never have to do the will of a man . . . because I'd be independent and happy."

At that, any hope John had of them together dimmed. In a voice brittle with disappointment, he asked, "What happened?"

She slowly turned toward him. "I got married."

five

THERE WAS NO REASON FOR ISABEL TO TELL JOHN ABOUT HER marriage . . . other than she had to know if he'd look down on her for it, if he'd find her unappealing. She'd been fast denying the feelings for him that had been blooming inside her since he'd almost kissed her at Rigby Glen. She'd wanted him to. She wanted him to now.

But he had to know who she was.

A lot of men were put off by divorced women. Not that she'd told a lot of men. In fact, John was only the second person she had told, Duster being the first, in that long night spent at the Blossom's kitchen table.

"Where's your husband?" John eventually asked.

It was a logical question. "I don't know. Down in San Diego, last I heard. He could be anywhere."

"You're still married to him?"

"No. I divorced him on the grounds of abandonment." She nervously plucked at the fringe on the colorful blanket. "I had every right to . . . but that doesn't change the fact that I'm a divorcée."

She waited for his disdain to show—his cool reception, the silent distance he would put between them. Rather than reacting the way she expected, he asked another question.

"How'd you meet him?"

Isabel looked at her lap, then out the tent's opening to watch the rain fall in little beads that bounced off the meadow. "I was an operator for the City of Angels Telephone Company. He would call the same numbers daily and I happened to get him most of the time. After a week, he began asking for me to connect him. I fell in love with his voice before we ever met." That last part she probably shouldn't have said, but it was true.

"The marriage wasn't any good from the start. Those

calls he made were to bookkeepers—and I don't mean the legal kind. He wasn't reliable . . . only I was too blind to see it at the time. We barely lasted a year. Then after he was gone for two, I filed for the divorce." Meeting John's eyes, she shrugged. "And that's all."

Again, the disapproval never came, no condeming eyes. Maybe she'd been hoping to scare him off, unable to face the facts: She was more than a little attracted to him. She enjoyed his strength and take-charge air. It was nice having a man do things for her, like when he'd watered her trees. She'd never had that before. Her husband had been quite self-centered. Money, the lack of it, had been the root of their problems. She'd always wondered if they would have stayed married if they hadn't been so broke.

"Well . . . ?" She could stand the quiet no longer. "Aren't you going to tell me I'm a ruined woman?"

"No."

"Why not?"

"Because I've been married before myself." His eyes darkened with distant memories. "So many times, I've lost track."

She hadn't been prepared for such a confession. Her pulse betrayed her and skipped several beats as she fought dismay. One marriage was bad enough—but numerous?

"Bartenders have married me to dozens of women, but come morning, I was single again." He ran a hand through his damp hair and gave her a slight grin that sent her heartbeat leaping. "None of my so-called marriages were legal. If a keep had been a bona fide minister, though, I would have been." Then his features went serious; the set of his mouth fell in a line and his brows leveled. "Mistakes happen, Isabel. It's not for me to judge."

"Then you don't care?"

"I care that you were left by your husband, and I wonder if you'll ever get over the hurt. Aside from that, your status doesn't mean squat to me. You're still Isabel. The woman I . . ." His words trailed off as if he'd meant to say more.

She'd hoped to hear more. But it wasn't to be. The tent's roof sprang a leak and a steady drip tattooed the floor.

John scrambled to his feet. "Hand me that slicker out of my pack," he said as he went outside. She quickly found the coat and gave it to him. With a few flicks of his wrists, he stretched the garment over the tent's top and came back inside.

Water dripped from the ends of his hair. He hadn't worn his hat—not that it would have mattered. His face didn't appear so hard and chiseled in the afternoon's cloudy light. He almost looked . . . boyish to her. She gave him a smile. He returned one of his own that made her feel disarmed and . . . pretty.

"We should get a fire going. I'll go see if I can find some wood dry enough to light."

"And I'll stick the coffeepot out in the rain for some water."

"Naw. You'll be holding your arm out to Christmas to get enough for a pot. Give me that and I'll fill it from the creek. I suspect it's chased us up here. I've seen a flash flood carry automobile-sized boulders then wash them downstream until they snag on an outcrop of granite."

"Really? Are we camped high enough?"

"We'll soon find out."

Then he went off and Isabel set out the lunch she'd brought. When she'd done all she could to make the shelter comfortable, she listened for every sound that could be from John. All she heard was the occasional nicker from the horses and the spatter of rain against the side of the tent.

It seemed as if he'd been gone hours before she spotted his familiar form coming toward her with an armful of timber and the coffeepot somehow anchored to his gun belt. He dropped the load at the tent's opening, gave her the pot, then crawled inside.

She handed him the blanket. He barely draped it over his shoulders. His arms were thick with muscles, the sleeves of his shirt torn out. He had a penchant for this particular style, which she'd thought slovenly . . . until now—when her eyes could see every bulge and swell of bicep as he ruffled the moisture from his hair with the blanket.

Isabel marveled, watching him dry off. She liked the play of splayed fingers as they wove through dark brown hair to tame the waves. She studied the planes of his face: the angle of his chin in comparison to his forehead, his straight nose. It had been a long time since she'd felt the stirrings of desire, the want of a man in a physical sense. She felt that now . . . and the pull that had grabbed hold of her with a fierce grip scared her.

She wasn't a loose woman by any means. But if John Wolcott had come into the Blossom right this minute and she'd still been one of the girls, she would have gone through with the hour he'd paid for.

He caught her staring and she forced away a blush. "I'll get the coffee ready."

His gaze lingered on her, as if he knew what she'd been thinking. Then he moved into action and assembled the wood beneath the canvas canopy at the tent's front. The flames from a small fire soon burned and they set the pot to simmer.

The space was confining. Their knees bumped because they both sat in the same manner. Her dress felt clammy against her hot skin. She wasn't cold, far from it. Even so, she couldn't dispel the shiver that ran down her arms when he reached over to poke the fire and coax it higher.

"Cold?" he asked once more.

She shook her head. "You?"

"No. But my boots are full of water. Mind if I take them off?"

"It's all right with me." She suspected he rarely asked if anyone minded anything he did.

First one then the other boot shucked free and she looked at his stockings. He had a hole in one of them at the toe. She kept a smile at bay.

"Yeah, well," he muttered self-consciously and tugged the end of his sock over his toes so she couldn't see the hole. "I was meaning to get to that. But a spool of thread is fifteen berries and I was tapped out."

"You don't have to explain."

"I sure as hell do. You think I'm a pig."

"I never said that."

"Tramp. Pig. Same thing."

This time she couldn't fend off the blush. "I'm sorry . . . I didn't know you then."

"Now you do?"

"Kind of."

"Well, Isabel Burche," he said leaning back on his elbow and extending his feet to the fire. "What do you kind of know about me?"

Taking in a breath, knitting her fingers together in her lap, and biting her lip she said, "You're lonely."

"Is that so?"

"I think you are."

"And why's that?"

"Because." She lowered her lashes, then lifted them to see his face expectant and waiting for her reply. "Because . . . I'm lonely, too, and I know how you feel."

He didn't move. Nothing in his eyes revealed how he felt. Then in a voice that was as deep as midnight velvet, he asked, "Do you ever want to get married again?"

She grew flustered. "I . . . I haven't ruled it out. But . . ."

"But what?"

"But I haven't found anyone I'd care to marry." Hastily she added, "What about you? Do you want to get married—for real? Legal, that is?"

"Never thought much about it."

Crestfallen, she swallowed the lump in her throat.

"Until recently," he went on. "I've thought some about it."

"Have you?"

"Yes. I figure after we win this contest, I'll have some money. Some kind of stability."

She nodded knowingly. "Me too."

The turn in the conversation was safer. No sense in talking marriage when neither of them was talking with the other in mind. Well . . . she'd been thinking of him. But he'd said nothing specific about her.

Isabel leaned back on her elbow, too, so that she faced him while propping her head in the palm of her hand. "What are you going to do with your share of the money?"

"Oil. That's where the future is."

"You think?"

"I know. Calco Oil's made a bundle. Only I don't expect to make as much as them. They've got the pipeline. I'll have to pay thirty cents a barrel to ship mine up to Santa Barbara on the train." A strand of hair fell over his brow and she had the strongest urge to tuck it back for him. But her hand remained still. "Start-up costs will be big, but I'll use oil to fire the boiler rather than coal. That'll save me some." His fingers caught the lock and smoothed it back. "What about you? What are you going to do?"

"Well, first thing, I'm going to have a well dug on my place so I don't have to keep going to the creek for water. Then I might add more trees because watering them won't be so difficult. And I'll fix my house up. I want to paint the porch white and put on a new roof. Of course, I'll be canning my lemon syrup and sauce. I may even open a little stand in my front yard—you know, like that widow woman over on Willow Street who sells eggs."

John regarded her with eyes that told her everything about how he felt. He understood her dreams, because he had the same ambitions. She was wrong about him. He wasn't a loafer. He just hadn't had the right opportunity come along to help him out. This contest was a godsend for both of them. And if they didn't win, she'd be almost hopeless again. He felt the same way. She could see it.

Her thoughts stalled when he leaned toward her as if he meant to cover her mouth with his. Firm lips were mere inches from hers. His breath mingled with the light sigh she made. Warmth from his hard body surrounded her even though they didn't touch. A fraction separated them and she waited . . . her eyelids fluttering closed.

Then he kissed her. His mouth moved over hers with a gentleness she hadn't expected. Warmth pooled in the bottom of her stomach and radiated outward with every beat of her heart. His kiss was a leisurely exploration that set her aflame in his arms—arms that had wrapped around her waist and pulled her close. She laid her own over his shoulders and skimmed the compact feel of muscle.

He must have sensed her total surrender, because his touch grew firmer. His lips pressed against hers in a possessive seal, coaxing a response from her that she had never experienced before. Could he know how shaken he made her feel? How desirable?

She leaned closer into him, and he molded his rock-solid body to hers. His hand reached into her hair, sifting and touching, caressing. She swept her own fingers at the nape of his neck, feeling the play of tendons as he slanted his head over hers.

Isabel trembled. Wanting John shattered her reasoning, her senses. Every thought she had focused on one thing: John Wolcott . . . and what he did to her, how he made her feel . . . special.

She could have lain back and given herself to him. She would have . . . if . . .

The coffeepot sputtered as water boiled over. Water that could put out the precious fire. John pulled back and Isabel felt cold for the first time.

His movements were jerky and restless, as if he was pent-up and frustrated. She could relate to that. But she hadn't been the one to move away. If it had been her, she would have damned the fire and let it go out. Who cared about coffee anyway?

Straightening and willing her jagged emotions to disappear, Isabel collected the cornbread and jar of stewed apples she'd packed.

"I suppose you're hungry." In spite of her best effort, she couldn't keep the tartness from her tone. Apparently, she wasn't as appealing as a hot cup of coffee.

"I could go for a bite." His voice sounded taut and edgy.

They ate in complete silence, Isabel wishing she'd never let herself think of John as more than a partner. Why had she let herself pretend there could be more between them? Pretend he liked her?

"Rain looks like it'll last for a while," John said at length. "We're stuck here until it lets up."

"I don't mind traveling in the rain." Her words were clipped.

"Neither do I. But that creek isn't a creek anymore. It's three times as wide as Main Street. To get back, we can't cross it for hours."

That sobered her out of her testy mood. "Really?"

"Yeah."

"But we're high enough . . . . right?"

"We are."

Their eyes came together, and Isabel felt sorry she'd been

so snappish. If she hadn't been longing for him, she could have been more civil. But her pride had been wounded. And, yet, her heart still wanted to reach out to him.

"Isabel . . ."

John's voice wrapped around her in a shimmering warmth, and his fingertip lifted to the seam of her mouth to lightly touch her. "You don't want to get tangled up with me. I'm no good."

"There's good in you," she whispered.

"Good for nothing. I can't hold a job for too long."

"Me either."

He cracked a slight smile.

She gave him one in return. "People like us do better working for ourselves."

"I reckon. But that takes money. We may not win."

"We have to win," she admonished. "We just have to."

She thought that if they didn't . . . what they had—or what was springing to life between them—would be gone, dead and buried. They'd have no reason to be with one another. But if they won . . . they'd have to divide the money. Then she'd want to see what land he bought, and watch how he drilled for the oil. In turn, she'd invite him to come over and see her porch painted up, show off her new lemon trees.

The contest was holding them together. If they walked away losers when it ended, both would go on with their lives . . . with nothing.

With no one.

Isabel didn't want to accept that.

John lowered his hand and gazed pensively out at the meadow. Isabel put the lunch away and watched the rain with him. He cradled her close with his arm, and she leaned her head onto his shoulder. After a while, he lay back and took her with him. She snuggled beside him, feeling as if she'd been made to fit perfectly in the contours of his body. Her palm rested on his chest, and beneath her fingertips, she could feel the thrum of his heartbeat.

Neither said anything, both heavily into thoughts, she supposed.

She stared at the tent's roof, her mind wandering to

Bellamy Nicklaus. She knew him ... she was sure ... the way he'd looked at her. He'd read through her and seen her past Christmases as if he'd been there. And she'd seen him, too. Maybe not in the physical sense ... but seen him just the same. In a book? In a *carte de visite?* A colored holiday card? There was something so familiar about him. So warm and cheery. So ...

Isabel bolted upright, her hair falling in her eyes. Brushing it away, she gazed straight at John and declared, "I know who Bellamy Nicklaus is!"

Skepticism rode his brows as he waited for her revelation.

"He's Santa Claus."

A dubious frown marred John's mouth. "Is that so?"

"He is! I'm telling you. It's been so long since I believed, I've forgotten about Santa Claus. But that's who Bellamy is."

"Yeah, well, I never believed in Santie Claus, so he's still Nicklaus to me."

"Oh, but you have to believe in him. I think the whole spirit of this contest revolves around believing. Those of us who truly do, will win. I know it."

He lifted himself onto his elbow. "What about the reindeer and elves? The Olds automobile shoots the first one down, and those two bruisers he had with him blows the elf theory straight to hell."

"I don't know. I can't explain that." Deadly serious, she insisted, "But he is Santa."

John stared at her long and hard. "Isabel, I pegged you wrong. I used to think you were crazy." He drew in a breath and ruefully shook his head. "Now I know you are."

John could tell Isabel was still mad at him for not buying into her Santa Claus idea.

And for calling her crazy.

The latter had slipped out, sort of. Maybe he'd really meant it so she could see she was being illogical. She obviously didn't think so. She'd been giving him the silent treatment ever since. And after a night spent in the tent, a ride back to Limonero, and half a day at her place, the quiet was getting on his nerves. He'd have taken his words back if he thought she'd yell at him. But Isabel wasn't the yelling type. Her anger came in concise movements and a peevish mask.

She sat in the shade on the porch of her house, counting berries and putting them into burlap bags. Tying off the tops of each with string, she stacked them against the house. Never once did she look up at him. He'd told her he'd help her count. After all, they'd designated today to do the counting. They had just over forty-eight hours left to collect berries and he wanted to know how they stood.

He still didn't know. Every time he asked her what the tally was, she raised her hand at him and waved him off—as if he were causing her to break the rhythm of counting in her head.

So be it.

Since he had nothing else to do, John had examined the ground in front of and behind the small lemon grove.

Isabel wanted a well.

John knew how to douse for water.

She hadn't asked him to find the well spot—she didn't know he could. Maybe it was the desire to make up to her for his remarks that made him leave and pick out a willow branch and come back. He doubted she even knew he'd been gone. Her head was still down in concentration, fingers nimble—that itty-bitty derringer by her side as if she were guarding a bank vault.

"Four hundred ninety-seven. Four hundred ninety-eight. Four hundred ninety-nine." She snuck a quick peek at him when he came up to the porch and leaned against the post.

Then, *plop,* the last berry went into the bag. "Five hundred."

A bowl loaded with berries sat in her lap. She went to reach for another bag and he drawled, "Where is it you want your well?"

An arch of her brow clearly said she thought he had ulterior motives. "Why?"

"Why?" he countered back, somewhat insulted. "Because I'm asking, that's why." Pushing the brim of his hat up, he motioned to her. "Get up and show me and I'll tell you if that's where you want it."

"What do you know about wells?"

"Enough to tell you whether or not the spot you've picked out will lead you to water."

She bit her lip, set the bowl aside, and stood. At least he'd won a little ground with her. "Well, I do have a spot I thought would be perfect."

He must have been temporarily forgiven, for she took the steps to the yard and walked to its weedy side. After picking up the stick he'd fashioned into a fork, he followed her.

Isabel had gone past the trees and toward the rear of the house in easy proximity to the back door. Stopping, she pointed. "Right here. This is where I want my well. It's close to my kitchen sink when I want water, and I would have to walk no more than ten paces to get to my trees. This is the perfect spot." Then in a voice he thought sounded placating, she asked, "Don't you think?"

"I can't say until I feel my way across it." He positioned the willow in his hands, palms up. The branches were limber enough to be responsive, yet stiff enough to resist all but a definite pull from the selected area. "Step aside and I'll see if you're right."

John had to relax and drift into a mental state that made him focus on only one thing: water. He chanted the word over and over in his head like his dad had taught him.

Dowsing wasn't something just anybody could do. Tom had tried, but he'd lacked the mental focus required. John could take himself inside a place where he felt only the energy coming off the ground, sending pulses to his hands, fingers, and palms. It was a strange thing, an electrically charged feeling he couldn't describe.

As he walked to where Isabel had stood, John watched the end of the rod and he closed off all noises and scenes around him. If there was water, the forked stick would react by a pulling motion, sometimes toward his body and sometimes away. He never knew. Either one meant he'd been successful.

Passing over the ground with its rocks and weeds, he felt no pulse. He tried coming in at a different angle. Again, no motion. Making two more attempts, he finally lowered the rod.

"You don't have water right here."

Disappointment mapped a pattern on her brows, mouth,

and the corners of her eyes. "I don't? But I really wanted a well in this spot."

"Well, hell, Isabel, you can put a well here if you want to, but all you're going to get out of your bucket is rocks."

"Rocks won't water my lemon trees," she all but snapped. So she was still too angry at him to be friends.

"No, they won't." John kept his tone even and strode in a different direction, looked at her trees and then the border of mustard weed that grew along the edges of her property. "You're going to have to settle for another spot."

"Like where?"

"Like where I tell you."

She folded her arms beneath her breasts, gnawing on the inside of her mouth in contemplation.

He set out once more and made several passes up and down the length of the grove and back to the house; to the front; by the back door, only on the other side; then beyond the lemon trees up the foothills. He was about to tell her she couldn't get water anywhere near her house on this gravel pit, when a golf ball arced out of the sky and dropped at his feet—right by a clump of bush poppies.

Turning with a jerk of his neck, John narrowed his eyes. Nothing stirred in the tall grasses. All he saw were the rooftops of the mill and Calco Café.

With a snort, John concluded Nicklaus was at it again. The way the ball's arc had a loop to it, it seemed that this time the old buzzard was using his lofting iron.

His attention shattered, John lowered the rod anyway for one last try. To his surprise, he got a reading—a strong one, enough to signal he'd hit pay dirt.

"I didn't need any help," he muttered. *Now why in hell had he said that? As if Nicklaus could hear him. As if Nicklaus were somebody . . . important.*

"Well?" Isabel walked up to him. "Did you get anything?"

"I got something, all right." He picked up the golf ball and shoved it into his Levi's pocket. "Almost hit in the head from a bogie by Santie Claus."

Her lips pursed. "Are you going to start that business again? You're going to ruin our chances."

Leaning his weight on one foot, John used the toe of his

boot to mark a large X in the dirt. "Money or no money for a well, you've got water. Right here."

Tempered excitement lit her eyes. "Really? This isn't where I wanted it to be." Then as the gist of it hit her, her whole face seemed radiant, softer, her mouth more kissable. "But I have water."

He thought about taking her into his arms and kissing her again. That kiss they'd shared yesterday in the tent had affected him like no other. He wanted to get to know Isabel better. Be with her. Explore all there was about her.

Funny how thoughts of the Republic Saloon dimmed as each minute with her passed. And he no longer felt as restless as he used to, so unsteady.

But at the end of this contest, if they didn't win . . . they'd have no reason to be together anymore. Unless . . .

He propped the diving rod on his shoulder, then angled the brim of his hat against the sun. "I tell you what, whether or not we win this contest, I'll dig your well for you."

"You will?"

"Consider it a Christmas present."

Her protest came out in a rush. "But I don't have anything for you."

With a smile, he reached up and touched the tip of her nose with his fingertip and said, "You don't know the half of what you've already given me."

Six

A GRAY CURTAIN OF FOG HAD COVERED THE LANDSCAPE EARLY IN the morning. But by mid-afternoon, the sun had broken through in enough places to warm Isabel's shoulders as she rode her horse. Clouds in wispy forms streaked through the sky as if a painter had put his brushstrokes here and there.

They were on their way to Moontide Ridge, a high precipice that overlooked a stretch of Ventura beach—a simple day's ride, no spending the night.

John rode ahead of her, leading the way. Every now and then she gave his broad back and narrow hips a slow perusal, admiring the taut display of muscles. She should have been boiling mad at him still. After all, he'd said she was nutty. And he'd denied Bellamy Nicklaus was Santa Claus.

Isabel was more sure now than she ever had been. Saint Nicholas. Bellamy Nicklaus. The same last name with a spelling variation. Why hadn't she caught on right from the start? It was so obvious. Had anyone else guessed besides her?

When she and John had stopped for a lunch of beans wrapped in tortillas along with dried figs, she'd tried to get him to see things through her eyes. But he'd have none of her reasoning.

A nonbeliever, that's what John Wolcott was.

She wished she could still call him a slouch. But after he'd found water on her place and offered to dig the well, she couldn't make a slanderous reference to his character. John did have a human side. That was the problem.

Even though he didn't believe her, she still found him thoroughly irresistible. Darn it all anyway.

John led the way to Santa Paula Creek, the very one that had been so full a day ago that their crossing had had to wait until morning. The night had slowly ticked away. She'd lain awake for most of it, listening to John breathing, sleeping. How could he sleep when he was angry at him? Didn't he want to talk about why they were mad at each other? Apparently not. Why was it men could roll over and get a good night's rest when a woman stewed over the argument and thought up all the things she should have said but hadn't been fast enough to think of at the time of the fight?

She would have given him what for in the morning if he'd made one Bellamy Nicklaus insult. But he hadn't. In fact, he'd acted as if nothing was wrong so she'd decided not to talk to him.

Simple.

Until he said he'd find water for her.

Then she couldn't ignore him anymore.

And when he'd touched her nose with the tip of his finger . . . she'd wanted to say she forgave him—even though she didn't, not all the way, at least . . . somewhat. Oh, she hated staying mad! But he was making her.

The creek ran in a placid flow here, close to the mountain that separated the inland from the shore. She wouldn't have thought the torrent could have dried up so quickly, but it had. The only evidence of the downpour were the broad sandbars and deeply rooted willows along the banks; they were limp and coated with grit. The banks had wavy ripples in the sand that marked the receding flow.

John dismounted and single-handed his reins. "We'll walk the horses across. After a flood, the river bottom's not too stable."

She gave him a slow nod, then scanned the water. The shallow trickle didn't look ominous to her. But she heeded his advice and hopped down from her horse to take the reins in her gloved hand.

He let her go ahead of him.

The rocky gravel gave way to silt that stuck to her boots, making a suction sound when she lifted her foot. On the opposite side was a shoulder of hills, and over them, the ridge that led to the coast. It was on the coastal side of Moontide Ridge where berry bushes grew in abundance. This far northwest from town, the chances of their still being lush with fruit was strong.

"You know, I've been thinking about Bellamy," she said in what she hoped came across as an offhand manner. Choosing her steps carefully, she went on when John didn't prompt her to divulge what exactly she'd been thinking about Bellamy. "He said he was in Pago Pago last year for Christmas. I looked up Pago Pago in the mercantile atlas. Do you know where it is?"

"Cross on the rocks," John directed, not answering her question.

She frowned and took a short leap onto a rock as the mare behind her sloshed through the water. "Pago Pago is on the southern coast of Tutuila Island, in Samoa." She paid little attention to her next step, trying to get him interested in the relevance of what she had to say. "You know where Samoa is?"

"On the rocks!" he barked at her. "Don't walk on the sandbars."

Isabel pitched him a glare over her shoulder. "I asked if you knew where Samoa was."

"What do I care? I'll never go there."

With a toss of her chin, she faced forward. "Well, you could go there if you were Santa Claus. Pago Pago is in the Pacific Ocean somewhere, this same ocean we have here. And they have pineapples. That's fruit."

"Your left foot, Isabel. Watch it."

Frowning, she stomped her left foot purposefully into the sandbar. "All I was trying to say is Pago Pago is far away. And for Bellamy to have been there he had to travel on a boat—I think . . . but I doubt it. You know, the books say Santa Claus can fly—"

The last words whooshed out of her as her right leg sunk straight down into an ooze of sand and she fell forward. Her hold on the horse released, and then both her hands were in front of her trying to push herself back to her feet. But she became caught in the quicksand.

Isabel was too stunned to do anything but sputter and gasp for air. The sand started to pull her under quicker than she could think.

Vaguely aware of John's voice and the light splash of creek water as he leapt from one rock to the other to reach the other side, she called out to him.

"Isabel, don't fight it! Stay still!"

She tried to find him on the shore, but she'd lost her hat and the sunlight was in her eyes. "John?!" She had to get out. Wiggling her feet and legs did no good.

"Don't move! You'll dig yourself in faster!"

"Help me!" But her cry sounded lost to her as she lowered nearly to her chin. Everything was happening so fast. Somewhere in her mind, she found the strength to do as John asked. She went still.

Then hands caught her beneath her arms. John's face loomed over hers and he never looked more handsome or heroic. Even if he couldn't save her . . . he'd tried, and she . . . loved him for his effort.

"Hold on to me!"

She wasn't a weak woman, but her strength was all but sapped. She did the best she could, her limp arms draping over his shoulders.

"You have to hold tight, Isabel! I can't pull myself out if I've got to hold you, too."

She barely nodded, seeing for the first time that he'd fastened a rope around his middle that reached the other side of the creek and was anchored to the limb of an oak.

In what seemed like forever, John made the slow journey with her out of the sand and onto the banks, where he went to his knees to help her get her bearings. She could hardly move other than to tighten her grasp around his neck and cling to him as if she'd never let him go.

"You saved me," she murmured against his ear. "You could have left me and had everything for yourself . . . but you saved me."

"Isabel." Her name grated from his throat in a pained whisper. "I would never have left you. Isabel . . . I couldn't. I . . . care too much. Everything wouldn't be anything to me . . . without you."

To her embarrassment, she began crying—softly, gently, against his strong shoulder.

They were wet and muddy and had nearly been pulled into the sand. But she couldn't think about that. The words swirling in her head weren't only the ones of gratitude and affection. There was a silent declaration she was too afraid to speak.

I love you, John.

John Wolcott had fallen in love for the first time in his life.

He loved Isabel.

Standing at the railing of the Pierpont Inn and gazing out at the ocean, John got used to the idea. Not that he needed to—he'd been in love with her for days, but he hadn't recognized how strongly until he'd nearly lost her.

What would she say if he told her?

It seemed too soon, too sudden. But sometimes a man just knew. She was the woman for him, the one he wanted to spend the rest of his life with. Hell, he'd been waiting for her *all* his life. And because of a contest . . . he'd found her.

Waves crashed beneath the deck, lapping against the pilings and creating a serenade that was to John's liking. The waning sun bronzed the white of his shirt. He'd bought himself and Isabel new clothes. His shirt had embroidery on the cuffs with full, billowing sleeves and an open neck where lacings lay undone. The pants were snow white as well, making him feel somewhat uncomfortable—too pristine. But it was the best he could do. The boardwalk vendor's price was right, not to mention that he was the only one around selling clothes.

Isabel was in one of the rooms cleaning up and changing. He'd paid for an hour's use with a bath and an attendant to help Isabel if she needed it. They'd had to come to the hotel on one horse. That mare he'd rented for her had taken off when she'd let go of the reins. No doubt the piebald was back to Limonero by now—with its panniers empty of berries. At least they hadn't picked any yet for somebody else to make off with when they caught the horse.

John had thought of booking the room for the night and staying in Ventura. But he hadn't wanted Isabel to feel trapped with him—he'd sensed she'd felt that way in the tent. He wasn't easily goaded into an argument. He didn't like them; he'd watched his parents have too many.

Tonight would be different, though. They weren't mad at each other. In fact, he felt as if they were closer now than they'd ever been. They could travel at night. He'd bought a set of blankets and a small lantern. Picking berries in near-dark wasn't a picnic. It could be done, though, if necessary. He was willing if that's what Isabel wanted.

Turning and resting his elbows on the railing, John looked through the magenta bougainvillea-covered arch that led to the hotel's rooms, to catch a glimpse of Isabel. He stood in the courtyard, where a single table and two chairs had been set up at his request. All around, palm tree fronds whispered in the breeze. Bird-of-paradise surrounded a softly trickling fountain. A gull cried overhead. Hibiscus flowers were in bloom in every color.

A slip of white caught his eye, and he turned.

Isabel walked toward him wearing her black hair in a high twist with many braids forming a loose effect at the top of her head. Pink flowers had been pinned in various places, adding a sweet softness he longed to breathe in. The three-tiered skirt and white blouse he'd picked out for her hadn't looked nearly as good on the vendor's table as they did on her.

The skirt had a wispy fullness to it and came only to her ankles. On her feet she wore Mexican sandals. The colorful embroidery on her blouse made a marbled splash at her bare throat and the crook of her arms. The ivory skin on the column and slope of her neck seemed almost golden in the sunset. A lacy shawl of fine white wool draped about her shoulders.

She was a vision. . . .

John left the railing and went to her to take her hands. She let him. "Isabel, I don't know what to say. 'Beautiful' isn't enough."

Shyly, she looked down, then at him. "Lupe told me this skirt isn't too short, and the blouse is worn off the shoulders, but I feel . . . undressed," she confessed; then she added, "All over. If it wasn't for the shawl, I wouldn't have come out."

"Shawl or no"—he brought his fingers beneath her chin and lightly brushed his lips over hers, as if it were natural to do so—"you're exquisite."

Her cheeks pinkened. "Look at you . . . all dressed up."

"Yeah." He shrugged, uncertain she really liked how he looked and wanting to impress her.

"You look handsome."

He gave her a half smile, pleased. "Well, we're all gussied up so I reckon we should do something about it."

"What?" Her voice was breathless; her eyes shone as soft as purple irises.

"Enjoy the sunset."

"I'd like that." She made a move toward the railing and he stopped her.

"No, Isabel. This way." Her hand still clasped in his, he guided her to the table with its flickering amber globe and red oil lantern. "We'll have dinner, then we can do whatever you like." He held a chair out for her.

With indecision, she paused. Her tone was low when she said, "But we don't have any berries to pay for this. . . ."

"They don't take berries here. Only money. And I had some. Enough for the room and clothes. And the dinner."

He thought back to Monday when his paycheck had been wearing a dent in his wallet, waiting for him to drink it away. He'd left the bar early and hadn't spent a cent since the Jolly Holly contest began. A damn good thing. He wanted to give Isabel a night she'd never forget.

"If you're sure," she murmured, then let him help her sit. Rounding the table, he sat across from her. "I'm sure."

The last vestiges of the sun were slipping into the ocean and the air felt soft. For a December evening, only a slight chill surrounded them.

Everything had to be perfect for Isabel. He didn't want to mess it up. He'd never wooed a woman and really meant it before.

She glanced at him, the fiery sunset shimmering off her hair.

He remembered something.

"S'cuse me," he said in a rush as he yanked his hat off and plopped it beneath the table. "I forgot I had it on."

Her laughter sounded as silky at the palm fronds. "You're forgiven."

He could tell she was making light of him. But he didn't care.

A waiter came to the table with a tray carrying a pitcher and two glasses. He bowed and set the table.

"For the *señorita,*" he said as he poured sangria for Isabel. Then to John he said, "*Señor.*"

John nodded, watching the sliced oranges spill into his glass along with the red wine.

Isabel didn't take a sip until John grasped his glass. Gazing into its depths, he could have sworn he saw a golf ball. Knitting his brows together, he gave the wine a swirl. What he thought had been a ball turned out to be an orange slice. But he would have made a bet there was a golf ball in his drink.

A warmth filled him . . . a kind of peace. Even though it was unsettling, he didn't feel as if he needed the liquor. He'd gone without and had craved a stiff drink for days. Now that he had one . . . he didn't have the need.

He lifted his eyes to Isabel's. "You go ahead. I quit drinking."

Curiosity caught the corners of her mouth. "You did?"

"Yeah, only I didn't know it until now."

"Then I won't have any."

He reached out and laid a hand on her wrist. "No. Have some of the sangria if you want it."

"It's all right."

She set her glass aside as four men playing instruments strolled toward them from the hotel. Reaching the table, they gave John a nod, then began singing.

Isabel smiled as she watched them.

John stood and held out his hand. "Care to dance, Isabel?"

"Oh . . . but I don't know how to dance to this. They're singing in Spanish."

"You don't need to know what they're saying. Just move with me in my arms and you'll do fine."

She went with him and they embraced, dancing to the music in a slow waltz. Isabel rested her cheek against the side of his neck. She was softer than anything he'd ever held and smelled like floral bathing salts. John savored the moment and let it embed into his memory for eternity.

"What are they saying?" Isabel asked, her breath warm next to his ear.

The band's lilting song with its accordion and guitar was a romantic ballad.

"Amor . . . quieres que te acompañe?"

John translated. "Love . . . may I walk with you?"

"Amor . . . eres tan bonita."

"Love . . . you are so beautiful."

"Suspiro por ti."

"I yearn for you."

"Sueño con tus besos."

"I dream of your kisses."

"Ven a mis brazos."

"Come to my arms."

"Amor . . . deseo de mi corazon."

"Love . . . my heart's desire."

"Angel de mi amor."

"My angel love."

His cheek came next to hers as the ballad continued

243

without words. The song said everything he felt in his heart. Could Isabel tell when he'd spoken the words . . . he'd been saying them to her?

Their dance ended just as several waiters brought a meal to the table—a feast was more like it. John escorted Isabel back and they explored the plates of seafood and salads with slices of avocado. All the while, they traded glances . . . smiles . . . no words other than the ones spoken from their eyes.

The third course was halibut with carrots. Then a bowl of baby lima beans in a peppery broth of milk and butter and fried potato slices. For desert, they had a choice from the tray of Mexican pastries. Isabel chose strawberries and cream. John picked the flan. They traded bites, leaning across the table with spoons lifted to the other's mouth.

When the meal was over, they drank *café con leche* and listened to the music as the moon rose.

John hated to bring up the contest, but he did because Isabel was so certain they had to win. "Isabel . . . we can collect berries and then ride back to town. We could be there by morning. I bought a lantern and blankets. They're on the beach with the rest of my gear. I'll get my horse, if you want."

She exhaled a long sigh of contentment. "I don't want to. Can't we stay here a little while longer?"

"Sure . . . sure."

Her lashes lowered, and she whispered, "Ask me to walk with you. Like the song."

John's heart thundered. "*Amor . . . quieres que te acompañe?*"

"Yes," she returned, gazing into his face. "I'll walk with you."

He rose from his chair and tucked her shawl about her shoulders. Before she stood, she reached down and grabbed his hat and put it on *her* own head. John put his arm through hers and they walked down the boardwalk and onto the soft sand.

The musicians stayed behind, but their melodic notes followed. Soon, the sandy beach sunk beneath the couple's feet, and the mellow night enveloped them as they strolled . . . hand-in-hand.

The hotel's outdoor cookfire had turned the moon into an orange wedge that resembled half a face. Wispy thin clouds slowly drifted across its mouth, then the light streaks of gray were carried on the breeze toward the water.

Isabel and John sat on the blanket listening to the surf as it washed up the sand and went back down again. The rhythm was gentle and soothing, a sound Isabel enjoyed but seldom heard.

"Did you get to the beach much when you lived in Los Angeles?" John asked, as if reading her thoughts while tucking her closer within the crook of his arm.

"Not as often as I would have liked. I never seemed to have the extra time." She rested her head on his shoulder. "Time is something I'm always chasing. Even now . . . we don't have much time left."

As she said it, she was referring to the contest, but in a way, the statement was more of a reflection on them—of how their relationship was drifting closer to being defined one way or another. After the contest, what would happen?

She didn't want to think about Christmas Day.

All that mattered was tonight and how wonderful John had made everything for her: the dinner, the dancing, and now the ocean and moon.

He'd made a cozy place for them in a secluded area where ice plant grew in the dunes that kept them hidden. A natural hedge of tree mallow acted as a wind break, its rosy lavender hollyhock flowers in bloom and fragrantly mingling on the sea air.

John's strength beside her comforted her. His arm felt right around her. This was the best time she'd ever had. She didn't want tonight to end. She wanted to take the moment farther . . . to have a memory above all else that she could treasure.

With her fingers meshed through John's, Isabel ran her thumb over his thick-skinned knuckle. It was the smallest of pleasures, one to be savored. With his free hand, he tilted her face to his.

"Isabel . . ." He breathed her name on the lightest of kisses.

Their lips brushed and danced, much as the two of them had to the music—a courtship of kissing. She needed this. She didn't know how badly until now.

Their fingers unlinked to give the hands freedom to explore.

Cupping his face in her hands, she kissed him with everything in her heart, all she felt, but couldn't say. He lifted her legs so that they rested over his knees and he could hold her close.

The kiss held a lifetime of romance, for in this one fragment of time, she was loved as she never had been. She understood his desire, for she felt the same. In intensity, they were equaled.

Isabel wanted to give herself to him; vows between them weren't necessary. In this, their own special place, nobody judged.

John trailed his fingers down her shoulder and over the curve of her breast, erupting sparks of desire through her. As he traced her taut nipple through the thin blouse that hung loosely around her, the kiss changed. It was dizzying, electrifying, deeper, with an intimacy she'd never dared before—all those passionate things she'd heard the girls in the Blossom talking about wanting—all those things she'd never experienced.

They lay back on the blanket without breaking the kiss, John on his side next to her. They lingered and pleased each other, until Isabel grew weak with need.

Then John lifted his head. Moonlight bathed him. "Isabel . . . do you—"

She brought her forefinger to his lips to silence him. "I do. Now, let's not talk anymore."

The surf crashed into the night, but Isabel barely heard it above the thunder of her heartbeat. Clothes were shed and naked skin kindled with caresses and kisses. Hands meshed. Mouths met. Touching became a sensory delight.

John aroused her senses to a fevered pitch that made her toes curl and had her wrapping her legs around his. Their legs intertwined, they joined and became one. She gasped in sweet agony. The pleasure was pure and explosive, new and different. It made her feel so very much alive . . . and cherished.

She clung to him as he made her his. He moved in strong and smooth strokes that sent her toward the edge, that made her lift to him and meet him. She gazed into his face, sweeping across his features: the tight control he exuded by the set of his mouth; the flare of his nostrils; the hooded slant of his eyes as he read into her soul.

He continued the rocking movements until she couldn't stop the shattering. Surrender came and riveted her, exploding and filling her with splendor. At that moment when everything inside her skittered and became charged, he met her with his own release and held her close, his mouth next to her ear . . . kissing . . . breathing.

Her own breathing labored and spent, Isabel embraced him.

The fire of completion spread to her heart. How easy it would be to say the words: I love you. But in the moment of passion . . . they might sound trite and expected. So she kept her silence and let her love for him fill the tears of joy that spilled out from the corners of her eyes.

Seven

JOHN STEERED HIS HORSE, WITH A PACK MULE STRUNG BEHIND, into Isabel's yard. As the tall weeds cleared his view, he saw the cabin and Isabel. She stood on the porch with a small cup of white paint, brushing snowflake patterns on her windowpanes. Her back was to him, and his gaze roamed the length of her as she worked.

Rich black hair coiled in a bun at her nape. He relived the sensation of sifting through the silky strands with his fingers . . . touching her satiny skin . . . kissing her . . . holding her . . . making love to her.

They'd returned to town that afternoon with holly berries in the baskets on his horse—but not nearly as many as they

247

could have collected if they hadn't spent the night in each other's arms. The hours on Ventura beach were the best in his memory. He'd wanted to tell her so, but he'd held back. Admitting the truth had never been easy for him.

She'd given herself to him freely and he could only hope she had no regrets. He didn't. Nor did he expect her to fall into a sexual relationship with him. That wouldn't be fair for either of them, and he surely didn't want Isabel to think that's all he cared about.

Although she'd once had house and hearth, she hadn't had it with a man who was right for her. John could be the one who showed her what marriage ought to be—if she let him.

But a single question continued to hammer in his mind, making him keep silent. Would she have him if he told her he loved her? Fearing she wouldn't caused him to be cautious.

When she heard his horse, Isabel turned and smiled. "Hello."

He gave her a smile back, stopped, and dismounted.

What he had tied on the pack mule was obvious, so he just came right out and said what had to be said about the fir tree that had taken him two hours to get and bring back. He felt a little self-conscious about it now, hoping the gift wasn't too presumptuous. "Isabel—" he shucked his Stetson and tucked it beneath his arm "—I noticed you didn't have a Christmas tree in your window. So I got you one."

"Oh . . ." She set the paintbrush aside and stepped down from the porch to look at her present. Walking to the mule, she lifted her hand and ran her fingers down the fir's blue-green needles. Her eyes shone with genuine gratitude when she turned toward him. "This is such a surprise. Thank you."

To his chagrin, his neck heated. Damn.

"You'll stay and help me decorate it?"

"Sure."

It didn't take John long to set the tree up in her front room—actually it was the great room. The cabin only had two: a large living area with a kitchen, and a bedroom off to the right. He could see the end of the plain poster bed with its quilt of colorful squares. He let himself wonder what it would be like to wake up in that bed with Isabel snuggled beside him.

The front door had been left open and sunshine spilled through the doorway as he worked to secure the tree in a bucket of rocks. No problem getting the rocks. Her yard was full of them. He'd noticed she used them to decorate the pathway to her door and the edges of her flower beds.

Pouring water into the bucket and giving the tree a slight shake to make sure it wouldn't topple, he stood back. "It's all set. You can put the doodads on."

Isabel lifted a garland of angels and snowflakes cut from white paper out of a crate. She handled them with care, gingerly giving him one end to hold. "You stay there and I'll walk around the tree."

He felt a little foolish. He couldn't recall ever having trussed up a Christmas tree before and having it mean something special.

"Put your end right there," she guided.

Tucking the last angel into the highest limb, the garland was in place. He stood back and examined the cut paper. "Who made that?"

"I did," she declared proudly. "When I was fourteen. My mother suggested the project, and both Kate and I sat at the table and began cutting out strips of paper." She made a few adjustments in the garland. "What about you? Did you and your brother ever do any Christmas things?"

John's brows rose in thought. "Nope. Tom and me, we're different. We don't stay in touch too good."

"I know. I should write my sister more. Maybe we ought to make a New Year's resolution."

"Maybe." Only he was into Tom for a hell of a lot of money—that's why he rarely wrote. He didn't want to have to own up to never being able to pay him back.

Feeling guilty and wanting to say something nice about his younger brother, John added, "Tom's got a sporting goods store in Harmony, Montana. Does a pretty good trade. Sells hunting stuff. Sporting gear—your big animal gewgaws. No golf clubs, though. Tom never did like the game."

"How is it that you know golf?"

"Well," he put his weight from one foot to the other, "I knew this cattle guy." John didn't mention that he'd rustled calves off him. That was during the prime of his trouble-maker ways when he still lived in Texas. "He was a rich baron type, a tycoon. Played it out in the pasture. Showed me how." After he'd caught John red-handed and hadn't turned him in to the sheriff, he made him work off the price of the calves as a hand for a whole damn year. But it had given John a sense of morality he hadn't learned at home.

Isabel produced puffs of cotton wool, and John changed the subject.

"What's that?"

"Pretend snow. Here, you can put some on." She laid a few tufts in his palm, their fingers connecting, which ignited in him the desire to take her into his arms and kiss her.

But he didn't readily move, too intent was he on watching her as she hummed a festive tune and placed cotton wool in strategic places on the branches.

In that instant, he could imagine spending the rest of his Christmases with Isabel—decorating the tree and house, sitting together and lighting the tree candles and enjoying the smell of pine as it filled the room. Morning would come and they'd wake up to wrapped gifts chosen with affection and love . . . perhaps have a child to toddle beside them. . . .

John shook his head and drew in a breath. It was a hell of a tall dream, one that he'd be lucky to have.

"Now we'll need that," she said, breaking into his musings as she pointed to the box behind him.

He turned and reached into the crate and took out stars cut from flattened tin cans. They hung those, and afterward, she went to the counter and gave him a string of popcorn and dried apricots.

"I was going to put these on the porch, then I remembered the birds. So there went that idea. But now I have a tree. You can put this on."

He did, taking care to string it evenly so as not to mess up her tree. Finally they wired on small tin candleholders and placed the candles in them.

Standing back together, his arm slipped over her shoulder. "Well." She sighed with awe. "It's a lovely tree, don't you think?"

He only had eyes for the woman beside him. "I think you're lovely, Isabel."

Then he took her into both arms, held her close, and kissed her. Melting into his embrace, she spoke against his lips, "Tonight, when the contest is over, we'll light the candles together."

"Together." The word turned into another kiss that sealed the promise.

An old midnight moon gazed down at the crowd standing in front of Bellamy Nicklaus's gingerbread-styled house. The clock had struck twelve, but that seemed an eternity ago to Isabel. She stood next to John, periodically biting her lip and standing on tiptoe to see if she could catch a glimpse of Bellamy through his front window.

Everyone had turned in their berries and he'd taken all the bundles, baskets, and sacks inside to have "Mother" count and string them. How she could manage to do all that in a short time baffled Isabel.

The tree in the yard glittered with a multitude of lit candles. Flickering red flames reflected off the sparkling trimmings that had been hung. Thankfully the air was still to keep the candles burning.

"How much longer, do you think?" Isabel asked John for at least the dozenth time.

"I don't know, Isabel. Soon, I hope."

Through the press of people, she reached out and found his hand, gripping it within her own. And they waited some more.

Finally the door opened and Bellamy came out.

Isabel stared at him with renewed reverence. Santa Claus. Saint Nicholas. How many Christmases had she tried to stay up to get a peek at the elusive man in the red coat? Funny how at the age of twenty-eight, when she'd stopped believing, she could now see him.

For a short few heartbeats, Isabel closed her eyes tight and whispered in her head: *I believe. I believe in you. I believe in Saint Nicholas. . . .*

Then she slowly opened her eyes to find Bellamy looking

directly at her and giving her a . . . wink! She smiled, broadly. They'd done it! They'd won! She knew it!

Voices fell quiet as Bellamy came to the front of the porch steps, where Yule and Tide stood like soldiers on either side. Bellamy gave them each a smile, then said, "What was that fruit again?"

"Pineapple," Yule reminded.

"Ja, pineapple," Tide nodded. "Good fruit."

"Juicy," Yule added.

"Sweet," Tide countered.

"You're making me want some," Bellamy said with a nod. "I think we ought to stop by Pago Pago on the way tonight and get us some."

"Ja," Yule agreed.

"Ja," Tide seconded with a broad grin.

"Folks," Bellamy began, addressing the gathering, "I'm glad you came out to see who would be the winner of the Jolly Holly contest."

Nods and glances to one another prevailed.

"I don't want to keep you in needless suspense, but Mother said it will take her just a minute more. I wanted to remind you about the spirit of the contest." He stepped through the crowd, and as it parted, Isabel noticed he'd changed out of house slippers and wore knee-high black boots polished to a brilliant gleam. He still wore knickers, though, and the funny hat with the pom-pom on the crown.

"The key to eternal happiness is clear to some of us. Not so clear to others," he said, walking with his hands clasped behind his back and looking into the faces around him. "How to find prosperity is a question that different people will give different answers for—when there is really only a single answer that will do."

Winding his way toward the mercantile owner, Bellamy stared directly into his eyes. "Reaping rewards doesn't mean cheating another. I saw the chaos that the contest created: berries being used as commodities; brother pitted against brother; friend opposing friend." He continued on, stopping at Saul, the bartender for the California Republic. "Drinkers going drinkless because berries couldn't buy liquor. Now that one I'm not so inclined to frown on."

He moved on, coming toward Isabel and John. She pulled

in her breath and squeezed John's hand. With a pause, Bellamy lit up his face with a smile for them. Even in the dimness, his eyes twinkled and his cheeks looked rosy. "There are some who believe," he said, holding Isabel's gaze with his own. "And then there are some who don't believe," he continued, this time pointedly staring at John.

Isabel felt his fingers go tense in her grasp.

"Believing is a mysterious thing. We only believe in what we think is capable of happening. Not what we want to happen. Why is that?" He absently scratched his full white beard and strolled forward. "And believing in ourselves is the last thing we do when we don't have the spirit of the season."

Once back on the steps, he turned around. The door behind him opened and Mrs. Nicklaus came outside, whispered in Bellamy's ear, then went back into the house.

"Well, folks," Bellamy announced with glee. "It's official."

A murmur rose in the crowd. Then came a shuffling of feet. Hatted heads fit close together. People leaned forward in anticipation.

Bellamy chuckled, that rolling laugh that made his tummy shake. "The prize goes to Isabel Burche and John Wolcott."

Isabel let out her breath and laughed—a short and choppy sound mixed with relief. She quickly turned to John, who looked down at her with an easy smile. "We did it," she whispered.

"Yeah, we did."

She desperately wanted to fling herself into his arms and kiss him soundly on the mouth. But she refrained. Later—when they lit the tree candles—she'd tell him she loved him, and everything was going to be wonderful!

Amid the groans of disappointment, Bellamy went on, "To the winners, as I promised in my flyer, the prize is unlike anything you've ever known."

Money! Lots of money! Isabel exclaimed inside her head.

Mrs. Nicklaus came outside once more. High in her arm, she carried a domed wire birdcage. Inside two birds anxiously flitted. Their coloring was creamy gray and green, and once they landed on their perch, their heads touched.

"Mother and I have had these birds since they left their broods. One's a male and the other's a female. They're lovebirds." He beamed at them, giving Isabel another wink.

This time Isabel's optimism took a plunge. *Lovebirds?* Where was the prize money?

"They can't be separated. Without the other, one will wither. But as a couple they're strong and healthy. Full of spirit."

Taking the cage from his wife, he came toward Isabel and John. "It's my pleasure to present you with the lovebirds as your prize for the Jolly Holly contest."

A few snickers resounded, then some moans of aggravation. Several people began to walk away.

Isabel didn't want to take the cage, but since John wasn't holding out his hand, she was obligated. Lifting the cage high enough to peek inside, she gazed at their winnings. The tiny birds flapped their wings and circled one another, then went back to the perch to nuzzle beaks.

It was humiliating at best to win a pair of birds when she had her heart set on currency. No doubt John was thinking the same thing. He hadn't said a word.

Bellamy put a hand on each of their shoulders, bringing them closer together. "I entrust you with my little friends. Keep them happy and you'll be happy for all your days. Merry Christmas."

Then he threw his head back and laughed, "Ho, ho, ho!"

Isabel didn't know whether to cry or sock him in the jolly old stomach.

Lovebirds! They'd been tricked. John was right. Bellamy wasn't Santa Claus. He was a demented old man who'd gotten his holidays mixed up. This was no Christmas prize. This was the trick in a Halloween trick or treat!

The crowd dispersed as Bellamy walked back up the steps to his house, his wife following and then the two bruisers, who waved to the crowd. Many waved them off with a grumble.

Isabel and John were the only ones left on the street. She lowered her arm and her shoulders sank.

"You were right," she dismally croaked. "Bellamy is a crackpot."

To her amazement, John didn't readily second her conclusion. After a long moment, he quietly took the cage from her and began walking. She went alongside him.

The wind kicked up out of nowhere. Warm gusts of the Santa Anas brought an unnatural shower of . . . *snow?*

Those scurrying down Main Street paused to see what was what.

Small white petals thickened the holiday sky and sprinkled down with the most delightful fragrance.

A gentleman off to Isabel's side shook his head. "Sun-Blessed," was all he said before running off to his home.

Of course. Lemon blossom petals from the Sun-Blessed groves. But how did there get to be so many of them? This had never happened before. It was a flurry of flowers that looked like real snow. The delicate smell of them filled the air with a magnificent perfume beyond description.

John glanced over his shoulder at Bellamy's house. Isabel followed his gaze. The residence had grown dark. The breezes must have blown the candles out on the tree.

"I'll walk you home," he said in a low voice.

He had distanced himself from her, she could tell. They hadn't won what they had thought and now he was angry. This was it, the end. They'd go their separate ways. It would be as if they had never known one another.

She should have known. Money had ruined her first marriage. Money had just ruined her chances for a second one.

But what about the birds . . . ?

Who would keep them? She didn't think she could. They'd always remind her of John. It would be too painful.

The road became covered with a snowfall of white blossoms. They clung to Isabel's shirtwaist and sleeves, they lay in her hair. She blinked several from her lashes.

Once at her cabin, John stopped at the base of the steps. She could barely face him. She'd been so sure everything would be perfect tonight.

"I'm sorry we didn't win like you wanted to, Isabel."

Tears filled her eyes. "That's all right. You said all along we were being fooled by a silly old man. I didn't listen to you. I should have."

John set the cage on the porch and put his arms around her from behind. He cradled her close and kissed the side of her neck. How easy it would be to lean into him and to let herself feel better. But kisses and embraces weren't the answer to anything.

"I was the one wrong about the contest," John said, tucking a wisp of hair behind her ear. "It was real."

"Why do you say that?"

"Because if it hadn't been for him, I wouldn't have known you, Isabel. For that, I'll forever be grateful. He said in his notice that the winner would be forever grateful. Well, I am." Then he moved away from her and she heard the shaky intake of his breath. Turning toward him, she brushed the tears from her eyes.

He stood with blossoms dusting his shoulders and hat, softness sifting on a man who'd shown her softness . . . kindness . . . love.

"You keep the birds, Isabel. They'd like your place a hell of a lot better than they'd like mine. You've got"—his voice clogged, and he cleared his throat—"got hope around here. They'll like that. Take care of them." Then with a lowering of his head and a shove of his hands into his pockets, he said, "Take care of yourself."

Tears slipped down her cheek as John followed the lane into the night.

When he was gone, she lowered herself onto the steps and buried her face in her hands. Hot tears spilled through her fingers.

Even with every emotion inside her in turmoil, a single thought surfaced and saddened her most.

They hadn't lit the candles on their Christmas tree.

A kerosene lantern burned on the bureau of John's room, giving off a mellow light. He lay stretched out on his bed, fully clothed and staring at the ceiling. In his hand, the golf ball he'd pocketed when he'd found water for Isabel. With a flick of his wrist, he pitched the ball upward. It soared back down and he caught it. He threw it again. Caught it again. He'd repeated this process some hundred times since returning home from Isabel's house.

He couldn't get her out of his mind. Her despair over the

contest playing out like that had been blatant. She'd wanted the money more than he did. Hell, he'd wanted the cash, too—maybe more than her. But he would have gladly given it all up.

Lovebirds.

Who did Nicklaus think he was kidding? Lovebirds were a pair. A couple that couldn't be parted. Nicklaus knew from the start of his damn contest that he was giving away a prize with complications. And he'd known they'd win and they'd have the birds to contend with.

Why?

Did the great Saint Nicholas know them better than they knew themselves? It was the only conclusion John could come to grips with.

Money would have bought him a lot of things he could use. Only it wouldn't have bought him Isabel's love. That, he'd have to earn.

He tossed the ball and it fell into his palm with a smack.

He should have told her how he felt, should have damned the consequences and just been honest for a change. He could live with rejection. He couldn't live without knowing if Isabel loved him in return, and he'd walked away from something.

Tomorrow morning, first light, he'd tell her. Get it all out in the open and let it be whatever it would be, future or no future. But for once, John Wolcott wasn't going to run from a commitment. He wanted to be a husband and a father, and if Isabel felt the same way, he'd marry her by sundown Christmas day.

On that thought, he forgot to catch the ball and it thwacked him on the brow. With the wincing impact, he had the oddest feeling that Nicklaus had slugged him for taking so long to see the light.

Isabel didn't sleep much at all that night. The birds rustled around in their cage for most of it. And this morning just before the sky turned golden, they began to chirp and coo at one another. They were so much in love, she could actually feel it overtaking the room.

Barefooted, she padded out of bed in the gray dawn. Finding the white shawl that John had bought for her, she went outside and sat in her rocking chair to greet the day—bleak as it would be for her.

She'd been so hopeful she'd win the money and her life would be everything she wanted, she could have the things she needed. But money didn't give her John. She'd been a fool to let him go. She was in love with him. Why hadn't she told him so? It hurt to think how much she longed to be in his arms. . . .

Wrapping the shawl tighter about her, she brought the ends to her cheek and rubbed the softness next to her skin.

She'd been selfish last night and she didn't like herself for it today. Telling John how she felt about him was worth the risk of his not returning her affections. At least she'd know.

The ripple of a chance stirred within Isabel. Yes . . . she'd tell him. Right away.

Several minutes later, Isabel dashed down the steps to the lane, but stopped shy to gaze at her lemon grove. Her mouth softly fell open.

Cardinal red ribbons were tied in bows around the branches of every single tree—just the color of ribbon she'd wanted as a child. Who had done such a thing? John? He hadn't known about the ribbons.

But somebody else had. . . .

About to turn and leave for John's bungalow, Isabel's pulse skipped when she saw him coming toward her up the drive. He carried a bucket and several of the clubs Bellamy used.

She didn't want to seem too anxious . . . too eager.

"Merry Christmas," she said softly, remembering what day it was.

"Same to you, Isabel," he returned, his tone pleasant yet guarded.

The lump on his forehead, just above his eyebrow, distressed her. She feared he'd gotten into a fight. "What happened to your forehead?"

John's grimaced. "I hit myself shaving."

"What . . . ?" That made no sense.

"Never mind."

Isabel let the matter drop. She raised her arm toward the grove. "Did you do that?"

John took in the ribbons, then shook his head. "Nope."

Then he lifted his arm with the bucket of golf balls. "What about this? Did you leave these on my doorstep?"

"No."

"Well . . . damn. Who did?"

Both were quiet a long moment. Then together: "I think I know—" They broke off and laughed, nervously.

"Isabel." The way he said her name had her shivering with wanting. "I need to talk to you."

She raised her eyes to his. "Me, too." Before she lost her courage, she went on, "It's about the birds. I don't think it's fair for just me to have them. And I don't think it's fair for only you. We won them together . . . so I think we should stay . . . that is . . ." He looked at her so intently she could barely breathe, much less think. All the things she planned on saying tripped over her tongue and she grew flustered and near speechless. "Oh . . . help me," she said more to Bellamy than to herself. It came out naturally . . . as if he knew she needed him.

John took a step toward her. "You mean, keep the lovebirds together because we're together?"

Slowly, she nodded. "Yes . . . that's what I want."

To her surprise, John dropped the iron sticks and bucket with a thud and took her into his arms. He lifted her off the ground and gave her several twirls in the dawn light that fanned across the yard in rays of honey and brass.

"I love you, Isabel Burche," John confessed.

Through her laughter she returned the avowal. "I love you, John Wolcott."

Setting her back on her feet, John gave her a hard kiss on the mouth; then he cupped her cheeks within his strong hands.

"I should have told you last night how I felt."

"I should have, too. I'm sorry about the way I acted. I don't care about the money. Only you."

"Me, too."

He kissed her once more, this time with a lingering caress over her lips. "So what if we don't have Nicklaus's stale money? Who cares? I've got my job at Calco."

"And I've got my lemon sauce and syrup to sell. We'll make do."

"Damn right."

Through a light rain of kisses, he asked, "Isabel, will you marry me?"

"Yes," she said back through feathery kisses of her own. "I'll marry you."

Then he picked her up once more and swung her around in his strong arms to her delighted laughter.

Epilogue

TWO WEEKS HAD PASSED SINCE JOHN MADE ISABEL HIS WIFE.
Dressed in the clothes they'd worn in Ventura, their private
ceremony had taken place in front of her lemon trees all
decked out with ribbons. The reverend hadn't been too keen
on preforming the nuptials outdoors, but he made an
exception on account of the fact that it was Christmas
day—though it was more likely due to Isabel's promise to
deliver him a case of her syrup at no charge.

Sunday sprung forth bright and cloudless, the air dry but
not dusty. John looked forward to the one day a week that
he could spend entirely with Isabel. Workdays were long on
Ferndale No. 8, and from there he headed to the livery to
muck the stalls and pay for that piebald mare. Sundays he
dug the well. He didn't mind the exhausting labor because
he was working toward something.

Making a home for Isabel.

John had changed—for the better. He'd even sent Tom
five dollars with a letter and a promise to pay him back
every last cent he'd borrowed.

Although he'd given up liquor, John hadn't given up his
dream to drill for his own oil. So this morning, he'd had
Duster come out and assess the place to give him his
opinion on the possibilities.

Duster had walked the property and sadly shaken his

head. Too many rocks. Not enough grasses, he'd said. The skeptic now sat in the porch rocker drinking a glass of Isabel's lemonade. Beside him, the birdcage hung with the lovebirds softly singing.

John called for his wife, who walked through the grove with a basket picking lemons. It seemed as if the trees had been producing bushels of lemons overnight. Isabel hadn't taken the ribbons off. She claimed she'd keep them on those trees forever as a symbol of their love.

"Hmm?" Isabel said as she set her basket down and came toward him.

John had selected the niblick club and a Perfect Flight golf ball—the very one that had dropped out of the sky at the well spot.

"Darlin', I'm going to line you up, and I want you to hit this ball as hard as you can."

She shaded her eyes with her hand. "How come?"

"Because wherever this ball lands is where I'm going to find oil."

"No petroleum on this property," Duster declared with a slow rock and a sip of lemonade.

"We'll see," John called to him. Then he handed the club to Isabel and set the ball on a tiny mound of dirt he'd made. "All right, darlin', you give it your best shot."

"But I don't know how to hit it."

"I'll show you." He cuddled her in front of him and made her lean back into his hips. "There you go. Sway a little. Loosen up."

She did so, pressing her shapely behind into him. He had to fight off the urge to forget about hitting the ball, tell Duster to go repark himself at the Republic, and take Isabel into the house and lie over her on the bed.

"Well, if that isn't the backward way to do things," Duster hollered, breaking John out of his thoughts.

"Just you watch," John replied without looking up.

"Really, John, I think we'd have better luck if you hit the ball."

"Darlin', you are my luck. Now you're going to do fine."

He put his hands over hers to fit around the club's handle. Then he helped her shift her weight and get into the right position. "Just swing your hips, Isabel, and lay into it."

"All right."

He straightened and backed away from her, giving her room to move. She didn't. She got out of position and turned to face him. "You know who gave you these clubs and balls, don't you?"

They'd been through this before. He'd never come out and admitted that he thought Bellamy Nicklaus had left him the golf gear and put the ribbons on her trees. Deep down, he knew the crafty buzzard had done it. How, he didn't know.

Because on Christmas day, that house on Ninth and Mill had been deserted as if nobody had ever lived there at all. The only thing remaining was the tree in the yard, all decked out with holly berries.

"Yes, I reckon I do, Isabel," he finally said.

"I just thought we ought to clear that up before I go hitting the ball. If we don't believe, this won't work." The silk poppies on her hat waved with the bob of her head as she turned around once more. "So, are you going to admit Bellamy Nicklaus is a legend?"

He drew up behind her and corrected her stance. Whispering into her ear, he said, "I believe that somewhere in time, the name Nicklaus will be a legend linked with golf. How's that?"

After a moment's silence, she nodded. "It's a start."

"Good." Backing away again, he gave Duster an encouraging nod.

Duster merely snorted.

"Go ahead, darlin', whack the hell out of it."

On that, Isabel sliced the club through the air and the ball sailed high in the sky. She came to stand beside John and he pulled her close with his arm.

Together, they watched the golf ball sail toward the ground, each knowing that whatever the outcome, they were already rich.

STEF ANN HOLM is the author of ten published novels and has been featured in various newspapers, including the *Los Angeles Times* and *USA Today*. Recently nominated for a Career Achievement Award as Storyteller of the Year by *Romantic Times,* she's just completed her eleventh romance. *Harmony* is the first book in the Brides for All Seasons Series, and is the story of Tom Wolcott, John's brother from "Jolly Holly."

She's been married for sixteen years and has two daughters (three if you count the dog). The early years of her writing career were spent sneaking time at the typewriter in between changing diapers and putting her daughters down for naps. Now that her girls are older and in school full time, she has the entire day to create what *Publishers Weekly* calls a "fine sense of atmosphere" in her novels. She loves to cook gourmet meals—especially desserts. Whenever she travels, she orders asparagus because nobody in the family likes it but her.

While Stef Ann is working on her next installment in the Brides for All Seasons series for Pocket Books, she invites you to write to her at P.O. Box 5727, Kent, WA 98064-5727.

Mariah Stewart

If Only in My Dreams

For Katie and Becca,
who make all my seasons bright

One

WITH HER LAND ROVER HAPPILY EATING UP THE MILES IN THE afternoon sun, Quinn Hollister headed north on Route 191 about sixty miles outside of Billings, Montana, determined to be home before dinner. Praying that no unannounced storm would ambush her to slow down her progress, she depressed the accelerator and prepared to make tracks. Fumbling in her big blue nylon zippered bag, she rejected first one, then another tape of Christmas music until she found just the right songs to sing along with as she drove toward the small town of Larkspur, and, just beyond the town limits, the High Meadow Ranch, where her family would gather to celebrate the holidays.

Quinn had left Missoula literally at the crack of dawn, her car already packed and ready to go. She would have two weeks at home before returning to Montana State, where she had spent the first semester filling in for a professor who had been injured in an automobile accident and was unable to teach his scheduled creative writing course. In four more weeks the class would end and the regular professor would return for the second semester, but Quinn hadn't quite made up her mind whether to stay in Missoula or to come back to the ranch. As a writer and illustrator of children's books, she could work just about anywhere. Presently between contracts, she hadn't quite settled on which of her possible projects to pursue next. For the next two weeks, however, she planned to put work aside and simply enjoy being with her family.

No matter where their lives had taken them, all of Catherine and Hap Hollister's offspring came home to spend Christmas with the family. Not that any of them had ever wanted to be anyplace else for the holiday. The High Meadow Ranch was home, and home was always filled with chatter and memories and wonderful things to eat. The old log and stucco house would smell like Christmas, like fresh-cut pine, like cinnamon and vanilla and ginger, and would look like a magazine photo, with greens draping every window and doorway. Claret red poinsettias, for which a special trip to Billings would have been made, would stand massed under the big dining room windows overlooking the valley. Catherine's Christmas village would grow from the flat plain of the piano in the great room, and the lights from the tiny porcelain houses would twinkle like tiny stars. On Christmas Eve, they would all gather in front of the fireplace, and whoever's turn it was that year would read "The Night Before Christmas" to the rest of the family. The beloved faces would glow in the firelight, and for a while, even the sibling bickering and baiting inevitable in a large family would cease. Just thinking about it kinked the corners of Quinn's mouth into a smile, and she unconsciously pressed a little more firmly on the gas pedal.

In her rearview mirror, the Crazy Mountains, where the Crow Indians once summoned the spirits, rose unexpectedly from the flat broad prairie, and up ahead, to her right, the isolated Snowy Mountains lifted toward the clouds. At Harlowtown she crossed the Musselshell River and passed the sign for Martinsdale, where, in recent weeks, many a Montanan would have sought the Hutterite colony to purchase their Christmas grain-fed goose from the German-speaking communal farmers who had fled religious persecution in Russia and Austria in the late 1800s. The Hutterites were as much a part of the Montana landscape as were the Amish in Pennsylvania Dutch country, and as well known for the quality of their produce and livestock. Quinn knew that family tradition dictated that the Hollister Christmas buffet would boast at least one fine Hutterite goose, and more likely than not, some specialty relishes as well. One fat goose . . . a roast of beef with Yorkshire pudding . . . a dining room table that would truly be a groaning board of holiday specialties to share with family and friends. The Dunham cousins from the other side of the mountain would be there, perhaps a few neighbors, and whomever else any one of the Hollisters might have added to the list this year. It was all part of Christmas at the High Meadow.

Tapping her fingers on the steering wheel to the Little Drummer Boy's "pa rum pa pa pum," she glanced at the clock. She had made excellent time. One never knew at this time of the year what the weather might do. The sun was just beginning its slow drop toward the hills as she took a right off the highway onto the last leg of two-lane paved road that would lead into Larkspur. Passing the district high school on the outskirts of town, she slowed down to reminisce, as she always did. On the playing fields behind the school, her brothers had won all-state honors in baseball and football. Around the perimeter of the football field ran the track, where Quinn had competed in the long-distance events and her sister Susannah—Sunny for short—had been a sprinter, and farther back beyond the boys' playing fields were the diamonds where the girls could play softball. The youngest Hollister, Elizabeth—Liza—had made the girls' all-state teams three years running. It all seemed so long ago.

It was long ago, she mused.

She slowed down as she approached the town limits, which were distinguished by the fifteen-mile-an-hour speed limit sign that was posted right there on the corner of Hemlock and Spruce. The tidy storefronts were all as familiar to her as the ranch she'd grown up on five miles outside of town. Rows of colored Christmas lights lined either side of the wide street that marked the business section. There, across the street on the first corner, stood Hiller's General Store, which served as both food market and pharmacy. Next came the Jewel Café, which was as close to fine dining as one was likely to come across for the next fifty miles or so and was also the only spot in town where one could purchase newspapers, magazines, and paperback books. Directly across the street from Jewel's one would find Chambers Sporting Goods ("Outfitters for the Sportsman Since 1874"), which was certain to be doing a booming business this time of year, and next to it, the little white clapboard complex that served as municipal building, library, and post office. Doc Bellows, the local veterinarian, had an office on the next corner, and across from him was the small medical building that served the town's human population. Down that same block was The Corral, Larkspur's only nightspot—that is, the only establishment open after ten P.M. The Towne Shop—a clothing store that prided itself on the variety of jeans it carried—and Tilstrom's, which had for generations sold farm equipment, pretty much rounded out the town of Larkspur, Montana, population 3,127.

On the other side of the business district lay the residential area, five blocks of neat streets lined with equally neat houses, many dating from the days when Larkspur was a boomtown, when the gold, lead, and silver mines had been active, and the sapphire mines had yielded some of the finest clear blue gems in the world. When the mines had settled down a bit, the region turned to cattle or sheep ranching, and many, such as the Hollisters and their close relatives on the other side of Blue Mountain, the Dunhams, had made their money in ranching as much as in mining. Down two blocks on Alder, off Main, were Larkspur's architectural treasures, the homes of those early men of foresight who had left the mining fields with their pockets full and moved into town, where they established themselves in trade, building fine mansions for their families and contributing much of their fortunes to the betterment of their growing community.

On a whim, Quinn took a left, slowing down to take in the sights of the large houses, each more elaborate than the one before it, all elegantly festooned for the holiday season. Quinn grinned to herself, recalling a time when she had been twelve or so and could not understand why the Hollisters had to live so far out of town, on a *ranch,* when so many of her friends lived amid the quiet splendor of Alder Lane. The fascination with living in town was a brief one, and she had never really regretted her country upbringing.

Once past Alder, each new block saw the houses growing smaller and smaller, less and less significant architecturally, until the last small streets, with their tiny bungalows and narrow one-story houses of concrete block, led down to the lake that served as the northernmost boundary of the town. At this time of the day, Quinn knew, the frozen lake would be thick with skaters. Unable to resist the pull, she allowed the Land Rover to drift down toward the tiny parking area just there on the right, where she turned off the engine and rested her arms over the top of the steering wheel for just a moment before getting out and following the frozen path to the lake.

Standing half-hidden by the row of small white pines that the Russell's Lake Improvement Committee had planted two summers ago, Quinn shoved her gloved hands into the pockets of her jeans and watched the late-afternoon show that had been running on this lake every winter since blades were first strapped to the bottom of the human foot here in the valley. The ice was deeply grooved in spots, pocked just enough to make the skating a little dicey for those who weren't watching where they were going. A line of teenagers passed in front of her on the ice, a boisterous whip being cracked across the center of the lake. Quinn watched, amused, as the boy on the very end of the whip appeared to hit a groove in the ice, sending his feet flying out from under him and his butt on a steady descent toward the hard surface of the ice. It hurt, she knew, but he laughed anyway, gleeful at having taken with him a goodly portion of the skating chain as many young bottoms skidded across the lake. Quinn took a step back into the shadow of the pines, smiling as she recalled many a cold afternoon spent engaged in exactly the same activities that this most recent crop of Larkspur teens enjoyed—skating, having fun, flirting, freezing their butts off, but laughing and yes, most definitely, flirting. Many a relationship had had its start right here— why, Quinn's own father had first courted her mother here, and Quinn herself had been chased around the ice by her own high school sweetheart, just like . . . just like *that*.

She watched in fascination as one of the girls fairly flew past on thin silver blades, the hat snatched off her head by an eager young man who raced off with it. The shrieking girl chased after him, her long auburn hair trailing behind her like a veil, her face flushed with the chase. Overcome with a sense of nostalgia, Quinn sighed. Hadn't she once been the girl who had streaked determinedly across the lake in pursuit of the boy who had challenged her to ignore him, knowing full well she would chase him until he permitted himself to be caught? And would not the chase end in one of the more remote spots where the boy could steal a hurried kiss, branding her with cold lips before leading her back to the chain that was reforming, where they would replay the same scene over and over until dark? Oh yes, Quinn knew the drill quite well.

Quinn wondered where her old skates might be, and if she could possibly talk her sisters into joining her on the lake one afternoon over the holiday week. It would be fun to soar across the ice again, she thought, as she dug into her jacket pocket and fished out a crumpled dollar bill. She walked the rock-hard ground to the little refreshment stand, where an acne-pocked girl sold hot chocolate under a green and white painted wooden sign that announced *All Sales Benefit Larkspur Youth Groups.* Quinn held up one finger and the girl poured a cup of steaming liquid, the top of which she zapped with a fat dollop of whipped cream before slapping a lid on and nudging it across the narrow counter to Quinn.

Late afternoon was rapidly fading into dusk, and several of the skaters had come to the edge of the lake to take those first awkward steps onto the snow-packed ground. It was getting near time for the young skaters to head home before dark. Several of the teenage girls called to their younger siblings, bending over to untie skates or to help the small ones with their boots. The girl whose hat had earlier been snatched, who had laughed and flirted while retrieving it, now leaned down to assist her little sister. The scene was so achingly familiar. It could have been Quinn there, leaning over to help a struggling Liza, so many years ago. . . .

There were some things that never seemed to change.

It was time for Quinn to head home, too, and she turned her back on the lake and walked the short distance to her car, her hands warmed by the hot drink. She shivered as she got into the car and turned on the heater. It was a cold day, and the temperature was dropping rapidly along with the failing sun. She made a U-turn onto Russell's Lake Road and paused briefly, her eyes locked on the little green house that was set back from the road. That same little green house she'd been trying to ignore since she had decided to stop at the lake.

The shabby garage that had once stood at the end of the gravel driveway was gone, as was the family that had once lived there, the boy and the girl and their grandmother, and sometimes their father, when he remembered where he had left them. Quinn had been to the house only once, when the grandmother had died. Sixteen years old and totally in love with the boy, Quinn had arrived with flowers and a cake, much as she had seen her mother do when there had been a death in a neighbor's family. She had stood on the cracked front steps and knocked on the door feeling very grown up. The boy had opened the door just enough for Quinn to see that the house held little furniture, and that his father had passed out in the one old chair in the dingy living room. The boy had seemed embarrassed that she had come, and had not invited her in. Later, at the old woman's funeral, Quinn had stood between her father and mother, watching the boy's face twist with loss, with pain, as the light coffin was lowered into the ground, all the while aching to put her arms around him and comfort him.

Well, Quinn reminded herself brusquely, *that boy is long gone, and so is the girl I was when I loved him.*

Quinn completed her turn crisply and headed back toward town and the road that would take her home.

The Land Rover crunched effortlessly over the occasional patch of dirty, compacted snow that covered the five miles of narrow gravel road leading toward the Big Snowy range. Just to the left of the slight bluff about half a mile ahead Quinn could see the lights from the ranch house burning yellow against the snow-covered hills. She could almost smell the pot roast her mother had promised to make for dinner, the cranberry-raisin pie there would be for dessert. Her mouth watering, she headed for home.

Two

CALEB McKENZIE STOOD ON THE PORCH OF THE CABIN THAT HAD
been built by a great-great-uncle over a hundred years ago,
and stared out into the stillness of the night. From somewhere in the pines beyond the cabin there was a dense
rustling, and he wondered what manner of beast might be
lurking in the darkness. There had been a time, once upon a
time, when he would have recognized the night moves of the
creatures who shared the mountain, but not anymore. He'd
been gone too long, had spent too many years in the cities of
the East. He wasn't even sure that he knew what inhabited
the mountain these days, what had been driven out or
endangered during the years since he had left Larkspur.

From across the rugged distance of the hills he could see
the amber lights from the Hollister ranch, tiny bright
candles in the night, down in the valley below. For a split
second he had considered stopping there when he had
driven past two days earlier. Hap and Catherine Hollister
would have welcomed him, he felt certain. As the local
Little League coach, it had been Hap who taught Cale how
to hit and how to throw, how to field. Cale and Sky Hollister
had been best friends back then, had played on the same
baseball team, and had spent endless hours practicing on
the makeshift playing field behind the Hollisters' barn.

They could have played on the field down in Larkspur—
as a town boy, it had been a long, dusty bike ride out to the
ranch in the merciless heat of those Montana summers—
but Sky's home had all the warmth that Cale's had lacked.
With a truck driver father who spent his infrequent sober
times on the road, and a mother who had walked out on all
of them years ago, Cale and his younger sister, Valerie, had
spent more time in the homes of their friends growing up
than they had in their own. Mrs. Hollister had always

welcomed Cale to their table, and Coach Hollister, who had seen the extraordinary athletic ability latent in the boy, had spent endless hours coaching him, teaching him. By the time Cale was in high school, he knew that, barring injury, a career playing professional baseball awaited him. He wondered where he would have been had it not been for Coach Hollister's tutoring. Probably not, he reckoned, playing in the majors.

As a youth, he'd spent many a summer night there at the Hollister ranch. Sometimes the boys all slept in the barn, or in one of the old bunkhouses. As he grew older, Cale recalled, sleeping in the bunkhouse had held a lot less appeal than sleeping in the ranch house, where he could, if luck was with him, run into Sky's sister. All of the Hollister girls had been knockouts, from CeCe, the oldest, right down to Liza, the baby. But as a young boy growing up, there had only been one girl who had caught his eye and fueled his adolescent fantasies.

Cale could not recall a time in his life when he had not been in love with Quinn Hollister. In his eyes, she had been the most beautiful girl in the world. Tall and exotic, with long dark auburn hair and eyes the same pale, luminous green as the piece of sea glass an aunt had sent him from Florida one year, Quinn had been his first love, his only love. Even now, so many years later, Cale could close his eyes and see her riding that big palomino mare of hers across the hills, her bright hair glowing like a halo and flowing like a river behind her. Beautiful. Beautiful as the pastel glow of the sun he now watched slide that last notch behind her family home.

And the wonder of it had been that Quinn had loved him, too.

If he had worked hard to achieve honors status in school, it had been to prove to Quinn that he was worthy of her. If he had spent hour after endless hour practicing hitting and catching to perfect his skills, it was as much to secure his future with her as it was to fulfill his dreams of being a star outfielder in the majors. He had even forgone his last two years of college to accept an offer from the Baltimore Harbormasters professional baseball team so that he could support her in style.

Cale had been convinced that he was the luckiest guy in the world back then, when, on his twentieth birthday, he had signed his first major league contract and proposed marriage to the then seventeen-year-old Quinn and she had thrown her arms around his neck to accept. Coach and Mrs. Hollister, however, had taken a dim view of their daughter skipping college and jumping into matrimony. Despite Quinn's promise to her parents that she would attend and complete school in Maryland where Cale would begin his major league career, the elder Hollisters were adamant. As much as they cared about Cale, there would be no wedding until the bride had graduated from college.

Quinn had argued and cried, but had been unable to convince her parents to permit her to marry at so young an age. And so, Quinn had told Cale, they would have to take matters into their own hands. Chart their own course. Follow their own star.

On the day she turned eighteen, they would elope.

It never failed to amaze Cale that, so many years later, the pain had barely diminished. His heart still hurt, his head still pounded, every time he thought back to that day, when he'd waited for her *right here,* in the very spot where he now stood on the porch of the old cabin where they had agreed to meet. And waited. And waited until the sun had begun its soft descent into the pastel hills and he knew there was no longer any reason to wait. Had he really believed that a girl like Quinn would give up everything that she had for the son of a hard-drinking truck driver from the wrong side of town? Cale had taken the plane ticket from his pocket—the one he had bought for his bride—and ripped it into a hundred pieces before climbing into the cab of his old black pickup and slamming the door. The truck had screamed down the gravel road and past the Hollister ranch as he had fought the tears of loss, of humiliation, and headed for the Gallatin Field about eight miles west of Bozeman. If he drove fast enough, he'd still make his flight to Denver, and from there, he'd fly to Baltimore. Alone.

Cale had gone on to fame and glory in the majors, but he never went back to the Montana hills or the cabin where he'd left his dreams of happily ever after with the only woman he'd ever really loved. Until now.

Cale rubbed his shoulder, as if to rub away the injury that plagued him, the injury that had, on a hot August night in Cleveland, ended his career. He had watched the film of the midair collision of the two men in the outfield almost dispassionately, as if it had been happening to someone else. Over and over he had played it, hoping against hope that the two bodies would not crash into each other, would not fall, one badly angled, to the earth. But each time it ended the same way. Each time he watched, he could feel the ground beneath his shoulder, could hear the crunch as bone gave way to turf. Two surgeries later, he had begun to regain his strength, but not his mobility. He would never play ball again, and that was that.

So here Cale stood, on the porch of an old mountain cabin, looking off into the dark night, wondering if it had been such a good idea to come here after all. Over the past year, his sister had hired a crew of contractors to rebuild the structure that had been for so long little more than an abandoned shell. The renovations having been completed in the fall, Val had spent two months here alone, escaping from the big city life she had never really adjusted to, seeking a haven from the demands of her modeling career that sometimes threatened to overcome her.

Although Cale and Valerie had grown up in town, they had spent many a summer day in the hills, and had been as proud of their connection to the old, dilapidated cabin as they had been of the legends that had grown up over the years surrounding its original inhabitant, Jed McKenzie. Surely the changes Val had made to the cabin would have mystified and amused their bachelor great-great-uncle, an early conservationist, who had spent most of his adult life here alone, and had died here alone years ago. Valerie had discovered that nothing really restored her the way a trip back to the hills could do, and this year she managed to convince Cale that some time up in the hills would be as good for his soul as it had been for hers. She had stocked the freezer and the pantry before leaving right after Thanksgiving, and had planned to meet her brother and his sons here for Christmas.

"It'll be great, Cale, you'll see," Valerie had promised.

"Just you, me, and your boys. You'll wish you'd come back sooner. . . ."

Cale doubted that, especially since he was beginning to wonder if Val's plane would make it to the airport in Lewistown before the storm that threatened to blow down from the mountains would arrive and close not only the airport but the roads as well. And he could do without the memories being in this cabin brought back. Banging his feet on the step to shake off the snow, he went back inside.

The warmth from the fire greeted him like an old friend, and he sat on the chair near the door to pull off his boots. In thick woolen socks he crossed the old pine floorboards as quietly as he could, lest he waken the twin sleeping devils who were his sons. Eric and Evan slept, one at each end of the sofa, each a four-year-old lump under the big black and tan hand-knitted afghan that their next-door neighbor, Mrs. Lindley, had made for Cale when he had left for college in Bozeman. Cale stoked the fire, then added another log, wondering if he should wake the boys for dinner. Clearly, they had been totally tuckered out from their hike in the deep snow that afternoon. Cale had been tempted to nap for a while himself, but his nights had been so restless lately that he feared an afternoon snooze would just be an invitation to one more long, sleepless night.

He went into the small kitchen and boiled some water for coffee, hoping that, this time, he'd get it right. Spoiled by all the conveniences that money could buy, he'd forgotten how to perk coffee on the top of the old stove, although this morning's efforts had been a big improvement over yesterday's. Funny, Val had modernized so much of the cabin, but had yet to replace the old stove. There was, she had told him, something about the way food tasted when she cooked on it that she wasn't ready to give up just yet. It made her feel like she hadn't quite lost that pioneer spirit. Just one of Val's little quirks, he figured. We all have them. He poured a little milk into his cup and tasted the hot, dark brown liquid. Better. He'd get it just right before too much longer.

Quietly placing the cup on the battered maple table, Cale pulled the old wing chair—his great-uncle Jed's favorite—closer to the fire and opened the book he had started the night before. You could hear a pin drop in here, he thought. There was no quiet as deep as that which you find in the hills. It both comforted him and made him jumpy. He'd been away too long to feel at home, but was discovering that he still had enough sense of the hills that the silence was a familiar one. He sighed and leaned back, and started to read the new legal thriller everyone was talking about.

The top log thumped dully against the back of the firebox, and he quietly rose to replace it. Eric stirred softly, his little foot in its little white sock pushed out from under the blanket. They were so cute when they were sleeping, Cale mused. And such little demons when they were awake. He wondered ruefully if perhaps the secret to raising two such children might not be lots and lots of exercise, much like the hike they'd taken that afternoon. Without wanting to, Cale's mind trailed back to last Christmas, to the big fancy house his wife, Jo Beth, had talked him into buying outside of Baltimore. As big as it was, as expensive as it had been, it had never been enough for her.

Jo Beth Wilkins had pursued Cale McKenzie from the night she first met him till the night he finally married her. Even then, in the midst of the ceremony, he had had the sinking feeling that he was going to regret it. But Jo Beth had been insistent and he had been tired of dodging the marital bullet, tired of discussing it. Tired of being asked about it. In a weak moment he had agreed to marry her, and it seemed from that moment on there'd been no turning back. She had been totally annoyed to have found herself pregnant, but once she found out she was having twins, she had come to accept the fact that if she had two at once, her job would be done and she'd never have to do *that* again. As soon as the boys were born, she hired a nanny, joined a spa, and set about the business of being a professional baseball wife again. She had been good at that, he'd give Jo Beth that much.

On the day it had been confirmed that his playing days were behind him, she'd packed and gone back to Tennessee—with a quick stop at a Nevada divorce-atorium—leaving Cale with the boys, the nanny, and the house, which he promptly sold, sending her a check for exactly half. She'd sent him a copy of the divorce decree in his birthday card, and he hadn't heard from her since.

Waking in her old room—the room she had shared with CeCe as a girl—never failed to bring Quinn face-to-face with the past. At dawn she had yawned and stretched and turned over, hopeful for a few extra hours of sleep on this first day of her Christmas vacation. But every time she closed her eyes, another memory would call itself forth. In this room she had written poetry and love letters and long wordy pages—alternating between bliss and despair—in a diary. When she was twelve, she had argued with CeCe and divided the room in half with an imaginary line neither of them had dared to cross for weeks. Later that same year she and Sunny sat on the edge of this very bed and watched as CeCe transformed herself from ranch hand to princess as she dressed for the sophomore dance at the high school down in the valley. Two years later, Quinn herself had been dressed in a flowing dress of palest lavender and had put her hair up and had felt very much the sophisticate on the arm of Caleb McKenzie.

That had been their first real date, after months of casual "hi's" exchanged in the hallways at school or at the ball field where Quinn had trailed behind her father and brother, ostensibly to watch Sky play, though Quinn couldn't have said what position Sky played. She'd never taken her eyes off Cale. When he'd shyly asked her to be his date for the big dance at school that spring, she'd thought the heavens had opened up and dropped the most precious of gifts into her waiting arms.

The dance had been everything a first big dance should be. Quinn and Cale had danced and talked and danced and talked, and finally—finally!—had kissed in the backseat of the car Billy DeWitt had borrowed from his big brother for the occasion. Later Cale had admitted that the only reason he hadn't wanted to double-date with Sky—who was, after all, his best friend—was because he'd been afraid that Sky would have decked him if he'd caught him kissing his little sister the way Cale had been planning to.

They had been inseparable after that, Quinn recalled. Quinn and Cale. For his remaining two years of high school, and his first two years of college, she and Cale had been desperately in love and the very best of friends. They had known each other's secrets, each other's dreams. Cale had been her first and best and biggest love. It had never occurred to Quinn that they wouldn't always be together. They had planned such a wonderful life, and she couldn't wait to begin it.

Though Cale had been hounded by professional teams from the time he'd been a junior in high school, he'd accepted a scholarship at Montana State down in Bozeman because it was close to home, and to Quinn. By his sophomore year, he'd known he couldn't wait much longer to marry her. As young as she and Cale were, Quinn had been confident that her parents would support them in their wedding plans—after all, her mother hadn't been much older than Quinn when she'd married.

No one had been more surprised than Quinn when her parents were appalled by their seventeen-year-old daughter's announcement that she and Cale would be getting married the week following her high school graduation. But she had it all worked out, she had told them tearfully when they flatly refused to give their blessing to her plans. She and Cale would both go to Montana State, and when he graduated in two years, she would simply transfer to a college in whatever city he'd be playing professional baseball.

"Quinn, for heaven's sake, you're only seventeen," Catherine had sighed.

"Mom, I love Cale. . . ."

"I'm sure that you think you do, sweetheart. But your father and I really believe that you're simply far too young to make a decision like this. Quinn, you've barely been out of Montana. You need to see more of the world—go places and do things."

"The only place I want to go is to Bozeman with Cale. The only thing I want to do is marry him."

"Quinn, listen to me." Catherine had sat on the edge of her daughter's bed. "Give yourself a little more time. At least wait two years. . . ."

Two years! They might just have well as asked her to wait two lifetimes.

And so Cale had contacted the coach for the Baltimore

team who had been pursuing him and the deal was struck. He would leave Montana, but he'd be taking Quinn with him. They'd get married as soon as they hit Maryland. Hap and Catherine would come around, Quinn had promised. She would enroll in a college nearby while Cale tried to make his mark in professional baseball. Life would surely be wonderful.

Quinn had never stopped wondering if, in fact, life would have been as blissful as those dreams, if he hadn't stood her up.

She had waited at the cabin that day until after dark, until she could no longer deny the fact that he had decided not to take her with him after all. She had gone home and forced herself to inquire casually if Cale had called. He had not.

Quinn had slowly climbed the stairs to her bed in the second-floor loft and, as quietly as she could, cried until there were no more tears left to be shed. The next day she had ridden out into the hills and, in a gesture her seventeen-year-old heart had thought suitably dramatic, threw his high school ring off the side of Boldface Rock, and had vowed never to speak his name again unless she had to. Too embarrassed to tell her family that she had been stood up, she had pretended that she and Cale had broken up following an argument, and she had refused to do more than mutter a vague reply or shrug noncommittally when asked about him. Eventually, the questions stopped, and as far as her family was concerned, the entire episode was past history. Which was exactly what Quinn wanted them to think

Of course, over the years it had been impossible to avoid knowing that he'd made his mark on the sport he loved. Quinn had stopped watching the game altogether and never read the sports pages. She didn't want to know where he was playing or how he was doing, but, of course, the local paper followed his every move, complete with photographs, from every game-winning play to his marriage to a former beauty queen from some Southern state a few years earlier.

"Looks like Cale finally settled down," her mother had told her tentatively on the telephone. "Saturday's paper had a picture of him and his bride right on the front page."

If Only in My Dreams

"How nice for Cale," Quinn had replied flatly, then inquired after the health of one of Sky's mares that had been sick the week before. Later she had hung up the phone and licked her wounds in private, as she had always done.

From time to time, Quinn caught a glimpse of him as he was being interviewed on television, and for that one moment, time would stand still, and he would still be her Cale, but only for a moment, only until she collected her wits and changed the channel. Oh, if hard-pressed, she'd have grudgingly admitted that she was proud of him, proud for him, that he'd managed to overcome an uncertain start in life and had followed his dream. On the other hand, she'd never been able to forgive him for letting her give her heart so completely, only to break it.

And she'd never once, in the twelve years that had passed, awakened in that bed in her old room without thinking of him and the nights she had spent crying for him. And somehow, all these years later, the memories still had the power to hurt.

I guess he just didn't know how to tell me that he'd changed his mind about me, she thought as she threw her legs over the side of the bed and reached for her robe.

It would be really nice if, just this once, I could get through a holiday season without having to hear about him.

She sighed, knowing that was unlikely. Cale McKenzie was the only bona fide, home-grown celebrity to come out of Larkspur, Montana. Sooner or later, over the next two weeks, someone—more accurately, *lots* of someones, family and friends alike—would be certain to bring up his name.

It's okay, she reassured herself as she rummaged through her suitcase for her jeans and a clean sweatshirt, *I can handle it. I always have.*

As if to convince herself, she forced herself to whistle a merry Christmas tune as she headed off down the hall toward her morning shower.

Three

". . . AND SANDY OSBORNE'S BEEN DIVORCED NOW FOR THE third time," Catherine was saying as she watched Quinn roll out sugar cookie dough on the marble countertop she'd had installed for just that very purpose. "She finally threw in the towel on marriage, I guess, 'cause she moved back into her folks' home in town."

"Poor Sandy," Quinn mused. "She never really did know what she wanted, did she?"

"Only on a temporary basis, it would seem," Catherine muttered. "There now, Quinn, flatten out that corner there, so all the dough's the same thickness."

Quinn did as she was told, secretly smiling. In her search for perfection in all things, Catherine would continue to instruct until her kids got it right.

"Stars?" Quinn asked, holding up the old tin cookie cutter, and her mother nodded absently. Quinn proceeded to press the cookie cutter into the dough, and Catherine lifted the little stars and placed them on the waiting baking sheets.

"I cannot wait until Susannah gets here with that darling little Lilly of hers," Catherine sighed, then grumbled. "To think I'd end up with only one grandchild, after all these years."

"Mom, you haven't 'ended up,'" Quinn reminded her. "None of us are even married yet."

"Don't think I don't realize that." Catherine held up her hand. "Goodness, six children and no sons- or daughters-in-law."

"Sunny was married for a while."

"Please, him I'd rather forget." Catherine shook her head. "I just don't understand why none of you has found someone to fall madly in love with so I could go to my grave knowing at least one of my children would live happily ever after."

"Mom, your grave isn't ready for you, and we all will live happily ever after. Eventually."

"Well, I wish you'd get on with it." Catherine opened the oven and slid the sheet of white-dough stars inside. "A house should be filled with children on Christmas."

"The house will be filled with kids, Mom, since we'll all be home," Quinn reminded her, "and we're all just little kids at heart."

Catherine raised her eyes above the oven door and glared at her middle child. "You've all long passed that cute, cuddly stage where you believed in Santa and couldn't wait to get up on Christmas morning to see what toys he brought you. I miss that excitement, Quinn. It's been all too many years since little hands have tapped my cheek to wake me at dawn." She brightened, adding, "At least I have Lilly to spoil, though every year I look at you and your brothers and your sisters and wonder if I've raised a bunch of crabby old maids and grumpy old bachelors."

Quinn laughed and kissed her mother's cheek. "You worry too much, Mom. We're just all taking our time to find the right person, that's all. Now, how long will those cookies take?" She peered at the recipe book. "Twelve minutes. Just enough time to go up to the attic and bring down a few boxes of Christmas decorations."

"Well, it might be a good idea to do that now. Your dad is afraid that the storm they've been predicting for tomorrow might hit early, so he wanted to go out after lunch to cut down the tree."

"CeCe will be disappointed if we go without her."

"She'll be more disappointed if we end up with no tree at all because we waited too long to go."

"True." Quinn turned on the light to the attic and opened the door, setting loose a cold whoosh of frigid, musty air. She climbed the steps and set about the task of selecting the boxes that would be stacked and carried to the first floor to trim the family tree. One of the advantages of being the first one home, she mused, is that you got to choose what decorations would go on the tree. She peeked through this box and that, piling up the ones that held her personal favorites. After several trips up and down the steps, she had several piles of boxes assembled in the great room. She began to lift lids, and to reminisce.

The timer from the kitchen signaled that this present batch of Christmas cookies had finished baking. She heard the oven door open, then close, smelled the pure vanilla aroma. Her mother would finish up the batches of sugar cookies, then start on the oatmeal raisin cookies, the orange drops, the shortbread. Everyone's favorites would be made, from her father's chocolate chip to those of Lilly, the youngest member of the family, who had a preference for the butterscotch brownies she had sampled the last time she had visited. Sky would want gingersnaps, Liza would want lemon squares, Susannah chocolate thumbprints, and Trevor and CeCe, the twins and oldest of the Hollister brood, would be scouring the cookie tins until they found the big, soft molasses cookies they both loved. Her mother would continue baking for days, and from now until Christmas, the old ranch house would smell like a fine bakeshop.

"Hey, Sis," Schuyler called from the doorway, "if you're planning on going with us to find the tree, you'd better start to get ready now."

"Can't you wait another hour or so, Sky? Mom and I were going to make the dough for the gingerbread houses next."

"Dad and I are thinking we should go before lunch." Schuyler pointed out the window and frowned. "It's getting white back toward the mountains. Dad thinks the storm might come early, and he'd just as soon take care of the tree now."

"I think I'll pass, then. Mom wanted to have a little village of gingerbread houses all baked so that when Sunny gets home, Lilly can have fun decorating them." Quinn lifted the lid off a box. "Look here, Sky. All the old colored-glass Christmas balls."

"You mean all the ones that didn't get broken the year the cat jumped onto the Christmas tree," her brother called from the kitchen, where he would be snitching a few golden sugar cookies off the cooling racks. "Good idea Liza had, to tie a ribbon around the cat's neck and take her for a walk."

The young orange tabby had taken off across the room, jumped onto the back of the sofa, from which it had been a mere hop onto the back of the Christmas tree, which had smashed forward onto the hardwood floor with all the might of a falling timber. Liza had been six or seven at the time, and had never lived it down. Knowing how upset Catherine had been to have lost so many of *her* mother's fragile glass balls, the children had spent the next several days making things to hang on the tree to take the place of those that had shattered. Paper chains and popcorn balls, diamond shapes made of aluminum foil and toothpicks, clothespin dolls and stars made of drinking straws, all had been hung on the tree to surprise their mother. Quinn would never forget the look on her mother's face when they led her into the great room and turned the lights on the tree. Liza had been vindicated, and the integrity of the family tree as a sort of family journal had remained intact.

From the pink tissue lining of the box that lay open on her lap, Quinn uncovered a stack of white paper hearts. She lifted it and let the paper chain unfold, remembering the year she had been ten and a bad case of chicken pox had kept her confined to her bed. Catherine had done double duty that year, supervising the tree decorating downstairs and trying to keep Quinn entertained in her sickroom at the same time. To make Quinn feel a part of the family effort, Catherine had brought her stacks of paper and a pair of scissors. With careful folding and a few quick snips, Catherine had shown her how to transform the paper into a chain of hearts. Quinn had spent all of Christmas Eve making chain after chain, and Catherine had patiently taped them together into one long chain before hanging them on the tree. Over the years this one or that section of Quinn's heart-chain had been ripped or torn or mistakenly tossed out, but here, in the corner of the box, cushioned by pink tissue, the last of the paper chain rested.

I could probably still do this in my sleep, Quinn thought, as she folded the chain back into itself again, *I made so many of them that night.* Holding the hearts in her hand brought that night back to her so vividly, and for the briefest second, Quinn felt that if she closed her eyes, she could still hear her mother's gentle voice, feel the cooling touch of those soothing fingers, taste the cold tartness of the orange juice Catherine had brought her.

The timer buzzed rudely from the kitchen and Catherine turned it off. It was time to start another batch of cookies if they were to be done by the end of the week. Quinn loved having this little bit of the morning to spend alone with her mother, just as she loved sorting through the old boxes that contained the fragments of Christmases past, as she loved the little pieces of herself and her family that she found within them.

Wasn't that what coming home for Christmas was all about, the memories, the love?

"Quinn." Sky tapped her on the shoulder.

"What?" She looked up at him.

"I said, Mom's calling you."

"Oh, I guess she's ready to make the gingerbread."

"You're sure you don't want to join us, Quinn?" Her father asked.

"I'm sure, Dad." She smiled back at the big man who filled the doorway. He was still tall and broad-shouldered, though not quite so tall as Sky, nor as muscular as Trevor, both of whom had played high school football before going on to play at the University of Montana at Missoula. Though well into his sixties, their father still had all of his hair, much of which was still chestnut brown, like that of both his sons. His eyes still twinkled and his laughter still filled this house and his face still softened when he looked at his beloved Catherine.

It had only been recently that Hap had started taking the first steps toward retiring, talking about turning the ranch over to his sons, to give him more time to spend with his wife. They spoke of taking a cruise come February, maybe even fly to Florida, then book a ship to the islands over there on the opposite side of the country. Their children not only encouraged them but had, as a Christmas surprise, chipped in for that very trip for their parents. Trevor had driven into town just that morning to see if the tickets had been delivered to the post office box.

Quinn had set the box of ornaments on the floor and stood up, preparing to drop the chain of hearts into a basket on the table next to her, when she realized the basket was filled with Christmas cards.

"I can never get over how many people find the time to mail Christmas cards each year," she said to her father.

"It's not something you find time to do," her mother corrected her from the nearby kitchen, "it's something you *make* time to do. And we received some lovely cards this year."

Quinn lifted the stack of cards and sorted through them, reading the names of the senders. Mostly relatives and old friends of the family, she noted.

"Who is 'Valerie'?" she asked, holding up the environmentally correct card depicting the endangered timber wolf on the front.

"Valerie McKenzie." Hap grinned. "She was here over Thanksgiving. Spent most of the fall up at old Jed's cabin, cleaning it up. Had a bunch of workmen up there every day. Had all sorts of new stuff delivered. New refrigerator, some new furniture. First time in years there's been a McKenzie back up here. You probably heard that she made it real big as a model in New York. Yep"—he nodded—"she's grown into one beautiful young woman, wouldn't you say, son?"

Sky shrugged noncommitally.

"Oh, right, I'll just *bet* you didn't notice her." Quinn laughed. "Just like you didn't notice how well she filled out those little bathing suits when she was sixteen and she and Liza used to go swimming down at Golden Lake."

Quinn ducked the rolled-up piece of paper that Sky threw in the direction of her head.

"Well, she's a lovely girl, and we're looking forward to seeing her over the Christmas holidays," Catherine told them. "She and Liza are planning on getting together. They were the best of friends for so long, you'll remember."

"Val is going to be staying at the cabin over Christmas?" Quinn asked.

"She said she would be. Said she enjoyed being home so much that she was sorry she'd stayed away so long," Hap told her.

"Did she now?" Quinn grinned meaningfully at Sky, who was just about to tell her that Valerie wasn't the only McKenzie who'd be around over the next few weeks.

Quinn was still smirking at her brother as she dropped Val's card into the basket.

On second thought, Sky thought, rubbing his chin thoughtfully, maybe we'll just let Little Miss Smart Mouth make that discovery on her own.

He just hoped that he wasn't around when she did.

"Daddy, we want cartoons." Evan McKenzie leaned over his father's shoulder and directly into his face to make his announcement.

"Yeah." Eric nodded. "We're bored."

"How can you be bored?" Cale glanced across the room to the clock on the mantle. It was barely ten o'clock in the morning. This had, he grimaced, all the makings of a *very* long day.

"We want television," the twins chorused.

"Guys, guys, for the last time, there is no television here. You're in the wilds of *Montana,* just like the hearty pioneers. Look"—Cale stood up and pulled back the homespun curtain on the living room window and pointed outside—"you stand right here and watch, and I'll bet that before too long a deer or an elk will go right by."

"We saw elk yesterday," Evan reminded him.

"I'd rather see the Grinch," Eric grumbled.

"Or *Sesame Street.* I miss Bert and Ernie, don't you?" Evan tumbled on top of his brother and brought him down with a thud.

"Elmo. And Oscar." Eric sat on his brother's chest. "And Beavis . . ."

"And Butthead."

"How do you guys know about Beavis and Butthead?" Cale asked over his shoulder.

"Cathy let us watch it with her when you were in habili . . . that place. After you got hurt," Evan told his father.

"You mean rehabilitation." Cale frowned and made a mental note to speak with Mrs. Mason, the nanny, about what her eleven-year-old daughter was watching on television these days.

"Yeah. That." Eric nodded as he struggled to slip out of his shirt and escape from his brother, rolling over the back of the sofa their Aunt Valerie had had delivered a month before.

Evan dove for his twin, who, being a master of evasive action, turned in time to send Evan crashing into the table and pitching the lamp onto the floor.

Cale considered his roughhousing offspring, and figured it would take them another twenty minutes more to pretty much destroy all the work it had taken his sister several months to accomplish. There would be hell to pay when Val arrived. Oh, he could explain a broken lamp—make that two broken lamps, he thought as he flinched at the sound coming from their bedroom—but as proud as she had been of the fact that she had transformed the old cabin into a cozy retreat, she was not likely to have more than two lamps' worth of forgiveness to spare.

A crash from the small dining area raised the ante to two lamps and one vase.

"Boys, get your gear, we're taking a walk." He caught the little hellions as they tried to flee back down the hallway that led to two small bedrooms.

"We took a walk yesterday," Evan protested loudly.

"Well, we're taking another one today." Cale dumped the squirming bodies onto the sofa. "Get your boots and your jackets and your gloves. Let's move it."

"We don't want to go for a walk. We want to watch cartoons." Eric folded his arms across his chest and did his best to scowl.

"Yeah." Evan mimicked his twin brother's stance and his facial expression.

"Tough. We're walking. Get ready." Cale, not to be out-scowled, pointed firmly to the pile of boots inside the back door.

Still grumbling, the boys reluctantly did as they were told.

"Maybe we'll see a bald eagle," Cale said to encourage them.

"I'd rather see a bear," Eric sulked.

"Yeah. Or a wolf." His brother moped along behind him.

"Trust me, fellas," their father told them as he held the back door open, "you don't want to see a bear or a wolf from the wrong side of the window."

"We're not scared," Eric said bravely.

"Well, you should be." Cale closed the door behind them. "Here, Evan, you can carry the binoculars and Eric can help me shake the snow off the rope."

"Why do you need to tie rope to the house?" Eric asked as he followed his father's lead and pulled the length of rope loose from the snow that had drifted to cover it.

"You tie the rope from the house to the shed where the wood is stacked," Cale explained, "so that if there's a really bad storm, you can go out and get firewood and not get lost in the snow."

"How could you get lost? The house is right there." Eric pointed.

"Sometimes the wind blows the snow around so much you can't see your hand in front of your face," Cale explained, "so you would hold on to the rope and use it to lead you back to the house. Come on, guys, let's go real quietly and we'll see what just landed in that big pine tree. . . ."

Dolefully rolling their eyes at each other, the sullen little boys trudged reluctantly through the snow behind their father.

Four

"Are you sure you don't mind that I go out for a while?" Quinn wrapped the scarf around her neck and searched the pockets of her parka for her thick fur-lined gloves. "I haven't been up to Elizabeth's cabin in months."

"Of course I don't mind," Catherine assured her daughter, "just don't get stuck up there. We haven't had near as much snow this year as we did last, and the latest report said that the storm may not arrive until tomorrow, but you never know."

"I have four-wheel drive. I won't get stuck." Quinn stole a cookie from the cooling rack. "And if the snow is too deep, I'll just turn around and come back."

"Well, you won't want to stay up there for too long anyway. There's no heat in the cabin, and it hasn't even been opened in months. You'll more than likely have to clear a path to the front door."

"Right. I'll take a shovel."

"Here, take this, too, just in case you get cold." Her mother handed her a thermos of hot coffee with one hand and a large wreath of fresh greens with the other.

"Thanks, Mom. And maybe I'll take a few of these, too, in case I need a snack." Quinn wrapped a few more cookies in a napkin, pitched an apple into her nylon shoulder bag, which was already bulging—cleaning cloths, candles, her cellular phone, pruning clippers—and headed out the back. "I won't be long. I just want to make sure that Elizabeth gets her wreath this year."

The cold mountain air was jarring once outside the house, and Quinn hurried across the densely packed snow toward her vehicle, which she had parked out by the barn. She opened the driver's door, tossed her bag onto the front seat, and laid the wreath on the backseat. Returning to the house, she took a broom from the pantry and a snow shovel from the open back porch and slid them both onto the floor in the back of the car before climbing in. She turned on the ignition, giving the engine a minute to warm up before making a wide circle and heading toward the road, driving tentatively, testing the depth of the snow. Finding her traction, she headed on up into the hills, to the old stone cabin that was built by her great-great-grandparents over a century earlier, where every year, Quinn or one of her siblings had gone to hang a wreath on the door to commemorate not only the date on which their great-great-grandmother had been born, but the date she had wed, as well.

They all called it Elizabeth's cabin, although in truth it had been both Elizabeth and Stephen Dunham who had, together, hauled endless stones from the beds of mountain streams to build their sturdy one-room shelter where they had begun their married life. As Stephen prospered as a trapper, the cabin had been expanded to accommodate their growing family. Years later, when Stephen's father had died back East in Philadelphia, he had with the greatest reluctance made the decision to return to take his place in the family shipbuilding business. Elizabeth had known that her husband's blue-blooded family was not likely to welcome her, a full-blooded Cherokee, with open arms, but she had promised to keep an open mind for Stephen's sake and for the sake of their children. And so she had accompanied him on the train across the country, the children all dressed in new "city" clothes, the boys tugging at their stiff collars, the girls confused by the number of undergarments they were forced to wear. The Dunhams had tolerated Elizabeth's presence while Stephen lived, but after his demise following a tragic carriage accident on Broad Street, Elizabeth had packed her belongings, and left her children with their grandmother to be educated as their father had wished. Taking the stash of gold coins Stephen had set aside for her, intending that she would never have to ask her in-laws for money, Elizabeth returned alone to the hills she had loved, to the cabin where she and Stephen and the children had been so happy, and it had been there that she remained until she died at the ripe old age of ninety-two.

Behind the cabin a small stone rose from the grass to designate Elizabeth's final resting place, a smaller stone nearby marking the grave of a daughter, Mary, who had not survived an outbreak of measles. Stories passed down through the family told of Elizabeth's oldest daughter's, Selena's, fight to bring Stephen's body back to the hills to bury him beside his beloved wife, but her efforts had been blocked by her brother Robert. Having taken his place as a Philadelphia Dunham, Robert had refused to permit the moving of their father's body from the cemetery in the city Stephen had never really known, and surely had never loved as he had loved the Montana wilderness. Elizabeth's heart would have broken, seeing her children divided, her son Avery siding with Selena, and Sarah and John siding with Robert. To this day, the descendants of one faction had no communication with those of the other.

It was said, too, that Elizabeth had never left the hills, that she waited still for Stephen's return. Several of Elizabeth's descendants had, at one time or another, claimed to have seen her, usually at a time of danger. Her daughter Selena was said to have seen her innumerable times, as had

Quinn's mother and aunt, Catherine and her sister, Charlotte. In Quinn's generation, both Liza and CeCe had claimed to have seen her once when they were swimming and a mountain lion had stalked them on the way home. Susannah swore she had seen her once when a momma bear had decided that Susannah was picking huckleberries all too closely to the den wherein her cubs slept. Each time, it seemed, Elizabeth had appeared to lead her descendants to safety. Quinn alone of Catherine's girls had yet to see the old woman, who had always been described in the same manner: dark hair, gently streaked with gray, hanging over one shoulder in a fat braid that reached past her hips, a green woolen blanket wrapped around her against the chill of the mountain air.

A random snowflake fell here and there as Quinn headed farther up the hill. Over the tops of the trees to her left, a trail of smoke twined toward the sky. She stopped momentarily, then recalled that the McKenzie cabin sat back in the woods a little off the road, back behind the pines. Val must already be there, she thought as she headed on her way.

"I love this place," Quinn announced aloud to the silence inside her car. "I love the way the road winds around through the trees, and I love the way the trees look up here when they are covered with snow, like puffy, soft sculptures, white and quiet and still. And I love the way the air smells, sharp and intense and drenched with pine."

She slowed, then stopped the car in front of the old one-room structure, the original section of the cabin that had been all to survive a fire twenty years earlier.

"And most of all," she proclaimed as she hopped out, "I love *this* place."

Despite the fact that she had spent some of the most painful moments of her life in this very spot—had spent several hours pacing the stone path leading to the door, waiting for a man who never came—Quinn's love for the cabin had never diminished.

With the shovel she dug a narrow path through the snow to the thick wooden door marking the front of the old stone structure that had weathered more than a hundred winters. Through her heavy gloves her fingers sought the nail upon which she would hang the wreath. She returned to the car and slid the shovel in the backseat with one hand, and with the other, grabbed the wreath and the broom. Slinging her bag over her shoulder, she returned to the cabin and placed the circle of greens on the door. With fingers already cold through her gloves, she searched her bag for the key ring she had removed from the cupboard in the ranch house, and finding the key marked "E," she slid open the lock that hung from the old wooden door handle.

As if a simple lock would keep anyone out who wanted in, she thought, as she pushed the thick door open into the small room, then closed it behind her. Dropping the bag to the floor, she leaned down to retrieve the candles and matches she had packed to lend a little extra light to that which the small windows afforded. One by one she lit the candles, placing them around the room to brighten and cheer the dark space.

"Happy birthday, Grandmother."

Rummaging in her bag again, she found the clippers she had packed, then pulled her hood up and went outside to clip a few sprigs of holly from the tall bush that sheltered one side of the cabin.

Though the air was bitterly cold, Quinn welcomed its sharpness even as it stung her nose and throat just to breathe it in, reminding her of all those many winters Elizabeth had spent here alone. Quinn thought perhaps she understood why Elizabeth had brought her broken heart here, why she had stayed with nothing but the wind to keep her company. Had Quinn herself not sought the silence of the hills, and come to this place to nurse her own broken heart?

Piling up the clipped branches, Quinn went back inside and dropped them onto the floor, then pulled a cloth from her bag and, singing Christmas carols, proceeded to dust the furniture and the window ledges. Starting as children, each of the Hollister girls had taken their turn at this small task, cleaning Elizabeth's cabin, several times each year. Although all grown women now, they still continued with the tradition. It didn't take long, there being little furniture left to dust. Quinn cleaned a few dead bees from the window ledges, then dusted a few spiders from the mantle before placing the holly branches there, wondering if perhaps

Elizabeth might have, once upon a time, done the same thing. Sweeping cobwebs from the corners and dust from the floor and removing the dead leaves from the unused fireplace pretty much completed the job.

"And now, we can visit," Quinn announced. Opening the thermos, she poured herself a cup of coffee. The cookies tempted her, but her hands were grimy from cleaning, so she decided to forego the snack until she arrived back at the ranch. "Are you here, Elizabeth?" she asked softly.

The air inside the unheated cabin was cold enough that Quinn's breath puffed from her face in tiny white clouds. She sat on one of the backless benches near the front window and sipped at her coffee, feeling the past—familial as well as personal—nipping at her heels. It had been in *that* very doorway she had stood watching for Cale's beat-up old black pickup truck that day, *this* exact bench on which she had sat and sobbed, her heart breaking at the truth she had had to face. Not once since that day had she entered this room without imagining that she could sense the vestiges of her own heartache, as if the walls had absorbed her sorrow and held it there, along with Elizabeth's.

"I suppose more than one of us has wept our share of tears here," she said aloud, as if to include the spirit of her grandmother in her reverie.

She drained the last bit of cool liquid from the cup and returned it to the top of the thermos, where it served as a lid. Pulling her jacket around her against the chill that seemed to seep through the thick walls, she gathered her things and snuffed out the candles.

"Good-bye, Grandmother, and merry Christmas to you. I'll be back in the spring. I hope your birthday is a happy one, and that wherever you are, Grandfather Stephen is with you to share your anniversary."

Quinn opened the door, and stepped into a swirl of white wind that all but lifted her from her feet. While she had cleaned Elizabeth's cabin, the storm had hit with a ferocity she had not seen in years. She put her head down against the driving wind, her feet seeking the path she had made, grateful that she had shoveled so narrow a trail, because only by following the path she had made was she able to find the car, so dense was the snowfall.

How could I have been so oblivious, she chastised herself. *How could I have been so foolish to allow myself to lose track of time like that?*

She climbed into the cab and huddled against the seat, trying to decide what to do. Perhaps if she waited a few minutes, the storm would subside as quickly as it had struck. For a long fifteen minutes, Quinn sat staring out through the windshield, but the storm only seemed to intensify. Some heat would be welcome right about now, she thought, as she turned the engine on and shivered heartily as the frigid air filled the cab. Knowing it would be some minutes before the vehicle warmed up, she decided to call home and let her family know where she was. Cold fingers punched the number on the cellular phone that she had dug out of her bag.

"Trevor? Hi," she said, trying to sound as nonchalant as possible.

"Quinn? Where are you? You sound so far away."

"I'm sitting outside of Elizabeth's cabin. The storm came up so quickly. I never even heard the wind pick up."

"Really? There's a storm up there? Hasn't hit the valley yet," he told her. "Are you all right?"

"Right now, I am. I thought I'd give it a few minutes to see if things settled down before I headed for home. Is it snowing there at all?"

"Not a flake. I guess it'll move down the mountain soon. Which means I should probably leave now if I'm going to make it to the airport to pick up Sunny and Lilly and whoever else is flying in today." He paused thoughtfully. "You're sure you're okay, Quinn?"

"Well"—she hesitated—"the snowfall is pretty dense right about now."

"On a scale from one to ten . . . ," Trevor asked, his standard barometer.

"Thirteen," she replied grimly.

"That bad, eh? Maybe Sky should take the truck and come up for you. . . ."

"No. No sense in both of us being stuck up here. Look, tell Mom and Dad I'll keep in touch. I do have some gas left, so I can keep the heater running, and I have some hot coffee, so I can stay warm."

For a while, anyway. She bit her lip. *What to do when the gas tank is empty and the coffee is gone?*

"Well, then, as soon as the snow lets up even a bit, head back on down slowly. Just keep the pines on either side of you and try to make it down to the hanging rock. If you can get that far, you can probably make it to the old McKenzie cabin. Val's been fixing it up. . . ."

"So I heard," she said wryly, thinking back to Sky's reaction to the mere mention of Valerie's name the night before.

"Yeah, well, if you can get to the cabin, you should be fine. Get a good fire going and wait out the storm."

"I think Val must already be there. I saw smoke from the cabin when I drove past. I just hope there's enough wood to get us through the storm."

"There's plenty." Even through the phone line, she could see Trevor's lopsided grin. "Seems like Sky spent most of the past six months chopping wood and stacking it next to Val's back door."

"I see. Well, then, the cabin should be nice and warm, and I can sit out the storm safely with Valerie."

Assuming I can get there.

"Quinn?" Trevor asked as she was about to say good-bye.

"What?"

"Call back when you get there so we know that you made it."

"I will. Tell Mom not to worry," she assured him. "I'll be fine."

Or I will be, once the snow lightens up.

It was almost twenty minutes more before the storm appeared to ease. She opened the car door tentatively, then slammed it in the face of the vicious wind. Another fifteen minutes passed before she tried again. This time the wind had died down a little, and so she grabbed the ice scraper from under the front seat and set about cleaning off her windows. In so brief a time, a blanket of snow had wrapped around the car, and it took her several minutes to clean the windows sufficiently to allow her to see. With the defroster on full steam, she shifted into first gear and headed toward the void between the towering shadows of the pines that marked either side of the makeshift road. Inch by careful

inch she crept along through a snowfall as thick as clotted
cream, straining her eyes to distinguish shape from shadow,
keeping her speed slow but steady as she made her way
down the mountain. It seemed that an eternity had passed
before she could distinguish the hanging rock there in the
distance. If she could make it just a little farther, she would
find shelter in the old McKenzie cabin.

The car continued its tedious crawl until she was close
enough to the rock to touch it. She pressed a little harder on
the gas pedal until she had passed the landmark, then eased
her foot onto the brake. The car rolled to a soft stop, and she
slid the gearshift into neutral. Rolling down the window,
she looked out onto an icy world that had suddenly turned
totally white. The cabin could be but twenty feet from her
face and she could miss it in this blizzard. She sighed glumly
and turned off the engine, hoping to preserve what little gas
she had left, and had started to roll the window back up
when movement just slightly to the left caught her eye.

Quinn squinted, trying to get a better look through the
churning white, thinking perhaps she had not seen anything
after all. But there, there again, just off the front of the car to
the left . . .

She leaned half out the window, certain that she was
hallucinating. Who in their right mind would be out in this
storm?

A tall, slender woman stood straight against the wind,
and appeared to stare directly at the car. Quinn could not
see her face clearly, but she could see the dark slash of
braided hair that hung to the woman's waist. A dark blanket
wrapped around the figure, which, even as Quinn watched,
pulled the blanket up around her head like a hood. Quinn
knew instinctively who the woman was, and why she was
there.

Elizabeth. Come to lead me through the storm.

Without a second's hesitation, Quinn cut the engine,
pulled the hood up on her down jacket, grabbed her bag,
and stepped out into a swirl of white. All she could see with
any certainty was the woman, who appeared to be waiting
patiently for her to catch up, but with each tedious step that
Quinn took through the deep snow, the woman seemed to

take three. No matter how quickly Quinn tried to walk, her guide managed to stay ahead of her. With the wind whipping around, stinging her face with keen icy needles, Quinn tried to keep up, but soon found herself near exhaustion and totally disoriented, questioning her sanity as she stood in the midst of a world so white that nothing appeared to exist beyond the tip of her nose, which right now was in serious danger of frostbite. And suddenly, in the blink of an eye, Elizabeth was gone.

Stunned to find herself totally alone, Quinn's eyes searched frantically for the figure she had unquestioningly followed, but there was neither form nor shadow to be found in the endless white landscape that surrounded her. The figure that had guided her had vanished without a trace.

"Elizabeth!" She screamed, but not even an echo returned. More frightened than she had ever been in her life, she desperately scanned the white for the shape of the woman in the blanket.

What in the name of heaven had come over her, that she had gotten out of the car in a blinding blizzard to follow a . . . a what? A spirit? Who in their right mind would leave certain shelter, guided only by something or someone who may not even exist, to venture into a world where nothing was certain but snow and wind?

Looking over her shoulder, Quinn sought her car, but knew, even as she squinted into the wind, that she would not find it. She was too turned around to know from which direction she had come, and in the storm, the white car had totally disappeared.

She had, she realized, two simple choices. She could remain where she was, where she would most certainly freeze to death on the spot, or she could search for shelter. Cursing her stupidity for giving credence to what was, after all, merely family legend, she lifted her right foot over the high snow, and fell face forward onto the wooden steps of Jed McKenzie's cabin.

"Thank you, Grandmother," she half laughed, half sobbed through a mouthful of snow as she pulled herself up. Her legs heavy with fatigue, she climbed the other three steps and crossed the porch to the front door. She tapped lightly, then looked through the windows. There did not appear to be anyone there. Turning the door handle, she pushed slightly, and was surprised to find it swing open quietly.

"Hello?" she called into the unlit room that opened up before her. "Val?"

When no one answered, Quinn closed the door against the storm and stepped inside. A big deep fireplace of native stone ran along one wall, and it was there that she automatically headed. Glowing embers in the firebox gave testimony that someone had been there recently enough to have had a fire going.

Val must have headed into town not knowing about the storm, Quinn thought. *I'm sure she won't mind if I wait here till it passes.*

Shivering and cold clear through to the bone, Quinn stacked several logs and fanned the embers until the warm glow began to grow and the flames came alive to warm her. As her hands began to thaw, she removed the gloves and held her hands up close to the fire. The warmth felt so good. She had thought she would never be warm again.

She rummaged in her bag for her phone, and punched in the numbers with fingers that were still stiff and stinging with cold. When the answering machine picked up, she left the message she knew her family would need to hear, that she was safe and warm and out of the storm.

Sitting on a low stool, Quinn removed her boots and wet socks. Her jacket came next, and she hung it on a hook she found inside the front door. She stacked another few logs on the fire, then wrapped herself in the two afghans that she found, one on each end of the sofa. Having fought her way through a piercing wind, she was as exhausted as any soldier fresh from battle. Shivering with the lingering cold, she snuggled down into the cushions and closed her eyes. That she was trespassing into a quiet cabin in the woods made her feel a little like Goldilocks, and her last conscious thought was of looking for something to drink, something not too hot, not too cold. And she would, as soon as she slept off the cold.

five

QUINN'S DEEP SLEEP AND VAGUE DREAMS WERE INTERRUPTED BY a foreign tugging somewhere in the area of her feet. She tried first to kick it away, then to turn over, but somehow, she could not, and her groggy mind struggled to move against something that seemed to hold her. A panic crept over her, and through the dense fog of sleep, she heard voices, deep and gravelly whispers in the near-darkened room. Forcing her eyes to open, she saw two small figures—dwarfs or demons, very possibly both—watching her, their arms folded across their chests in a gesture of gleeful satisfaction. She tried to sit up, but could not.

She had to be dreaming.

Attempting to speak, Quinn found that something thick and soft filled her mouth, which was now desert dry. She started to gag, her throat constricting against the presence of the alien thing that stuck to the sides and the roof of her mouth. She began to choke, and the two dwarflike creatures jumped back in surprise.

"What are you two doing?" a male voice asked from somewhere in the dark.

A tall figure stepped out of the shadows and leaned over the back of the sofa to peer down at her.

"Look what we caught!" one of the gravel-voiced demon-dwarfs answered with obvious pride.

Cale's breath caught in his throat, and for a long minute, he thought he must be dreaming. His heart pounding in his chest, he leaned closer, not trusting his eyes. Even in the dim light, he knew her.

Miracle of miracles. It was her. Here. In his cabin.

Quinn.

Twelve and a half years late.

"Well, then," he said, forcing a nonchalance he did not feel. "Look who stopped by to say 'hey.'"

She glared up at him, her auburn hair spread around her head like a soft fog.

Yep. Those were her eyes, all right. Big and green and throwing off sparks when she was angry. Just like now.

"Mmphfmprhm." She seemed to be speaking directly to him. Through her teeth.

Frowning, Cale leaned forward to take a closer look. Something white protruded from her mouth.

"What in the . . . ?" He tugged at the white thing until her mouth released it, then held up the small white sock and asked with studied patience and practiced composure, "Whose is this?"

Eric pointed at Evan. Evan pointed at Eric.

"His," they both said.

"How did it get into her mouth?" Cale asked sternly.

"He did it," they both replied.

"Well, I guess it could have been worse." Cale held the sock up to examine it. "At least it's clean."

"That makes me feel so much better," Quinn told him dryly. "There aren't five more of them, are there?" She eyed the two boys warily, certain that they, too, were part of this ridiculous dream. And it was, of course, a dream, wasn't it?

How could it be otherwise?

"What?" Cale asked. He sounded real enough. Looked real enough . . .

"Weren't there seven dwarfs?" she heard herself ask.

Cale's laughter was unexpected.

Good grief. It wasn't a dream. It *was* him. She'd know that laugh anywhere.

Mortified, Quinn straightened herself up and, going for dignity—as much as one could muster when the man who'd dumped you twelve years ago had just removed a linty sock from your mouth—cleared her throat and leveled her chin.

"Well then, if you would just untie me and get me a glass of water so that I can rinse the cotton out of my mouth, I think I'd like to mosey on back to the ranch about now." Quinn sought to sound as nonchalant as possible, searching for just the right note, trying to ignore the fact that her heart was attempting to pound its way out of her chest in heavy, erratic thumps.

Pulling back the afghan to reveal rope looped tightly around her wrists and ankles, Cale scowled, then turned to his sons. "Would one of you like to explain this? And it had better be good, fellas. This one had better be *real* good."

Eric pointed to Quinn and said darkly, "She's an invader."

"He means an *intruder.*" Evan nodded.

"Boys, this is no way to treat company."

"She's not company. She's a *girl.*"

"Yeah." Eric nodded. "A *stranger* girl."

"Well, this girl just happens to be an old friend of mine, so she's not a stranger at all." Cale unloosened the rope with fingers that were close to shaking at the sudden nearness of this woman who had appeared in his dreams so many times he knew every line of her face, every curve of her body.

He cleared his throat and helped her up, as if was the most natural thing in the world to have the woman of his dreams show up, bound and gagged, on the sofa in a remote cabin in the Montana hills in a blinding blizzard.

"Boys, you obviously do not know who this woman is," Cale told them, forcing his eyes onto them and away from her. From those green eyes that still, he had noticed, held that spark of gold.

They shook their heads and asked in unison, "Who?"

"This is the daughter of Hap Hollister," he announced gravely.

"Hap Hollister!" one gasped.

"The greatest Little League coach in the world!" the other exclaimed.

"The very one."

Quinn looked down at the two small faces that were staring up at her, open-mouthed and wide-eyed. She wondered what Cale had told them about her father.

"My sons." Cale turned to her. "Eric and Evan. Boys, say hello to Quinn Hollister. Then apologize."

"Hello. Sorry." Eric stared at his feet, from which dark socks trailed.

"Like you mean it." Cale's eyes narrowed.

"We're sorry. We thought you were a robber."

"Well, I guess I can understand why you might have thought that, finding a stranger sleeping on your sofa. But didn't you hear me when I came in? I called. . . ."

"We were out cold," Cale said over his shoulder as he disappeared through a doorway momentarily. "Napping. I took the boys for a long walk this morning, and I guess it knocked us all out."

"You took your sons out to play in a blizzard?" she asked. "Isn't that a form of child abuse?"

"It was before the blizzard hit. Ever spend three days in a remote cabin with no TV and two four-year-olds who have had electronic baby-sitters all their young lives?" He returned and handed her a glass of water.

"Can't say that I have." She accepted the glass and drank greedily, hoping the water would wash away the lint that had attached to the roof of her mouth.

"Walking in the snow is the only thing that keeps them moving and tires them out enough that they're not bouncing off the walls." He smiled, and Quinn felt something in her chest begin to tighten.

He still had a killer smile. It was impossible not to notice.

"But what," he was saying, "are you doing up here in the midst of a blizzard?"

"I went up to put the wreath on Elizabeth's cabin. Every year, one of us . . ."

"I remember," he said softly, recalling a time when he had accompanied her to do that very task. Had she forgotten?

Ignoring the reference to another Christmas, when they had not been strangers, she said, "While I was inside, the storm came up, and I got stuck coming back down the mountain. My brother told me that Val was coming back for Christmas, so I thought I'd see if she was here. The door was open, so I came in and built up the fire and wrapped up in the blankets. I was very cold."

"You're lucky you made it. Quinn, what ever possessed you to get out of the car in a storm like this? How could you have seen the cabin from the road in all this snow?" His eyebrows arched upward just slightly, the right higher than the left, in a gesture she suddenly remembered all too well.

"My car is right there, at the end of the lane. It's not that far. And I have a very good sense of direction." Her chin lifted just a bit. No point in telling him about Elizabeth. . . .

His eyes caught hers and she turned away from his gaze, which she was not ready to meet. Here was the man who had broken her heart and changed her life. The very least she deserved was to feel hard, cold anger.

All she felt at that moment was awkward and unprepared to share the confines of a cabin with him.

All she wanted was to get away, to retreat from those hazel eyes that changed with the light, and that were now turning a soft blue.

Not ready, she told herself. *I'm not ready for this.*

She forced her eyes from his face—dammit, the very least he could have done was to have gone bald and paunchy—forced herself to look around for her boots. There. By the door. Right where she left them. "I have to go."

Cale walked to the window and drew aside a dark green and white checked curtain. "Quinn, you wouldn't make it ten feet from the door in this storm."

"I have to get home." She felt awkward and nervous, wanting to flee.

"Not for a while, I'm afraid."

Walking to the front door, Quinn peered out onto a totally white world. Cale was right. She wouldn't make it past the porch without losing her direction. She stared into the dense whiteness, searching for a shadow. Perhaps Elizabeth would come back, and lead her away from here. But there were no shadows to be found, no dark figures waiting to guide her from the cabin and back to her car. With a sigh she turned back to the room, the words she had been about to speak forgotten in the blink of an eye.

Cale was tending the dying fire, building it up to send warmth and light into the room. The dark blue sweatshirt stretched across his broad back and shoulders as he lifted one log after another and stacked them evenly. Even as a teenager his arms had always been strong and hard, overdeveloped from baseball. She wondered how much more so now, after twelve seasons of playing in the majors. He looked wonderful. Everything about him looked wonderful.

She wondered where his wife was. Still napping, no doubt, in one of those rooms at the end of the hallway.

Without warning, he turned and smiled at her, totally disarming her with that same warm smile she had lived for once upon a time. Touched in ways that terrified her to recall, Quinn backed up involuntarily as if to place as much distance between them as possible. So many times throughout the years she had dreamed of this moment when she would see him again, had so carefully planned what she would say. And though she might *want* to grab him by the throat and demand an explanation, of course, she would not. She'd never give him the satisfaction of knowing how deep the pain had gone, how long it had lingered. Oh, no. She'd be mature. Witty. Sophisticated.

But now, so unexpectedly face-to-face, she could not recall even one word of the clever monologue she'd carefully rehearsed so many times over the years.

A crash from the back of the cabin made her jump.

"Excuse me," Cale said with a grim expression as he headed down the hallway.

He was back in two minutes with one small boy under each arm. He deposited one at each end of the sofa and said sternly, "And you will sit there until I say you can get up."

Two small freckled faces levied silent curses in Cale's direction.

"So." Cale turned to Quinn and folded his arms. "I bet you'd like something warm to drink. Can I get you some tea? Coffee? Cocoa?"

"Well, a cup of tea would be great. My mouth is still a little dry," Quinn said, uneasily awaiting the appearance of the boys' mother at any moment. She couldn't possibly sleep through the racket her sons had made. Quinn kept one eye on the doorway, waiting for Cale's wife to appear. What did she look like? What was she like? Quinn was at once dying to know and sick with the thought of meeting the woman who had, after all, taken her place in Cale's life.

He walked through the doorway behind her into the small kitchen. She heard a cupboard door open, then close.

"Regular or herbal?" he asked.

"What kind of herbal?"

"Umm, let's see." Cale looked up to see her in the

doorway, and he held up several boxes of teas. "Val has some mint, some chamomile, and something called 'Roast-aroma.'"

Suddenly clumsy, he dropped all three boxes on the floor. Quinn bent to pick them up at the same time he did.

Trying to ignore the fact that she was close enough that he could smell some delicate, enticing scent—lilac, maybe?—he stacked the boxes of tea, which his sister had brought at Hiller's General Store back in November, onto the counter, and stepped back, away from her.

"Mint is fine. Thank you." She tried to be casual, and thought she wasn't doing too badly, right then.

He filled the blue enamel pot with water and set it atop the stove. "I don't know why Val didn't replace this old wood stove," he muttered.

"Probably so that when you lose electricity up here, you can still eat."

"Well, it's a pain in the butt." He reached into a large black bucket by the back door and pulled out a few pieces of wood. Opening a door in the front of the stove, he stuffed in the wood, which had been cut to fit perfectly.

Cut to fit by my brother, she could have told him.

"When's dinner?" Eric poked his head around the door-jamb.

"What did I say about staying on the sofa till I said you could get up?"

"We're hungry." Evan appeared behind him.

"Okay. I'll start dinner."

"What?" They eyed him suspiciously.

"Spaghetti."

"You made spaghetti last night. It was hard."

"We want pizza."

"Sorry, boys. No pizza up here. But I will try to time the spaghetti better tonight. I promise. Now, back on the sofa. You're still doing penance for having tied up Quinn and stuffed a sock in her mouth."

Dejected and grumbling, the two little boys shuffled sullenly back into the living room.

"We're bored."

"We want TV."

Cale grimaced and shrugged his shoulders. "It's hard to keep them amused sometimes. They're used to video games and cartoons."

"I'm sure your wife will have some ideas to keep them busy," Quinn leaned against the doorway.

"Oh, she has some ideas, all right," Cale laughed grimly. "All of which conveniently leave her out of the picture."

Quinn looked at him blankly, not comprehending.

"My wife left me. We're divorced." He said it simply, with the same amount of emotion as when he had told his sons what was on the dinner menu.

"I see," she said, not at all seeing how any woman could leave a man like Cale.

There was a crash from the living room.

Then again, Quinn silently acknowledged, *there may have been other considerations.*

Six

THE WATER IN THE TEAPOT BEGAN TO BOIL, EMITTING A HOSTILE whistle. On his way into the living room to assess the latest damage inflicted by his offspring, Cale hesitated, debating which to tend to first.

"You finish with the tea. I'll see what's going on in there," Quinn said, grateful for an opportunity to flee the kitchen's close quarters and the overwhelming nearness of him. It was far too much too soon, after way too long.

Hearing her approach, the boys scurried back to their places on either end of the sofa.

"So, guys," Quinn asked as she righted the lamp, "what's doing?"

"We are being bored," the one on the right told her, his arms folded across his chest in much the same way as Cale had done earlier.

"Yeah," said the one on the left, narrowing his eyes

meaningfully, "and you know what happens when little kids get bored."

"No." She pulled up a small ottoman and sat down facing them. "What happens when little kids get bored?"

"They *bounce off walls*," one said, repeating the phrase he had heard his father use earlier.

"They get *carried away*," the other told her.

"Well, I wouldn't know, not having any little kids," she said. "But if I did, there would be no wall-bouncing. And no one would have time to get carried away."

"Why not?" they asked in unison.

"They'd be much too busy."

"Like watching TV and stuff, right?" One nodded approvingly.

She shook her head. "We'd be doing much more fun things."

They exchanged an uneasy glance. Grown-ups never referred to TV as a *fun thing*.

"Like what?"

"Yeah, what's more fun than watching cartoons?"

"Who's art kit is that on the table?" Quinn pointed to a box on the table under the front window.

"It's Eric's," the boy on the left told her.

Quinn smiled. Now she knew that Eric had the cowlick and Evan did not.

"Eric, may I look at it?" she asked.

"Sure." He shrugged. "I don't use it. My Aunt Val sent it to me."

Quinn retrieved the box and unsnapped the closure. "Ah, look at all these goodies."

The twins rolled their eyes. What was so neat about a bunch of paper and colored pencils and crayons and such?

Quinn drew out a sketch pad and the colored pencils and smiled.

"Well, you boys may go back to whatever walls you were planning on jumping on."

"*Bouncing*," Evan said meaningfully, craning his neck to see what she was doing.

"*Off*," Eric added. "*Bouncing off*."

"Whatever," she said casually, without taking her eyes

from the sketch pad on her knees, and the lines and curves she was making with a light brown colored pencil.

It wasn't long before both boys had hopped down from their perches to lean over her shoulder, as she had intended.

"It's Miss Jane Mousewing." Eric pointed to the figure emerging from Quinn's rapidly moving pencil.

"How do you know how to draw Miss Jane so good?" Evan asked.

"Because that's what I do." She looked up at them, and seeing that they did not understand what she meant, she added, "I write the Miss Jane stories, and I draw the pictures, too."

They looked at each other, then said in unison, "S. Q. Hollister writes the Miss Jane books."

"Right. Selena Quinn Hollister. That's me. Quinn is my middle name, but I use it as my first name."

"Why?" Eric leaned ever closer until he all but hung over her shoulder, fascinated as the picture of the little mouse-girl became more defined.

"I guess 'cause my mother liked it." She shrugged as Evan closed in on her other side. "And because I have a cousin named Selena and it would be confusing if there were two of us."

"Then why didn't your mother just name you Quinn? Why did she name you Selena if she was going to call you 'Quinn'?"

"Because in my mother's family, the first girl is always named Selena, after my mother's great-aunt. But my mom's brother had a little girl before I was born, and he had named her Selena. So my cousin got to be called Selena and I got to be called by my middle name."

"Hmmm." They both nodded, and leaned just a little closer.

"So, do you have any of the Miss Jane books?" Quinn asked.

"No," Eric told her, "but our teacher read them to us at nursery school sometimes."

"They're *girls'* books," Evan sneered. "We don't read *girls'* books."

"Miss Jane is not just for girls." Quinn fixed him with a stare. "What makes you think she's just for girls?"

"'Cause she's a *girl* mouse. And because she does *girl* things."

"Like what?" Quinn asked him, really wanting to know.

"Like she always wears a dress and dances or plays the flute and stuff." Evan shrugged.

Quinn looked down at Miss Jane, a vision in a little flowy dress, her flute raised to her lips.

"She plays to the bees and to the butterflies," Quinn told them, as if needing to explain, "so that they can fly to music."

"She has tea parties," Evan said with a mild touch of disdain.

"She's a girl mouse," Eric repeated, as if that said it all.

"Well, then, if you were writing the Miss Jane books, what would you do to make them more interesting to boys?"

Eric and Evan sat uncharacteristically still for an overly long moment.

"I know!" Eric hopped up and down on one foot. "You could give her a brother!"

"A *twin* brother," Evan added.

"Hmmm." Quinn contemplated the possibility. "And if I gave her a brother, what would I call him?"

"You could call him . . ." Eric bit his bottom lip, pondering the very important task of naming Miss Jane's only brother.

"Jed! For Jedidiah!" Evan shouted gleefully. "Like Jedidiah McKenzie!"

"Perfect!" Quinn exclaimed. "Jedidiah Mousewing. Now, what do you suppose he looks like? Describe him for me, so that I can draw him. Help me to put him on paper. . . ."

For the next fifteen minutes, Quinn bent over the sketch pad, a small boy at each elbow, totally oblivious to the man who stood in the doorway, her forgotten cup of tea in one hand, his heart on his sleeve. After all the nights he'd dreamed of her, all the times he'd unconsciously sought her face in every crowd in every airport he'd walked through, in every stadium he'd ever played in, there she was, calmly sitting there sketching away, looking for all the world as if she belonged there with his sons. As if this was her place, her cabin, her family.

This is the way it should have been all along, he told himself. *The way it would have been, if only she had been here that day. . . .*

"Is that my tea?" she asked, her eyes bright with the excitement of creating a new character as she sketched to the boys' specifications.

"Ahhh . . . it might be a little cool," he told her, realizing that he'd been standing there staring for much longer than he'd intended.

"That's okay." She smiled at him, and he thought for a moment that the cabin seemed to tilt at an odd angle. "Would you like to meet Jed Mousewing?"

"Sure." He cleared his throat as he crossed the small distance between the kitchen and the ottoman and peered over her shoulder, much as his sons had done.

"See, Dad, he's a pioneer, just like Jed McKenzie was," Eric told him.

"He sort of looks a little like Davy Crockett," Cale noted, trying to ignore that scent of lilac again. "If Crockett had had a tail, two big front teeth, and big round ears."

"It's the buckskin," Quinn explained, tensing at his nearness. "The boys gave me an excellent idea for my next book. If it works, I'll give them credit."

"What does that mean?" Eric asked.

"It means that inside the book, it will say something like, 'Thanks to Evan and Eric McKenzie, for all their help in bringing Jed to life.' Something like that."

"You mean our names would be in the book?" Evan asked, wide-eyed.

"Yep."

"Wow."

"Of course, you'll have to help me think up things that mice-boys might like to do."

"We can do that. We're good at thinking up things to do."

"I think Quinn means things that do not involve rough-housing or breaking things. Or watching TV," Cale offered.

"Does Miss Jane have a TV?" Evan asked.

"No, she does not," Quinn replied. "We'll just have to think of other things mouse children would like to do."

"Well, why don't you two think about old Jed here while you wash up for dinner," Cale suggested.

"Okay." They nodded, and, miraculously, flew from the room without argument.

Alone with her, Cale hesitated, feeling awkward. Until she smiled up at him and his knees began to unravel. He sat on the sofa before they could betray him.

"So, that's Jed, eh?" he said, to have something to say.

"Jed Mousewing." She smiled, her heart pounding, and she blushed, certain that he could hear it banging against her chest.

"Where did the *Mousewing* come from?" He licked dry lips with an equally dry tongue.

"Actually, her original name had been *Mouseling,* as in *small mouse.* But the daughter of a friend of mine, who had trouble with her *l*'s, pronounced it Mouse*wing.* I thought it was cute, so I kept the name." She shrugged, feeling trapped all of a sudden. While the boys had been there with her, it had been easier to ignore the fact that he was here, and she was here, and after all this time, they were together. Just as she had dreamed they would be someday. It was a dream she had never had much faith in. Until today.

"I guess you've done well for yourself, then," he said.

"I'm doing what I like to do." She shrugged and tried to sound nonchalant.

"So was I," he told her, the slightest hint of shadow darkening his face.

"I was sorry to hear about your accident," she said softly. "I know how much it must have meant to you, to have been able to play . . ."

He started to shrug it off as perhaps not so big a deal, as he had done so many times over the past six months, then stopped, suddenly feeling no need to pretend.

"It hurt like hell to give it up," Cale said quietly, his words barely above a whisper.

"I'm sorry, Cale." Instinctively, she had placed a hand upon his, and the softness of it, the tenderness of the gesture, shot through him like a bolt.

"Well, so am I." He stood abruptly and her hand fell away. The place where her fingers had touched his wrist seemed marked as if by fire. He cleared his throat again—a nervous gesture that he hadn't found the need to use for years—and backed away from her in the direction of the kitchen. "Dinner will be ready in about two minutes. I hope you don't mind having your spaghetti sauce come out of a jar."

"Not at all," she assured him.

Cale fled back into the safety of the small kitchen, where he would not have to look into her eyes.

"How 'bout if I set the table?" Quinn was just a few steps behind him.

Cale resisted the urge to sigh openly. Nowhere to run. Nowhere to hide. . . .

"Sure." He forced a smile and pointed to the cupboard behind him. "Plates and glasses in there."

He tried to pretend that her presence wasn't disconcerting, that he wasn't watching her, but it was impossible not to in so confined an area. Their backs collided mildly as she reached for plates from the shelves above her head. She brushed against him when she sorted through the flatware drawer for knives, forks, and spoons. His awareness of her was closing in on him at a pace that was rapidly accelerating.

He turned and brushed aside the curtain at the kitchen window. If anything, the storm had intensified. There was no chance she would be leaving before the morning.

How would he last a whole night with her here, under the same roof with him?

She looked up and smiled again, and he felt his insides begin to twist and twitch.

This could very well be the longest night of his life.

Seven

"WOULD YOU LIKE SOME MUSIC?" CALE STOOD IN THE MIDDLE of the living room, his hands on his hips, wondering just what to do next. Quinn was emerging from the kitchen, where she had offered to clean up from dinner while Cale put his sons to bed.

"Sure." She nodded.

"What's your pleasure?"

"What are my choices?"

"Whatever we can get on this old radio." He slowly turned the dial, distracted by her nearness. "Not much of a variety tonight, I'm afraid."

"That's fine, right there. Christmas music would be nice."

Cale adjusted the dial to eliminate the static, taking his time while he tried to figure out what to do with her.

In his dreams, he had known exactly what to do. Now that she was really here, he had changed into a bumbling adolescent in the space of a few hours.

"I was listening to this on tape while I was driving up the mountain today," she told him as "I'll Be Home for Christmas" began to play.

"I've always liked it," Cale said awkwardly.

"Me, too." She nodded.

"Ah, why don't you sit down"—Cale folded up the blankets on the sofa to give her room—"and I'll . . ." He looked around wildly for something to occupy himself with. "I'll . . . put more wood on the fire."

Quinn sat on the sofa, pulling her feet up under her and easing back into the cushions. Cale lifted a few logs from the stack and placed them on the fire, using the bellows to build up the flames. Quinn exhaled, a long silent stream of air. Her face was beginning to hurt from having forced a carefree smile for the past several hours. Her chest and stomach hurt from having been so close to him after so long. She watched him, his back to her, and though she tried to will her eyes away from him, she could not. It had been too long a drought, and now that she could, she drank in every bit of him. The way his dark hair curled over the back of his collar. The way his hands grasped the logs as if they were twigs, the way the bottom of his jeans rounded when he leaned back on his haunches to stack the logs . . .

She rose abruptly and went to the window to look out. Maybe a miracle had occurred while they were eating dinner and the snow had stopped.

Fat chance.

"I'm afraid it's only gotten worse, Quinn," he said from behind her.

"I guess I should call home." She turned slightly and found him closer than she had anticipated.

"That's probably a good idea," he agreed, telling himself to back away so that the scent from her hair would not be able to reach his nostrils, but his legs seemed unable to obey the command to move.

"I left a message on the answering machine earlier, but I think my mother will worry until she actually speaks to me," she said. The urge to reach her hand up and touch his face was so powerful that she had to force her hands behind her back.

She was the first to move, the first to step away. Averting her eyes, she stepped around him and reached for her bag. Refusing to look at him again while she searched for the phone, she turned her back while she dialed the number and spoke softly and paced nervously while she explained the situation to her mother.

"My mother said to tell you hello and to thank you for giving me shelter from the storm," Quinn said as she dropped the cell phone back into the bag.

Cale nodded. "It's my pleasure."

If you only knew, Quinn. . . .

"So," Quinn said, forcing herself to sound perky. "What book are you reading?" She walked to the chair and lifted the hardback he had left there the night before and inspected the cover. It was a thriller, written by a favorite author of Quinn's. "Oh. I heard this was great."

"It's pretty good," he told her, looking for something to do with himself. "But I liked his last one better."

"I loved that book," she agreed. "Had you figured out that Janelle was the murderer before the last scene?"

"No." He shook his head. "I thought it was Desmond."

"So did I." Quinn laughed. "He sure had me fooled."

"Me, too." Cale nodded.

That common ground having been exhausted, silence began to surround them.

"I'm sorry about the boys. I mean, tying you up and stuffing the sock in your mouth," he said awkwardly, at a loss for words now that she was really here.

"I'm sure they thought they had bagged a felon, that they

had done something really good." She couldn't help but smile. "They certainly seemed proud of themselves."

"You may be giving them too much credit," he said with a wry smile.

"They're just little boys, Cale."

"Quinn, my sons are spoiled, undisciplined little hooligans," he told her bluntly. "And while I find it all too easy to blame their mother, I can't deny that I've had as much of a hand in their turning out to be hellions as she did."

Quinn leaned back, watching his face.

"I spent very little time at home, Quinn. I played ball during the season, then spent the off-season rehabilitating whatever injuries I had accumulated over the previous few months. Then it would be time for spring training, then the season would start all over again. I spent no more time with them than their mother did. I hardly knew them at all, so it really isn't fair for me to place all the blame on her."

"And you're trying to make up for it now."

"I'm all they have, Quinn." He ran nervous fingers through his dark brown hair. "She left them months ago and has never looked back. She has not asked to see them, hasn't even called."

"That's so difficult to understand, why a woman would leave her children. . . ."

"It's probably a lot easier when you never wanted them in the first place," he said, his eyes turning grim. "And when you don't care much for their father, I guess it's even easier."

How could any woman not love you, the thought rang in her head, so loudly she startled, certain he must have heard.

"I'm so sorry," she said softly, wondering what the confession might have cost him.

"Marrying Jo Beth was a mistake. It just *seemed* like a good idea at the time. The boys were the only good thing that came out of the relationship."

"They must miss her."

"Actually, I don't think they do," he said, adding, without apology, "any more than I do."

"That's very sad for them."

"I can't argue that, but that's how it is." He tried to lean back in his chair, tried to act real casual, telling himself that she was just any old friend from high school that he happened to run into. His pounding heart and frazzled nerves told him otherwise. "But I am determined to make up for all the time I didn't spend with them. If that's possible. Sometimes it's a little difficult to keep them busy. More than a little, actually. They've had years of electronic baby-sitters. I'm trying to wean them from the television, as you've probably noticed."

"I guess taking them to the wilds of Montana must have sounded like a good idea."

"It did when Val suggested it. Now I'm not so sure. It gets harder every day to find something new for them to do. But what about you, Quinn? Any spouse or children waiting for you back at the High Meadow?"

"No," she said, not bothering to elaborate. Why bother telling him that she had never fallen in love with anyone else? Oh, there'd been a few close calls, but nothing that had set her heart and blood on fire the way he had, but why go into that?

"You write children's books and live . . . where?"

"Right now I'm renting an apartment in Missoula. I'm substituting at the university this semester through the end of January."

"And then . . . ?"

"I'm not sure." She shrugged. "I might stay in Missoula, I might come back to the ranch. I might go someplace else. I haven't decided yet." *This isn't really so difficult after all,* Quinn told herself. *If I just look at that spot on the wall behind him, right there above his head, instead of at his face, I'll be fine.*

"I guess that's an advantage of doing the type of work you do. You can live just about anywhere."

"Anywhere there's postal service and electricity for my PC." She nodded. "How 'bout you? What are your plans?"

"You mean beyond accepting the fact that my ball-playing days are over?" His eyes darkened and the crevices near the corners of his mouth seemed to deepen.

"It must be very difficult for you to have to start over."

He stood up and paced just a little, like someone who had been confined to a very small space for far too long. "Everyone says, you can coach. You can get a job with radio, or TV. You can be a broadcaster."

"It's not just about a job." She stated what to her was obvious.

"No. It's not just about a job. Baseball is so much a part of what I am, that I don't know who I am without it." He paused, then added, his voice barely above a whisper, "Maybe I'm afraid to find out who I am now. Maybe I'll find out that I'm really no one at all."

His solemn candor stunned her and took her breath away.

Before she could reply, he turned his back and said, "I guess it's a good time to turn in. You must be tired from walking through the storm."

She could only nod, suddenly grateful to know that within a few more minutes, she would be alone, away from his haunted eyes and the sorrow that seemed to overtake him, away from her sudden urge to put her arms around him and comfort him, to reassure him.

"You can have my room. I'll sleep out here."

"If it's all the same to you, I'd rather sleep out here. I don't want to put you out of your bed," she said, knowing there was no way she would be able to sleep in a bed where he had lain. No, thank you. Sleeping in Papa Bear's bed might have worked for Goldilocks, but Quinn Hollister would stick to the sofa.

"I really don't mind. . . ."

"I'd really rather," she said firmly.

"I'll get some blankets." He nodded as if he understood and went off down the hall, returning a few minutes later with a pile of blankets and a pillow, which he dropped on the sofa.

"I thought maybe you might be more comfortable sleeping in these." He handed her a dark gray thermal shirt and a pair of light gray sweatpants. "Val left a few nightgowns, but I doubt they'd be warm enough."

"These are fine. Thank you. Where can I change?"

"The bathroom is the first door on the left." He pointed toward the hallway.

She hesitated before asking, "Is there a shower?"

"Yes."

"Do you mind if I use it?" She felt sweaty from the exertion of her walk.

"Not at all. I'll get you some towels."

Quinn nodded her thanks and followed him the short walk to the bathroom. He removed several fluffy towels from a small closet and handed them to her. "Soap's in there." He pointed through the open door as he reached behind her to turn on the light.

Cale tried to concentrate on preparing a bed for Quinn on the sofa, piling the blankets and fluffing the pillow, and not on the fact that she was, at this moment, in his shower. That the water he could hear running on the other side of the wall was sliding down her back, across her shoulders . . .

He had added yet another log on the fire, and poked energetically at the embers, when he heard the bathroom door open, heard her soft footsteps behind him as she came into the room. Turning to her, his words stuck in his throat. He watched her as she placed her folded clothes into her bag, his stomach tightening, and he tried in vain to look away. Even with her long hair damp from the shower and wrapped in a towel, Quinn was, if possible, even more lovely than she had been as a girl. She had filled out just a little, rounding here and lengthening there, until she was, as he could plainly see, nearer to perfection than any woman had a right to be. He could not help but notice, too, that she filled out his old gray thermal shirt in ways it was never intended to be filled.

Feeling his eyes on her, Quinn practically leaped under the blankets and drew them up to her chin.

"Anything else I can get you?" he asked.

"Just your promise that I won't be bound and gagged when I wake up in the morning." She tried to make light of it.

"You've got it." Cale did his best to smile.

"Well then," she said, rubbing the wet strands of hair with the towel, "I guess I'll see you in the morning. And thank you."

"For what?"

"For taking me in."

"Right." He backed away from the sofa as if it were on fire. "Good night, Quinn."

"Good night, Cale."

Sweet dreams, she wanted to call after him, but did not. Instead, she lay in silence and listened to his footsteps echo on the wooden floor. Hearing his bedroom door close, Quinn sat up and took a deep breath, then got up quietly, creeping across the rag carpet to the fire, where she bent forward to let her hair dry the best it could. When she had finished, she draped the towel along the stone mantel, and tiptoed back to the sofa, grateful to be alone for the first time in hours. Alone to contemplate what the fates had delivered to her. Had anyone told her that she would spend the days before Christmas in a remote cabin with Cale McKenzie she'd have laughed in their face.

And yet here she sat, wearing his clothes and bundled in blankets a mere fifteen or twenty feet from where he slept, right down that hallway. And with him out of sight, it was easier for her to dwell on him, on how well he had filled out over the years. His face had changed so little, maybe a little less angular, but his eyes still had that glow and his smile still carried that same old warmth, that same sweet promise. . . .

That promise he had never kept, she reminded herself. Tortured by the memory, she wished she had the nerve to ask *why,* but then again, surely he'd think her a fool to have harbored *that* all these years. Better, perhaps, to pretend that the episode never happened, than to open those old wounds.

Old wounds that never really healed, but that's mine to deal with. He doesn't need to know that. . . .

Quinn sighed deeply and lay back down, pulling the covers around her to make a nest of sorts, knowing that there would be little sleep for her while the man who had filled her dreams for so many years was *really* here, under the same roof. In the flesh. Just seeing Cale had touched her in places she hadn't even known were still alive and well.

She sighed again and turned over to stare at the fire,

watching its dancing tongues lick the sides of the brick
firebox and the shadows move slowly, sinuously across the
room, like lovers dancing in the dark.

Arrrghhh.

Wrong image.

She turned her back to the fire and punched the pillow,
then began to count backward from one thousand. Anything to keep her mind off the beautiful man with the hazel
eyes who slept just a short stroll down a darkened hallway.

Cale turned over for what must have been the four-
hundredth time. Sleep, which was, for him, always hard to
come by, was, on this night, a total impossibility. Not with
her curled up on his sofa, just thirty-two steps away. He'd
counted after he'd turned his back and walked to his room.

The reality of it stunned him and almost made him giddy.
Quinn was there. His golden girl was *there*, under his roof.
How different things could have been—*should* have been—
if things had gone the way they had been intended. They
would be cuddled together under this down quilt right now,
sharing their warmth and sharing the night, instead of being
separated by thirty-two steps.

Why, he had wanted to ask her. *Why*, his heart had
wanted to know. But surely, after all this time, it should not
matter. And would it not hurt more to find that he had had
his heart bruised by the whim of a schoolgirl? Why embar-
rass himself now by demanding from the woman an explanation for the actions of the girl she had once been?

He turned restlessly once again and closed his eyes, but all
he could see was that face, eyes green like new grass, mouth
ripe as mountain berries . . .

Cale groaned and turned over again, knowing that this
was a night that was not likely to pass quickly.

Quinn had sensed him before she saw or heard him.
Opening one eye into a mere slit, she watched as he bent
down to lift a log and leaned over to place it on the
diminished pile of smoldering wood. He added a second
log, then a third. He brushed his hands on his dark
sweatpants, then softly crossed the rag rug to straighten her
blankets. Pausing just slightly, he reached down and
touched the side of her face, touched her lips with his

fingertips in a gesture of longing that took her breath away. Drawing his hand back abruptly, he turned and padded back down the hall.

Raising one hand to her face, Quinn traced the path his fingers had made on her skin, and with the other, she wiped the tears from her cheek.

Eight

SENSING THAT A NEW DAY HAD ACTUALLY MANAGED TO DAWN somehow through the intensity of the storm's fury, Quinn stretched her arms over her head and looked around. It hadn't been a dream after all. She was really here. And that meant that Cale was here, too. What a strange twist, she thought as she slid the blankets off and went to the window. As suspected, the storm still raged outside. Funny, though, that it seemed to confine itself to the mountain. Her mother had said they had had but an inch or so of snow, not even enough to keep Trevor from picking up her sisters at the airport.

Grabbing her clothes out of the bag, she tiptoed to the bathroom and washed her face and dressed in the same brown wool tweed pants and heavy oatmeal-colored sweater she'd worn the day before. Standing in the hallway, she listened for sounds from either of the two bedrooms. Hearing none, she went into the kitchen and poked in the cupboards.

Val had most certainly stocked up. There were several bags of flour and sugar, lots of herbal teas, and several packages of pudding mix, cans of soup and jars of spaghetti sauce, and boxes of pasta. In the refrigerator she found milk, several boxes of butter and eggs, some apples, oranges, and raisins. The freezer held packages of frozen food, and she poked through them. Remembering the boys' complaint about Cale's spaghetti, she lifted out a bag of mixed vegetables and a package of rock-hard beef. Guessing that Cale might welcome a little help as much as the boys would welcome the variety, perhaps she would suggest a simple stew for that night.

In a basket near the back door, she found small pieces of wood for the stove, and soon she had a pot of coffee on. By the time the two small tousled faces had appeared in the doorway, she had already planned the breakfast she would make. It was the least she could do, she reasoned. Cale clearly did not enjoy cooking, and she did. Besides, she was up and he was not, the boys were there and hungry.

"Pancakes?" she asked, and they nodded enthusiastically. "Go get dressed, and by the time you get back, there should be a few ready for you."

"Yea!" they shouted as they ran from the room and down the hall.

Within minutes, their father had emerged, and following his nose to the kitchen, he, too, soon stood in the doorway.

"I hope you don't mind, but I come from a long line of take-charge types," she told him. "Besides, I was awake and I just thought . . ."

"Thank you. I appreciate the help. You probably noticed that I'm not exactly James Beard." He smiled, and her knees turned to jelly. "What can I do?"

Just stand there and let me look at you for a while. A few days might be enough.

She swatted at the thought and handed him a cup of coffee, saying, "Nothing. It's all done. Look what I found in the cupboard. Chokecherry sauce. Val must have bought it at the Larkspur Fall Festival in October."

"I can't remember the last time I had this on pancakes." Cale lifted the jar to give his hands something to do and pretended to read the homemade label. The scent of lilac was gone, he noted regretfully, and had been replaced with the musky smell of his own soap. It was just as well, he told himself. That soft flowery scent had brought back too many memories of too many nights he was better off not thinking about right now. Time enough to look back, when the snow stopped and she would leave him to go back to the ranch.

He watched her break eggs into the batter. She looked beautiful. He wished he could tell her so. Instead, he cleared his throat and said, "Pancakes are a big step up for us this week. You'll have to give me lessons."

"Be glad to." She turned her back to shield herself from his eyes. The urge to reach out and touch him had been so strong, so real, that it spooked her. If there had been a place to run to, she might have fled, but the storm whistled and sang outside the small cabin, and so she merely squared her shoulders and stirred the pancake batter.

"Yea! We're having pancakes!" Eric of the cowlick sang as he ran into the room.

"Yippee!" Evan dashed in, hot on his brother's heels, and slid in his stocking feet into the solid wall that was his father. Looking up, he asked earnestly, "Does this mean we don't have to eat cold cereal or gloppy eggs today?"

"What are you, a budding food critic? Sit." Cale pointed toward the little wooden table, and the two boys hopped over and seated themselves expectantly.

Cale forced his hands steady as he held the plate upon which Quinn layered pancakes. Forced himself to pretend that it had not been her leg that had touched his under the table. Forced himself not to grin like a total and complete idiot when she blinded him with a smile from across the room. Forced his hands to remain at his side rather than follow their natural course to her hips when she turned her back to rinse dishes at the sink when breakfast was over. Forced his lips not to seek the back of her neck . . .

"Daddy, we have nothing to do." Eric's little freckled face frowned hard, to emphasize the extent of grumpiness.

Cale paused. He was damned near out of options.

"Can't we rent just one movie?" Evan asked earnestly.

"No VCR, guys," Cale reminded them of the obvious fact that their four-year-old brains refused to accept, "and no TV."

"Why didn't Aunt Val buy a TV?" Eric lamented.

"Montana's a dumb place," Evan told his father. "It's cold and it snows all the time and there's nothing to do. It's dumb."

"I beg your pardon"—Quinn sat down on the edge of the wing chair—"but if I could put my two cents in . . ."

"Take your best shot," Cale invited.

"Montana is far from being a dumb place. As a matter of fact, they call it the 'Treasure State' because of all the great stuff that you can find here."

"Like what?" Eric's eyes narrowed.

"Like sapphires and copper . . ."

"What are sapphires?" Eric asked.

"Pretty blue stones that people set into jewelry. And of course, there are gold mines and silver mines. . . ."

"Real gold mines?"

"Yes. And there are lots of great things to see in Montana. Get your dad to take you to one of the ghost towns one day when the weather clears up."

"Ghost towns?" Eric looked up at his father, his eyes widening. "Real ghost towns?"

"Oh, yes," Cale told them. "Several not far from here."

"They're making it up, Eric," Evan told his brother.

"No, we are not. Why, not two miles from here, at the bottom of the other side of the mountain, is Settler's Head."

"Settler's Head?" the boys asked in unison.

Quinn nodded. "If you want to hear the story, you have to sit down."

They sat, and listened as Quinn and their father traded tales of this ghost town or that.

Maybe Montana wouldn't be so bad, they concluded, if the snow ever stopped and they could get to see all those neat places with the neat names like Anguish and Celebration, Indian Toes and Crow Skull.

Talking about it kept them entertained until twelve-thirty, when they had a lunch of tuna sandwiches and canned soup.

"Now what can we do?" the boys asked.

Quinn looked across the room to Cale to see if he looked like he had any suggestions. The panic settling in his eyes told her he was fresh out of ideas.

"Hmmm. I have an idea. Cale, do you mind if I poke in your kitchen?"

"Be my guest," he said gratefully.

She went through the cupboards, taking down everything she thought she might be able to use. Just as the boys began to wrestle across the living room floor, Quinn appeared in the doorway and asked, "Would anyone like to make Christmas cookies?"

Three male McKenzies froze where they stood.

"You mean, real ones?" Eric asked.

"Yes. We have everything we need out here. Who wants to help?"

330

It was tight quarters, the space in the kitchen being limited, but before long, the cabin was filled with the smell of cinnamon and vanilla and citrus. Cale scraped oranges for the rind to go into a special orange cookie that Quinn's grandmother used to make. The boys took turns stirring batter and cutting little shapes out of sugar cookie dough with a butter knife. By the time the afternoon had ended, they had stacks of cookie stars and baseballs, footballs colored brown with cocoa and little half-moons. The boys were delighted with their efforts.

And all the while, the snow continued to swirl and the wind continued to blow.

"Really?" Quinn frowned, looking out the window while she talked with her sister Sunny, who had arrived at the ranch the day before. "It's not snowing at all down there? Sunny, it's total whiteout up here. You can't see beyond the window. . . . No"—Quinn lowered her voice—"I am *not* making it up. And nothing is happening between Cale and me . . . we're sharing space, that's all. Exactly. Shelter from the storm. Of course not . . . we're old friends. Yes, that's *all,* Sunny. Of course, I'm sure," she fairly hissed at her sister, who, despite Quinn's assurance, didn't sound at all convinced.

"How is Sunny?" Cale looked faintly amused.

"She's fine. She has a darling little girl named Lilly whom she adopted about two years ago," Quinn told him, wondering if he'd been eavesdropping. "When she divorced her husband, she let him buy out her share of their business—a move we all questioned at the time, but she was adamant. Right now, she's looking for something else to do. Eventually, I imagine she'll probably start another business."

"And your other sisters?" Cale sat in the high-back chair, and Quinn took a seat on the sofa, pushing the pile of blankets aside to make a space.

The cabin was oddly quiet, the boys having gone to bed without fuss after Cale told them a rousing, though slightly embellished, story about how the ghost town of Settler's Head *really* got its name.

"Liza has her own radio talk show in Seattle—I guess Val

told you that—and CeCe is hawking jewelry on television."
She grinned.

"She's what?"

"CeCe is a sales host on a shopping channel."

"You're kidding." He laughed.

"No, I am not. And if you see her, you will be wise to
wipe off that smirk. She takes her job very seriously, and
loves every blessed minute of it. She's having a better time
than she ever did reporting the news in Abilene."

"Well, I'm glad to hear that she's happy. I always liked
CeCe. She was sort of like everyone's big sister. I remember
when she used to catch for Sky and me when Trevor wasn't
around."

"I remember. You would never let me play."

"Not while you were little, anyway," he said, ancient
memories flooding back, of Quinn throwing wobbly pitches
to Cale, which he would hit into the woods. Of the two of
them, chasing after the ball and taking their time in finding
it . . .

So long ago.

She blushed, as if she'd lifted the memory from his mind.

Sensing her discomfort, he changed the subject abruptly.
"You were great with the boys today."

"They really are a lot of fun, Cale. I enjoyed them."

*And you. I loved being with you again. Loved watching
your face and making you laugh, loved seeing you covered
with flour, and watching your sons taking turns patting you
on the back to make little white handprints on the back of
your sweater. It's breaking my heart all over again, but I
wouldn't trade a minute of this time with you. I'll carry these
days with me forever. . . .*

"I've spent more time doing things with them this week
than I ever did before," Cale was saying, "and I have to
admit, it has been fun."

"I think the secret may be just to keep them busy with
something they like to do."

"I'm just starting to learn what they like to do." His face
sank into a frown. "I hate admitting that, that my sons are
four years old already and I hardly know them at all."

"Some fathers never get to know their children," she told
him.

"Daddy, I can't sleep." A very small voice emerged from the dark hall.

"What's the matter, little buddy?" Cale's face softened as Evan appeared tentatively, his face flushed, his fisted hands rubbing his eyes.

"I had a bad dream."

"Oops." Cale walked to his son and picked him up, resting the little head on his shoulder. "Maybe ghost stories at bedtime weren't such a good idea, after all."

"Will you stay with me?" Evan yawned into his father's neck.

Cale looked at Quinn and she nodded. "I'm kind of tired anyway," she told him. "I'll just get ready for bed and turn in."

"Well . . ." He hesitated for just a second, then nodded slowly, saying, "I guess I'll see you in the morning."

"Sure. Good night, Cale." She stood and patted the little boy gently on the back. "Good night, Evan."

" 'Night, Quinn," was the sleepy reply.

Cale's footfall echoed softly on the old pine floor as he carried his son back to his bed. Quinn piled logs onto the fire, and changed into the clothes she had worn to bed the night before. Not stylish, certainly not sexy, she noted, but they were warm. And warm was no small thing in the midst of the storm that continued to rage outside the cabin. She hoped that it would stop tomorrow. She just didn't know how much longer she could stand being here with him. She had held on so tightly to the pain he had inflicted on her that, for years, it had been all she had left of him.

Now, being here with him, seeing his face, hearing his laughter again, hearing him say her name, had eroded the wall she had built to keep him out, to make certain that he—that no one—ever came close to her heart again. But it was no use, she knew.

If anything, she thought as she sighed and punched her pillow, the past two days had taught her something she had suspected for years.

If love is deep enough, true enough, it never dies. No matter what.

Nine

"WHAT ARE WE GOING TO DO TODAY?" EVAN POUNCED UPON Cale from behind.

"There is nothing to do," Eric whined.

"Christmas is in two days." Evan counted on his fingers. "This is the worst Christmas ever."

"How do you figure that?" Cale asked.

"We're stuck in this dumb cabin. Santa Claus will never find us here." Eric's eyes widened at the realization.

The twins looked at each other in horror.

"No Christmas presents?" Evan whispered.

"We don't even have a tree," Eric moaned.

"I wish we'd never come here," Evan announced. "I want to go home."

"We want to go home," Eric repeated.

Just finishing up washing the breakfast dishes—Cale having made his world-famous gloppy eggs that morning—Quinn paused at the sink, then dried her hands on the towel.

"Get your coats on, boys," she told them.

The boys groaned in unison.

"No. Not a walk," Eric protested. "Daddy, don't let her make us go for a _walk!_"

"We are going to build a snowman on the front porch," she told them. "There's plenty of snow. Come on."

Without giving anyone an opportunity to protest further, she pushed the boys to the door and assisted Cale in getting them dressed for the outside. After bundling themselves up, Cale and Quinn led the twins through the front door onto the porch.

"Quinn's right," their father told them, "there's more than enough snow for a good snowman."

Soon the snowman began to take shape, and the boys

wanted features for the frosty face. A pile of pinecones found under the snow in one corner of the porch supplied eyes, nose, and mouth. The boys admired their creation, but, cold and bored, now that the distraction had ended, they began to complain again.

"We want a Christmas tree, Daddy," Evan told him solemnly. "If we have a tree and Santa does find us, he'll have a place to leave our presents."

Cale had planned on chopping one of the small pines from the back to bring into the cabin. He hadn't counted on a blizzard. A Christmas tree wasn't too much for his sons to ask, he knew. Of course, if Val couldn't get here with their presents, there wouldn't be anything to put under the tree, but he'd worry about that later.

"Guys, go inside with Quinn and warm up. I'll be in in a few minutes."

"What are you going to do, Daddy?"

"It's a surprise. Go on." Cale opened the door and shoved them through. "Maybe Quinn can make something hot for you to drink."

"Sure, Cale, but what are you . . . ?" she asked as he scooted her through the door behind the boys.

"You just go on." Cale motioned for her to follow behind his sons, and closed the door. He turned to the snowman and asked, "What would Christmas be without a tree?"

"Well, boys, what do you think?" Cale stood the little tree upon its cut trunk and gave it a twirl.

The boys looked at it in horror.

"What's wrong?" he asked.

"What's *that?*" They frowned.

"This," Cale told them, "is our Christmas tree."

"That's not a Christmas tree!"

"That's a twig!"

Crestfallen, Cale stepped back to take another look at the little tree he had chopped from where it had grown at the foot of the porch steps, trying to see it through his sons' eyes. It had been the only tree he could get to without running the risk of being lost in the storm.

It was a bit . . . *scraggly.*

"Why, that tree's just right," Quinn announced, having

seen the look of disappointment cross Cale's face. "It'll be wonderful, once we decorate it. You'll see, guys. It'll be perfect."

"We don't have any decorations," Evan wailed.

"Then we'll make them," she told them. "Eric, get out that art kit of yours."

"Oh, brother," the boys moaned joylessly.

"Here." Quinn handed Eric a pair of scissors and a pile of construction paper. "You cut out strips, like this." She folded the paper into strips of equal width, then cut out the first two.

From the art kit, she withdrew a container of paste and, removing the lid, told Evan, "And you can glue the strips together into a chain, see?"

She demonstrated, then held up the two resulting circles. Cutting one more strip, she added the third circle and handed them to Evan.

"We used to do that, Val and I did," Cale said softly from behind her. "With our grandmother. We never had anything on our tree that we hadn't made."

Quinn turned to him, wanting to put her arms around him. From somewhere across the years, the old Cale had come back. She recognized every fiber of him now, recalled all the hurts he had shared with her, all the pain of his mother leaving and his grandmother dying, the shame of having a father who came home only when he had nowhere else to go.

"We made things, too," she told him as she sorted through the pile of colored paper until she found the white. Sitting next to him at the table, she cut wide strips, then folded the strips into squares, over and over until the entire strip was little more than two inches wide. With the scissors, she clipped and trimmed, then unfolded the strip and held it up for him to see.

"It's a chain of hearts," Quinn said simply, holding it out to him.

He met her eyes from across the table, then reached out and took the simple gift she offered, his hand lingering on hers for just a moment.

"Hearts are for girls," Eric said, looking over his father's shoulder.

Cale frowned, and began to fold one of the white strips that Quinn had cut and laid upon the table. When the paper was nothing more than a square, he cut as he had seen her do, then held the paper up so that the hearts unfolded, as hers had done. Smiling, she took his chain and pasted it to the one she had made, and for a long moment, it seemed that time stood still, and they were alone.

"Daddy, are you going to let her hang *hearts* on our tree?" Eric asked suspiciously.

"I would let her hang whatever she wants on our tree," Cale said softly.

"Boy," Evan grumbled, wondering what had gotten into his dad.

"How might Christmas cookies look on the tree?" Quinn asked.

"Christmas cookies?" The boys asked in unison. Now she had their attention. "Like the ones we made yesterday?"

"Different ones today. Special ones to put on the tree," she told them.

"Yea!" They clapped their hands, and the little demons turned back into little boys again.

"You guys finish the chain," she instructed. "And while you do that, I'll make us some lunch and get stuff ready for cookies."

"How long does the chain have to be?" Eric frowned.

Quinn tried to gauge how long it would take her to make soup from a can and the first batch of cookie dough.

"The chain should reach from the door to the sofa." She nodded, figuring that ought to buy her a little time and keep the boys occupied.

Cale watched her later as she worked with his sons, as she rolled out the dough and patiently showed them how to cut shapes. He watched the small faces of the boys, so intent on learning the new skills, so pleased with their efforts, so eager for Quinn's attention and approval. Their faces were wonders to behold, the boys' and the woman's, and the simple joy of the scene settled around him. As the warmth of the day spread through him, it occurred to him that he could not remember the last time he had been this happy. He wanted to hold on to it with both hands. Instead he leaned against the counter and willed himself not to weep at the sight of the beautiful woman and the two beautiful boys who were busy cutting uneven stars out of cookie dough.

It was all exactly the way he had dreamed it would be. He wondered if it was true what they said, that it was never too late for dreams to come true.

"The tree looks pretty good, fellas," Quinn commented as Cale prepared to carry one young boy under each arm into the waiting tub of warm water.

"It's a great tree," Eric sang gleefully, "and we made it ourselves."

"It doesn't have any sparkly lights," noted Evan.

"It doesn't need lights." Eric tried to swat at his brother. "It's like a pioneer tree, and pioneers didn't have 'lecticity. Right, Dad?"

"Right, son." Cale hoisted the slipping boy a little higher and headed down the hallway.

While Cale was tending to his sons, Quinn cleared up the kitchen and made two cups of tea, which she placed on the table near the fire. It was all so right, it all *felt* so right, that she wanted to cry. She felt too much at home here. If things had turned out differently, she might have actually belonged here, been a real part of their lives.

She touched the ornaments gently, one then the next. The boys had been so cute making their little cookie ornaments. Lacking food coloring to make colored dough, they had added cocoa to some of the batter, and from the light brown dough had made little bears and wolves, and deer like the ones they had seen in the mountains. Then, from the plain batter, they had made baseballs and bats to hang on the tree for their father. Lastly, they had made mittens in the shape of their hands out of red and blue construction paper, insisting that Cale and Quinn trace and hang their hands, too. Then they had hung them all on the tree together.

They looked so dear to her, the four hands of colored paper, like Poppa Bear, Momma Bear, and the two Baby Bears. Dear enough to set her heart to breaking if she dwelled too long on the sight. She wondered what would happen to the decorations once Cale took his sons back to Maryland.

"The boys would like you to come say good night," Cale told her as he came into the quiet room.

"Okay," she said, and set off toward the end of the hall.

It was twenty minutes before she returned to the front of the cabin, the boys having talked her into a story before letting her turn out the light. Cale was stacking wood on the fire and had already made her bed for her.

"The boys had such a great time today," he said without turning around. With the boys in bed, there was little to focus on but Quinn. On her eyes, on her face. On her body. It was only a little less difficult if he couldn't see her. Knowing she was there, behind him, was hard enough.

"I had a great time, too. They are really a lot of fun," she said to his back. "When they're not tying you up, of course."

"I'm sorry about that." Cale laughed, then made the mistake of turning to face her. The nearness of her pierced him to his soul.

His laughter died in his throat and he rested the fire poker against the stone of the face of the fireplace.

"Quinn . . ." He searched for words, then realized he wasn't even certain of what he had wanted to say, beyond speaking her name. He cleared his throat. "Thanks for all you did with the boys today. I can't remember when I saw them have so much fun. I'll see you in the morning."

Abruptly he turned, and she was alone in the room.

A wave of disappointment rolled over her. She had hoped for some time alone with him, had looked forward to discussing the day, and all they had shared. Everything they had done had seemed so natural. Talking it over at the end of the day felt like the natural thing to do.

And I guess, in a normal happy family, that *would* be the natural thing to do, she told herself as she changed into the thermal shirt and sweatpants she had slept in the night before. If, in fact, you are a normal happy family. Which we are not. The boys are Cale's and another woman's, and I'm just a . . . what had Evan called her? An intruder.

With an unhappy sigh, she turned off the light and stared into the darkness, and permitted herself to face with a sinking heart the undeniable fact that, after all these years, she was still in love with Caleb McKenzie.

The temperature in the cabin having dropped another few degrees, Cale thought it might be a good idea to throw a few more logs on the fire. And he might as well take another quilt in for Quinn, just in case she needed it.

Quietly, he followed the thirty-two steps to the sofa, then placed the quilt over the sleeping woman. He added some logs to the fire, which had all but gone out, then fanned the flames for a few minutes. Turning back to the sofa, he fought off the urge to awaken her, to tell her that he was still hopelessly in love with her.

There had been a time when he had been certain that he could never forgive her for having hurt him so very deeply. It had only taken her smile to prove him wrong.

Wondering if it could ever be possible to make it right again, if there was such a thing as a second chance, Cale walked to the window and stared out into the winter night.

The blizzard seemed to have stopped, although the wind still whipped the snow around in a powdery swirl. The night was still draped in hazy white, and the faintest trace of moonlight dusted the hills. He was just about to turn away, when a shadow out beyond the trees caught his eye. He leaned closer to the glass. What could be out on a night like this?

The figure moved easily through the snow, as if out for a stroll on a summer night. Frowning, he went to the door and opened it, not believing his eyes.

There, *there* near the hanging rock. He could see her so clearly now. But how . . . ?

"Are you lost?" He called to her across the night. "Can you make it to the cabin by yourself?"

The figure appeared to move slightly away, toward the trees.

"No, no, don't go into the woods. Wait right there, I'll come for you." But even as he spoke, the figure seemed to disappear into thin air. Confused, he stood in the open doorway, looking out into a whirl of white.

"Cale?" Quinn called to him from the sofa. "What's wrong?"

"Nothing," he told her, closing out the night as he closed the door behind him. "I guess it was nothing."

"Who were you talking to?" She sat up sleepily.

"I'm not certain that I was speaking to anyone." He hesitated, wondering what he had, in fact, seen. "I thought I saw . . . I don't know, a figure . . . but of course, I didn't. I couldn't have. No one could survive out on a night like this. . . ."

"Was it a woman?" she asked. "A woman wrapped in a blanket?"

"How do you know . . . ?"

"Because I saw her. She led me here, to your cabin."

He stared at her. "A woman in a blanket led you through a blizzard to this cabin and you didn't find that remarkable enough to mention?"

"Not really." She smiled in the darkness and added, "It was Elizabeth."

"Elizabeth?" He frowned. "You mean your great-great whatever?"

"Yes."

"Are you telling me that a ghost led you here?"

"We don't really think of her as a ghost. But yes. I do believe it was her spirit."

"Remind me to thank her," he said in the safety of the darkness.

"I already have," she told him.

From across the room, he could see the way her hair turned to copper flames in the fire's glow, and the way the light played with shadows across her face, and he knew in that moment, without doubt, that they were inevitable.

"Quinn."

He dropped to the floor next to the sofa, and took her face in his hands. Their eyes met, measuring each other for a very long time. He leaned forward and kissed her, tentatively at first, to give her the option of pulling away, just on the outside chance he had misunderstood the message he thought he read in her eyes. Quinn pulled him closer, deepening the kiss as she had in a thousand dreams, while his fingers traced the sides of her face and down the fine-boned jawline to her throat and back to her mouth, just as he had longed to do through all those sleepless nights. Sinking back into the cushions, she took him with her, until he half-covered her body with his, and his hands began to explore the body that arched beneath him and drew him like a magnet.

"Quinn," he whispered, hating to stop, but needing to know, "Quinn, why didn't you come that day?"

"What?" Her eyes snapped open. He couldn't possibly have said what she thought he said.

"If you had changed your mind, why didn't you just tell me?"

"What are you talking about?" She pushed at his chest.

"Don't tell me that you've forgotten, Quinn. Even after all these years, I don't think I could take that." He sat up and ran a restless hand through his hair.

"Cale . . ."

"Did your parents find out that we were planning to elope? Or did you get cold feet? I need to know, Quinn. Why did you leave me waiting here?"

Quinn pushed him away and shot up from the sofa on a bolt of remembered pain. "What are you talking about? *I waited.* I waited all day. I watched and waited and paced . . ."

She began to do just that, reliving those agonizing hours.

"Quinn, I was here all day. I stood right there, on that porch . . ." He stood and pointed to the front of the house.

"Here?" Her face twisted into a frown. "Why would you have waited *here?*"

"Because that's what we had agreed upon. July 27, at three o'clock. At the cabin."

"At *Elizabeth's* cabin."

"Elizabeth's cabin?" He frowned. "Why would you have gone all the way up there?"

"Because *cabin* means Elizabeth's . . ."

"No, Quinn. When I said, *Meet me at the cabin,* I meant *this* cabin. . . ." Cale's mouth went dry. "You were there? At Elizabeth's? You actually were there . . . ?"

"All day. Until dark." She blinked, not believing. "You were here . . . ?"

"Till the last possible moment. Until I had just enough time left to catch my plane."

"Oh, Cale. Oh, Cale." The enormity of it overwhelmed her and took her breath away. "All these years, I thought . . . I thought . . ." She backed up toward the fireplace, choking on words she could not speak.

". . . that I didn't love you? That I'd changed my mind about you?" He spoke as if the very words singed his tongue.

She nodded. "Yes."

"That's exactly what I thought," Cale whispered.

Tears as clear as glass and big as pearls welled in her eyes and rolled down her cheeks.

"Quinn, I never stopped loving you. Never. Not for a day." He gathered her into his arms, and her sobs broke his heart. "I thought that maybe you had gotten cold feet about leaving with me . . . that you were afraid to take that chance."

"Never, Cale. I was never afraid to love you."

"Even now?"

"Especially now."

He lifted her off her feet, and with one hand, grabbed a comforter from the sofa and spread it on the floor in front of the fireplace. Gently resting her on the blanket, he lay down beside her and wordlessly began to kiss the tears from her face. Soon there were no tears left to be kissed away, and his lips began a descent the length of her throat to the place where her collarbone met the buttons of the old thermal shirt, which one by one, she opened to lay bare the skin beneath, inviting him to feast on her flesh the way she had dreamed he might have done. Moaning through slightly parted lips, she offered more, and then more of herself to the heat of his mouth, crying out softly as his hands and seeking lips found those places that had so ached for his touch for so very long.

Reality being ever so much more wonderful than fantasy, she pulled the shirt over her head, and removed his own, needing desperately to feel his skin against hers. She felt her bones begin to melt away, the resultant liquid, thick and hot and bright, seeming to spread through her like lava. Wordlessly they moved together, caught up in the rhythms of an ancient dance, until he filled her as completely as she needed him to, and the sweet power of their dreams engulfed them both and dragged them down into the magical heart of the night.

Ten

FOR THE FIRST TIME IN YEARS, CALE SLEPT LIKE A BABY. WAKING to find Quinn curled up next to him had brought him to tears, proving that the wonders of the night had not been a dream after all. He kissed her shoulders to awaken her just as the sun rose through the trees to spread the first early arms of light into the cabin, and she rolled into his open arms, urging him to love her into the new day. He had needed no encouragement.

"Cale." She spoke into his chest, where her head had fallen, her neck being too languid, refusing to hold up its weight.

"What, sweetheart?" he whispered into the cloud of auburn curls that rested just below his chin.

"I think we should get up." She tried to stir, as if to be the one to make the first move, but found she could not. Her bones, it would appear, had been stolen while she slept, making it difficult for her to rise.

"Why?"

"Because your sons will be up soon," she said. "We should not be lying here, wrapped in little more than each other."

"Ummm," Cale replied.

"I take it that means you agree."

Forcing her body into action, she sat up and searched for her shirt and sweatpants amidst the rumpled blankets, which at some point had made their way from the sofa onto the floor. Finding her shirt, she pulled it over her head, then realizing he was watching her, asked, "What?"

"I can't believe you're here with me. After all these years of loving you, of missing you, I can't believe you're really here."

"Twelve years too late . . . ," she said wryly.

"Better late than never," he told her. "It's a miracle."

"A Christmas miracle." She smiled.

"Not many people get the second chance that we've been given, Quinn," he said softly.

"Do you really think it could be the same?" Her fingertips played with the dark hairs on his chest.

"No," he told her. "Better. It will be much better."

"What do we do now?" she asked.

"What we should have done before"—he drew her down to kiss her mouth—"only this time, we don't need your parents' permission."

"You want to *elope?*"

"Actually, I think maybe we could plan on something a little more elaborate than the sitting room of the local justice of the peace." He ran his hands slowly up and down her arms. "Maybe something with all the Hollisters in attendance."

Quinn let that sink in for a moment before asking, "You still want to marry me?"

"I never stopped wanting to marry you. Not for a day. I never loved anyone but you, Quinn. I don't want to lose you again."

She smiled and cradled his head against her chest. "I never loved anyone but you, either. I thought I would die when—"

A crash from the back of the cabin jolted them both.

"Guess we'd better get moving," she sighed.

"Want to toss a coin to see who makes breakfast today?" he asked as he pulled on his sweatpants and stood up.

"Ah, would that be a choice between my perfect pancakes and your 'gloppy' eggs?"

"She's not back seventy-two hours and already she's making fun of my cooking."

"Shall we ask your sons which they would prefer?" Quinn batted her eyelashes innocently.

"You do breakfast. I'll"—he paused as a second crash followed the first—"just see what the boys are doing."

"Quinn, why'd you sleep on the floor?" Evan stood by the kitchen door and pointed to the tangle of forgotten blankets in front of the fireplace.

Without turning around, Quinn replied from in front of the stove, "It was warmer by the fire."

"Good save," Cale murmured, reaching around her to grab a slice of buttered toast off the plate.

"What does that mean?" Eric plopped himself into one of the wooden chairs. " 'Good save'?"

"It means eat your breakfast." Cale buttered the pancakes on first one, then the other of his sons' plates.

"It looks like it's cleared up a lot." Quinn looked out the window and squinted, the sun playing off the snow nearly blinding her. "But the report on the radio warned of another storm."

"Gee, too bad," Cale deadpanned. "I guess you'll be stuck here for a while."

"I should call home." She looked at the clock. It was ten o'clock in the morning. "It's Christmas Eve, Cale. I have to be home for Christmas."

"I understand," he said without looking at her.

Quinn started to speak, then apparently thought better of it. She disappeared into the living room, and he could hear her voice, though he could not make out what she was saying. The thought of her leaving made his hands shake and his head pound, so fearful was he of losing her again. The hole he had carried around inside him for the past twelve years, the one that had only so recently begun to mend, began to open again. Stitch by painful stitch.

"My brother Trevor is going to drive up on the tractor," she told him happily as she sat at the table and sipped at her coffee.

"Is he going to take you away?" Evan asked.

"He's going to plow a road so that I can drive down the mountain to our ranch."

"You're going to leave?" Eric's bottom lip began to quiver unexpectedly.

"Well, actually, I thought I'd take you all with me." She

looked into Cale's eyes. Under the table, her foot, soft in its wool sock, followed the length of his leg to his knee and back again. "Since there is another big storm coming. And since my mother is all prepared for the holiday." She turned to the boys and added, "And since your Aunt Val is already there with perhaps something special for her two favorite boys."

"Would Santa be able to find us there?" Eric asked, worried that a last-minute change of address might confuse the jolly old elf.

"Absolutely." She grinned at Cale. Her mother had told her that Val arrived the night before with all the presents for the boys that Cale had bought and mailed for Val to bring with her. "What do you say, Cale? A wonderful Christmas is waiting, just a mile down the mountain."

"Maybe for some. But me, I had my Christmas," he told her softly. "And it was wonderful. Every bit as wonderful as I dreamed it would be."

"Come home with me, Cale." She reached across the table to rub his face gently with the back of her hand. "Let me have it all this year. Let me share it all with you and the boys."

Two little pairs of eyes met across the table. What was going on? Dad was acting like one of those guys on the soap operas that the nanny used to watch, and Quinn was looking all melty.

Yuck.

On the other hand, she had made cookies and a tree and was going to put their names in a book. That stuff should count for something.

As much as Cale wished to keep her to himself for a few more days, he could not deny the light in Quinn's eyes as she described the scene that would greet them at the High Meadow Ranch. She wanted, at long last, to share him with her family, to share the holiday with all of those she loved. She deserved to have it all. And it would be wonderful to see her family again, to bask in the glow of that large and happy group, to see her parents and to introduce his sons to the man they knew only as a legend. To see Sky again, and to spend the holiday with Valerie for the first time in years.

"Well, then, shall we pack up some clothes for the boys

and me before we dig out your car?" He stood up and took her hand, drawing her out of her seat to hold her to him. "I suspect this will be but the first of many Christmases we will spend together at the Hollister hacienda. I'm ready, if you are."

She rocked against him, filled with the wonder of all the miracles that had somehow found their way into her life over the past few days. True Christmas miracles, of a certainty.

"What about our tree?" Eric wailed as left the cabin.

"It will be waiting for us when we come back," Quinn assured him.

"Will you come back with us?" Evan queried Quinn.

"Of course, I'll come back with you. You think I'm going to let you eat all those Christmas cookies by yourselves?" She ruffled his hair as she closed the front door, telling him, "Go get your hat. It's cold out here."

Pulling the wool hat down over his ears, Evan turned solemnly to look at his brother.

Finally, Eric said, "Is she going to be, like, you know"—he looked up at Cale, gesturing awkwardly with his hands—"like our mother?"

"There's a good possibility that we might let her do that." Cale knelt down to face his sons. "What do you think?"

The boys looked at each other for a long moment.

"She does make pretty good breakfasts," Eric said.

"And she knows how to make paper chains." Evan nodded.

"It might be okay," Eric told Cale.

"I hear the tractor." Quinn stuck her head back inside the cabin and looked at the three McKenzies, huddled together conspiratorially. "What are you guys up to?"

"Nothing," the three replied in unison.

"Uh-oh." Quinn rolled her eyes. "What have I gotten myself into?"

It was midafternoon by the time the Land Rover made it down the mountain past snow-gilded trees that sparkled in the sun and fence posts that leaned wearily into the heavy drifts. A trail of smoke fled the massive stone chimney and thinned as it reached the sky; even as they followed the plowed path, the warmth of the High Meadow Ranch reached out toward them with arms filled with love. Quinn bit her bottom lip anticipating the joy of reunion with her sisters and the glow that seemed to surround the family home this time of the year.

From the big kitchen window, Catherine studied the caravan of tractor and Land Rover as it played follow the leader down the narrow, newly plowed road. She sighed heavily. Who would have thought that after all these years, Cale McKenzie would be back?

Anxiously, she watched the Land Rover pull into the yard and stop. From the passenger side, the man emerged. He looked taller, leaner than she had remembered, but the face with its boyish smile had barely changed at all. He always was a handsome thing, Catherine recalled. Handsome enough to have had a string of girls back in high school, had he wanted them, though she knew he had only wanted one.

A tide of maternal guilt washed over Catherine, and a kink of uncertainty pricked her conscience. She had never really known just what exactly had caused her daughter's breakup with Cale that summer so long ago. To be sure, Catherine had made gentle inquiries, but Quinn had chosen to respond in vague, one-word answers that had told Catherine nothing. All Catherine had known was that Quinn had not been the same since the day Cale had left Larkspur for Baltimore.

Had Catherine known how heavily Quinn would carry the burden of heartbreak for so many years, would she have been so quick back then to brush off her daughter's declaration of undying love? And more importantly, how badly bruised was Quinn from having been forced to spend the last few days in the company of the man who had broken her heart, but had never been replaced in her life?

Merciful heaven, why did he have to come back, after all these years?

Quinn opened her door and slid from behind the driver's seat to jump into the hard-crusted snow just as Sky and her father fled the house from the side door to greet the newcomers. The three men greeted each other tentatively at first, but in a heartbeat Hap had embraced Cale and a fine reunion was in progress. At least that went well, Catherine thought, nodding, knowing how proud Hap was of his famous protégé.

Cale rounded the side of the vehicle to where Quinn appeared to be fussing with something in the backseat. The way he touched the small of Quinn's back, the familiarity of the simple gesture, and the manner in which Quinn had turned to look up at him, squinting into the sun but grinning happily, gave Catherine cause for thought. Good grief, one would think that they . . . that they . . .

Could it be . . . ?

Catherine peered out the window, looking more closely at her daughter's face, seeking her eyes. With Quinn, it had always been in her eyes.

And yes, there it was. That same look of love, of trust, of total devotion she had worn twelve years ago. The glow, the sparkle that came from within.

Oh dear.

Catherine sat down on a stool near the window, tears of regret forming in her eyes. Quinn must have loved him immensely for it to have lasted, untouched, all this time. Catherine sighed heavily. Do parents ever really know if the decisions they make for their children are, after all, the right ones? And if called upon to make the same decision for a seventeen-year-old daughter again, would her answer be different?

Probably not, she told herself.

Feeling slightly redeemed, Catherine rose to go to the door to welcome her daughter home, when two little figures out in the snow caught her eye. She leaned closer to the window to get a better look. Of course. Val had said that Cale had two little boys.

Catherine watched the two little bundled fellows chase each other toward the house and smiled as one tripped the other, who fell flat into the snow. Weighted down by what must have felt like pounds of clothing, the one in the snow flailed about while the other, laughing, tried to help him up. Soon both boys were rolling in the snow. Catherine laughed out loud. How many times had she watched her own sons frolic just so?

Maybe Trevor could go out to the barn to look for the old sleds he and Sky used to have. These little ones were just about the right age for them.

The front door opened and Catherine reached the hallway in time to see young Lilly greet the two tousled, snow-covered little boys with freckles on their faces and mischief in their eyes.

Maybe Cale's coming back wasn't so bad, she mused.

"Hi. We've been waiting for you to get here." Lilly pushed the door open wide.

"Who are you?" one of the little snow-boys asked.

"I'm Lilly. And I'm making a gingerbread village with my grandma. Want to help make little houses?"

"Do we get to eat them?"

"Of course not," Lilly replied as if the boy was daft. "It's for the village. To go in the dining room. Come see. . . ."

Snowy boots made snowy prints from the front door to the kitchen. Not for the first time, Catherine remembered. And, God willing, not for the last. . . .

"Mom," Quinn called from the doorway, "I'm home. Come see who's joined us for Christmas. . . ."

It had been a gala Christmas Eve, the best ever, to Quinn's way of thinking, with all of the people she loved most gathered under the sturdy roof of the old ranch house. As always, there had been tons of wonderful things to eat and drink, games to play and songs to sing, old memories to share and new memories to be made. At eight o'clock, they all crowded around the fireplace in the great room, the merry chatter subsiding as Catherine rang the little silver bell that had served the purpose since the year the twins were born and every Christmas Eve since.

"Loved ones," a beaming Catherine addressed her family, "it is time for the reading. Schuyler won the toss this year." She handed her son the worn copy of "The Night Before Christmas."

Standing at one end of the room, his back against the stone hearth, Sky began to read the words they all knew by heart.

Quinn settled back in the armchair near the window and

counted her many blessings in the faces that surrounded her in the comfortable room. Her eyes danced from one to the other.

It was certainly turning out to be a Christmas filled with surprises, a Christmas she would never forget.

I can't wait to see Mom's and Dad's faces when they open their gift. Quinn smiled at the thought of her parents, stretched out on the clean soft sands of St. Thomas, with palm trees behind them and a perfect pastel blue sea open to the horizon.

Across the room, Aunt Sarah, hard of hearing but unwilling to admit it, leaned forward to catch every one of Sky's words. Her daughter Selena had whispered to Quinn and Sunny that she and her siblings had bought their mother a ring set with the birthstones of her children, all of whom were present and accounted for. Selena's brother, Christian, had announced his engagement that night to his longtime girlfriend, and their sister, Alexa, announced that she was carrying twins.

From one sibling to the next, Quinn's loving eyes trailed around the room. CeCe, who with her twin brother, Trevor, never seemed to age. Gorgeous dark-haired Sunny, with her beautiful little Lilly, the pride of the Hollister clan. Liza, looking surprisingly sophisticated. Ruggedly handsome Sky, blushing as he looked up to meet the eyes of the very elegant Valerie McKenzie from across the room.

And, miracle of miracles, there was Cale, who sat on the big square ottoman in front of her chair, his back to her, his sons sitting uncharacteristically still on the rag rug at his feet. Even they seemed to belong, to have been absorbed into the welcoming warmth of the family. She touched his back, and without turning around he leaned back into her, and she rested her forehead on the small of his back. How wonderful to have him here, to share this night with him. It was all so right.

Sky completed his reading, signaling bedtime for the young ones. Following a giddy round of good-night kisses from all of her aunts and uncles, Lilly was carried from the room over Sunny's shoulder to the big loft bedroom upstairs. Eric and Evan were relegated to Sky's old room and the same old bunk beds that Cale himself had slept in many a night as a boy. The older "boys"—Sky, Trevor, and Cale—would later be shipped across the yard to the old bunkhouse for the night. As soon as the children were tucked in, the business of hanging their stockings and bringing their presents out of hiding to place under the tree began. Soon the room was filled with laughter and the space under the tree was filled with gifts. Champagne was poured, as was the tradition, and another round of Christmas cookies circulated on silver trays.

There being little room left under the tree, Quinn stacked her family's gifts here and there around the room. Feeling Cale's fingers on her arm, she turned to him and said, "I have no gift for you."

"You can make it up to me later." He grinned. "When we get back to the cabin. I'll sure you'll think of something. But in the meantime, I have something for you."

"You do?"

"Um-hmm." He took her by the hand and led her to the doorway, where just that morning her mother had hung a sprig of mistletoe.

"Now, give me your hand."

Puzzled, she held them both out to him. Around the ring finger of her left hand, he began to twist a piece of tinsel that had fallen from the tree.

"It's not much, I know," he said, "but as soon as we can get into Bozeman, we'll find something that's a little more permanent. But for now, it will have to do."

"I always thought it would be so romantic to get engaged on Christmas Eve," she told him. "But are you sure . . . ? Cale, please don't rush into anything you're not sure of. . . ."

"Well, after having twelve years to think about it, I'd say I'm about as sure as I could be. And you, Quinn . . . ?"

"I've always been sure, Cale. I've never loved anyone but you."

"Well, then, I guess that settles it. Maybe we should try having that little talk with your parents again."

He took her in his arms and swayed to the slow sweet Christmas music on the stereo. She had never tried dancing to "I'll Be Home for Christmas" before, but it seemed to fit.

Later, as she helped clean up the plates and glasses, she stopped in front of the window that overlooked the hills.

The moon was big and bright, lending a luster to the all-white landscape that seemed to stretch endlessly into the night. How perfect it all was. How wonderful. She had never known just how much love her heart was capable of holding until tonight. Her family, Cale, the boys, all had . . .

She blinked, then leaned closer to the window, and a slow smile crossed her lips. There, by the fence, a shadowy figure stood, as if gazing at the ranch house.

Quinn touched the frosted pane with the fingers of her right hand.

"Thank you, Grandmother," she whispered.

"What are you thinking?" Cale's face was reflected in the glass, his arms wrapping around her from behind, drawing her close into a secure and loving circle. "Are you thinking about all the Christmases we missed spending together?"

"Oh, no," she told him, turning in his arms and pulling his face close enough to kiss, "I'm thinking of all the Christmases yet to come."

MARIAH STEWART is the author of several award-winning contemporary romances. *Moments in Time,* her first book, was the winner of the prestigious Golden Leaf for Best Single Title of 1995, and was a nominee for *Romantic Times* magazine's Reviewers Choice Award for Best Contemporary Novel of 1995. Her second book, *A Different Light,* was the recipient of the 1995 Award of Excellence for Best Contemporary Romance. *Carolina Mist* was a bestselling romance in 1996, and was a finalist for the highly regarded Holt Medallion. *Devlin's Light,* released in the summer of 1997 (an Amazon Top Pick for August), begins a three-book contemporary family saga for Pocket Books. Also, watch for *Moondance* in early 1999.

A native of Hightstown, New Jersey, Mariah Stewart currently lives in Lansdowne, Pennsylvania, with her husband, two daughters, and one very large golden retriever in a century-old country Victorian home, which is, alas, still being renovated.

Linda Howard

White Out

One

It was going to snow.

The sky was low and flat, an ominous purplish gray that blended into and obscured the mountaintops, so that it was difficult to tell where the earth stopped and the sky began. The air had a sharp, ammonia smell to it, and the icy edge of the wind cut through Hope Bradshaw's jeans as if they were made of gauze instead of thick denim. The trees moaned under the lash of the wind, branches rustling and whipping, the low, mournful sound settling in her bones.

She was too busy to stand around staring at the clouds, but she was nevertheless always aware of them hovering, pressing closer. A sense of urgency kept her moving, checking the generator and making sure she had plenty of fuel handy for it, carrying extra wood into her cabin and stacking even more on the broad, covered porch behind the kitchen. Maybe her instincts were wrong and the snow wouldn't amount to any more than the four to six inches the weather forecasters were predicting.

She trusted her instincts, though. This was her seventh winter in Idaho, and every time there had been a big snow, she had gotten this same crawly feeling just before it. The atmosphere was charged with energy, Mother Nature gathering herself for a real blast. Whether caused by static electricity or plain old foreboding, her spine was tingling from an uneasiness that wouldn't let her rest.

She wasn't worried about surviving: she had food, water, shelter. This was, however, the first time Hope had gone through a big snow alone. Dylan had been here the first two years; after he died, her dad had moved to Idaho to help her take care of the resort. But her uncle Pete had suffered a heart attack three days ago, and her dad had flown to Indianapolis to be with his oldest brother. Uncle Pete's prognosis was good: the heart attack was relatively mild, and he had gotten to the hospital soon enough to minimize the damage. Her dad planned to stay another week, since he hadn't seen any of his brothers or sisters in over a year.

She didn't *mind* being alone, but securing the cabins was a lot of work for one person. There were eight of them, single-storied, some with one bedroom and some with two, sheltered by towering trees. There were four on one side of her own, much larger A-frame cabin, and four on the other side, the nine buildings curving around the bank of a picturesque lake that was teeming with fish. She had to make certain the doors and windows were securely fastened against what could be a violent wind, and water valves had to be turned off and pipes drained so they wouldn't freeze and burst when the power went off, which she had absolute faith would happen. Losing power wasn't a matter of *if*, but *when*.

Actually, the weather had been mild this year; though it was December, there had been only one snow, a measly few inches, the remnants of which still lingered in the shaded areas and crunched under her boots. The ski resorts were hurting; their owners would welcome even a blizzard, if it left behind a good thick base.

Even the infamously optimistic slobber-hound, a golden retriever otherwise known as Tinkerbell even though he was neither female nor a fairy, seemed to be worrying about the weather. He stayed right behind her as she trudged from cabin to cabin, sitting on the porch while she worked inside, his tail thumping on the planks in relieved greeting when she reappeared. "Go chase a rabbit or something," she told him after she almost stumbled over him as she left the next to last cabin, but though his brown eyes lit with enthusiasm at the idea, he declined the invitation.

Those brown eyes were irresistible, staring up at her with love and boundless trust. Hope squatted down and rubbed behind his ears, sending him into twisting, whining ecstasy as he all but collapsed under the pleasure. "You big mutt," she said lovingly, and he responded to the tone with a swipe of his tongue on her hand.

Tink was five; she had gotten him the month after Dylan died, before her dad had come to live with her. The clumsy, adorable, loving ball of fuzz seemed to sense her sadness and had devoted himself to making her laugh with his antics. He smothered her with affection, licking whatever part of her was within reach, crying at night until she surrendered and lifted the puppy onto the bed with her, where he happily settled down against her, and the warmth of the little body in the night somehow made the loneliness more bearable.

Gradually the pain became less acute, her father arrived, and she was less lonely, and as he grew, Tink gradually distanced himself, moving from her bed to the rug beside it, then to the doorway, and finally down to the living room, as if he were weaning her from *his* presence. His accustomed sleeping spot now was on the rug in front of the fireplace, though he made periodic tours of the house during the night to make certain everything in his doggy world was okay.

Hope looked at Tink, and her lungs suddenly constricted, compressing as an enormous sense of panic seized her. He was five. Dylan had been dead *five* years! The impossibility of it stunned her, rocked her back. Hope stared, unseeing, at the dog, her eyes wide and fixed, her hand still on his head.

Five years. She was thirty-one, a widow who lived with her father and her dog, who hadn't been on a date in . . . God, almost two years now, and there had been a grand total of only three dates anyway. There weren't any neighbors nearby, the motel kept her busy during the summer when travel was easier, and she made it a point not to get involved with any of the guests, not that she had met any with whom she *wanted* to get involved.

Stricken, she looked around as if she didn't recognize her

surroundings. There had been moments before when the reality of Dylan's death hit hard, but this was different. This was like being kicked in the chest.

Five years. Thirty-one. The numbers kept echoing in her mind, chasing each other in circles like maddened squirrels. What was she *doing* here? She was living her life secluded in the mountains, so immersed in being Dylan Bradshaw's widow that she had forgotten to be herself, running the small, exclusive resort that had been Dylan's dream.

Dylan's dream, not hers.

It had never been hers. Oh, she had been happy enough to come to Idaho with him, help him build his dream in the wilderness paradise, but her dream had been much simpler: a good marriage, kids, the kind of life her parents had enjoyed, piercingly sweet in its normalcy.

But Dylan was gone, his dream forever unfulfilled, and now hers was in danger too. She hadn't remarried, she had no children, and she was thirty-one.

"Oh, Tink," she whispered. For the first time she realized she might never remarry, might never have a family of her own. Where had the time gone? How had it slipped away, unnoticed?

As always, Tinkerbell sensed her mood and thrust himself closer to her, licking her hands, her cheek, her ear, almost knocking her down in his frenzy of sympathy. Hope grabbed him and regained her balance, laughing a little in spite of herself as she wiped away the slobber-hound's latest offering. "All right, all right, no more feeling sorry for myself. If I don't like what I've been doing, then change, right?"

His plumy tail wagged, his tongue lolled, and he grinned his doggy grin that said he approved of her speed in figuring out what she should do.

"Of course," she told him as she headed down the trail toward the last cabin, "I have others to consider. I can't forget Dad. After all, he sold his house and came out here because of me. It wouldn't be fair to uproot him again, to say, 'Thanks for the support, but now it's time to move on.' And what about you, goofball? You're used to having plenty of room to roam, and let's face it, you aren't dainty."

Tink trotted after her, gamboling at her heels like an overgrown puppy, his ears pricked up as he listened to her tone. It was conversational, no longer sad, so his tail happily swished back and forth.

"Maybe I should just make an effort to get out more. The fact that I've only had three dates in five years *could* be my fault," Hope allowed wryly. "Let's face it, the drawback to living in a remote area is that there aren't many people around. *Duhh.*"

Tink stopped dead, bright eyes fastening on a squirrel scampering across the path in front of them. Without even an apologetic look for abandoning her, he tore out in furious pursuit of the squirrel, barking madly. Clearing Idaho of the villainous squirrels was Tink's ambition in life; though he had never caught one, he never stopped trying. After fruitlessly trying to break him of the habit, fearing he would tangle with a rabid squirrel, Hope had given up the effort and instead made certain he always got his rabies vaccination.

The squirrel scrambled up the nearest tree and stopped just out of reach of Tink's lunges, chattering at him and spurring Tink to even more barking and jumping, as if he suspected the varmint was mocking him.

Leaving the dog to his fun, Hope went up the steps to the long front porch of the last cabin. Though the little resort had been Dylan's idea, his dream, going into one of the cabins always gave her a sense of pride. He had designed them, but she was the one who had decorated them, took care of them. The furnishings were different in each one, but similar in their simplicity and comfort. The walls were decorated with tasteful prints, rather than ratty deer heads bought at garage sales. The furniture was comfortable enough for a couple on a honeymoon and substantial enough for a hunting party.

She had tried to make each one feel like a home instead of a rented cabin, with rugs and lamps and books, as well as a fully equipped kitchen. There were radios but no televisions, because reception in the mountains was so spotty and most of the guests mentioned how peaceful their stay was without it. There was a television in Hope's cabin, but it pulled in only one station during good weather and none at all during bad. She was considering investing in a satellite dish, because the winters were terribly long and often boring, and she and her dad could play only so many games of checkers.

If she did, she thought, she might add an extra receiver or two so a couple of the cabins could have television service to offer as an option. Things couldn't stay the same; if she kept the resort, she would have to continually make changes and improvements.

Taking a wrench from her hip pocket, she turned the valve that shut off the water to the cabin, then set about draining the pipes. The cabins were heated electrically, so when the power went off, they would be quickly become icy inside. Each cabin did have a fireplace, but if a blizzard came, she certainly wouldn't be able to battle her way from cabin to cabin, building fires and keeping them fed.

That accomplished, she secured the shutters over the windows and locked the door. Tink had given up on the squirrel and was waiting for her on the porch. "That's it," she told him. "All finished. Just in time too," she added, as a snowflake drifted past her nose. "C'mon, let's go home."

He understood the word "home" and leaped to his feet, panting eagerly. A snowflake drifted past *his* nose, and he snapped at it, then was off on another manic tear, running back and forth, jumping at snowflakes and trying to catch them. His expression invited Hope to laugh at him, and she did, then joined him in a snowflake chase that turned into a game of tag, and ended with her running and jumping through the falling snow like a five-year-old herself. By the time she reached the big cabin, she was exhausted, panting harder than Tink and giggling at his antics.

He reached the door before she did, of course, and as always he was impatient to get inside. He turned his head to bark at her, demanding she hurry and open the door. "You're worse than having a child," she said, leaning over him to turn the doorknob. "You can't wait to get out, and once you're out, you can't wait to get back in. You'd better enjoy the outdoors while you can, because if this snow gets as bad as I think it will, it'll be a couple of days before you can go for a run."

Logic made no impression on Tink. He merely wagged his tail harder, and when the door opened, he lunged through the widening crack, yipping a little as he trotted around the spacious, two-story great room, checking all the familiar scents before darting into the kitchen and out again, then coming over to Hope as if to say, "I've checked things out and everything's okay." She patted him, then shed her heavy shearling coat and hung it on the hall tree, sighing in relief at the immediate sense of freedom and coolness.

Her home was beautiful, she thought, looking around. Not grand, not luxurious, but definitely beautiful. The front of the A-frame was a wall of windows, giving a wonderful view of the lake and the mountains. A big rock fireplace soared the entire two stories, and twin ceiling fans hung from the exposed-beam ceiling, circulating the warm air that gathered at the top back to the ground floor. Hope had a green thumb, and luxurious ferns and other houseplants gave the interior of the house a lush freshness. The floor was wide wood planking, finished to a pale gold and covered with thick area rugs in rich shades of blue and green. Graceful curving stairs wound up to the second floor, and the white stair railing continued across the balcony. For Christmas she always wound lights and greenery up the stair banisters and across the balcony, and the effect was breathtaking.

There were two bedrooms upstairs—the master bed and bath and a smaller bedroom, which they had intended to use for a nursery—and a large bedroom downstairs off the kitchen. Her dad used the downstairs bedroom, saying the stairs were hard on his knees, but the truth was the arrangement gave them both more privacy. The kitchen was spacious and efficient, with more cabinet space than she would ever use, a cook island she loved, and an enormous side-by-side refrigerator-freezer that could hold enough food to feed an army. There was also a well-stocked pantry, a small laundry room, and a powder room, and after her dad had moved in, Hope had added a small full bath to connect to his bedroom.

The total effect was undeniably beautiful and comfortable, but every time the electricity went off, Hope wished they had made better decisions about what would or would not be hard-wired to the generator. The refrigerator, cooktop, and water heater were connected. To save money by buying a smaller generator, they had decided not to connect the heating unit, the lights, or any wall plugs except those in the kitchen. In a power outage, they had reasoned, the fireplace in the great room would provide enough heat. Unfortunately, without the ceiling fans working to keep the air circulated, most of the heat produced by the fireplace went straight to the second floor. The upstairs would be stifling hot, while the downstairs remained chilly. The situation was livable, but not comfortable, especially for any length of time.

Forget the satellite dish, she thought. The money would be better spent on a larger generator and some electrical rewiring.

She looked out the windows; though it was only three o'clock, the clouds were so heavy it looked like twilight outside. The snow was falling faster now, fat, heavy flakes that had already dusted the ground with white just in the short time she had been inside.

She shivered suddenly, though the house was perfectly comfortable. A big pot of beef stew would hit the spot, she thought. And if the electricity was off for a long time, well, she might get awfully tired of beef stew, but reheating a bowl of it in the microwave drained a lot less power from the generator than cooking a small meal from scratch each time she got hungry.

But maybe she was wrong. Maybe it wouldn't snow that much.

Two

SHE WASN'T WRONG.

The wind began howling, sweeping down from the icy mountaintops, and the snowfall grew steadily heavier. With nightfall, Hope could no longer see out the windows, so she opened the front door to peek out, and the savage wind slammed the door into her, almost knocking her down. Snow all but exploded into the great room. She couldn't see anything out there but a wall of white.

Panting, she grabbed the door and braced all her weight against it, forcing it shut. The wind seeped around the edges in a high-pitched whine. Tink sniffed at her legs, assuring himself she was okay, then barked at the door.

Hope pushed her hair out of her face and blew out a deep breath. That was a full-fledged blizzard, a complete white-out, where the wind whipped the snow around and blotted out visibility. Her shoulder ached where the door had hit her, and snow melted on her polished floor. "I won't do that again," she muttered, going in search of a mop and towel to dry the floor.

As she was cleaning up the water, the lights dimmed, then flickered brightly again. Ten seconds later they went off.

Having expected it, she had a flashlight close to hand, and switched it on. For a moment the house was eerily silent, then the generator automatically switched on and in the kitchen the refrigerator hummed to life. Just that faint noise was enough to banish the alarming sense of being disabled.

Anticipating, Hope had put out the oil lamps. She lit the lamp on the mantel, then put the match to the dry kindling and rolled newspapers under the logs she had already laid. Small blue-and-yellow flames licked at the paper, then curled up the sticks of kindling. She watched the fire for a moment to make certain it had caught, then moved around lighting the other lamps, turning the wicks low so they didn't smoke. Normally she wouldn't have lit so many lamps, but normally she wasn't alone, either. She had never thought herself timid and she wasn't afraid of the dark, but something about being alone in a blizzard was a little unnerving.

Tink settled down on his rug, his muzzle resting on his front paws. Perfectly content, he closed his eyes.

"You shouldn't get so worked up," Hope advised the dog, and he responded by rolling onto his side and stretching out.

Television reception had been nonexistent all afternoon, and the radio was picking up mostly static. She had turned it off earlier but now switched it over to battery operation and turned it on again, hoping the reception was better. It wasn't. Sighing, she switched it off. Why, at this rate, it might be a couple of days before she learned there was a blizzard.

It was too early to go to bed; she felt as if she should be doing something, but didn't know what. Restlessly she prowled around, the shrill whistle of the wind getting on her nerves. Maybe a bath would help. She climbed the stairs, peeling out of her clothes as she went. Already the heat was intensifying upstairs, and because her bedroom door was open, that room was toasty.

Instead of showering, she ran a tub of water and lolled in it, her blond hair pinned on top of her head and the mellow light of a lamp flickering over her. Her naked flesh gleamed in the water, oddly different in lamplight; the curves were highlighted and shadows deepened, so that her breasts looked more voluptuous, the hair between her legs darker and more mysterious.

It wasn't a bad body, for thirty-one, she thought as she inspected herself. In fact, it was a damn good body. Hard work kept her slim and toned. Her breasts weren't large, but they were high and well-shaped; her belly was flat, and she had a nice butt.

It was a body that hadn't had sex in five long years.

Immediately she winced away from the thought. As much as she had enjoyed making love with Dylan, on the whole she wasn't tormented by horniness. For a couple of years after his death she hadn't felt even the slightest flicker of sexual need. That had gradually changed, but not to the extent that she felt frustrated enough to do something about it. Now, however, her loins clenched with a sharp surge of need. Maybe the tub bath had been a mistake, the warm water lapping at her naked body, too much like a touch, a caress.

Tears stung her eyes and she closed them, leaning back and sinking even deeper into the water, letting it envelope her. She wanted sex. Hard-thrusting, sweaty, heart-pounding sex. And she wanted to love again, to *be* loved again. She wanted that closeness, that warmth, to be able to reach out in the night and know she wasn't alone. She wanted a baby. She wanted to waddle around with bloated breasts and an extended belly, her bladder under constant pressure, feeling their child squirming within her.

Oh, she wanted.

She allowed five minutes for a pity party, then sniffed and briskly sat up, using her toes to open the drain. Standing, she pulled the curtains closed and turned on the shower, rinsing away both soap and the blues.

Maybe she didn't have a man, but she did have nice, thick flannel pajamas, and she put them on, reveling in their warmth and comfort. Flannel pajamas possessed the same powers of reassurance as a hot bowl of soup on a cold day, a subliminal "there, there."

After brushing her teeth and hair, moisturizing her face, and pulling on an extra-thick pair of socks, she felt considerably better. Indulging in a hot bath, the sniffles, and a bout of self-pity was something she hadn't done in a long time, and it had been way overdue. Now that the ritual was behind her, she felt ready to deal with a blizzard.

Tink was lying at the foot of the stairs, waiting for her. He wagged a greeting, then stretched out in front of the bottom step so she had to step over him. "You could move," she informed him, as she did on a regular basis. He never took the hint, assuming it was his right to lie wherever he wanted.

After the warmth of the upstairs, the downstairs felt

chilly. She poked up the fire, then microwaved herself a cup of hot chocolate. With the chocolate, a book, and a small battery-operated reading light, she installed herself on the couch. Cushions behind her back and a throw over her legs added the perfect touch. Soothed, pampered, comfortable, she lost herself in the book.

The night hours drifted by. She dozed, woke, eyed the clock on the mantel: ten-fifty. She should go to bed, she thought, but getting up so she could lie down again seemed ridiculous. On the other hand, she had to get up anyway to tend the fire, which was low.

Yawning, she added a couple of logs to the fire. Tink came over to watch, and Hope scratched behind his ears. Suddenly he stiffened, his ears lifting, and a growl rumbled in his throat. He tore over to the front door and stood in front of it, barking furiously.

Something was out there.

She didn't know how Tink could hear anything over the howl of the wind, but she trusted the acuity of his senses. She had a pistol in the drawer of her nightstand, but that was upstairs and her father's rifle was much closer. Running into the bedroom, her socks sliding on the polished floor, she grabbed the rifle from its rack and the box of bullets from the shelf below it. Carrying both out into the great room where she could see, she racheted five bullets into place.

Between the wind and Tink's barking, she couldn't hear anything else. "Tink, quiet!" she commanded. "C'mere, boy." She patted her thigh, and with a worried look at the door, Tink trotted over to stand beside her. She stroked his head, whispering praise. He growled again, every muscle in his body tense as he shoved in front of her and pushed against her legs.

Was that a thump on the porch? Straining her ears, patting Tink so he would be quiet, she tilted her head and listened. The wind screamed.

Her mind raced, running through the possibilities. A bear? Normally they would be in their dens by now, but the weather had been mild. Cougar, wolf . . . they would avoid humans and a house, if possible; could a blizzard make them desperate enough for shelter that the shy, wary animals would ignore their instincts?

Something thumped against the door, hard. Tink tore away from her, charging at the door, barking his head off again.

Hope's heart was pounding, her hands sweating. She wiped her palms on her pajamas and gripped the rifle more securely. "Tink, be quiet!"

He ignored her, barking even louder as another thump came, this one hard enough to rattle the door. Oh, God, was it a bear? The door would probably hold, but the windows wouldn't, not if the animal was determined to get in.

"Help."

She froze, not certain she had heard the muffled word. "Tink, shut up!" she yelled, and the tone of her voice briefly silenced the dog.

She hurried over to the door, the rifle ready in her hands. "Is anyone out there?" she called.

Another thump, much weaker, and what sounded like a groan.

"Dear God," she whispered, transferring the rifle to one hand and reaching to unbolt the door. There was a *person* out in this weather. She hadn't even considered that possibility, because she was so far from a main road. Anyone who left the protection of their vehicle shouldn't have been able to make it to her house, not in these conditions.

She opened the door and something white and heavy crashed into her legs. She screamed, staggering back. The door crashed against the wall, and the wind blew snow all over the floor, then sucked the warmth from the cabin with its icy breath.

The white thing on her floor was a man.

Hope set the rifle aside and grabbed him under the arms. She braced her legs, trying to drag him across the threshold so she could shut the door, and grunted as she moved him only a few inches. Damn, he was heavy! Ice pellets stung her face like bees, and the wind was unbelievably cold. She closed her eyes against the onslaught and braced herself for another effort. Desperation gave her strength; she threw herself backward, hauling the man with her. She fell, his weight pinning her to the floor, but his legs were over the threshold.

Tink was beside himself with worry, barking and lunging, then whining. He thrust his muzzle at her face for a quick lick of reassurance, for her or himself she couldn't begin to guess; then he sniffed at the stranger and resumed barking. Hope gathered herself for one more effort, and pulled the man all the way inside.

Panting, she crawled over to the door and wrestled it shut. The wind hammered at it, as if enraged at being shut out. She could feel the heavy door shuddering under the onslaught. Hope secured the bolt, then turned her attention to the man.

He had to be in bad shape. Frantically she knelt beside him, brushing away snow and ice that crusted his clothes and the towel he had wrapped over his face.

"Can you hear me?" she asked insistently. "Are you awake?"

He was silent, limp, not even shivering, which wasn't a good sign. She pushed back the hood of his heavy coat and unwrapped the towel from his face, then used it to wipe the snow from his eyes. His skin was white with cold, his lips blue. From the waist down, his clothes were wet and coated with a sheet of ice.

As swiftly as possible, given his size and the difficulty of wrestling an unconscious man out of wet clothing that had been frozen stiff, she began undressing him. Thick gloves came off first, then the coat. She didn't take the time to inspect his fingers for frostbite, but moved down to his feet and began unlacing the insulated boots, then tugged them off. He wore two pairs of socks, and she peeled them away. His feet were icy. Moving back up, she began unbuttoning his shirt and only then noticed that he wore a deputy sheriff's uniform, the shirt stretched tight across his chest and shoulders.

Under the shirt he wore a thermal pullover, and under that a T-shirt. He had been prepared for cold weather, but not for being caught out in it. Maybe his vehicle had slid off the road, though she didn't see how he could have made his way such a distance under these drastic conditions. It was nothing less than a miracle, or sheer chance, that he'd managed to stumble onto the house. By all logic, he should be dead out in the snow. And unless she could get him warm, he might yet die.

She tossed the three shirts into a heap, then attacked his belt buckle. It was coated with ice, the belt itself frozen stiff. Even the zipper of his fly was iced over. Unable to see in the storm, he must have stepped into the lake; the wonder was that he had managed to stay on his feet and not completely submerged himself. If he had gone under and gotten his head wet, he wouldn't have been able to make it to the house; most of the body's heat was lost through the scalp surface.

She fought the stiff fabric, using sheer force to get his pants off. The thermal underwear underneath was even more difficult, because it clung. Finally he lay on her floor in a puddle of melting snow and ice, clad only in his white shorts. She started to leave them on, but they were wet too, and getting him warm was more important than preserving his modesty. She stripped them down his legs and tossed them onto the pile of wet clothes.

Now she had to get him dried off and wrapped up. She ran to the downstairs bathroom and gathered up some towels, and then stripped the blankets off her father's bed. She raced back. The man hadn't moved from his sprawled position on the floor. She dragged him out of the puddle, hastily dried him, then spread a blanket on the floor and rolled him onto it. Wrapping it around him, she then dragged him in front of the fire. Tink sniffed at him, whined, then lay down beside him.

"That's right, boy, snuggle close," Hope whispered. Her muscles were trembling with exertion, but she ran to the kitchen and stuffed one of the towels into the microwave. When she got it out, the cloth was so hot she could barely hold it.

She raced back to the great room and wrapped the hot towel around the man's head. Then, grimly, she stripped off her own clothes. She was naked beneath her pajamas, but when this man's life depended on how fast she could get him warm, she wasn't about to waste time running upstairs to put on underwear. Grabbing up the other blanket, she held it in front of the fire until it was toasty. Throwing open the blanket wrapped around the man, she placed the warm blanket over him, tucking it around his cold feet; then she slid under it with him.

Shared body heat was the best way to combat hypothermia. Hope pressed herself close to his cold body, forcing herself not to flinch as his icy skin touched hers. Oh, God, he was so cold. She got on top of him, put her arms around him, pressed her warm face to his. She massaged his arms and shoulders, tucked his hands under her belly, cupped her hands over his ears until they warmed. She slid her feet up and down his legs, stroking away the cold, massaging the blood through his veins.

He moaned, a faint sound whispering past his parted lips.

"That's right," she murmured. "Wake up, sweetie." She stroked his face, his beard stubble scraping across her palm. His lips weren't as blue, she thought.

The towel around his head had cooled. Hope unwrapped it and slipped out from under the blanket, then ran to the kitchen and reheated the towel in the microwave. Back to the great room, put the towel around his head, crawl under the blanket with him again. He was tall, and she wasn't; she couldn't reach all of him at once. She slid down and warmed his feet with hers, curling her toes over his until his flesh caught some of her body heat.

Slithering back up his body, she lay on top of him again. He was hard with muscle, and that was good, because muscles generated heat.

He began to shiver.

Three

HOPE HELD HIM, MURMURING TO HIM, TRYING TO GET HIM TO talk to her. If she could get him awake enough to drink some coffee, the heat and caffeine would go a long way toward rousing him, but trying to pour hot coffee into an unconscious man was a good way to both choke him and burn him.

He moaned again, and sucked in a quick breath. He made a sharp movement with his head, dislodging the towel. The heat had dried his hair; it was dark, glistening with bronze lights in the glow of the fire. Hope tucked the towel back around his head to keep him from losing any of the precious body heat he had gained, and stroked his forehead, his cheeks. "Wake up, honey. Open your eyes and talk to me." She whispered to him, unconsciously using endearments to both reassure him and entice him to respond. Tink's ears perked up, because he was accustomed to that sweet tone being used when she spoke to him. He moved down to the man's feet, crowding against them when he lay down again. Maybe he could feel their chill through the blanket; with his thick fur, that would feel good to him. Or maybe it was instinct that led him to warm the man. Hope talked to Tink too, telling him what a good dog he was.

The faint, occasional shivers began to intensify. They wracked the man's body, roughening his skin, contorting his muscles. His teeth clenched and began chattering.

Hope held him through the convulsive shaking. He was in pain, barely conscious, groaning and breathing hard. He tried to curl into a ball, but she held him too tightly. "You're all right," she kept telling him. "Wake up, please. Open your eyes."

Unbelievably, he obeyed. His lids half lifted. His eyes were glazed, unfocused. Then they closed again, dark lashes resting on his cheeks. His arms swept up and locked around her, desperately clinging to her warmth as he was wracked by another bout of uncontrollable shaking. His entire body was tense, shuddering.

He was as strong as an ox; his arms were like steel bands around her. She murmured soothingly to him, rubbing his shoulders, pressing as close to him as she could. His skin definitely felt warmer now. *She* was hot, sweating from exertion and being swaddled in the heated blanket. She was exhausted from the effort of dragging him inside and wrestling him out of his clothes, as well as from the stress of knowing he would die if she didn't get him warm.

He relaxed beneath her, the bout of shivering over. He was breathing hard. He moved restlessly, shifting his legs, shrugging the towel away from his head. The towel seemed to annoy him, so she didn't replace it. Instead she folded it and lifted his head to slide the towel underneath, giving him more padding between his head and the hard floor.

At first he had been too cold, and the situation too urgent, for her to notice, but for some moments now she had been growing more aware of the sensations produced by his naked body against hers. He was a tall, well-built man, with a nice hairy chest and even nicer hard muscles. Good-looking too, now that his features weren't pinched and blue. Her nipples tingled from the rasping of his chest hair, and Hope knew it was time to get up. She pushed gently against him, trying to rise, but he groaned and tightened his arms, shivering again, so she let herself relax.

The shaking wasn't as violent this time. He swallowed and licked his lips, and his eyes flickered open again, just for a second. Then he seemed to doze, and because he was warm now, Hope wasn't alarmed. Her own muscles quivered from exhaustion. She closed her eyes too, resting for just a minute.

Time drifted. Half-asleep, warm, boneless from fatigue, she didn't know if a minute had passed, or an hour. His hand moved down to her bottom, curving over one rounded cheek. He shifted beneath her, muscled legs moving, sliding between her thighs. His engorged penis prodded at her exposed opening.

It happened so fast that he was inside her before she was fully awake. He rolled, pinning her beneath him on the blanket, mounting her, squeezing his penis into her and driving it deep with quick, hard shoves. After five years of chastity the penetration hurt, stretching her around his thick shaft, but it felt good too. Disoriented, unbelievably aroused, Hope arched her hips and felt him prod deeply, nudging her cervix. She cried out, gasping, her neck arching back as the sensation rocketed through her nerve endings.

There was no finesse, no lingering arousal. He simply began thrusting, his heavy weight holding her down, and she wound her arms and legs around him and met his thrusts with mindless ones of her own. In the mellow light of fire and lamp she saw his face, his eyes open now, very blue and still dazed, his expression set in the hardness of physical absorption. He was operating solely on animal instinct, his body aroused by the closeness of hers, by the naked intimacy that had been necessary to save his life. He was aware only of being warm and alive, and of her bare body in his arms.

On a purely physical level, the pleasure was more intense than any she had ever known. She had never felt more female, never been so acutely aware of her own body, or of the hard masculinity of a man's. She felt very inch of his smooth, hard shaft as he rocked back and forth inside her, felt the excited, welcoming cling of her inner flesh as each stroke took her closer and closer to climax. She was unbearably hot, her skin scorching, trembling pleasure lingering just out of reach. She grabbed his buttocks, holding him tight and grinding herself as deeply onto him as she could, crying out as the already intense pleasure became even more so. He gave a hoarse cry and convulsed, bucking, hips pumping, spurting hot semen, and Hope dissolved on an agonizing pulse of sensation.

He sank down on her, trembling in every muscle, his heart pounding violently, his breathing hard and fast. As shaken and dazed as he, she put her arms around him and held him close.

Unbelievably, they slept. Wrung out, emptied, hollowed, she felt the darkness descending on her and could do nothing to resist it. He was limp and heavy on top of her, already asleep. She managed to touch his cheek, stroke his dark hair back from his forehead, and then surrendered to the overwhelming need for rest.

The collapse of a log woke her. She stirred, wincing as her muscles protested the hard floor beneath her, the heavy body weighing her down. Confused, at first she thought she was dreaming. This couldn't be real, she couldn't be lying naked on the floor with a strange man, who was also completely naked.

But Tink was snoozing in his accustomed place, and the howling wind, the gently flickering lamplight, recalled the blizzard. Everything clicked into place.

And just as abruptly she realized he was also awake. He was lying very still, but every muscle was tense, and the penis still nestled inside her was growing thicker and longer by the second.

If she was confused, she could only imagine how disoriented he was. Gently she touched his back, smoothing her palm up the muscled expanse. "I'm awake," she murmured, her touch telling him she was there because she wanted to be, that everything was okay.

He lifted his head, and their eyes met. She felt an almost tangible shock as she stared into those blue eyes, eyes that were completely aware and revealed the sharpness of the personality behind them, as well as his comprehension of the situation.

Hope blushed. Her cheeks heated and she almost groaned aloud. What should she say to a man she was meeting for the first time, when she was lying naked beneath him and his erection was firmly lodged inside her?

He trailed one fingertip across her lips, then lightly stroked her hot cheek. "Do you want me to stop?" he whispered.

The first time had caught her unawares, but Hope was always brutally honest with herself, and she didn't allow herself to pretend she had been unwilling. This time, however, they were both fully cognizant of what they were doing. She didn't stop to analyze or question her response; she simply gave it. "No," she whispered in return. "Don't stop."

He kissed her then, a kiss as gentle and searching as if nothing had ever passed between them, as if he wasn't already inside her. He wooed her as if it were the first time, kissing her for a long time until her mouth slanted eagerly under his, until their tongues twined together. His hands were tender on her breasts, learning how she liked to be touched, teasing her nipples into tight peaks. He stroked her belly, her hips, between her legs. He licked his fingertips and stroked them over the ultrasensitive bud of her clitoris, drawing it out, make her gasp and arch her hips upward. He grunted at the resulting sensation as she took him even deeper.

She thought she would die from sensual torment before he finally began moving, but she enjoyed it so much she didn't urge him to hurry. She hadn't realized how hungry she was for this, for a man's attention, for his body, for the exquisite release of lovemaking. Even her frustration earlier, in the bath, hadn't prepared her for her total surrender to sensuality. She reveled in every kiss, every touch, every stroke. She clung to him and returned the caresses, trying to return some of the pleasure he was giving her, and judging from his groans she succeeded.

The time came when they no longer needed the gentle touches, when nothing mattered but the pounding drive to orgasm. Hope let herself get lost in the urgency of the moment, let her body drown in pure pleasure . . . and then he aroused her again, whispering, "Let me feel it again, let me feel you come."

His self-control held, barely. When the pulses of her third climax began, he made a deep, helpless sound in his throat and shuddered over her.

This time she didn't allow herself the luxury of sleep. This time he gently withdrew and collapsed on the blanket beside her. His hand sought hers, clasping her fingers against his callused palm.

"Tell me what happened," he finally said, his voice low and even. "Who are you?"

An introduction at this point seemed unbearably awkward. Hope blushed again, and cleared her throat. "Hope Bradshaw."

The blue eyes searched her face. "Tanner. Price Tanner."

The fire was getting too low. She needed to put another couple of logs on, but getting up and standing naked in front of him was somehow impossible. She looked around for her pajamas and, in an agony of embarrassment, realized she needed to bathe before putting them on.

He saw where she was looking, and he didn't suffer any such modesty. Unfolding his long length from the floor, he stepped over to the stack of wood and replenished the fire.

Hope did exactly what she had been embarrassed to let him to do to her, looked him over good, from head to foot. She liked what she saw, every inch of him. His muscles were delineated in the firelight, revealing the slope and curve of broad shoulders, wide chest, the long bulge of strong thigh muscles. His buttocks were round, firm. Even flaccid, his penis was intriguingly thick, and his testicles swung heavily below them. *Price Tanner.* She repeated his name in her mind, the syllables strong and brisk.

Tink looked a little grumpy at having had his sleep disturbed. He got up and sniffed at the stranger, and wagged his tail when the man leaned down and patted him. "I remember the dog barking," Price Tanner said.

"He heard you before I did. His name is Tinkerbell. Tink, for short."

"Tinkerbell?" He glanced at her, blue eyes incredulous. "He's gay?"

Hope sputtered with laughter. "No, he's just an eternally optimistic, goofy dog. He thinks the world is here to pet him."

"He may be right." He studied the sodden mass of his clothing, the water puddled on the floor. "How long have I been here?"

She looked at the clock. Two-thirty. "Three and a half hours." Too much had happened in such a short length of time, and yet she felt as if only an hour or so had passed instead of almost twice that. "I dragged you in and got you out of your clothes. You must have stepped into the lake, because you were wet from the waist down. I dried you off and wrapped you in a blanket."

"Yeah, I remember going into the water. I knew this place was here, but I couldn't see a damn thing."

"I don't know how you made it this far. Why were you on foot? Did you have an accident? And why were you out in this weather anyway?"

"I was trying to make it down to Boise. The Blazer slid off the road and broke out the windshield, so I couldn't stay there. Like I said, I knew this place was here, and I had a compass. I didn't have much choice except try to get here."

"You're a walking miracle," she said frankly. "Logically, you should be dead out in the snow."

"But I'm not, thanks to you." He returned to the blanket and stretched out beside her, his gaze somber. He caught a tendril of blond hair, rubbing it between his fingers before smoothing it behind her ear. "I know when you got under the blanket to get me warm, you weren't expecting me to jump you as soon as I was half conscious. Tell me the truth, Hope: Were you willing?"

She cleared her throat. "I—I was *surprised.*" She touched his hand. "I wasn't unwilling. Couldn't you tell?"

He briefly closed his eyes in relief. "I don't have a real clear memory of anything that happened until I woke up on top of you. Or rather, I remember what I did and what *I* felt, but I wasn't sure you felt the same." He spread his hand on her belly and lightly stroked upward to cover her breast. "I thought maybe I'd lost my head, waking up with such a pretty, brown-eyed little blond naked next to me."

"Strictly speaking, I wasn't *next* to you. I was on top of you." Her face got hot again. Damn those blushes! "It seemed the best way to get you warm."

"It worked," he said, and for the first time a smile curved his mouth.

Hope almost lost her breath. He was ruggedly attractive rather than handsome, but when he smiled, her heart did a crazy loop. It must be chemistry, she thought dazedly. She had seen many better-looking men; Dylan had been better looking, in a clean-cut, classical way. But what her eyes saw and her body felt were two different things, and she had never experienced such a strong sexual response to any other man. She wanted to make love again, and before she gave in to the need, she forced herself to remember he had been through a harrowing, physically exhausting ordeal.

"Do you want some coffee?" she asked hurriedly, getting to her feet. She carefully didn't look at him as she gathered up her pajamas. "Or something to eat? I made a big pot of stew yesterday. Or how about a hot bath? The water heater is wired to the generator, so there's plenty of hot water."

"That sounds good," he said, also standing. "All of it."

He reached out and caught her arms, turning her so she faced him. Bending his head, he gave her another of those sweet, tender kisses. "I also want to make love to you again, if you'll let me."

Nothing like this had ever happened to her before. Hope looked up at him. Her heart did another crazy loop, and she knew she wasn't going to call a halt to this now. For as long as the blizzard lasted, she and Price Tanner were together, and she might never have another chance like this.

"I'd like that too," she managed to say.

"Maybe on a bed instead of the floor?" He circled her nipple with his thumb, making it harden and stand erect.

"Upstairs." She swallowed. "It's warm up there, because all the heat rises. I couldn't get you up the stairs, though, so I put you in front of the fireplace."

"I'm not complaining." He tugged the pajamas from her arms and let them drop to the floor. "On second thought, let's forget the coffee and the stew. The bath too, unless you planned to be in the tub with me."

She hadn't, but it was a darn good idea. She went into his arms, forgetting everything except the earthy magic their bodies made together.

four

HOPE WOKE BESIDE HIM IN THE MORNING AND LAY WATCHING him sleep, her body more deeply contented than she could remember it ever being before. She didn't wonder how or why she responded so strongly to a man about whom she knew little more than his name; she simply accepted the joy this chance encounter had brought her. The warmth of his body made the bed a cozy nest she didn't want to leave, especially since the chill in the room told her the fire in the fireplace had burned out.

It had been so long since she had been able to enjoy such

a simple pleasure as lying beside a sleeping man, listening to the slow, deep rhythm of his breathing. She wanted to cuddle close to him, but was reluctant to wake him. He was sleeping deeply, evidence of his exhaustion. After nearly freezing to death, he hadn't exactly spent a restful night.

One muscled arm lay draped over the pillow, and she could see the dark bruises on his wrist. On top of everything else, he had been in a car accident. The wonder wasn't that he slept now, but that he had been so energetic during the night.

She surveyed the other details available to her. He had beautiful hair, dark and thick, with streaks of bronze glinting through it as if he spent a lot of time in the sun. His face was turned toward her in his sleep, and she smiled, wanting to trace her finger along the bridge of his nose, which was high and a little crooked, maybe as the result of a fight. His mouth was wide and well-shaped, his lips soft. His jaw was angular, his chin nothing less than stubborn. Good-looking, rugged, attractive; definitely not handsome, as she had noticed before. Just looking at him made her breasts tighten.

She felt almost dizzy from the force of her attraction to him. She had forgotten how heady infatuation could be, and how powerful. If she had met him under normal circumstances, no doubt she would still have been attracted to him; but without the overwhelming physical intimacy that had been forced between them, she might not even have encouraged him. The necessary contact of their nude bodies, however, had established a link even before he had regained consciousness. She had stroked him, knew the textures of his skin, from the roughness of his beard-stubbled cheeks to the sleekness of his muscular shoulders. Her nipples had been tight from rubbing against his chest, her legs had tangled with his, and though she hadn't touched him sexually, she had inescapably felt his genitals against her own. She hadn't let herself think about it, but nevertheless she had been almost unbearably aroused.

Her sexual attraction wasn't due to simple deprivation. If she had thought it was, before, now she knew differently, because she was certainly no longer deprived and she still felt the same. Their sexual fit was devastating in its perfection. It was as if he had been born knowing exactly how to touch her, as if his body had been crafted specifically to bring her maximum pleasure.

She thought it must be the same, at least sexually, for him. As exhausted and drained as he had to have been, still he had turned to her time and again, his hands literally shaking with need as he drew her under him.

Her breath sighed gently, rapidly, between her lips.

The wind still blew, rattling the windows. She couldn't see anything beyond the glass but an impenetrable white curtain. While the blizzard raged, the world couldn't intrude, and he was hers.

What a difference one day made. Yesterday she had been panicked by the sense of time passing her by, thinking she had lost all opportunity to get out of life what she had always wanted most, a family. Then Price Tanner had blown in on a snowstorm, and abruptly the future was bright with promise.

He was a deputy. He had said he was heading to Boise, so he could be from there, but he had known the resort was here, which meant he was familiar with the area, so he might be local. She would ask him when he woke.

Despite the heady lovemaking of the night, and more she hoped to enjoy while he was here, she was afraid to automatically assume they were a couple. The circumstances that had brought them together were extreme, and once the weather cleared he might be on his way without a backward look. She had known that from the beginning, and accepted that risk. She, who had never had any lover other than her husband, had gone into this with her eyes open.

If this situation between them grew into something permanent, she would be happy beyond belief. She didn't let herself think the word "love," for how could she love someone she didn't really know? He was a tender, generous lover, and during the night she had seen signs of a sharp sense of humor, both qualities she liked, but she was too cautious to imagine either of them were in love.

The truth was, she had seized the opportunity to have a child.

Even beyond her own powerful attraction to him, the physical pleasure he had given her, she had been acutely aware of the lack of birth control. She hadn't taken birth control pills in five years, and there wasn't a condom in the house. She was a healthy, fertile woman, the odds were he was equally fertile, and the time was roughly right. He had climaxed inside her five times during the night, with no barrier—chemical, hormonal, or otherwise—between her and his sperm, and the knowledge was so erotic she trembled with need.

This morning, her head clear and the stresses of the emergency behind her, she felt guilty about what she had done. She didn't even know if he was married! He didn't wear a ring, and the thought hadn't occurred to her the night before. She cringed inside at the thought of sleeping with a married man and didn't want to think how much it would hurt if he did turn out to be an unfaithful jerk. But even assuming he was unmarried, the hard truth was she hadn't had any right to take such an enormous step without his consent. He hadn't asked about birth control, but he had been through quite an ordeal and could be excused for having other things on his mind, such as being alive.

She felt as if she had stolen his free will from him. If she did get pregnant, he might be, justifiably, very angry. If there was such a thing as unauthorized use of sperm, then she had committed the offense.

Being a single mother wouldn't be easy, assuming she had gotten pregnant. If she had given herself time to think about it, caution would have prevented her from taking the chance. But she *hadn't* taken the time, Price hadn't given her the time, and all she could feel now was a guilty joy that a child might be the result of their lovemaking. Her father wouldn't like it, but he loved her, and it wasn't as if she was a teenager unable to support herself or her baby. She would prefer being married, but as she had so sharply realized the day before, time was running out. She had taken the chance.

Hope slid out of bed, careful not to waken him. Her thighs trembled, and she ached deep inside her body. Her first few steps were little more than a hobble, as long unused muscles and flesh protested their treatment during the night. Silently she gathered her clothes and tiptoed out of the room.

Tink trotted from the kitchen as she came downstairs, his eagerness telling her she was late, he was hungry, but he forgave everything for the joy of her company. She poured some food into his bowl, then immediately went to rebuild the fire. It had burned down to embers, and the house was cold. She relaid the fire, the kindling catching immediately from the glowing embers, and carefully stacked three logs on the grate. Then she put on a pot of coffee and, while it was brewing, went into her father's bathroom and stepped into the shower. Thank God for hot water, because otherwise she couldn't have tolerated the cold!

The shower went a long way toward relieving her aches and pains. Feeling much better, she pulled on a pair of sweatpants and an oversize flannel shirt, put on two pairs of thick socks, and padded out to have her first cup of coffee.

Cup in hand, she went into the great room to mop up the water she had left puddled on the floor the night before and straighten Price's clothing.

The best way to dry them would be to hang them over the balcony railing, where the heat was. She hung his coat over a chair and set his boots beside the fireplace, because they needed to dry more slowly, but carried the rest of his clothes upstairs. Until Price's clothes dried, she supposed he would have to sit around naked. He was too tall for her father's clothes, and all she had left of Dylan's clothing was a couple of shirts she wore herself.

No—come to think of it, her dad had bought a pair of black sweatpants that had evidently had the wrong tag attached to them, because they were several inches too long for him. Returning them would have cost more in gasoline than the pants were worth, so he had just folded them away in the top of his closet. Buying by size being as iffy as it was, she was fairly certain she could lay her hands on an extra large sweatshirt too.

She straightened out the uniform to minimize wrinkles and, as she was doing so, noticed a tear in the left pants leg.

Lifting the garment for a closer inspection, she saw the faded red stain below the tear, as if whatever had made the tear had also brought blood. But she had undressed Price, and she knew he wasn't hurt anywhere. She frowned at the stain, then mentally shrugged and draped the pants over the railing.

Something was missing. She stared at the uniform for a moment before it hit her: where was his pistol? Had he lost it somewhere? But he didn't have a holster, either, so he must have taken the gun off and . . . . left it in the Blazer? That didn't make sense. He didn't have a wallet with him, either, but that was easier to understand. It could have fallen out of his pocket at any time during his hazardous trek through the blinding snow; it might even be in the lake.

Even if he had lost the pistol, would he then have removed the gun belt and holster and left them behind? They were part of his uniform. Of course, who knew what shape he had been in when he left the Blazer? He could have hit his head and not realized it, though if he *had* been addled, it had taken an even bigger miracle than she had thought for him to find his way here.

Well, the missing pistol was only a small mystery, and one that would wait until he woke. The house was warming, the coffee was ready, and she was hungry.

Downstairs again, she picked up the phone just to check it, but the line was dead, not even static coming through. She turned on the radio and picked up the same thing— static. Given the conditions outside, she hadn't expected anything else, but she always checked periodically during power failures, just in case.

The rifle was where she had left it, propped beside the door. She retrieved it and returned it to the rack in her father's bedroom, before Tink knocked it down with an exuberant swish of his tail.

Carrying a cup of hot coffee with her, she then tidied the great room, putting the blankets and towels she had used in the laundry room to be washed whenever power returned. She cleaned up the puddles of melted snow and ice. Tink had been back and forth through the water several times, of course, leaving wet doggy tracks all over the house. She followed his trail, crawling on the floor and blotting up paw prints.

"I thought I smelled coffee."

Her head jerked up. He was standing at the balcony railing, his hair tousled, his jaw dark with beard stubble, his eyes still heavy-lidded from sleep. His voice was hoarse, and she wondered if he was getting sick.

"I'll bring a cup up to you," she said. "It's too cold down here for you to be walking around without clothes."

"Then I think I'll stay right here. I'm not ready to be cold again, just yet." He gave her a crooked smile, and turned to pet Tink, who had bounded up the stairs as soon as he heard a new voice.

Hope went into her dad's room and searched until she found the long sweatpants. Then she collected a pair of shorts and some thick hunting socks, but try as she might she couldn't locate the extra-large sweatshirt she knew was here, somewhere. It was a gray University of Idaho shirt, and she had worn it once with leggings, but the thing had been so big she looked as if she were lost inside it. What had she done with it?

Maybe it was in the closet of the extra bedroom upstairs. She rotated her winter and summer clothing between that closet and the one in her room, but she didn't necessarily move everything.

With the small stack of clothes in her arms, she detoured to the kitchen and poured a cup of coffee, then carried everything up the stairs.

The roaring fire had rapidly warmed the upstairs. The bathroom door was open, and Price was in the shower. Hope set the cup on the vanity. "Here's your coffee."

He pulled the curtain aside and stuck his head out. Water streamed down his face. "Would you hand it to me, please. Thanks." He drank deeply, sighing as the caffeine jolted through him.

"I brought you some clothes. I hope you don't mind wearing my father's shorts."

"I don't if he doesn't." Blue eyes regarded her over the rim of the cup. "I'm glad you said they belonged to your father and not your husband. I didn't ask, last night, but I don't fool around with married women, and I sure do want to fool around some more with you."

"I'm a widow." She paused. "I had the same thoughts about you this morning. That I hadn't thought to ask if you were married, I mean."

"I'm not. Divorced, no kids." He took another sip of coffee. "So where is your father?" he asked, his tone casual.

"Visiting his brother in Indianapolis. Uncle Pete had a heart attack, and Dad flew out. He's supposed to be gone another week."

Price handed the cup back to her, smiling. "Think the blizzard will last another week?"

She laughed. "I doubt it." Both his wrists were bruised, she noticed.

"Damn. At least there's no question of leaving today, though I guess I should let some people know where I am."

"You can't. The phone lines are down too. I just checked."

"What rotten luck." The blue eyes twinkled as he pulled the shower curtain closed. "Marooned with a sexy blond." From behind the curtain came the sound of cheerful whistling.

Hope felt like whistling a tune herself. She listened to the wind blow and hoped it would be days before he would be able to leave.

She remembered something. "Oh, I meant to ask, are you hurt anywhere? I didn't see any blood last night, but your uniform is torn and has blood on it, or at least I think it's blood."

A few seconds lapsed before he answered. "No, I'm not hurt. I don't know what the stain is."

"Your pistol and holster are missing too. Do you remember what happened to them?"

Again there was a pause, and when he spoke, he sounded as if he had his face turned up to the spray. "I must have left them in the Blazer."

"Why would you have taken off your gun belt?"

"Damn if I know. Ah . . . do you have any weapons here? Other than the rifle I saw last night, that is."

"A pistol."

"Where do you keep it?"

"In my nightstand drawer. Why?"

"I might not be the only person to get stranded in the storm and come looking for shelter. It pays to be careful."

Five

WHEN HE CAME DOWNSTAIRS, HE WAS FRESHLY SHAVED, WITH her father's borrowed razor, and he looked alert and vital in the sweat clothes she had provided. The big sweatshirt had been in the other closet after all, and it fit him perfectly, just loose enough to be comfortable.

She would normally have just eaten cereal, but with him there she was cooking a breakfast of bacon and eggs. He came up behind her as she stood at the island, turning bacon with a fork, and wrapped his arms around her waist. He kissed the top of her head, then rested his chin there. "I don't know which smells best, the coffee, the bacon, or you."

"Wow, I'm impressed. I must really smell good, if I rank up there with coffee and bacon."

She felt him grin, his chin moving on top of her head. "I could eat you right up." His tone was both teasing and serious, sensual, and a wave of heat that had nothing to do with embarrassment swept over her. She leaned back against him, her knees weak. He had a serious swelling in the groin area, and she rubbed her bottom against it.

"I think we need to go back to bed." There was no teasing at all in his voice this time.

"Now?"

"Now." He reached around her and turned off the cooktop.

Ten minutes later she was naked, breathless, trembling on the verge of climax. Her thighs were draped over his shoulders, and he was driving her, with his tongue, to absolute madness. She tried to pull him up and over her, but he pinned her wrists to the bed and continued what he was doing. She surrendered, her hips lifting, her body shuddering with completion. Only when she was limp did he move upward, covering her, sliding his erection into her with a smooth thrust that took him all the way in.

She inhaled deeply, having already forgotten how completely he filled her.

He began a gentle back-and-forth movement, gripping her shoulders, watching her face.

Guilt and her innate honesty nagged at her. "I'm not taking birth control pills," she blurted, knowing this wasn't exactly the best time to bring up her lack of protection.

He didn't stop. "I'm not wearing a rubber," he said equably. "I would stop, but that would be like closing the barn door after the horse is out, wouldn't it?"

Afterward, while she was in the bathroom, he finished dressing—again—and called out, "I'll go down and start breakfast again."

"I'll be there in a minute." She still felt incredibly weak-kneed, and relieved. She stared at her face in the mirror, her brown eyes huge. She was going to get pregnant. She knew it, sensed it. The prospect both terrified and exhilarated her. From now on, her life would be changed.

She went out into the bedroom and collected her scattered garments, pulling them on again. After a lifetime of caution and careful behavior, taking such a deliberate risk was nerve-racking, like climbing on board a space shuttle without any previous training.

It pays to be careful, Price had said, but sometimes it paid to be careless too. And, any way, she was doing this deliberately, not carelessly.

One of her socks had ended up between the bed and the nightstand. She got down on her knees to retrieve it, and because she was there, because she had just been remembering what Price had said, she opened the nightstand drawer to make certain the pistol was there.

It wasn't.

Slowly she stood, staring down at the empty drawer. She knew the pistol had been there. When her dad had left, she had checked to make certain it was loaded and returned it to the same place. Living in such an isolated place, where self-defense was sometimes necessary, she had learned how to use the weapon. Idaho had more than its share of dangerous wildlife, both animal and human. The ruggedness of the mountains, the isolation, seemed to be a magnet for nut groups, from neo-Nazis to drug runners. She might happen upon a bear or a cougar, but she was more worried about happening upon a human predator.

The pistol had been there, and now it wasn't. Price had asked where she kept it, not that finding it would have been that difficult. But why hadn't he simply said he wanted it close to hand? He was a cop; she understood that he was more comfortable armed than unarmed, especially when he wasn't on his own turf.

She went downstairs, her expression thoughtful. He was standing at the island, taking up the bacon. "Price, do you have my pistol?"

He slanted a quick, assessing look at her, then turned back to the bacon. "Yes."

"Why didn't you tell me you were getting it?"

"I didn't want to worry you."

"Why would I be worried?"

"What I said about other people coming here."

"*I* wasn't worried, but you seem to be," she said pointedly.

"It's my job to worry. I feel more comfortable armed. I'll put the pistol back if it bothers you."

She looked around. She didn't see the weapon lying on the cabinet. "Where is it?"

"In my waistband."

She felt uneasy, but she didn't know why. She herself had thought that he would feel more comfortable armed, and he had said so himself. It was just—for a moment, his expression had been . . . hard. Distant. Maybe it was because he worked in law enforcement and saw a lot of things the average person never even dreamed of seeing that he expected the worst. But for a moment, just for a moment, he had looked as dangerous as any of the scum with whom he dealt. He had been so easy and approachable until then that the contrast rattled her.

She shoved the uneasiness away and didn't say anything more about the pistol.

Over breakfast she asked, "In what county do you work?"

"This one," he said. "But I haven't been here long. Like I said, I knew this place was here, but I hadn't had time to get up here and meet you and your dad—and Tinkerbell, of course."

The dog, lying on the floor between their chairs in obvious hopes of doubling his chances of catching a stray tidbit, perked up when he heard his name.

"Table scraps aren't good for you," Hope said sternly. "Besides, you've already eaten."

Tink didn't look discouraged, and Price laughed.

"How long have you worked in law enforcement?"

"Eleven years. I worked in Boise before." His mouth quirked with amusement. "For the record, I'm thirty-four, I've been divorced eight years, I've been known to have a few drinks, and I enjoy an occasional cigar, but I'm not a regular smoker. I don't attend any church, but I believe in God."

Hope put down her fork. She could feel her face turning red in mortification. "I wasn't—"

"Yes you were, and I don't blame you. When a woman lets a man make love to her, she has a right to reassure herself about him, find out every detail right down to the size of his Fruit of the Looms."

"Jockeys," she corrected, and turned even redder.

He shrugged. "I just look at sizes, not brand names." The amusement turned into a grin. "Stop blushing. So you looked at my briefs; I looked at your panties this morning, didn't I? I bet you just hung mine over the railing to dry, instead of sniffing them the way I did yours."

He had sniffed, drawing an exaggeratedly deep breath and rolling his eyes in pretended ecstasy, making her laugh, before he had tossed the garment over his shoulder with a flourish.

"You were goofing around," she mumbled.

"Was I? Maybe I was turned on. What do you think? Was my dick hard?"

"It was hard before we went upstairs, so you can't use that argument."

"It got hard when I thought about sniffing your underwear."

She began to laugh, enjoying his teasing. She was beginning to suspect arguing with him would be like swatting at smoke.

"I do have a really bad habit," he confessed.

"Oh?"

"I'm addicted to remote controls."

"You and about a hundred million other men in America. We can pick up one station here—*one*—and when my dad watches television, he sits with the remote control in his hand."

"I don't think I'm that bad." He grinned and reached for her hand. "So, Hope Bradshaw, when conditions are back to normal, will you go out to dinner with me?"

"Gee, I don't know," she said. "A date, huh? I don't know if I'm ready for that."

He chuckled and started to answer, but a sunbeam fell across their hands. Startled, they both looked at the light, then out the window. The wind had stopped blowing, and patches of blue sky were visible.

"I'll be damned," he said, getting up to walk to the window and look out. "I thought the storm would last longer than this."

"So did I," Hope said, her disappointment more intense than she wanted to show. He had asked her out, after all. The clearing weather meant he would be leaving sooner than she had anticipated, but it wasn't as if she wouldn't see him again.

She went over to the window too, and gasped when she saw the amount of snow. "Good heavens!" The familiar terrain was completely transformed, disguised by drifts of snow that appeared to level out the landscape. The wind had piled snow to window level on the porch.

"It looks like at least three feet. The ski resort operators will love this, but it'll take the snowplows a while to clear the roads." He walked to the door and opened it, and the frigidity of the air seemed to suck the warmth from the room. "Jesus!" He slammed the door. "The temperature has to be below zero. No chance of any of this melting."

Oddly, the improved weather seemed to make Price uneasy. As the day progressed, Hope noticed several times that he went from window to window, looking out, though he would stand to one side as he did so. She was busy, as being confined to the house didn't mean there weren't any chores to do, such as laundry, but doing it without electricity was twice as hard and took twice as long.

Price helped her wring out the clothes she had washed by hand, then braved the cold long enough to carry in more firewood while she hung the clothes over the stair railings to dry. She checked his uniform, picking up the shirt and feeling the seams, which would be the last to dry. Another hour would do it, she thought, as hot as Price was keeping the fire. The temperature on the second level had to be close to ninety.

She started to drape the shirt over the railing again when her attention was caught by the tag. The shirt was a size fifteen and a half. That was odd. She *knew* Price was bigger than that. The shirt had in fact been tight on him; she remembered how strained the buttons had been last night. Of course, he had been wearing a thermal shirt underneath, which would make the uniform seem tighter than it was. But if she had been buying a shirt for Price, she wouldn't have looked at anything smaller than a sixteen and a half.

He came in with a load of wood and stacked it on the fireplace. "I'm going to clear off the steps," he called up to her.

"That can wait until the weather's warmer."

"Now that the wind isn't blowing, it's bearable for a few minutes, and that's all it'll take to clear the steps." He buttoned his heavy coat and went back outside. At least he was wearing a pair of her dad's sturdy work gloves, and if his boots weren't completely dry, at least he had on three pairs of socks. Tink went with him, glad for the chance to do his business outside instead of on a pad.

With the weather clearing, perhaps she could pick up something on the radio now. Going downstairs, she switched it on; music filled the air, a welcome relief from static, and she listened to the song as she got the beef stew out of the refrigerator to warm it up for lunch.

The weather was the big news, of course, and as soon as the song ended the announcer began running down a list of closings. Her road was impassable, she heard, and the highway department estimated at least three days before all the roads in the county were cleared. Mail service was spotty, but utility crews were hard at work restoring service.

"Also in the news," the announcer continued, "a bus carrying six prisoners ran off County Road Twelve during the storm. Three people were killed, including two sheriff's deputies. Five prisoners escaped; two have been recaptured, but three are still at large. It is unknown if they survived the blizzard. Be alert for strangers in your area, as one of the prisoners is described as extremely dangerous."

Hope went still. The bottom dropped out of her stomach. County Road 12 was just a few miles away. She reached over and turned off the radio, the announcer's voice suddenly grating on her nerves.

She had to think. Unfortunately, what she was thinking was almost too frightening to contemplate.

Price's uniform shirt was too small for him. He didn't have a wallet. He had blown it off, but she was certain now that the stain on his pants leg was blood—and he had no corresponding wound. There were bruises on his wrists—from handcuffs? And he hadn't had a weapon.

He did now, though. Hers.

Six

THERE WAS STILL THE RIFLE. HOPE LEFT THE STEW SITTING ON the cabinet and went into her father's bedroom. She lifted the rifle from the rack, breathing a sigh of relief as the reassuring weight of it settled in her hands. Though she had loaded it just the night before, the lesson "always check your weapon" had been drilled into her so many times she automatically slid the bolt—and stared down into the empty chamber.

He had unloaded it.

Swiftly, she searched for the bullets; he had to have

hidden them somewhere. They were too heavy to carry around, and he didn't have pockets in his sweat clothes anyway. But before she had time to look in more than a couple of places, she heard the door open, and she straightened in alarm. Dear God, what should she do?

Three prisoners were still at large, the announcer had said, but only one was considered extremely dangerous. She had a two to one chance that he wasn't the dangerous one.

But he had taken her pistol and unloaded the rifle—both without telling her. He had obviously taken the uniform off one of the dead deputies. Damn it, why hadn't the announcer warned people that one of the escaped prisoners could be wearing a deputy's uniform?

Price was too intelligent to get thrown in jail over some penny-ante crime, and if by some chance he had, he wouldn't compound the offense by escaping. The common criminal was, by and large, uncommonly stupid. Price was neither common nor stupid.

Given her own observations, she now thought her estimated chance of being snowbound with an extremely dangerous escaped criminal had just flip-flopped. What could "extremely dangerous" mean other than he was a murderer? A criminal didn't get that description hung on him by taking someone's television.

"Hope?" he called.

Hastily she returned the rifle to the rack, trying to be as quiet as she could. "I'm in Dad's room," she called, "putting up his underwear." She opened and closed a dresser drawer for the sound effect, then plastered a smile on her face and stepped to the door. "Are you about frozen?"

"Cold enough," he said, shrugging out of his coat and hanging it up. Tink shook about ten pounds of snow off his fur onto the floor, then came bounding over to Hope to say hello after his extended absence of ten minutes.

Automatically she scolded him for getting the floor wet again, though bending over to pet him probably ruined the effect. She went to get the broom and mop, hoping her expression didn't give her away. Her face felt stiff from strain; any smile she attempted must look like a grimace.

What could she do? What options did she have?

At the moment, she wasn't in any danger, she didn't think. Price didn't know she had been listening to the radio, so he didn't feel threatened. He had no reason to kill her; she was providing him with food, shelter, and sex.

Her face went white. She couldn't bear having him touch her again. She simply couldn't.

She heard him in the kitchen, getting a cup of coffee to warm himself. Her hands began shaking. Oh, God. She hurt so much she thought she would fly apart. She had never been more attracted to a man in her life, not even Dylan. She had warmed him with her body, saved his life; in some primitive, basic way he was hers now. In just twelve short hours he had become the central focus of her mind and emotions, and that she didn't yet dare call it love was an effort at self-protection—too late. Part of her was being ripped away, and she didn't know if she could survive the agony. She might—dear God—she might even be pregnant with his child.

He had laughed with her, teased her, made love to her. He had been so tender and considerate that, even now, she couldn't describe it as anything except making love. Of course, Ted Bundy had been an immensely charming man too, except to the women he raped and murdered. Hope had always thought herself a fairly good judge of character, and everything Price had shown her so far said he was a decent and likable person, the type of man who coached Little League teams and danced a mean two-step. He had even, good-humoredly, given her his "stats" and asked her out on a date, just as if he would be around for a long time, be part of her life.

Either it was just a big game to him, or he was totally delusional. She remembered the moment when his expression had suddenly altered to something hard and frightening, and she knew he wasn't delusional.

He was dangerous.

She had to turn him in. She knew it, accepted the necessity, and the pain was so sharp she almost moaned aloud. She had always wondered why women would aid their husbands or boyfriends in eluding the law, and now she knew why; the thought of Price in jail for most of his life, perhaps even facing a death penalty, was devastating. And yet she wouldn't be able to live with herself if she did nothing and someone else died because she let him go.

Maybe she was wrong. Maybe she was jumping to the most ludicrous conclusion of her lifetime. The radio announcer hadn't said *all* the deputies on the bus had been killed, but that two of them had. On the other hand, neither had he said that one of the deputies was missing, which surely would have been in the news if that was the case.

And now she was grasping at straws, and she knew it. The deputy's uniform drying on the railing was too small for Price, and there was no logical reason for him to have exchanged his own uniform for one that didn't fit. Price was one of the escaped prisoners, not a deputy.

She had to keep him from knowing she knew about the bus wreck. She didn't have to worry about anything being on the television until the electric power was restored, and the next time he went to the bathroom, she would take the batteries out of the radio and hide them. All she had to do was periodically check the phone and, when service to it was restored, wait for the opportunity to call the sheriff's department.

If she kept her wits about her, everything would be all right.

"Hope?"

She jumped, her heart thundering with panic. Price was standing in the door, watching her, his gaze sharp. She fumbled with the broom and mop and almost dropped them. "You startled me!"

"So I see." Calmly he stepped forward and took the broom and mop from her hands. Hope took an involuntary step back, fighting a sense of suffocation. He seemed even bigger in the small laundry room, his shoulders totally blocking the door. She had reveled in his size and strength when they were making love, but now she was overwhelmed by the thought of her utter helplessness in a physical match against him. Not that she had entertained any idea of wrestling him into submission, but she had to be prepared to fight him in any way possible, if necessary.

Running would be the smartest thing to do, if she had the chance.

"What's wrong?" he asked. His expression was still, unreadable, and his gaze never left her face. He stood squarely in front of her, and there was no way past him, not in the narrow confines of the laundry room. "You look scared to death."

Considering how she must have looked, Hope knew she couldn't try to deny it; he would know she was lying. "I am," she confessed, her voice shaking. She didn't know what she was going to say until the words began tumbling out. "I don't . . . I mean, I've been widowed five years and I haven't . . . I've just *met* you, and we—I—oh, damn," she said helplessly, dwindling to an end.

His face relaxed, and a faint smile teased his mouth. "So you just had one of those moments when reality bites you on the ass, when you look around and everything hits all at once and you think, holy shit, what am I *doing?*"

She managed a nod. "Something like that," she said. and swallowed.

"Well, let's see. You're caught alone in a blizzard, an almost dead stranger falls in your front door, you save his life, and though you haven't had a lover in five years, somehow he ends up on top of you for most of the night. I can see how all that would be a little disconcerting, especially when you didn't use any birth control and might have gotten pregnant."

Hope felt as if there were no blood left in her face.

"Ah, honey." Gently he set the things aside and caught her arms, his big hands rubbing up and down as he eased her into his arms. "What happened, did you check the calendar and find out getting pregnant is a lot more likely than you'd thought?"

Oh, God, she thought she might faint at his touch, the combined terror and longing so intense she couldn't bear it. How could he be so tender and comforting when he was a criminal, an escaped prisoner? And how could the feel of his strong body against hers be so right? She wanted to be able to rest her head on his shoulder and forget about the rest of the world, just stay with him here in these remote mountains where nothing could ever touch them.

"Hope?" He tilted his head so he could better see her face.

She gasped for breath, because she didn't seem to be getting enough oxygen. "The wrong time—is now," she blurted.

He took a deep breath too, as if reality had just taken a nip out of his ass too. "That close, huh?"

"On the money." She sounded a little steadier now, and she was grateful. The sharp edge of panic was fading. She had already decided she wasn't in any immediate danger, so she should just stay cool instead of jumping every time he came near. That would definitely make him suspicious, given how willingly she had made love with him. She had been lucky that his insightfulness had given her a plausible reason for her upset, but at the same time she had to remember exactly how sharp he was. If he knew she had been listening to the radio, it wouldn't take him five seconds to put it all together and realize she was on to him.

"Okay." He blew out a breath. "Before, when you told me you weren't on the pill, I didn't realize the odds. So what do you want to do? Stop taking chances, or take our chances?" Suddenly, impossibly, she felt him tremble. "Jesus," he said, his voice shaking. "I've always been so fucking careful, and vice versa."

"Do you feel reality nibbling?" Hope mumbled against his chest.

"Nibbling, hell. I've got fang marks on my ass." He trembled again. "The hell of it is . . . Hope—I like the idea."

Oh, God. In despair, Hope pressed her face tight against him. He couldn't be a killer, he simply couldn't, not and treat her so sweetly, and tremble at the thought of being a father. He would have to have a split personality, to be both the man she knew and the man she feared he could be.

"Your call," he said.

He was aroused. She could feel the hard bulge of his erection. Talking about the possibility of pregnancy hadn't scared him, it had turned him on, just the way she had felt earlier, knowing they were making love without protection. And her body was already so attuned to him, so responsive to his sexuality, that she felt the inner tightening of her own desire. She was shocked at herself, but helpless to kill her reaction. All she could do was refuse to satisfy her need.

Her mouth was dry from tension, and she tried to work up some saliva. "We—we should be careful," she managed to say, thankful he had given her this out. Even if he was one of the other escaped prisoners and not the one considered so dangerous, it would be criminally irresponsible of her to continue sleeping with him. She had already been irresponsible enough. She could live with what she had already done, but it couldn't continue.

"All right." Reluctantly he released her. His face was tense. "Call me when lunch is ready. I'm going to go shovel some more snow."

Hope stood where she was until she heard the door slam behind him; then she covered her face with her hands and weakly sagged against the washing machine. Please, please, she prayed, let the telephone service be restored soon. She didn't know if she could stand another hour of this, much less *days*. She wanted to weep. She wanted to scream. She wanted to grab him and slam him against the wall and yell at him for being stupid and getting himself in trouble to begin with. Most of all, she wanted none of this to be true. She wanted to be completely mistaken in every conclusion she had reached.

She wanted Price.

Seven

WHILE THE STEW WAS WARMING IN THE MICROWAVE, HOPE TOOK the batteries out of the radio and hid them in one of her lidded saucepans. She checked the phone, but wasn't surprised when she didn't hear a dial tone. The wind had died only a couple of hours ago, so the utility crews wouldn't have had a chance yet to begin work in her area; they would have to work behind the road crews.

The bus wreck, she thought, must have happened before the weather got so bad, otherwise no one would yet know about it. The authorities had had time to reach the scene and ascertain the two deputies were dead, as well as recapture two of the escaped prisoners. Price might not have eluded them if the blizzard hadn't interfered. The radio report had said the bus ran off the road during the storm, but what was reported wasn't always accurate, and the timing of events didn't really matter.

The microwave *ping*ed. Hope checked the stew, then set the timer for another two minutes. She could hear the thud of the shovel against the wooden porch, but Price was working on a section that wasn't in view of the windows.

If she could hear the shovel, could he have heard the radio earlier?

Sweat broke out on her forehead, and she sank weakly into a chair. Was he that good an actor?

This was making her crazy. The only way she could make it through was to stop second-guessing herself. It didn't matter whether Price was a murderer or a more ordinary criminal, she had to turn him in. She couldn't torment herself wondering what he knew or guessed, she had to proceed as best she could.

She thought of the rifle again and hastily left the chair to return to her father's bedroom, to search more thoroughly for the bullets. She couldn't afford to waste any of these precious minutes of privacy.

The box of cartridges wasn't in any of the bureau drawers. Hope looked around the room, hoping instinct would tell her the most likely hiding place—or the most unlikely. But the room was just an ordinary room, without secret panels or hidden drawers, or anything like that. She went to the bed and ran her hands under the pillows and mattress, but came up empty again.

She was pushing her luck by remaining any longer, so she hurried back to the kitchen and began setting the table. She had just finished when she heard Price stomping the snow off his boots, and the door opened.

"Damn, it's cold!" he said, shuddering as he shed his coat

and sat down to pull off his heavy boots. His face was red from exposure. Despite the cold he had worked up a sweat, and a frosting of ice coated his forehead. It melted immediately in the warmth of the house, trickling down his temples.

He wiped the moisture away with his sleeve, then added another log to the fire and held his hands out to the blaze, rubbing them briskly to restore circulation.

"I'll make another pot of coffee, if you want some," Hope called as she set the large bowl of stew on the table. "Otherwise, you have a choice of milk or water."

"Water will do." He took the same kitchen chair he had used earlier. Tink, who hadn't been allowed out with Price the second time, left his spot by the fire and came to stand beside Price's chair. With a hopeful look in his eyes, he rested his muzzle on Price's thigh.

Price froze in the midst of ladling a large amount of beef stew into his bowl. He looked down at the soulful brown eyes watching him, and slanted a quick look at Hope. "Am I eating out of his bowl?"

"No, he's just giving you a guilt complex."

"It's working."

"He's had a lot of practice. Tink, come here." She patted her own thigh, but he ignored her, evidently having concluded Price was a softer touch.

Price spooned some of the stew to his mouth, but didn't take the bite. He looked down at Tink. Tink looked at him. Price returned the spoon to his bowl. "For God's sake, do something," he muttered to Hope.

"Tink, come here," she repeated, reaching for the stubborn dog.

Abruptly Tink whirled away from Price, his ears pricked forward as he faced the kitchen door. He didn't bark, but every muscle in his body quivered with alertness.

Price was out of his chair so fast Hope didn't have time to blink. With his left hand he dragged her out of her chair and whirled her behind him, at the same time reaching behind his back, drawing the pistol from his waistband.

She stood paralyzed for a second, a second in which Price seemed to be listening as intently as Tink. Then he put one hand on her shoulder and forced her down on the floor beside the china cabinet, and with a motion of his hand told her to stay there. Noiseless in his stocking feet, he moved over to the window in the dining area, flattening his back to the wall as he reached it. She watched as he eased his head to the edge of the window, moving just enough that he could see out with one eye. He immediately drew back, then after a moment eased forward for another look.

A low growl began in Tink's throat. Price made another motion with his hand, and without thinking, Hope reached out and dragged her pet closer to her, wrapping her arms around him, though she didn't know what she could do to keep him from barking. Hold his muzzle, maybe, but he was strong enough that she wouldn't be able to hold him if he wanted to pull free.

What was she doing? she wondered wildly. What if it were law officers out there? They couldn't have tracked Price through the blizzard, but they could be searching any places where he might have found shelter.

But would deputies be on foot, or would they use snowmobiles? She hadn't heard the distinctive roar of the machines, and surely the cold was too dangerous for anyone to be out in it any length of time, anyway.

There were also two other escaped prisoners unaccounted for; would Price be as alarmed if one or both of them were out there? Had he seen anything? There might not be anything out there but a pine cone falling, or a squirrel venturing from its den and knocking some snow off a tree limb.

"I didn't check the cabins," Price muttered savagely to himself. "God damn it, I didn't check the cabins!"

"I locked them up yesterday," Hope said, keeping her voice low.

"Locks don't mean anything." He tilted his head, listening, then made another motion for her to be quiet.

Tink quivered under her hand. Hope trembled too, her thoughts racing. If anyone had stayed last night in one of the cabins, he wasn't a deputy, because a deputy would already have come to the house. That left another escapee. Praying she was right, she clamped her hand around the dog's muzzle and hugged him close to her, whispering an apology.

Tink began fighting her immediately, squirming to get free. "Hold him," Price mouthed silently, easing toward the kitchen door.

From where she crouched beside the china cabinet, Hope couldn't see the door, and she had her hands full with Tink. The door exploded inward, crashing against the wall. She screamed and jumped, and lost her grip on Tink. He tore away from her, his paws sliding on the wood floor as he launched himself toward the unseen intruder.

The shot was deafening. Instinctively she hit the floor, still unable to see what was happening, her ears ringing. The sharp stench of burned cordite stung her nostrils. A hard thud in the kitchen was followed by the shattering of glass. Her ears cleared enough for her to hear the savage sounds of two men fighting, the grunts and curses and thuds of fists on flesh. Tink's snarls added to the din, and she caught a flash of golden fur as he darted into the fray.

She scrambled to her feet and ran for the rifle. Price knew it was unloaded, but the other person wouldn't.

With the heavy weapon in her hands, she charged back toward the kitchen. As she rounded the cabinets, a heavy body slammed into her, knocking her down. The sharp edge of the counter dug into her shoulder, making her arm go numb, and the rifle slipped from her hand as she landed hard on her back. She cried out in angry pain, grabbing for the rifle and struggling up on one knee.

Price and a stranger strained together in vicious combat, sprawled half on the cabinets. Each man had a pistol, and each had their free hand locked around the other's wrist as they fought for control. They slammed sideways, knocking over her canister set and sending it to the floor. A cloud of flour flew over the room to settle like a powdery shroud over every surface. Price's foot slipped on the flour, and he lost leverage; the stranger rolled, heaving Price to the side. The momentum tore Price's fingers from the stranger's wrist, freeing the pistol.

Hope felt herself moving, scrambling to grab the man's hand, but she felt half paralyzed with horror; everything was in slow motion, and she knew she wouldn't get there before the man could bring the pistol down and pull the trigger.

Tink shot forward, low to the ground, and sank his teeth into the man's leg.

He screamed with pain and shock, and with his other foot kicked Tink in the head. The dog skidded across the floor, yelping.

Price gathered himself and lunged for the man, the impact carrying them both crashing into the table. The table overturned, chairs broke, chunks of meat and potatoes and carrots scattered across the floor. The two men went down, Price on top. The other man's head banged hard against the floor, momentarily stunning him. Price took swift advantage, driving his elbow into the man's solar plexus, and when the man convulsed, gasping, followed up with a short, savage punch under the chin that snapped the man's teeth together. Before he recovered from that, Price had the pistol barrel digging into the soft hollow below his ear.

The man froze.

"Drop the gun, Clinton," Price said in a very soft voice, between gulps of air. *"Now,* or I pull the trigger."

Clinton dropped the gun. Price reached out with his left hand and swiped the weapon back toward himself, pinning it under his left leg. Tucking his own pistol in his waistband, he grabbed Clinton with both hands and literally lifted him off the floor, turning him and slamming him down on his belly. Hope saw Clinton brace his hands, and she stepped forward, shoving the rifle barrel in his face. "Don't," she said.

Clinton slowly relaxed.

Price flicked a glance at the rifle, but he didn't say anything. He wasn't going to reveal it wasn't loaded, Hope realized, but neither would she let on that she knew it. Let him assume she didn't know.

Price dragged Clinton's arms behind his back and held them with one hand, then took the pistol out of his waistband, jamming the barrel against the base of Clinton's skull. "Move one inch," he said in a low, guttural tone, "and I'll blow your fucking head off. Hope." He didn't look at her. "Do you have any thin rope? Scarves will do, if you don't."

"I have some scarves."

"Get them."

She went upstairs and searched through her dresser until she found three scarves. Her knees were trembling, her heart thudding wildly against her ribs. She felt faintly nauseated.

She held on to the railing as she shakily made her way back down the stairs. The two men didn't look as if they had moved, Clinton lying on his belly, Price straddling him. The carnage of wrecked furniture and food surrounded them. Tink was standing at Clinton's head, his muzzle down very close to the man's face, growling.

Price took one of the scarves, twisted it lengthwise, and wound it around Clinton's wrists. He jerked the fabric tight and tied it in a hard knot. Then he jabbed the pistol into his waistband once more, took Clinton's pistol from under his knee, and levered himself to his feet. Leaning down, he grabbed the collar of Clinton's coveralls and hauled him to his feet, then slammed him down into the only chair left standing upright. He crouched and secured Clinton's feet to the legs of the chair, using a scarf for each ankle.

Clinton's head lolled back. He was breathing hard, one eye swollen shut, blood leaking from both corners of his mouth. He looked at Hope, standing there pale and stricken, still holding the rifle as if she had forgotten she had it.

"Shoot him," he croaked. "For God's sake . . . shoot him. He's an escaped murderer. I'm a deputy sheriff . . . He took my uniform . . . Damn it, *shoot the bastard!*"

"Nice try, Clinton," Price said, straightening.

"Ma'am, I'm telling the truth," Clinton said. "Listen to me, please."

With one smooth movement Price reached out and tugged the rifle from Hope's nerveless hands. She let it go without a protest, because now that Clinton was tied up, there was no one she could intimidate with the empty weapon.

"Shit," Clinton said, closing his good eye in despair. He sagged against the chair, still breathing hard.

Hope stared at him, fighting off the dizziness that assailed her. He was almost Price's height, but not as muscular. If she was any judge of men's clothing—and after doing all the clothes shopping for first Dylan and now her dad, she had had plenty of experience—Clinton would wear a size fifteen and a half shirt.

Price wasn't unscathed. A lump was forming on his right cheekbone, his left eyebrow was clotted with blood, and his lips were cut in three separate places. He wiped the blood out of his eye and looked at Hope. "Are you all right?"

"Yes," she said, though her shoulder hurt like blue blazes where the cabinet edge had dug in, and she still wasn't at all certain she wasn't going to faint.

"You don't look it. Sit down." He looked around, spotted an unbroken chair, and set it upright. His hand on Hope's shoulder, he pressed her down onto the chair. "Adrenaline," he said briefly. "You always feel weak as hell when the scare's over."

"You broke into one of the cabins, didn't you?" Price asked Clinton. "Built a fire in the fireplace, stayed nice and warm. With the blizzard going on, we wouldn't be able to see the smoke from the chimney. When the weather cleared, though, you had to let the fire go out. Got damn cold, didn't it? But you couldn't head off into the mountains without heavier clothes and some food, so you knew you had to break into the house."

"Good scenario, Tanner," Clinton said. "Is that what you would've done if you hadn't stolen my uniform?" He opened his eye and flicked a look around. "Where's the old man? Did you kill him too?"

Hope felt Price looking at her, assessing her reaction to Clinton's tale, but she merely stared at the captured man without a change in her expression. Maintaining her composure wasn't difficult; she felt numb, absolutely drained. How did Clinton know about her father? Was he from the area? She was not, she thought, cut out to be an action hero.

"Hey." Price squatted in front of her, touching her cheek, folding her hands in his. She blinked, focusing her gaze on him. His brows were drawn together in a small frown, his blue eyes searching as he examined her. "Don't let him play mind games with you, honey. Everything's going to be all right; just relax and trust me."

"Don't listen to him, ma'am," Clinton said.

"You look pretty shaky," Price told her, ignoring Clinton. "Maybe you should lie down from a minute. Come on, let me help you to the couch." He urged her to her feet, his hand under her elbow. As she turned, he uttered a savage curse and hauled her to a halt.

"What?" she said, shaken by the abrupt change in him.

"You said you weren't hurt."

"I'm not."

"Your back is bleeding." His face grim, he force-marched her into her dad's bedroom. He paused to replace the rifle in the rack, then ushered her into the bathroom. After jerking open curtains so he would have sufficient light, he began unbuttoning her shirt.

"Oh, that. I scraped it on the cabinet edge when I fell." She tried to grab his hands, but he brushed her hands aside and pulled off her shirt, whirling her around so he could examine her back. She shivered, her nipples puckering as the cold air washed over her bare breasts.

He dampened a washcloth and dabbed it on her back, just below her shoulder blade. Hope flinched at the pain.

"You've got a gouge in your back, and from the looks of it, a monster bruise is forming." Gently he continued washing the wound. "You need an ice pack on it, but first I'm going to disinfect that gouge and put a gauze pad over it. Where are your first aid supplies?"

"In the cabinet door over the refrigerator."

"Lie down on the bed. I'll be right back."

He guided her to the bed, and Hope willingly collapsed facedown. She was cold without her shirt, though, and tugged the cover around her.

Price returned in just a moment with the first aid box. Blood was dripping in his eye again, and he paused a minute to wash his own face. Blood immediately trickled down again, and with an impatient curse he tore open an adhesive bandage and plastered it over his eyebrow.

Then, holding the box on his lap, he sat beside Hope and gently dabbed the wound with an antibiotic ointment. As gentle as he was, even the lightest touch was painful. She bore it, refusing to flinch again. He placed a gauze pad over the wound, then covered her with one of her dad's T-shirts.

"Just lie still," he ordered. "I'll get an ice pack."

He improvised an ice pack by filling a zip-lock plastic bag with ice cubes. Hope jumped when he gently laid it on her back. "That's too cold!"

"Okay, maybe the T-shirt's too thin. Let me get a towel."

He got a towel from the bathroom, and draped it over her in place of the T-shirt. The ice pack was tolerable then, barely.

He pulled the cover up over her, because the room was chilly. "Are you too cold?" he asked, smoothing her hair. "Do you want me to carry you upstairs?"

"No, I'm fine, with the cover over me," she murmured. "I'm sleepy, though."

"Reaction," he said, leaning over and brushing a kiss on her temple. "Take a nap, then. You'll feel fine when you wake up."

"I feel like a wuss right now," she admitted.

"Never been in a fight before?"

"Nope, that was my first one. I didn't like it. I acted like a girl, didn't I?"

He chuckled, his fingers gentle on her hair. "How does a girl act?"

"You know, the way they always do in the movies, screaming and getting in the way."

"Did you scream?"

"Yes. When he kicked in the door. It startled me."

"Fancy that. Did you get in the way?"

"I tried not to."

"You didn't, honey," he said reassuringly. "You kept your head, got the rifle, and held it on him." He kissed her once more, his lips warm on her cool skin. "I'd choose you for my side in any fight. Go to sleep, now, and don't worry about the mess in the kitchen. Tink and I will clean it up. He's already taken care of the beef stew."

She smiled, as he had meant her to, and he eased up from the bed. She closed her eyes, and in a few seconds she heard the quiet click of the door closing.

Hope opened her eyes.

She lay quietly, because the ice pack was easing the soreness in her shoulder. Fifteen minutes on, fifteen minutes off—if she remembered accurately how ice therapy worked. She might need all the flexibility in the shoulder she could muster, and she estimated Price wouldn't check on her for at least an hour. She had a little time to take care of herself.

She heard him moving around in the kitchen. Broken glass tinkled as he swept it up, and she heard the crackle of shattered wood when he picked up the smashed remains of some of her chairs. She didn't hear the captured Clinton utter a sound.

The flour had made quite a mess. Cleaning it up would require vacuuming and mopping, and washing it off everything else would take a lot of time.

Hope threw back the covers and eased off the bed. Silently she opened the closet door and took down one of her dad's sweatshirts, gingerly pulling it on over her head and wincing as her abused shoulder and back muscles protested the movement.

Then she began searching for the bullets.

Half an hour later, she found the box, in the pocket of one of her dad's jackets.

Eight

HOPE HAD SEVERAL OF HER DAD'S OLD, NO-LONGER-USED NECK-ties dangling from the waistband of her sweatpants when she left the bedroom. The rifle was in her hands.

Clinton was sitting silently, exactly as she had last seen him, not that he had much choice. He opened his good eye when he heard her, the single orb widening as he saw the rifle. He gave a faint, satisfied smile and nodded at her.

Price was standing at the sink, wringing out a dishcloth. He had most of the mess cleaned up, though she was woefully short of furniture now and there were still a few surfaces dusted with flour. He looked up, and whatever he had been about to say died on his lips when she raised the rifle.

"Keep your right hand where I can see it," she said calmly. "Use your left hand to get the pistol out of your waistband. Put it on the cabinet and slide it toward me."

He didn't move. His blue eyes turned hard and glacial. "What in hell do you think you're doing?"

"Taking over," she replied. "Do what I said."

He didn't even glance at the rifle. His mouth set in a grim line, he started toward her.

"I found the bullets," Hope said quickly, before he got close enough to grab the rifle. "In a coat pocket," she added, just so he would know she really had found them.

He stopped. The fury that darkened his face would have terrified her if she hadn't had the rifle.

"The pistol," she prompted.

Slowly, keeping his right hand resting on the sink, he reached behind his back and drew out the pistol. Placing it on the cabinet, he shoved it toward her.

"Don't forget mine," Clinton said from behind her, the words slightly slurred; his damaged mouth and jaw were swelling and turning dark.

"The other one too," Hope said, not flinching from the sulfurous look Price gave her. Silently he obeyed.

"Now step back."

He did. She picked up her pistol and laid down the rifle, because the pistol was more convenient. "Okay, sit down in the chair and put your hands behind you."

"Don't do this, Hope," he said between clenched teeth. "He's a murderer. Don't listen to him. Why would you believe him, for God's sake? Look at him! He's wearing prison coveralls."

"Only because you stole my uniform," Clinton snarled.

"Sit down," Hope told Price again.

"Damn it, why won't you listen to me?" he said furiously.

"Because I heard on the radio about a bus wreck. Two deputies were killed, and five prisoners escaped." Hope didn't take her eyes off his face. She saw his pupils dilate, his jaw harden. "Because your uniform shirt is too small for you. Because you didn't have a wallet, and even though your uniform pants were torn and bloody, you weren't injured anywhere."

"Then what about the service revolver? If I took a deputy's clothes, why wouldn't I have also taken his weapon?"

"I don't know," she admitted. "Maybe you were knocked out during the wreck, and when you regained consciousness, the other prisoners had already escaped and taken the weapons with them. I don't know all the details. All I know is I have a lot of questions, and your answers don't add up. Why did you unload the rifle and hide the bullets?"

He didn't blink. "For safety reasons."

She didn't either. "Bull. Sit down."

He sat. He didn't like it, but her finger was on the trigger and her gaze didn't waver.

"Hands behind your back."

He put them behind his back. Steam was all but coming out of his ears. Staying out of his reach, in case he should whirl suddenly and try to knock the gun out of her hand, she pulled one of the neckties from her waistband and fashioned two loose loops with it. Moving in quickly then, she slipped the loops over his hands and jerked the ends tight. He was already moving, shifting his weight, but he froze in place as the fabric tightened around his wrists.

"Neat trick," he said emotionlessly. "What did you do?"

"Loops, like roping a calf. All I had to do was pull." She wrapped the loose ends between his wrists, tying off each of the loops, and then knotted the tie in place. "Okay, now your feet."

He sat without moving, letting her tie his feet to the chair legs. "Listen to me," he said urgently. "I really am a deputy sheriff. I haven't worked in this county very long and not many people know me."

"Yeah, sure," Clinton snarled. "You killed those two deputies, and you would probably have killed her before you left. Untie me, ma'am, my hands are numb."

"Don't! Listen to me, Hope. You've heard about this guy. He's from around here. That's how he knew you lived with your father. Clinton"—he jerked his head toward the other man—"kidnapped the daughter of a wealthy rancher from this area and asked for a million in ransom. They paid him the money, but he didn't keep his part of the bargain. The girl wasn't where he said he had left her. He was caught when he tried to spend the money, and he's never told where he hid the girl's body. It was all over the news. He was being transferred to a more secure jail, and we thought it was worth a try to put me in with him, maybe get him to talk about it. He can be convicted of murder on circumstantial evidence, but the parents want their child's body found. They've accepted that she's dead, but they want to give her a decent burial. She was seventeen, a pretty little girl he's got buried up in the mountains somewhere, or dumped in an abandoned mine."

"You know a lot of possibilities," Clinton charged, his tone savage. "Keep talking; tell me where you hid her body."

Hope walked into the great room and added more wood to the fire. Then she paused by the telephone, lifting the receiver to check for a dial tone. Nothing.

"What are you doing?" Clinton demanded. "Untie me."

"No," Hope said.

"What?" He sounded as if he couldn't believe what he had heard.

"No. Until the phone service is restored and I can call the sheriff to straighten this out, I figure the best thing to do is keep both of you just the way you are."

There was a stunned moment of silence; then Price threw back his head on a shout of laughter. Clinton stared at her, mouth agape; then his face flushed dark red and he yelled, "You stupid fucking bitch!"

"That's my girl," Price chortled, still laughing. "God, I love you! I'll even forgive you for this, though the guys are going to ride my ass for years about letting a sweet little brown-eyed blonde get the drop on me."

Hope looked at those laughing blue eyes, shiny with tears of mirth, and she couldn't help smiling. "I probably love you too, but that doesn't mean I'm going to untie you."

Clinton recovered himself enough to say, "He's playing you for a fool, ma'am."

" 'Ma'am'?" she repeated. "That isn't what you called me a second ago."

"I'm sorry. I lost my temper." He inhaled raggedly. "It

galls me to see you falling for that sweet shit he deals out to every woman."

"I'm sure it does."

"What do I have to do to convince you he's lying?"

"You can't do anything, so you might as well save your breath," she said politely.

Half an hour later Clinton said, "I have to use the bathroom."

"Go in your pants," Hope replied. She hadn't thought about that complication, but she wasn't going to change her mind and untie either one of them. She gave Price an apologetic look, and he winked at her.

"I'm okay for right now. If the phone service isn't restored by nightfall, though, I'll probably be begging you for a fruit jar."

She would bring him one too, she thought. She wouldn't mind performing that service for him at all. She glanced at Clinton. No way; she wouldn't touch his with a pair of tongs.

She checked the phone every half hour, watching as the afternoon sun sank behind the mountains. Clinton squirmed, and she had no doubt he was in misery. Price had to be uncomfortable too, but he didn't let it show. He grinned at her every time he caught her eye, though with his bruised face the grin looked more like a grimace.

Just at twilight, when she lifted the receiver, she heard a dial tone. "Bingo!" she said triumphantly, picking up the phone book to look up the number of the sheriff's department.

Price rattled off the number for her, and though she had been almost certain he was telling the truth, in that moment she knew for certain. Light broke across her face, and she gave him a radiant smile as she punched in the number.

"Sheriff's department," a brisk male voice said.

"Hello, this is Hope Bradshaw, at the Crescent Lake Resort. I have two men here. One is Price Tanner and the other's name is Clinton. They both claim to be deputies and that the other is a murderer. Can you tell me which is which?"

"Holy shit!" the voice bellowed. "Damn! Shit, I'm sorry,

I didn't mean to say that. You say you have both Tanner *and* Clinton?"

"Yes, I do. Which one is your deputy?"

"Tanner is. *How* do you have them? I mean—"

"I'm holding a gun on them," she said. "What does Tanner look like? What color are his eyes?"

The deputy on the line sounded nonplussed. "His eyes? Ah . . . the subject is approximately six-two, two hundred pounds, dark hair, blue eyes."

"Thank you," Hope said, thankful that law officers were trained to give succinct descriptions. "Would you like to speak with Deputy Tanner?"

"Yes, ma'am, I would!"

Picking up the phone, she carried it as far as she could, but the cord wasn't long enough to reach. "Just a moment," she said, laying down the receiver.

She dashed to the kitchen and got her paring knife. Running back to Price, she knelt and sawed through the fabric binding his wrists, then turned her attention to his ankles while he rubbed feeling back into his hands. "You need a cordless phone," he said. "Or one with a longer cord."

"I'll take care of that the next time I go shopping," she said as she freed his ankles. The kitchen phone was closer, though that cord wasn't long enough to reach either. He hobbled over to it, his muscles stiff from sitting so long in a strained position.

"This is Tanner. Yeah, everything's under control. I'll give a complete briefing when you get here. Are the roads passable yet? Okay." He hung up and hobbled toward her. "The road is still blocked, but they're going to grab a snowplow. They should be here in a couple of hours."

He hobbled past. Hope blinked. "Price?"

"Can't stop to talk," he said, speeding up his hobbling, heading straight toward the bathroom.

Hope couldn't smother her laugh. Clinton glared at her as she walked past him to hang up the phone in the great room. She still had the paring knife in her hand. She paused and looked at him consideringly, and something must have shown in her face because he blanched.

"Don't," he said as she started toward him, and then he began to yell.

"You cut him," Price said, his tone disbelieving. "You really cut him."

"He had to know I meant business," Hope said. "It was just a teeny cut, nothing to make such a fuss about. Actually, it was an accident; I didn't intend to get that close, but he jumped."

That wasn't all Clinton had done; he had also lost control of his bladder. And then he had begun talking, babbling as fast as he could, yelling for Price, saying anything to keep her from cutting him again. Price had called the sheriff's department and relayed the information, which they hoped was accurate.

It was after midnight. They lay in bed, their arms around each other. She held an ice pack to his cheek; he held another one on her back.

"I meant it, you know," Price said, kissing her forehead, "about loving you. I know everything happened too fast, but . . . I know what I feel. From the minute I opened my eyes and saw your face, I wanted you." He paused. "So . . . ?"

"So?" she repeated.

"So, you 'probably' love me too, huh?"

"Probably." She nestled more comfortably against him. "Definitely."

"Say it!" he ordered under his breath, his arms tightening around her.

"I love you. But we really should take our time, get to know each other—"

He gave a low laugh. "Take our time? It's a little late for that, isn't it?"

She had no answer, because too much had happened in too short a time. She felt as if the past day had been weeks long. Thrown together as they had been under extreme circumstances, she had seen him in a multitude of situations, and she knew her first dazed, deliriously joyous impression of him had been accurate. She felt as if she had known him immediately, primitive instinct recognizing him as her mate.

"Marry me, Hope. As soon as possible. The chances we've taken, we've probably hit the baby jackpot." His voice was lazy, seductive.

She lifted her head from his shoulder, staring at him through the darkness. She saw the gleam of his teeth as he smiled, and once again she felt that jolt of awareness, of recognition. "All right," she whispered. "You don't mind?"

"Mind?" He took her hand and carried it to his crotch. He was hard as a rock. "I'm raring to go, honey," he whispered, and his voice was trembling a little, as it had earlier when they discussed the possibility. "All you have to do is say the word, and I'll devote myself to the project."

"Word," she said, joyfully giving herself up to the inevitable.

LINDA HOWARD has won many awards, including the Silver Pen from *Affaire de Coeur* and the *Romantic Times* Reviewer's Choice Award for Best Sensual Romance. She has captivated her vast audience with bestselling romances such as *A Lady of the West, Angel Creek, The Touch of Fire, Heart of Fire, Dream Man, After the Night, Shades of Twilight, Son of the Morning, Kill and Tell,* and *Now You See Her.*

UPON A MIDNIGHT CLEAR

Proof-of-Purchase

1584